Martin,
Reading this will
help those ribs heal.

P.S. THANK YOU,
FOR THE BEER!

Once Upon a Treatise

iUniverse

ONCE UPON A TREATISE

iUniverse books may be ordered through booksellers or by contacting:

iUniverse
1663 Liberty Drive
Bloomington, IN 47403
www.iuniverse.com
844-349-9409

ISBN: 978-1-5320-9874-1 (sc)
ISBN: 978-1-6632-2240-4 (hc)
ISBN: 978-1-5320-9873-4 (e)

Library of Congress Control Number: 2020906144

Print information available on the last page.

iUniverse rev. date: 02/04/2021

CONTENTS

PROLOGUE

QUERIES ANSWERED

Enrandl sat with his legs crossed in the middle of an aged ceremonial chamber. His eyes were closed beneath a thick mane of drenched and tangled black hair. His body was relaxed, his arms hung limply to each side of him, and his hands rested on the rough yet molded stone floor with his palms up. The flames from one hundred candles burned brightly around him while their smoke drifted silently toward the ceiling. The candles afforded the chamber illumination, and the warmth from them enticed rivulets of perspiration to flow from his forehead down his cheeks while he remained motionless.

The space encompassing him was immaculate. The magic user had taken several hours to personally clear away every speck of dust and arrange each candle in one of the four circular tiers so that the chamber would be balanced evenly. The twisted silver candlesticks along the walls in the highest level were six feet tall. This height tapered down with each row to the lowest candles, which had no holders, and had been placed directly on the floor. An unadorned path led from him to a pair of thick wooden doors. The cold gray of the stone walls absorbed most of the light but could not dissuade an uncomfortable heat that gradually mounted within the room.

Is it conscious to the potentiality of the tomes' cogency? His query mystically extended. This particular display of magic could not be seen by anyone observing him. The internal audience in progress was the result of an effect that he channelled to make his inquiries. This effect allowed him (at least his mind) to project out beyond the room. He seemed worlds away if any distance could define where his form sat and where his consciousness now questioned higher powers for their divine consultation. He perceived that no distance had been traveled to attain this destination, but he felt that he was nowhere near his body.

He heard a voice answering his question with, "Unknown." It was not a thought in response to his own, and it presented him with the strangest sensation. He was expressing his portion of the commune mentally, yet the answers to his proposed questions returned as an unmistakable voice that he could hear audibly, and this left him disconcerted.

The conversation had only taken several minutes. While the effect's magical display began to fade, leaving him with no more feeling of travel than before, his mind again united with his body. His aura weakened as the display from his powerful effect diminished. This deficiency would not impair him but would be instinctively noticeable. Weaker effects expended less of the source energy when channelled, while stronger ones could induce various intensities of fatigue. Genuinely formidable effects could even cause physical alterations to the channeller, including premature aging and possible death, when used without appropriate precautions.

The unseen source was always there. It floated and waited for a channelled effect's specific components to merge. Then it derived the desired magical display from it. Where the source originated was unknowable, even to those with the persistence to study it, and if studied, multiple theories clouded a researcher's investigation on the matter. The qualities of mystery and ambiguity were just too challenging to understand and interpret.

One constant proved accurate: Aggregate proportions of energy, which were allowed to pass through an aura, had set limits. Once they were depleted, only time could restore them. An aura's capacity would expand with consistent practice and meditation, which enabled it to tap into more substantial quantities; however, there was always a limit. No magic user truly knew his or her limitations, but Enrandl contended that he could channel as many of the weaker effects as he desired, with only minimal inconvenience.

So, he thought, *that bastard had not perjured himself.* "You would bargain a prevarication with your existence ventured," he accused his former mentor aloud.

Revolutions before, his master had enlightened him about an arcane volume of incredible power. This same man had pleaded relentlessly that his student should heed his veracity about the book. Enrandl assumed the ramblings were solely a vain attempt to prevent a dagger from ending his life. For many revolutions afterward, he carried reservations about the sincerity of his deceased master. Recent events and numerous divination effects (such as the one he had just finished) assured him of its existence.

Earlier in his life, the assumption of this proposed object, which supposedly allowed an unlimited amount of the source to be channelled without causing the aura to weaken, was inconceivable. He had believed it was irrational for anyone with magical aptitude to tell another about such an item.

Unless intention denotes falsification, he mused.

Now he knew there was no falsehood in his mentor's story, but the book currently had a resolute guardian or possessor, depending on one's viewpoint. There was not enough time for him to glean its age during his divine consultation, but a red dragon, with or without the book's power to aid the beast, would prove a dangerous foe. Attempting to retrieve the book from the creature would require help.

He opened his eyes. They were gray and had an almost kind demeanor to them. He brushed his tangled black hair from his cleanly shaved face, wiped the sweat from his forehead onto his sleeve, and stood. His tall frame was skinny, but his healthy features reflected his age accurately. He was beyond what most humans would call the middle of life. An average human would live close to eighty revolutions. Some humans lived beyond that, if they were lucky enough not to find an unfortunate and untimely passing. Other races of people had much longer life spans. Elves, for example, lived several hundred revolutions before a natural death would befall them.

The candlelight flickered and danced on his long, sparkling blue robe as he walked to the doors. The garment gave the appearance of floating just above the ground, never revealing the black leather boots on his feet. Halfway to the chamber's exit, he clapped his hands in front of him and uttered an unintelligible magic word. When he got closer, as part of his channelling, he pulled his hands apart and toward him to finish the effect and watched the display.

The doors opened inward as if his hands were on the handles. A slow, piercing screech emanated from their ancient hinges. Cool air rushed in past him as the high-pitched sound reverberated within and outside the chamber. He stepped between the doors and nodded his thanks to a short, burly, and bearded priest standing in the torch-lit corridor. The priest's brown robes rustled as he removed his hands from his pockets. He nodded back while the fingers of his left hand traced an expensive gold necklace that he wore.

Without looking back to witness the new display, he channelled a reversal—his hand gestures moved in opposition from before—to close the doors. The walls around them and the rest of the temple's lower levels were old and deteriorating, and a slight but apparent fresh crack near the upper hinge of the left door formed and spread for several inches.

Enrandl looked past the priest and regarded the wall behind him, where a screened hole, which was large enough for an average man to climb through, had been carved directly across from the doors of the chamber. Several of these holes had been placed sporadically throughout the halls, and they allowed a moderate amount of fresher air for breathing in the lower levels. Most of them had a crude mesh of metal bars to prevent any entry or exit through them. This particular aperture was missing one of those protective bars. He noted this so that he could remember which chamber he had used.

They ascended two flights of stairs to the main floor where the priest wandered off, and Enrandl was left alone to escort himself out. Other than those fading footfalls, the area was quiet and lifeless. Fourteen candles provided illumination against the darkness. Each was positioned on pews, and they formed two rows of light down the center aisle of the main floor. The temple was always open for anyone who wanted to come and worship, but not many direful followers of The Dark Gods' came this late at night unless the situation was extremely urgent.

The area where the congregation would sit was not nearly as impressive in the current light as it was near midday, but it still radiated tenfold with an impeccable appearance what the lower levels lacked in regular preservation. In those lower levels, ancient construction had been shoddily braced in most areas to keep the structure sturdy and, scattered everywhere, discarded objects no longer needed in the main temple lay covered with revolutions worth of layered dust.

He walked between the pews and headed for the exit. Each pew was made of oak, which had not been made in separate sections to fit together later but had been precisely carved in one whole piece from a tree. On each wall, these masterful carvings were combined with lancet arches of divinely hewn stone. They contained magnificent stained glass, which decorated the temple. Whether dedicated to Dark or Light, everything he saw here was the envy of any other temple or church in Jenerv. Nothing was too expensive for the taste and greed of Frederick Smythe.

The High Priest of the temple was no doubt asleep in his chambers. Enrandl had known him for a long time and had perhaps considered him a friend. He knew without a doubt that Smythe would frown upon Enrandl's use of the lower chambers for his effect.

What is the resultant impairment of my desire for his ignorance? Enrandl thought.

Winter-chilled air caused a shiver to run through him when he opened the main door of the temple. He took a deep breath of the brisk evening air before leaving the building.

Outside, the port city of Jenerv had a minuscule portion of dim light from the occasional unshuttered window. The dark moon, having just started its fifth cycle of revolution and promising warmer weather to come, could spare no accompanying light for the quiet city streets.

During the day, there were wagons pulled by animals, carts pushed or pulled by residents, and visitors, horses, and people walking the crowded streets of the port city. Here in the dark late-night hours before daylight, very few traveled them. Even in the upscale, high-class, cobblestoned portions of the city, it was not an appropriate time to take a stroll. A militia made regular patrols, but even an inexperienced rogue could mark its patterns and work around it.

He had walked down several streets and turned a few corners, but he had only encountered a black cat perched on a sill. The cat meowed and watched him turn down a narrow, trash-cluttered alley.

He heard a scuffling sound behind him but kept walking. He was far from surprised when, before long, a man garbed in ragged clothing and armed with a dagger moved into the lane in front of him.

"Give me your gold," the man ordered in a clear voice as he held out his filthy hand. The robber's face was shaven, but he was dirty. His hair was scruffy and light brown, and with several feet of distance between them, his stench still assaulted the chilly air.

"This endeavor shall reign you afoul at present," he answered.

Enrandl took delight in the disbelief of his opponent when the thief threw his dagger and then watched it fly far away from its intended target. He even allowed the other to compose himself, draw another blade, and charge forward to attack again. The knife of the second assault against him cut through his robe but deflected off something other than skin. The grungy man's surprise threw him off guard and close enough for Enrandl to act. He seized the man's throat, squeezing it tightly. After relieving him of the dagger, Enrandl positioned the thief between himself and his two accomplices who had moved in behind him. The captured man gasped for air.

"Retreat!" Enrandl ordered. "Your election determines his providence." The two men ran out of the alley leaving in opposite directions.

"Th-they are g-gone," the thief said, forcing his words out and struggling as the grip on his throat tightened. The magic user looked directly into the thief's eyes.

"The financial disbursement to reinstate this garment prevails against the significance of their insufficiency of aspect." A head nod indicated the retreating companions. As Enrandl spoke, his staring eyes narrowed, yielding a chilly expression that was even colder than the night air. The fear he reveled in would be the last thing this dullard knew. The struggling under Enrandl's grip weakened as he said, "Conceivably, your execution shall evidence a complimentary expense."

He dropped the lifeless body and considered his hand for a moment. His usual measures concerning physical confrontation were not to involve himself, preferring to use magic to further his ends. He felt that strangling the man had been harder than it should have been. *I should endeavor a solution for such nuisance,* he thought.

He continued through the alley, hurrying to avoid any other encounters with Jenerv's night crowd. Two streets away from where he had left the strangled thief, he stopped at the Goode Tavern and entered it.

The disposition inside the crowded tavern was relaxed and warm. It bustled with various activities from dagger tossing to small groups listening to painted minstrels spinning glorious tales. The odors from alcoholic concoctions and a cloud of musty gray smoke, which drifted in the air, filled his senses. Nevertheless, even in this cluttered place, it did not take him long to find the person he was looking for.

"Toran," he called across the room. Receiving no reaction, he tried again. "Toran," he called out much louder this time. Many people in the crowd stopped what they were doing and looked in his direction.

In the middle of a small huddle of half-drunken men and beside one of the two great fireplaces, which glowed with warm orange light, Toran Hensh stood upon a table. Obviously not a minstrel, the motions of his arms and the attention of the group around him proved that he had been spinning an exciting tale nonetheless. He looked away from his following, gazed at Enrandl, and shook his head. He ran his hand through his sandy-blond hair, stopped his story, made his apologies to his entourage, and worked his way across the tavern. The excellent brown vest and matching pants and boots that he wore stood out above the rest of the patrons' clothing.

"Too employed to venture across the taproom and greet me in a more common tone with less commotion drawn to you?" Toran asked as the crowd slowly returned to their own attentions.

"Your squandered civilities with me are pedestrian. You comprehend my aspiration of extravagant emergence." Enrandl looked around the tavern again. "An assemblage of cohorts is required. Four or five should be sufficient. An employment has come to fruition," he said.

"And should I have no interest?" Toran asked.

"Twenty gold finance," Enrandl answered.

Toran scowled.

Enrandl added, "Per day … each." Now he specifically paused, but Toran remained indifferent. "A ten-day excursion and all treasure discovered—with exception to my specific—divided among your company, will assuredly crown your approbation to investment."

"Indeed. The particulars of service to be rendered?" Toran asked.

"Protection."

"From?" Toran continued to question.

"Protective assurance for the journey. Are we sufficiently established?"

"Consider the matter concluded," Toran said and bowed slightly.

"Excellent. We embark two cycles hence. A more clement season for travel."

Toran muffled a cough as he watched the other man turn away. Enrandl left the tavern. Toran returned to his place atop the table to finish his interrupted tale.

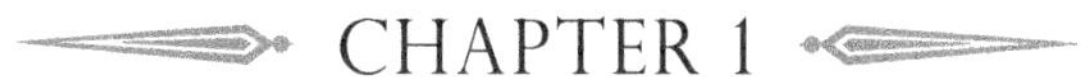

CHAPTER 1

TRAPPED TOGETHER

The rain was falling hard and soaking Kellik thoroughly. A mass of dark clouds had moved in just before the last light of the day had dwindled into the evening darkness, and rain had followed soon afterward.

His cold fingers reached upward for the next handhold of wet rock. When they found a firm grip, he pulled himself up a little higher and closer to his goal. He believed that travel through this mountain range was a necessity. His hope was that The Westlands would provide more finance for the pelts than the home he was leaving behind. The part of him that believed and hoped this was true trusted his reason for being here now, fighting against rain and cold to reach the destination above for shelter.

He was earning a moderate amount for the animal pelts that he had collected. However, he had convinced himself and others that the prospect of better finance and possible new and unique wares had finally worn away any resolve to stay in his homeland. Another part of him interpreted his necessity differently. The honesty within his spirit told him that his increasing desire to see what was out there and seek something fresh and exciting was the genuine compulsion for his leaving home.

One example of this was that he no longer hunted explicitly for pelts like most trappers he knew did. Their chosen profession made them an excellent income. When he initially believed this was his calling, he had thought that he could also do so. An unfortunate incident brought him to realize that the life of a hunter and trapper did not entirely suit him. Consequently, he decided that he would only use his skills to support his sustenance or protection during his travels. Should he require a meal, his efforts might grant him another pelt to sell.

He made the decision to undertake the journey, whether by belief or aspiration. His parents bade him farewell and GodsLight in crossing the mountains. This pass, if it was indeed defined as a pass, would have been challenging, even without the rain.

The story was that a clan of dwarves from the far side of the mountain had started engineering a way through it. The undertaking that they had outlined would be presumably advantageous to everyone. As their race was stubborn and born with pride, they had been forced to abandon the project after many revolutions and too many dwarves had died.

Kellik was determined to cross the piecemeal construction that had remained after the dwarves had relinquished it. The alternative was an additional cycle of travel, either north or south, to circumvent the massive expanse of mountain ranges known as The Unforgiving.

On his home's side of the mountain, there had been no construction whatsoever. However, after several days (what he believed to have been one-third of his way across), he could see signs of the dwarves' work: felled trees and rock that had been worked on. The crude production was decidedly rough, but he could not imagine, considering his current trek, the clan giving up when its objective appeared so close.

It may have been simple blind chance that he spotted the small cave above him during a flash of lightning, but he called it GodsLight. He hoped that it would bring him the shelter that he needed to last through the storm. It should have been a short and easy climb, but the weight of his chain mail and unreliability of the wet rock that threatened a lack of purchase with every move deemed otherwise. On a rainless day without armor to weigh him down, he would not have been struggling, even considering the cactus growing everywhere. The climbing equipment that he had in his pack would have helped tonight, but now that he was halfway up, it was too late to use that gear.

When he finally attained the goal of his climb and stood before the opening of the cave, he caught sight of a ledge, which led down the side of the mountain. He could not see where it would have combined with the path he had been traveling, but he was confident that it did. Another flash of lightning followed shortly by a low rumbling thunder greeted his entrance. He was shorter than most of his race, but he still had to crouch slightly inside the dark area. He paused, shook out his silver hair, and allowed his eyes to adjust to the darkness.

To any but true elves, he could hide his human heritage if he wanted. He was the son of a human father and an elven mother. Because of this, he enjoyed some of the gifts that had been given to his elven ancestors. Those gifts would help show him details of this cave, which would be bathed in a perfect blue light, as sunlight would give to a human.

When his eyes adjusted, he could finally see the cave around him. The air was cold, and the ground mostly wet. The remains of a small fire were there. Had it been burning, the water flowing on the floor of the cave would have extinguished it. He placed the pack from his back on a piece of the dry ground and then sat down for a moment. The moment turned into an hour when he dozed off.

He awoke a little refreshed but still cold and wet. His small nap had been from exhaustion, but he scolded himself for it anyway. He looked outside to confirm that the rain persisted and decided to wait out the storm in this awkward shelter, but he wanted to secure it first. He made preparations for a fire, found a spot that water would not reach, and soon after, a warm glow filled the small cave quickly.

He opened his pack, took out some of the furs that were inside it, and set them on dry ground near the fire. He took particular care to lay out a specific white albino pelt over the rest. It had been a few revolutions since he had acquired that one. Although some offers had been quite tempting, he had not found the heart to sell it. It was a beautiful pelt with only one imperfection. In the end, no amount of finance could replace its sentimental value. He stroked the hide a couple of times, staring into the fire as he remembered.

He had been traveling through the Turnpike Hills near Philter's Crossing, and winter had been in full bloom. The snow fell all day and showed no signs of stopping. His well-hidden traps, which had been placed the night before, now had a blanket of freshly fallen snow to veil them even more.

At that time, it was his habit to set a few traps around his camp before settling in and offering his prayers. The prayers were special to him, for when he offered them, The Gods' granted him small portions of their divine power. The essences of power that he could manage were minuscule and straightforward when compared to the wonders that clerics and priests of religious orders, whether they were Dark or Light, could produce. However, he appreciated the ability to use that which he had been given.

That night, through the course of time and faithful following, The Gods' granted greater force than they usually bestowed upon him. In many ways, these essences resembled magic displays from the effects that a magician might channel. Some of those displays duplicated the celestial influences. He knew several magicians and had heard from them how their effects weakened their auras—whatever that meant—and could render them other problems without the proper precautions. He had never experienced any complications similar to their descriptions. Perhaps the simplicity of his works was not enough to cause him any such hindrances. He decided that he would not want to change places with them.

When he awoke the next morning, the snow had stopped falling. He brushed the light covering off himself. A few moments of meditation told him that The Gods' responses to his prayers were different from what he had expected. He meditated for several more minutes to discover a reason for the misunderstanding in his prayers, but no answer came. He had been able to pray for specific essences every couple of days. Until that day, he had not been able to register a single disappointment in their granting.

There was a chance he had made some error in his evening prayers that he had not considered. He concluded that although a magician could channel the effects that he wanted whenever he wanted, The Gods' had their eminent purposes—reasons known only to them—and would grant what they deemed necessary. He accepted this faithfully and expected to find out, in time, what purpose they wanted him to fulfill.

He went about his morning routines, which included checking on the traps that he had lain the previous night. Three of his traps had been empty with one more to review. At first glance, it looked as though it would be the same as the others, but as he approached the last trap, he heard a low growl coming from its direction. He stopped immediately and drew a dagger from his belt. Then while crouching low, he looked around for the cause of the sound. He could see nothing that looked threatening along the ground or in the trees either. By then, the growling had stopped.

As he moved cautiously forward, he heard the growl again. This time, he was able to tell that it was coming from the trap itself. Then he saw a red contrast on the snow that surrounded the trap and guessed it was blood. He wondered what it could be from since his traps were not meant to harm animals. Damaged pelts were not worth much, so he did what he could to not ruin them.

The growling persisted as he inched even closer. As if from nowhere, the faint outline of a pure white snow leopard appeared before him. Its natural defense and reciprocal offense of blending perfectly with its surroundings had made it nearly invisible against the backdrop of snow. He marveled at the creature. It was an immense beast. If it had been standing, it would have been as tall as his waist. He moved closer while talking slowly and easily, trying to keep the animal calm. This creature was beyond any expectations of his trapping, and he only wanted to release this rare animal.

"Take it easy, girl," he said in a calm, clear voice. His green eyes met the leopard's eyes without fear, but the injured cat growled more. "Okay, boy then?" he recanted. Continued growling, bared teeth, and snarling met his every movement forward. When he was close enough, he could tell that its rear leg was hopelessly tangled. He could get no closer. Every vain attempt that he made to calm the creature down only made it more furious with him.

There was one more option. He reached into his pack, pulled out some fresh meat, which he had not had a chance to smoke the night before, and then sat in front of the leopard. He tossed the meat toward it, wincing as the cat started back a bit. Then he began to chant one of his essences.

Many minutes later, he finished his litany. When he opened his eyes, he found that the attitude of the leopard had changed. The meat he had offered was gone, and the cat weakly watched his every move but did not emit a single growl in protest.

Still moving slowly, he made his way over to it and then removed the animal's tangled leg from the trap. This closer observation of the damaged limb told him that the cat had tried to sever it to escape and that the leg was too damaged ever to be used again.

He started to speak to the leopard another time, recalled the modification of his previous evening's prayers, and the essence he had been granted instead. He placed one hand on his chest and the other upon the cat. Then he chanted the alternate essence. The mantra lasted only several seconds. Upon the completion of the final phrase, an intense pain overcame him. His right leg burned as if it had been torn away from his body. Reacting as if he had been attacked, he rolled in the snow and drew a dagger from his belt.

Only the leopard was there. Kellik looked at his leg and found no reason for the agony he felt. The pain faded slightly, and he urgently wanted to impart something to someone ... the other one. He could still feel the throbbing in his leg, but it had subsided as he had felt the new emotional compulsion.

He looked over at the leopard and realized that the desire to impart had not been his, but the cat's. He had not known the essence would work this way. This empathy between him and any animal (as its target) would require practice to use effectively. Then weakness overwhelmed him, and he was barely able to move. This time, he understood that it was not his own lack of strength. He found the resolve to overcome this empathic weakness and crawled back to the leopard. It growled at him again, but this time, it was not an angry growl.

Kellik looked up into the falling snow and pleaded, "Please don't let it die. I'll do anything!"

The leopard purred weakly, and he knew there was something else that he needed to do. He closed his eyes and waited. The animal sounded again, and he placed his hands on it.

"Promise you what?"

Then every sensation from the leopard faded from his mind, and at first, he thought that the power of the essence had run its course. When he opened his eyes again, he found the cat lying still, with no life left in its open eyes. The Gods' had not answered his plea.

He could not permit himself to leave it there like that, and he started to dig. He had no shovel but used branches from the surrounding trees to break up the frozen earth so that he could remove the soil.

Later that evening, he finally placed the last stone on top of the mound of rocks that covered the animal. As he set this one, he made a vow. He had not buried the whole beast (that would not only be a waste but also an insult). He had taken only what he could use, including the creature's pelt, and he wanted to leave something as a reminder that it had been and had died there. This memorial would only mean something to Kellik, for no one else would know what it represented.

From that day forward, he would trap animals for sustenance and not the finance that he could receive for selling their pelts. That had been his promise, and he would keep it rather than chance the sacrifice of another rare creature as that one.

Kellik now stood and looked away from the fire, shaking away the painful memory. He started to draw the bastard sword at his waist, only to realize that there was not enough room to use it if he needed to. He walked around his flame-lit shelter and found that it dived farther into the mountain. He could see well in the flame's light but not further into the cave.

He allowed his vision to meld with the darkness. The walls and floor of the cave started to angle downward, but he did not notice the place where he was walking becoming smoother as he advanced, in contrast to the walls and ceiling.

By the time he did realize this, it was too late.

The water on the floor of the cave made the smoothed rock slippery enough that his feet skidded out from underneath him. He tried all that he could to prevent his descent into the mountain, yet he still slid. Several times, he actually fell deeper into the depths. Fortunately, the times he fell gradually decreased back into sliding so that when he finally leveled out and fell from a hole six feet above the floor into a long narrow crevice, his momentum was considerably slower.

There was a sharp crack when he landed. He winced and waited to feel a pain that never came. Looking around, he found that the floor had returned to its rougher cave-like appearance. It was littered with the bones of others, who had not survived the fall. He and his weapons were intact. He still had both longswords on his back and the bastard sword at his waist. The pelts and everything else were lost above. Unlike the climb against the wet mountainside to the cave, he would not be able to return from here to there without his lost climbing gear.

Large chalcedonic eyes gleamed with excitement as Kayrahawkatzeena watched one of the openings to her sleeping chamber. Sounds had been coming from that direction. One helpless victim had fallen down, screaming all the way, and she had laughed at those screams. Then with barely a blink of her long life, a second had followed the first. This one had not screamed, but the sound of metal clashing against stone spoke to her of weapons that could be dangerous in the proper hands. A passing thought inspired her with a pleasant memory.

This was her home, and they were caught in her trap, which gave her the advantage over them. She shifted her red-scaled head slightly with the confidence that those who had been trapped had but one choice to follow. She had designed the lack of options for anyone who was caught. Whether they had been in the past or would be in the future, they became guests who were guided to meet her.

She had not constructed this all on her own. Her role had been mostly designing what she had imagined. Some of the magic had been hers, but the work of the dwarves had been paramount.

It had taken many revolutions and many of the dwarven population to have it brought into being. The clan dwarves who had thought to carve a swath through this range, one that would bring caravans a shorter distance and avoid long trips around The Unforgiving, had been quite helpful. She had watched them for several revolutions.

They had been working hard to cut a disastrously crude passage when she had finally confronted them. She had promised them finance for their creating of her design and a halt to any progress that was barely passable for most beings. She knew that many foolish beings would still try to pass here and was counting on this to happen. Having been grudgingly convinced to work for her and that the compensation she proffered them was in their best interests, the dwarves had immediately set to work on her vision.

The whole clan of dwarves had worked on the stone inside the mountain to her exact standards, as she knew they would. Dwarves were meticulous when it came to creation, construction, and battle.

When they completed her work, the dwarves wanted to finish their highway. This would not be prosperous for her designs. A significant thoroughfare would have her quickly discovered, but even an unfinished project—something that might make the journey weeks shorter—would still tempt those smaller groups that she was counting on away from the long voyage around The Unforgiving.

This notion enticed her considerably.

As for the dwarves that continued to work on the highway project, groups of them found misfortunes befalling them, or they just went missing. When they finally decided to relinquish their project due to weather and the number of mysterious accidents and disappearances that had already occurred, she could not allow them to leave. If any of them informed others about her or gave away her secret, their efforts to build her trap would be in vain. She decided that their indignation concerning the unfinished project would not be healthy for such a prideful race of beings. Instead of allowing them to suffer any vexation, it was her obligation to exterminate them immediately.

She knew that there was only one passage.

One way in.

One way to get by her.

With her head positioned to watch for her guests, she started to count by memory, every piece of treasure resting beneath her.

Kellik stumbled over the bones beneath his feet and put his hand against the wall to stay balanced. A strange powdery substance came off the wall and onto his fingers. His vision did not allow him to see color, but he could tell that the powder was dark against his fingers. He rubbed his thumb across his finger, feeling the substance fall away from the tips. As he resumed walking, he remained alert to his surroundings. Soon the cave widened before him. The ceiling here was beyond his sight, and the walls were just within the limits of what his eyes allowed him to see.

He had played in caves as a child. They had been smaller caves than this one and more like the one that he had entered earlier for protection from the rain. He had always wondered what could form something like this. Experience since then had granted him the knowledge of erosion, which made sense for the caves that he had played in and the one high above him, but this was an excessively large area; therefore, he doubted it was natural.

At the far end of the chamber, the cave narrowed again. He hoped that he would not have to use it but drew his sword from his waist as he made his way across the cavern. After several minutes in the new area, he could see some light ahead of him on the cave walls. He guessed that it was firelight by the way it danced along the side of the cave. He moved forward cautiously, but because of his armor, he was not quiet. Whatever lay ahead of him could already hear him coming.

He came around the last curve just before reaching the source of the light, and he was startled by what he saw. His first thought was that he was seeing a child who was less than four feet tall standing there holding a torch in one hand and a short sword in the other. This child wore a cloak with its hood pulled up over his head.

There were no signs on the trail outside indicating that anyone was traveling in front of him, but it was possible that another group might have been crossing from the other direction. As he considered this unusual sight, an afterthought occurred to him: the small washed-out fire he had seen.

The child stood nearly motionless, peering ahead into the cavern as if he was waiting for something. Any vision he had imagined of this being a child vanished in an instant when it finally looked back at him. Under the hood of the robe, the torchlight revealed a face filled with dark stubble. The eyes of this little person were glaring at him as if expecting something. Then, as the other looked again ahead into the cave, the hand holding the torch beckoned Kellik to come closer. Amused at this, he walked forward.

He had never seen one. They were rarely ever seen out of their native communities in warmer southern climates, but this creature fit the description of a minikin almost perfectly.

"Well met. I'm …"

"Are yuh daft?" was growled back in a hushed voice. "And nois'er thanan avalanche."

Kellik started to reply, but the minikin turned back to face him again, cutting his comment off. "Do yuh know whut's up thur?" The minikin pointed his sword arm in the direction of the cave.

"Uh, no?"

The gruff voice, with cheeks and chin dotted with patches of red stubble, had Kellik startled and speechless. The little man was wearing leather armor, which had been tailored to fit his trim frame and belied the more common definition of a minikin, but Kellik decided it must be true.

"I dunno eether, but we'yul shurinuff find out if yuh don't hush." The little man looked ahead into the cave. "Saigel."

"Kellik. Nice to …"

Saigel turned back to him. His hairy eyebrows scrunched together, and the glare in his eyes was silently demanding and unmistakable: *Hush!*

Kayrahawkatzeena listened to the loudly whispered conversation. The echoes from the walls gave her more than enough information about her prey. There was no mistaking that one of them had elven blood running within him. His smell was delightful, and she was prepared to enjoy him.

The one speaking human with a heavy dwarven accent had her confused though. He was probably a dwarf, but there seemed to be something wrong with his inflections, and she did not smell anything dwarven in the air passing by her.

This is not going to be much of a challenge, she thought. They were two distinctly different creatures that did not know each other's strengths and weaknesses. Therefore, they would not be able to compensate or complement one another and would offer an unorganized fight.

She decided that she would play with them for a little while, and if some parley ensued, she would speak archaically. Due to her immense size and because of what she was, the expectation of this chosen aspect would make her even more majestic than she already was. For now, she settled for positioning herself, this time favoring their only possible exit from her lair. She considered the chance that there might be no need for conversation.

CHAPTER 2

FIGHT OR FLIGHT

"What's that?" Saigel heard Kellik whisper from behind him. The half-elf pointed over his shoulder to a glint of silver reflecting in the torchlight ahead of them.

Saigel walked over, bent, and picked up a ring. He studied it for a moment and then tossed it to Kellik. "Jus' a silver band," remarked Saigel quietly. "Pro'bly dropped by suhm fool soul passin' by. Yuh spied it. Yuh keeps it."

Kellik looked at it for a moment and then put it on a finger of his right hand. The magical ring imperceptibly adjusted itself to his finger, which it would have done to anyone.

Saigel thought, *Wouldn't 'ave fit me anyway.*

Kellik was admiring the new ring in the torchlight, and Saigel was starting his march farther into the cave when they heard a loud snore from ahead of them. The two glanced at each other, concurrently entertaining the thought of turning back yet silently agreeing that an impossible climb was not an option for them. Another rumbling snore echoed from ahead. The signifying of continued slumber was a good sign. They must not awaken whatever was making it.

Saigel had been more disturbed by the sound, for he now had an idea of what may lie ahead. He did not know that Kellik had only heard stories of such dreaded beasts and said nothing to him about it. Had the minikin known the stories that the other had heard—stories that were meant to scare children into behaving rather than being true—it might have disturbed him further.

Most members of his race, who were generally considered by the other races as lazy and fun loving, would not have recognized the sound. Dwarves had raised Saigel for the majority of his life, forging him into a more mentally informed and physically fit minikin who could know and manage the everyday world better than the societies of his ancestors. The last time he had faced a dragon, it had been a black one, and about fifty dwarves hardened for battle had been with him. Even then, they had only driven the creature away. He was not looking forward to the prospect of facing another one with only a half-elf as a companion.

The snore had been closer than expected. Close enough that when they rounded the next bend where the cave widened again, Kellik caught sight of the giant beast. He stood motionless, as did his partner, and stared at the red-scaled form as the brilliant scales reflected torchlight back at them. The dragon's body was long and lean. There was apparent muscle under the mesh of scales, which shifted seamlessly with each continued breath. The creature dominated the back wall of the cavern. Its tail was curled around behind it out of his sight. The neck and head of the beast angled away from them, leaving just one closed eye to spot them if it opened.

Kellik's paralysis was due more to his awe of the beautiful creature than to any fear of it. The descriptions and stories he had heard in his youth could not compare to the spectacle his eyes beheld before him, and he was so entirely stricken by the dragon that he did not even notice the great mound of treasure beneath it.

They stood unmoving for a moment longer before Saigel finally elbowed him in the thigh, bringing him out of his reverie. He knelt down to hear what Saigel whispered in his ear. The dragon took another deep breath and then exhaled.

"Yuhr vishion'll 'elp mor'an mine." Saigel obviously had more experience with elven heritage than Kellik had with minikin. He accepted that his partner's vision was similar to that of a human's, so he needed light to see. "Keep yuhr eyes on it fuhr movement while I seek thuh exit." Saigel indicated the other end of the cave.

To achieve the full range of his vision, Kellik needed to move away from the light of the torch. He walked about ten paces away from Saigel while trying to remain directly between the flame and the large eye of the dragon. He guessed that the light might wake the sleeping form eventually, unless they could find a way out of the cave quickly. The two had made it halfway across the cavern when he thought he saw an exit ahead of him, but he remained vigilant to his purpose and left Saigel to his.

Kayrahawkatzeena listened patiently, peeking slightly through her mostly closed eye, as her two victims stole their way across the room. She was neither excited nor bored but merely patient. She had been wrong about one of them being a dwarf, and the little creature she heard speaking with the heavy accent amused her even more. She kept her breathing slow and even but stopped halfway through an exhale to enact an inhale when her prey was where she wanted them.

Fire spewed forth from her mouth without her even lifting her head. It stopped the intruders in their tracks. The burst had been short, but she knew the elf, who had been yards away from the searing flames, had felt the extreme warmth from it.

The little one, who also had not been caught inside her demonstration, had been much closer. The singe he received would not be as deflating as the information it would give him. He had almost entered the passage that she knew could free them, but her fiery breath had flowed well into it.

The transformed passage was now glowing with tremendous heat, and because of that detriment, an escape that way was impossible for quite some time. In addition, either of them retreating in that direction would find more of her dragonfire at their backs. She was confident that it would, even though she might need a bit of parley to allow her system some time to recuperate.

"Insolent guests! Will your premature departure have more strategic aesthetics?" The dragon purred with rhetoric clearly in her tone. When a moment of dead silence ensued, she almost believed that her diction had been too elaborate. She continued with a more limited style. "No? Then it is grand gesture to attend me for an interval, and I accept the honor of your presence, for I have been too long deficient in conversation."

How wonderful, Kellik thought, amazed that the creature before him had the ability, *but how would that dragon learn to speak?* Its soft feminine tones added to his reverence. After having seen the fire, fear had crept in to temper his thoughts as well. None of the stories he had heard had revealed that these magnificent beasts could speak. He looked up, sensing its gaze on him as the head of the creature was now raising and peering down at him.

He toned his fear down and replied, "I don't think we've much of a choice."

"Inaccurate! Your departure accompanies your convenience."

"With yuhr fire trailin' us as we go," said Saigel, startling Kellik. The minikin was standing next to him rather than across the room where the torch still burned. He wondered if all minikin were as stealthy as his new ally. When he noticed the little man had his hand on his sword hilt, it struck him that they were in a dangerous situation. Kellik's sword was in his hand, but his arm was relaxed, so it, with no regard, pointed to the ground. He had not even considered using it.

"Perhaps." Her head turned from side to side and then up toward the darkness that was above them.

"Whut yuh lookin' fuhr?" Saigel asked.

"Friends," she replied, which prompted Saigel to look around anxiously, but Kellik's attention remained on the dragon.

"Friends secretly located for an ambush." This was a lie, of course, for two reasons. First, they were unaware that she had been awake and listening to their whole progression through the cave. The second reason was something that she had never had a chance to use in the time since her cave had been built. A particular trap that needed specific conditions met for her to use. By moving forward, the accented little one had just fulfilled that very condition for her.

When Kellik turned to say something to Saigel, three things happened in rapid succession. Kellik saw an *X* scratched on the floor exactly where the minikin stood, from the corner of his eye he spotted something moving behind the dragon, and there was an echoing crack from above. At the sound of the snap, Saigel looked up along with Kellik in time to see a large boulder dropping down on them but not in time for either to react to it.

Kellik stood in shock and even dropped his sword as the boulder crashed down on the very spot where Saigel stood. Should Saigel have had time to cry out, the loud crash of rock against rock would have drowned out his words.

When the boulder hit the ground, the dragon pounced toward Kellik, landing right in front of him and then knocking him to the ground with a punch from its snout. This blow successfully awakened him. He was thinking clearly now while admiring the agility of the large beast. When he looked up, their eyes locked together. This connection did not break, so Kellik was acutely aware that the dragon observed him while he shook himself back to his senses, and then allowed him to get up.

He picked up his sword, gripped it with both hands, and prepared himself for what he already believed would be his last fight. Suddenly and without warning, a flash of light erupted in the cavern, effectively blinding him until his eyes adjusted to the lack of darkness. The next thing he saw was Saigel, now armed with a short sword and the smallest scimitar he had ever seen, rushing underneath the dragon.

The scimitar was the source of the light.

The dragon roared in pain as he watched both weapons hit their marks. Then the beast scraped one of its sharp claws at Kellik, leaving a gash across his forehead, but concentrated the rest of its attacks against the minikin. Saigel tumbled away from a claw that was scratching at him, and it had been GodsLight shining on him that the bite had only grazed his shoulder rather than the dragon picking him up and swallowing him whole.

Kellik was so caught up in the whirlwind of fast-moving events that he almost forgot he should be fighting to save his life. He might have been able to dodge the scratch to his face if his vision had not been temporarily impaired. He finally moved in and managed to swing his sword at the dragon, but the scales proved stronger than his attack.

Fortunately, his new companion was having more GodsLight than he was. Saigel's swords had created a cut in the dragon, and blood oozed from the wound, so it made sense that he was concentrating his attacks on the weakened area. His blades moved quickly and accurately as they cut deeper into the dragon's hide.

She was hurt but too proud to show it. Forgetting the elf completely, the minikin was going to pay for the pain that he had inflicted upon her. She focused on him with furious intensity. Each attack connected in order with absolute perfection. Her left claw scratched across the little one's chest—and also had spun him out from underneath her. Her right claw then knocked him prone, leaving him as a perfect target. She craned her head down, grasped him in her mouth, and this time, successfully lifted him with her razor-sharp teeth.

Kellik, aware that he was being of little help, hoped his partner had not noticed the hardened scales that still held against his heavy sword. After the dragon picked up Saigel, he recognized the opportunity to take advantage of where he had been, crossed over to the vacated spot, and attacked the already wounded break. His heavy weapon cut in deeply, causing the beast to roar in pain and drop the minikin before it could swallow him.

Saigel thought that his life had been ended. Despite his aching head and body, he had never been so glad to hit solid ground. Once the minikin did hit it, he found a way to roll dizzily away and stand. The word *run* entered his mind, and he tried to yell it out. He was not sure it had come out right, but he forced his feet onward and ran as fast as his injured body would take him down the way that they had entered.

Proud as he was at finally causing some damage to the dragon, Kellik recognized the wisdom in Saigel's advice. He moved in, set his sword for one last swing before running, realized he now had the creature's full attention, mentally shrugged his shoulders, and ran for an exit.

Opposite the one Saigel had chosen.

She welcomed the break as her trespassers ran off in opposite directions. If she could have launched a gush of flame to follow the elf, she would have. However, she knew that her insides were close to but not quite recovered enough to produce one. Now she considered her wounds. The little one had injured her more than she thought she could ever be injured. Then she realized the direction that he had run.

If dragons could smile, hers was ear to ear.

Saigel bumped into a few walls as he staggered his way through the caves. He was considerably weak from the fight and lucky not to be in the dragon's stomach. His scimitar lit the path, and he knew it was a dead end. He had made it all the way to where he had become trapped. Even his dwarven brothers, with proper climbing and rock-cutting tools, would be hard-pressed to perform the climb.

Every so often, he wondered why he had ever left the dwarves. Mining and drinking were just about the only worries that they had, unless the occasional goblin tribe, who was trying to extend their boundaries, needed turning away from where he had spent half of his maturing childhood. Saigel had never fought goblins personally. He had thrown rocks at one, and the thought of this produced a smile. The ageless prejudices of his clan against them had fueled his own hatred.

Stronger creatures, including the black dragon, had accidentally been stumbled upon while digging deep in the mountains for precious gems and metals. It took a few hundred dwarves, armed with pickaxes and hammers, with the taste and skill for battle, which was only rivaled by the urge and ability to create, to conquer those hindrances.

As usual, he always forced himself to remember his mission. He dredged up his sole reason for leaving the relative security that the dwarven sanctuary had given him, and after doing so, buried the memory as deep as he could.

He scolded himself again for having been caught in this trap in the first place. All the experience he had had in caves such as this, while mining gems and metals with his dwarven brothers, should have given him some insight and ability to notice that the upper cave had been set up that way for a reason.

He had not given a second thought to the way he should have run. The closest egress had been the only one that he could have escaped through anyway. The other exit was assuredly still a molten tunnel from the heat of the dragon's flames. When he slumped down next to the wall, a black-powder residue rubbed off and onto his brown cloak. He was wondering what was taking Kellik so long to get there when he heard the scratching claws of the approaching dragon.

His heart sank.

If the dragon was almost there before him, Kellik was surely dead. Saigel stood and faced the beast, confident that it could not enter the narrow area. When he heard the intentionally loud inhale, his shoulders sank along with his heart. He could do nothing but stand and receive the deadly dragonfire that was coming in his direction.

Kellik ran for what seemed like hours. In his hasty retreat, he had paid no attention to the red glow of the heated rock and had run right through the area. The caves that he ran through twisted back and forth, while widening and narrowing a few times. The caverns here seemed more natural than most of what he had previously come through. A trickling noise echoed from somewhere ahead. When another cave that extended out possessed a large pond of water, he understood why.

A thin, steady stream of liquid poured down from overhead, beyond his vision. This stream fell into a large pond of what he suspected to be water. Several other droplets from above also found their way into the same pool at alternating points.

He wondered if that water could offer him protection from the dragonfire. The sound of thunder did not answer his question but made his decision for him, so he ran farther.

Minutes later, he was out in the open, under the night skies. He looked around and up into the storm. The rain had not stopped, and the dark clouds still dominated his view. It did not take long for him to realize that he was just as trapped here as he had been in the cave. The edge of a cliff with a sheer drop into darkness was all he found at first. His only hope lay back toward the mouth of the cave. If he could climb up there, he might be able to drop onto the dragon's back, if it pursued him this far.

An easy climb followed, for there were plenty of handholds for him to work with. His plan changed when he arrived at the top of his ascent. The backside of this part of the mountain was a far more gentle descent than the sheer drop from a cliff edge. He decided to take his chances with the climb downward.

Kayrahawkatzeena came to the main exit of her lair. She had a few other exits available to her. These exits were not so easily noticed. She had used them to create many of those dwarven happenings, which had caused the dereliction of their highway project, but they were not as spacious as this one. This ledge provided a perfect spot for her, where she would frequently sit, bask in the sun, and not have anything bother her while looking over what she considered was her territory (conveniently being everything she could see). This night, the clouds blocked any view of the surrounding mountains or any other sight she would typically want to see.

Only one sight interested her. The elf calling himself Kellik was that interest, and he was nowhere in sight. She tracked him this far, employing all of her senses to do so, but the rain befuddled her here. It wiped away his scent and marred any tracks that he might have left behind.

She roared. This roar was sourced by anger and not pain this time. She did not feel wounds from the earlier battle where the minikin had hurt her, but she remembered them. That creature was gone now, and one adversary remained. She had followed the elf to this ledge and needed to know what had happened to him. She could only ponder two options. She spread her leathery wings and launched herself upward.

Kellik had not had time to think before he had heard the roar, and he knew he was in trouble when the sound of flapping wings filled the air. There was no place to hide on that side of the mountain, so he was going to have to make a stand. He found a landing with a little solid purchase where he could maneuver and drew the pair of longswords from his back.

A flash of lightning helped Kellik find the dragon, but he could tell that it had already spotted him. Thunder boomed while he steadied himself for a second round against the beast that was speeding toward him. The dragon was upon him so quickly that he could not direct his attacks at its previous injuries. His swords flashed immediately, and both struck her underbelly as he dodged claws that were aimed to snatch him into the air. He turned his head and tried to see a flight path.

The beast's tail thudded into him, spun him around twice from the force of its contact, and knocked him to the ground. He ended up on his back, skidding toward a rocky edge. Half his body was over the verge before the supine sliding stopped. The rain was pelting his face. He rolled onto his stomach and had to let go of his swords in order to catch himself from falling. One of the swords, released too near the brink, tipped over the crest, and fell for many seconds before he heard it crash on the rocks below. That was too many seconds more than he wanted to drop, and he pulled himself up onto solid ground to avoid doing so.

Kayrahawkatzeena was making her turn to come around for another pass when the sky lit up again. The bolt of lightning arced across the sky and struck under her left wing. Her body convulsed as the charge coursed through her. She overcame this problem as she realized a second one: Her wing had gone numb, and it was useless as she fell wildly toward the side of the mountain. With her working wing, she regained as much control as possible, but her crash was inevitable.

She thudded into the rock face, rolled downward, and came to rest next to where the elf's sword had done so only moments earlier. A few dazed minutes later when she was again coherent, she knew her wing would be no help to her. She stayed still and allowed her mind to clear a little more before she started her climb back up to her lair.

Kellik had seen the dragon struck by the lightning, though he had been too busy pulling himself back onto the ledge to watch the rest of the spectacle. The crash echoed all around him. One of his swords was gone, but he picked up the other, returned it to the hilt on his back, and climbed back to the cave where he might find Saigel.

As the rain fell harder, he heard the scratching of claws against the rock. Again amazed, this time by the power and resilience of this dragon, he wondered how much longer the beast could hold on. He rushed urgently inside. With or without his minikin partner, he decided that an ambush of the dragon was still his best course of action.

The exhausted Kayrahawkatzeena reached the mouth of her cave. All that she wanted to do was heal and be rested. Reduced to crawling speed, she struggled with every move. During it all, she knew that something was wrong. She had not forgotten about Kellik, but she had no idea where he had gone. Her movements were already slow from her wounds, but now she added caution to them as she crawled her way through the cavern to the room with the pool. His scent was still in the caves, but she could not discern whether it was from a previous time, or if he had come through again.

When Kellik found the room with a pool, he gave it more thought. He scooped up a handful of water, drank some, and splashed his face several times to clean away the caked blood from his forehead. He felt the gash begin to tingle. He reached up to trace the wound with his finger but only found a scar where the scratch should have been. The injury still hurt when he touched it, and it would probably need to heal correctly, but washing his face in the water had treated what might have taken weeks.

He forgot about his ambush until he heard the dragon coming through the cave. He hurried to the side with no time to draw either of his weapons. Taking a fortifying breath, he would have to hope the beast did not see him.

For several reasons, all of them due to her superior senses, she had thwarted his ambush. She already smelled his stronger scent in the open cavern ahead. His hurried steps to his hiding place could only have been louder if he had been wearing heavier armor, not to mention his breathing, which gave her his position as she came into the room with the pool. She was looking directly at him and already inhaling when he charged and drew the single longsword from his back. It would be his last futile effort as deadly fire flowed from her mouth directly at him.

Kellik burst through the flames barely singed. The astonished dragon, stunned beyond offering any opposition, did no more than watch as his sword pierced the place where the lightning had torn away scales from the underside of her weakened wing. The dragon's limp body had already surrendered as Kellik pulled the sword back, but he stabbed several times again for his own satisfaction.

He walked over to the pool and splashed water over his wounds. The fire had not burned him very much, but it had burned him. The water he had splashed onto himself did nothing to heal the new burns. He tried several times before he decided that this obviously magical substance would only improve him so far and that the rest would have to heal naturally.

After resting for a while and staring at the dragon, he remembered that Saigel was somewhere nearby. He wandered through the maze of caves, looking for him and finally finding him when he came to the place where they had both fallen into the trap. The smell of charred flesh filled the area. When he spotted the minikin, he thought he had lost him.

When he knelt down next to Saigel, a ragged breath escaped the minikin, and Kellik's heart leaped. After a short chant, Kellik put his hands on the other, performing a minor healing essence that he had learned many revolutions ago. He knew that the power was too weak for any noticeable difference, but it would help. The burns covered almost all of Saigel's small body, and his breathing continued to be erratic, but he might be able to pull through it.

He hoisted Saigel up on his shoulder and carried him to the room with the pool. He was going to lay him on the floor but then thought better of it. He removed his partner's gear and dunked him in the water.

Saigel abruptly sat up in the pool, coughing and gasping for breath. "Yuh tryin' to drown me?" he scolded weakly in the darkness.

"The water heals, so I was dowsing your wounds," Kellik replied.

"Oh, it's yuh. Can't see very well, can I? Healin' water yuh say, eh?" Saigel cupped his hands and drank water from them as Kellik retrieved a torch from the minikin's gear. Most of his burns faded away. With another handful, he was completely healed, with not a blister in sight. Kellik followed Saigel's lead, drank the water, and his wounds too were quickly recovered.

"That's how the dragon came back so strong," Kellik mused.

"Whur's thuh beast?" Saigel asked, and Kellik pointed to the perished form. Taking in the view, Saigel added, "Whur's thuh treasure?" The half-elf shrugged.

They walked back to the treasure room, and when they reached the narrow area where the dragon had flooded the cave with its fire, Saigel tested it carefully. The foundation had cooled enough to pass, but a thought came to him as he watched Kellik walk to the treasure. Saigel said, "Yuh never caught me. Whur'd yuh go when yuh ran?"

"The way we just came."

"How'd yuh get past thuh rock?"

"I just ran through. Why?"

Saigel looked at the other's feet. His boots, as hot as the rock surely was at that time, should have melted away yet showed no damage from the heat. However, he said, "No reason."

They gathered as much treasure as they could carry as Kellik recounted his ongoing battle with the dragon. He thought that Saigel was impressed, but he could not honestly tell. There was no reason to hurry the gathering process, so they took the time to separate gold coins from the rest. During the division, Kellik found an old book with a ragged green cover among the currencies and sifted through the pages to consider it for a moment. *Never can tell,* he thought and added it to the pile of already separated gold.

He listened in shock as Saigel recounted what had happened to him after Kellik had run off. When the tale was told and the gold was separated, they agreed that the only option for them was to climb down from the entrance cave. They did find some rope and minimal climbing gear in the pile of treasure.

When they came to the room with the pool on their way out of the dragon's lair, they found that they would have to climb over the dragon's body to get past it. Kellik took three steps up when one of the claws suddenly reached out and grabbed him. The dragon weakly raised its head and drew in a deep breath.

Saigel had almost died the last time and did not need to feel the death-dealing flames again. The minikin could do nothing, so Kellik did not blame him when he saw the little man dive behind the dragon's body for cover. Kellik was being held helplessly by the strong claw with nowhere to hide. He also had sampled the flames, but he had barely been affected. With the hope of being spared once again, he closed his eyes. The last breath from the dying dragon was a harmless cloud of black smoke. Saigel came out of hiding and helped pry Kellik free from the lifeless claw.

The rain had let up by the time they were outside, and the morning light was peeking through the clouds. Without hesitation, they started their descent of the mountain with an unspoken decision between them. There were too few instances where two different people formed an instant friendship. They decided that being trapped together, and having fought their way side by side past a dragon constituted one of those instances. Right now, the friends both wanted to get far from that place with their health and newly found wealth. But if possible, Kellik wished to retrieve his lost sword.

CHAPTER 3

A PAST REMEMBERED

It was midsummer, and not a cloud was in the teal-green sky. The afternoon sun bore down on six men. They were standing on a small ledge, which served as the path to the cave entrance that was currently under scrutiny. The elevation of the mountain pass was no protection from the heat, and there were no trees to provide shade. If this cave had been on the other side of the mountain, then shade would have been plentiful, but it was not, so the only relief was the mountain cacti.

Where most cacti grew in desolate desert regions of The Westlands and Southern Provinces, this type of cactus seemed to flourish at higher altitudes than most did and preferred a more temperate climate. The Northern Territory, which had very few mountains, rarely saw this cactus. When it did, it was because someone had removed it from its native region, and the plant never lasted long in the new climate.

This type of cactus was generally a late winter and spring plant, which usually curled within itself and hibernated during the extreme heat of the summer cycles. While most entered hibernation near the end of spring, some of the cacti survived during the summer cycles. They became short and stocky plants with many sharply pointed needles while in hibernation. In their seasonal presence, they blossomed like a flower, with many outstretched tentacles webbed together by a thin membrane.

Occasionally and more often on hot days, the seasonal plant sprayed a fine mist of liquid from its pores onto the tentacles. The meat from the plant was highly toxic, but the mist was crisp, refreshing, and not at all poisonous. Several cacti, which were along the ledge, had not entered hibernation, and all the men thanked them for their presence.

The first of the six men, who was dressed in sparkling blue clothing, cursed when he entered the cave because his robe caught on the rough rock wall and ripped. Toran heard the magician mumble something about the expense of the garment and chuckled to himself.

He did not like Enrandl. From the pompous, antiquated way he spoke, which Toran made every effort to mimic, to the consistent need to wear his customary robes, there was something off about him. He had worked for the magician before, but they had never actually worked together. Toran accepted his presence stoically this time. Besides, the magician was paying the bill for this trip, and it was already two cycles over what he had planned it to be. What was one more expense during this journey going to hurt?

Enrandl did not let Toran know it, but Toran had been one of the expenses incurred in the creation of the long blue glittering robe. Enrandl had hired him to obtain its materials, and he had been paid well for his services. It had taken two separate contracts to find enough material to permit the tailoring of several robes.

The jungles of The Southern Provinces were home to a common variety of spiders, which spun a web of tough, stringy fiber. The fiber glowed in the dark, but it was nearly imperceptible during the day. These webs were stronger than a normal spider would use to capture its prey, and the strands could be woven into clothing.

There had been something about this idea that had appealed to Enrandl, but only if he could tint the fibers with color. Enrandl had hired Toran to collect a large amount of the webbing. If Enrandl had done the smallest bit of research when he had first heard about the webbing, he might not have bothered.

When Toran delivered the strands to him, he found that they were far too tacky for his purpose. He tried several methods of neutralizing them but found no success in that endeavor or with his attempts to color them. He was almost ready to concede defeat when he noticed the accidental stowaway, which had been brought along with the mass of unworkable fibers, coming out of its hiding place.

The carnivorous light-brown arachnid watched his every move with its large black eyes. It was only about the size of a human thumb and mostly covered with fine white hairs, except around its eyes. These hairs were as black as the eyes that watched the mage were. He had no idea how potent the little creature was.

Their usual prey were small animals in the forests and jungles of The Southern Provinces, but its poison was far more deadly than these conditions warranted. Enrandl ignored it for the most part. When he moved closer, it tried to spray him with its poison, but he escaped untouched and smashed the little arachnid. Blood from the spider dyed the strands of the web blue wherever it touched it and neutralized the sticky fibers enough to be workable. So he then contracted Toran once again, this time to collect hundreds of the spiders.

He had studied the poison and had been kind enough to warn Toran about the toxic spray. If contact with the skin persisted for more than one minute, it would seep into the person's bloodstream and cause death in a matter of seconds. Once inside the body, nothing would impede its final outcome. However, a simple antidote of alcohol rubbed onto the sprayed area neutralized the poison. This remedy for one spray of a spider made perfect sense, but in a forest or cave where hundreds of spiders were around and ready to spray, rubbing alcohol on it within a minute was a problem. He and Toran had agreed that a higher fee would be more appropriate for such a dangerous mission.

Enrandl set to work dying the fibers and found that not only did the dye from the blood neutralize the stickiness of the threads but also canceled their glow for the most part. He sent the strands to a seamstress whom he had commissioned to make other clothing for him. After a week, she had completed five of the blue robes. The glow of the webbing material had not been eradicated entirely. Now small areas that glowed throughout the gown gave it a star-spangled and glittering appearance. Enrandl was so pleased with it that he paid the seamstress additional finance, even though she had nothing to do with the final result of the robe.

The magic user learned much later that Toran had completed this contract with too much leisure, gathering more than enough spiders for Enrandl's purpose and having GodsLight to escape from being sprayed. Toran had discovered on his first trip that smoke from any normal fire had killed them. Even during the bargaining, he withheld this information so that his employer would not know how easy it had been.

In contrast to his employer's fancier clothing, Toran was wearing an old suit of leather armor. He was feeling the temperature, even with the cooling spray of the cactus. The other four men were clad in chain mail. He knew they were being tortured more than he was. All of their armor was ordinarily clean and well kept, as was his leather, but the two cycles worth of searching mountain ranges was beginning to blemish the appearance of each person's armor. He had known all of these men for several revolutions and had adventured with them often. He was not a regular member of their party but was always welcomed as one if he decided to come along or as in this instance, gathered them together to join him.

Shawln, the tallest of the group on the mountain ledge, was third in their single-file line. He moved closer to Toran, who was second from the front. Shawln carried a small ax in one hand. This ax was much smaller than the battle-ax that was strapped to his back. His other hand steadied him against the rock. His bright flaxen hair fell just short of reaching the head of the battle-ax.

"Normally, those protecting go before those being protected," Shawln whispered into Toran's ear.

"Ordinary circumstance dictates the compensated make convention to not anatomize the deliberations of their benefactor," Enrandl shot back angrily before he continued into the cave. His attitude about searching for his prize had waned with each failure to find it. He had not counted on incorrect information from his consultation with the higher powers, and he was beyond anger on the matter. All the other information they had given to him had been correct, except the location of the cave. If he had interpreted the answers wrongly, which he must have done, surely the previously searched areas of The Unforgiving would have crossed the dragon's dominion.

From below, he had seen what now appeared to be a small cave. One of the others had spotted the ledge leading to it, so they had backtracked to find its origin. Inside and near the middle of the cave were the remains of two long-forgotten fires. He was not optimistic that there was much here. Beside one of the extinguished fires lay several animal pelts. He walked over to examine them as the other five men entered the cave behind him.

"I hope we do not have to duck the whole time we are here," Erick complained sarcastically. He was the shortest of them and the only one who could actually walk inside the cave without ducking. His hair had been shaved before they had left but had grown out to stubble during this expedition. The skin on his head had been burnt red by the sun, but he did not seem to notice it.

He was the least likely among them to appear to be a fighting man when he was not in armor. With his height and gaunt physique, no one would guess that he was an adventurer while in his everyday attire or place him as a magician. Fortunately, and contrary to his build, he was strong, and his skill with the sword defended his position as the group's best fighter.

"Toran, to accommodate a reduced quantity of complaint, would you construct a suitable exploit to mark their intermission? Evidence indicates the requirement of exploration elsewhere." Enrandl pointed toward the back of the cave, not realizing that Erick had made the statement. Then he tucked some tangled hair behind his ear and away from his face so that he could finish his inspection.

Toran did not like agreeing with Enrandl, but he was right. The two-day trip through the pass from Kershal had been uneventful, as most of this expedition had been.

"Shawln and Erick, guard the entrance. Gleason and Philip, track the cavern back fifty yards and report." Toran walked over to Enrandl. "What are your expectations of discovery here?" He asked, but no answer followed because a scream echoed from the back of the small cave.

"Gleason, Philip, report!" Toran called out as the scream faded away.

"Philip has fallen into the mountain," Gleason replied as he came into view. He was Toran's height and build, but Toran was his senior by several revolutions. Like Erick, he only carried a longsword.

Toran motioned to Shawln and Erick to follow him. Gleason led them to the point where Philip had fallen. Enrandl also followed as he slung a pure-white pelt over his shoulder.

"He just slipped and kept sliding down," Gleason reported when they reached the spot.

Toran yelled Philip's name but received no answer as Enrandl pondered the area. "There is magic displayed here," he said, indicating the floor farther ahead toward the interior of the cave. "Your fellow may have stumbled upon its convention. Anyone enticed to attend him?" Enrandl asked, but no one seemed amused or interested. "None would proceed to assess your associate's predicament?"

"To certain death?" Shawln added.

"Death? A conceivable consequence, but my certainty is not so convinced. The incidence of the effect displayed here certainly methods other contrivance. I can institute a more benign technique to shadow his advance, but if I alone endeavor presently, your excess will compose an arduous passage."

Three of the four men looked at each other quizzically. The magic user smiled as he watched Toran realize and understand him. *He does have his merits*, Enrandl mused.

Toran was ready to follow, nodded to the rest of his fellows, and said, "Let us advance."

"Leadership prevails once again," Enrandl said, "but quite correct. We advance." He pulled a white feather from a pouch and gathered everyone together. Then he whispered a quick phrase and brushed each man across the shoulder with the feather. He raised it above his head and let it go to complete his channelling. The feather dissipated into nothing before it reached the cave floor. Little aura was expended so he felt nothing.

All but one of the men watched in amazement as he walked deeper into the cave and then dove in.

The magician's actions did not impress Toran as much. "Come on," Toran said. "He is not going to dupe us if he still needs our help." He walked back and disappeared downward. One by one, three confused men followed him down, trusting that they would not be led astray.

Deep inside the mountain, the temperature was significantly colder and mildly damp. A small glowing disk beside Philip spread light through the cavern and revealed charred black walls throughout the five-foot-wide cave hall. In the upper cave, plenty of daylight had stolen in from the outside so that they could see. However, down here, he needed some other light source. It was times like these that he was glad to have the disk. It was glowing when it had been given to him revolutions ago, and the glow had never faded. His blond hair had been shorter then, and he had not yet learned the skill of the scimitar, which he wielded with the expertise that served him now.

When he had found the disk, he had been an apprentice to a popular magic user but had discovered the lifestyle did not suit him. It had been glowing from underneath a pile of leaves, and his teacher had instructed him to investigate. The mage had educated him on the effect only days before that, but when he had tried to channel a breeze to blow the leaves, nothing had happened. He had tried several more times, but the display had not come forth.

His master had finally lost patience and had channelled the effect for Philip. The leaves had blown in all directions, and the light disk underneath them had been revealed. The impatient mage had told him to keep it as an intended gift and never to let its light shine upon him again unless Philip was not present. He did just that. He walked away and never saw his tutor again. Philip thought that if he had had another master, maybe one with more patience, he would have fared better at a career in magic.

Philip screamed in pain as he set his own broken shin while Enrandl watched quietly. Then Toran slowly landed behind the magic user. Erick and Shawln followed and also set down lightly, but Gleason was not so lucky. The display from Enrandl's effect to decrease their rate of fall had worn off just before Gleason reached the bottom. He bowled over the four men blocking his way.

Philip, despite the pain, started to laugh as they untangled themselves and got back on their feet. Enrandl started to inspect the black walls that surrounded them as the rest of the men joined Philip in his laughter.

"Scorched," Enrandl said. "But a display here prohibits the embodiment from conceding to extreme calefaction." He placed his hand on the wall as he walked further away from the group. Black soot rubbed away from the wall as his hand dragged across it. The black soot rubbed away from the wall, and tiny amounts of the dust fell away as his hand dragged across it. Enrandl was almost at the coin's limit of the light, but he could see past the layers of grit to the actual color of the rock wall.

"Scorched by what?" Toran asked.

The magic user did not answer. He walked on from the group of fighters, studying the cave walls as he went. He thought that fire might have caused the scorching, but if a dragon's fire had caused it, the effect used there would have to have been very potent; otherwise, there would be melted rock.

"It is time that we merit our compensation," Toran said, "unless suspension to splint Philip's leg achieves your aversion."

Enrandl glared at him across the expanse lightened by the coin, and Toran returned the glare. The mage let Toran win the stare down. *For now,* Enrandl thought. He went back to inspecting the wall.

An idea occurred to Toran just as he decided that the dry bones they had used, though they were very brittle, would have to suffice as a splint until an alternate could be found. Something that he had long since forgotten now came to the forefront of his thoughts. He knelt, put one hand on Philip's knee, and the other on his ankle, closed his eyes, and peered into the darkness of his eyelids.

"What are you doing?" The injured man asked, but Toran gave no answer.

A few moments of concentration later, in the vision of his mind's eye, a pale colorless sphere replaced the darkness. Myriad pigments formed and danced around this field. Although what he was seeing was all happening in his mind, he felt himself flinch as the sphere washed over and bound itself to him. Within the field, as the colors surrounding it continued to entwine themselves around him, a vision of his surroundings formed.

Each pigment was represented by its own sphere. At one time, he would have been able to connect each one to a part of his surroundings, but his memory of them was foggy, so for the moment, he focused on one sphere as a picture of Philip's broken leg now formed within it. He could see the same view that he would have if he had been looking directly at the leg. His face contorted slightly as he concentrated harder, drawing the primary red hue to the injured leg. He did not flinch this time as the color enveloped him and replaced the colorless binding around him.

While this sphere altered what he saw, the new tint of his vision was a little unnerving. He looked beyond the outer leg and now saw what his eyes could not. He saw the bones in Philip's broken leg, which Philip had set back together himself. He knew that he could do better. He focused the sphere, centered the red hue on the leg, and directed a manipulation from his view. He watched the bones mend and also forced some of Philip's internal damage to be repaired, before his vision went colorless again. He opened his eyes and released his concentration. The sphere melted away from both his views.

"That should feel better," Toran replied after a moment.

"It does, but what did you do?" Philip asked. Everyone except Enrandl, who had continued farther down the passage, waited for the reply.

Toran checked that the magician was far enough away before whispering, "Something from a long time ago, my friend. I will explain later."

Philip limped along with the rest of the group. The healing that had been done was not completed. His leg would still be sore, and he would have to favor it in the makeshift splint.

Toran wondered if he should try healing him again, but they came around a curve in the cave and saw the mound of treasure. He smiled when wounded leg and all, Philip was the first to dive into the hoard, followed shortly by Gleason.

"All the treasure we find, we keep! That was the deal." Gleason shouted. "I love this deal!"

"A book," Enrandl said. "That is my expectation, Toran. The residual treasure division is as previously agreed."

The mage began a channelling. He waggled the fingers of both hands for a moment and whispered a phrase to himself until they began to sparkle with orange light. Then he covered each eye with the palms of his hands for a moment before he pulled his hands away. When he had finished, he looked at the mound of treasure. He scanned the whole pile twice and then made a slow, methodical 360-degree turn.

"No!" he yelled and threw the leopard pelt down at the base of the treasure. "Its presence must be valid!" Four men stood and watched him climb through the collection of treasure while muttering, "Obligation alludes to requirement. Its presence must be valid! Toran, your men have purpose to endure their investigation of the lair. Perchance a secondary locality for treasure disposition has been conceived."

"Lair? What do you mean?" asked Philip.

"Exactly what he said." The answer came from Shawln across the cave, who was kneeling beside charred and melted rock. The other men joined him.

"Red, by these marks," Gleason added.

"You were aware of this!" Toran accused. Preoccupied with healing Philip's leg and remembering more of his previous training, he had not considered the amount of treasure here or the creature that may have collected it.

"Of course not! I conjectured such. With allowance for the self-indulgence required to procure and hoard an accumulation approximating this, what speculation yields your theorization?" Enrandl replied. Toran, who was thinking of earlier comments, did not believe him. The magician said, "You have your own allowances. Your men should be reconnoitering at present."

"Correct! We are being paid." Toran was beyond mimicking now. "Another thousand each or my men stay right here." He did not consider himself a greedy man, but he and the others deserved an amount of finance that measured up to the risk, of what he now assumed, a red dragon would more than certainly provide.

"More supplementary resource than I have capacity to provide, abundantly present, and you would further negotiate additional? Agreed then, one thousand more each," Enrandl consented, but Toran felt that he had won this stare down with too much ease.

He gave the men their orders. Each one drew his weapons and started his search. He lit one of his torches before the others left with the light disk. Enrandl must have used some magic because from across the cavern, Toran saw the magician search the pile for more than a half hour with no other light source than his torch. He wanted to ask why this book was so important but did not figure that he would get an answer.

Let alone a true one.

Philip returned and tossed the bones from his splint at Toran. "Healing water. Dead red. Four cycles minimum," he commented. He motioned for Toran and Enrandl to follow him and jogged away.

The run, as they followed Philip, became a race. Toran had had a head start but carrying a torch had hindered his speed. Enrandl, quick on his feet and apparently needing no light to see, closed the distance and nearly overtook him. They had both already passed Philip by the time they reached the scene of the dead dragon.

Enrandl was too winded to continue the race much longer. He noticed that Toran only slowed to a jog and then joined the rest of his men near the dragon. The magic user stopped by the pool of water, which was fifty feet away, to gather his breath and allow time for Philip to also join the others. He reached into one of his robe pockets and removed a tiny ball.

"Dead?" Enrandl asked after a few moments to gather his breath.

"Very," Toran called back his reply.

"Good," he whispered to himself and started channelling. Gripping the tiny ball, he pointed his index finger at the group, which now surrounded the beast. Magic words rolled off his tongue, and the effect displayed. A flash of red-orange light drew a perfect line from the mage's finger to a point just above the decaying creature. Where the line stopped, a bubble developed and expanded.

An explosion of fire filled the passageway above the dead dragon as he felt his aura was drained. None of the five fighters remained standing. "So are you," the mage chuckled, waggled his singed hand, and blew on it to cool it off.

He had released more energy than the effect needed, allowing it to display much larger so that he would encompass them all. As a result, his hand had suffered the consequence along with his aura.

The smell of burnt sulfur, the remains of the tiny ball that he had used, filled the air immediately around him, and his palm was left with a moderate burn. A drink from the pool healed Enrandl's charred palm, and he walked over to pick up Philip's light disk, which appeared unharmed by his flashfire. He tucked it into a pouch and looked over the dead dragon's body. He needed a conversation with it—one he could not perform on his own.

He produced another feather, from somewhere on his outfit, started twisting it back and forth between his thumb and index finger, and channelled again. Shawln was lifted from the ground by the display.

Enrandl tried to raise a second body, but the effect was too weak to allow it.

A quick walk later, and he had moved the lifted body to the narrowed cave where Philip had broken his leg, but that was as far as one effect would get him. Expending additional aura (as he had done with the flashfire) to increase how much he could move would save him subsequent trips but would be a waste of aura, which he did not need to expend since he had the time.

He repeated the trip three more times. He was making his way to retrieve Toran when he heard some coins moving in the pile of treasure. He immediately retrieved a tiny crystal orb and a pinch of fur from a pouch. He held the orb in the palm of his right hand, pointed to the pile of coins, and snapped his left hand's fingers with the fur between them—as the channel dictated. The fur sparked at the snap, and the crystal shattered.

The cave was instantly and momentarily washed in a blue-white brightness as a crackling bolt of electricity, which he had assumed would conduct throughout the pile of metal coins, hit.

When he went to inspect the area for what he had heard, all he saw was gold, silver, and copper finance, which had been melted together in a twisted mass where the bolt had directly struck. Farther away from the impact point, fewer coins were fused, and most coins on the outer edges of the pile still held their individual forms. He found no sign of anything that would cause the coins to have moved. He was angry that he had wasted aura for a figment of his imagination.

But he had not imagined what he had heard.

Toran had been lying on the outer edge of the pile. His eyes had been closed, and his concentration had been balanced on three separate spheres at once. He had been looking for something to cover his naked body. His armor had been a casualty of the fiery blast, but had performed its duty well in protecting him.

Just before Enrandl had interrupted his search, he had found a cloak to wrap around him. While grabbing the black garment, he had jarred several loose coins. He had seen Enrandl start at the noise, had almost instinctively closed his eyes, and had waited for the orb to form. He had drawn a tertiary purple sphere to surround himself in silence, and the coins had made no more noise.

Then he had heard Enrandl channelling. Not wanting to be Enrandl's next target, he had slid down the backside of the hill of coins as his tertiary sphere had still sustained his silence. When the jolt of energy had hit the coins, its current had coursed through the pile and had electrocuted him. He had slumped down at the edge of the pile and had almost passed out from the pain. It was perhaps because he was entrenched in his talent that he had not already done so, but he would pass out soon if he did not do something quickly.

His scrambled senses somehow realized that he had not been the target of the electrical force. That meant the coins were. If that was true, he had not been seen yet. His head pounded again, as if the electrical current was still rolling through him. He nearly collapsed. A wave of nausea rattled his system. He knew that if he did not remain conscious, he would be found. There was no time to hesitate, but he was not sure how to proceed. Red, the sphere he had used for Philip's leg, would not be appropriate, but a warm pigment was still reasonable. Grasping for the first available option, he chose primary yellow. Instead of combining this pigment with the violet sphere, which was already bound around him, he sent it directly to his troubled brain and centered it there as he had done with the red one on Philip's leg. The choice was a good one. Like a waterfall, everything that was unsettling his head was washed away, and he could think clearly. He was not sure if this comfort was a momentary reprieve or permanent repair, so instead of letting it go, he held its focus.

He knew the next effort, just like he knew that he could heal Philip's broken leg and silence the space around himself. His mind reached out for the blue-green, grabbed it, and pooled it with the violet globe. The warm colors blended, each swirling in his sight, as he altered the vision behind his eyes. The multicolored sphere in his mind's eye showed a picture of the whole treasure room, including Enrandl searching.

What this mental image did not include was himself because he had removed his image from the vision.

His focus was almost faltering, and by the time Enrandl was done searching the pile and had left the cave, a dull ache started to form in his forehead. He had watched Enrandl go the opposite direction, so he knew that he was safe enough to go back to the room with the pool, before he investigated what the other was doing. The pain in his head was not from any queasiness or need to pass out. His use of the spheres had caused it, and he was sure that the water would heal only the wounds to his body and not the headache from their use.

It had taken two handfuls of healing water before he could return to the treasure room after he had regained consciousness from the flashfire. This time, it only took one handful.

Enrandl damned Toran several times as he walked back to the other bodies. The four were still there, and the mage was going to make sure they did not go anywhere. He found some lantern oil on one of the bodies and poured it all over them. Then he ignited them with a weak effect. He produced a flame from his right hand and extended it out to them. He studied and memorized this area of the cave while the bodies burned. Then he uttered a phrase to induce the channel for the next effect's display. He bowed his head and raised both arms as magical energy responded to his command. It swirled around him and engulfed him faster than any eyes could see.

Toran, invisible and silent again but no longer injured, had positioned himselfbehind the magician. His sword found only air when he swung it at Enrandl, who had vanished in front of him. If Enrandl was still close enough, he could find his mind. Toran remembered that he could search for him even without accessing a new sphere to do so and realized quickly that the other must have shifted away.

The magician was probably all the way back to Jenerv. What he had wanted had not been here. Toran relaxed and discontinued his search, invisibility, and silence spheres all at once.

He was correct about the water not helping his head. He had not used the Merea in a long time. He was not even sure that he had done so from memory or GodsLight. What he had remembered had been useful, but he had approached a barrier, and his headache reminded him of this fact. Healing Philip's leg had been an inspiration. The healing could have been completed if he had taken more time. He could not imagine why he had suddenly remembered it was something he could do or how he could have forgotten in the first place.

He had studied and had lived on the Merea ability to control his mind for nearly ten revolutions of his life until he had decided that a good weapon at his side had been more important in most situations than his Merea talent. Sometime during his training with sword and body, he had buried his mental exercise deep inside himself, favoring the physical.

"The spheres are important, but the formation is the key," Higoshi had always told him. "Form that which you desire in your mind, and then, will it to become so." He heard the words in his memory, spoken precisely because Higoshi had said them directly to him hundreds of times. He remembered Higoshi well and recalled snippets of his training. The old man had been ever so patient. Although he had acted impatiently at times with many of his students, Toran had known his master well. He had ignored the act and had learned at his own pace.

Higoshi's concept was simple, and if accurate with his representation, application of the Merea talent was nearly limitless. Toran had never gone beyond the foundation of already-experimented ability.

There were others in the realms who had no training for their talents. Some accidentally discovered that they were capable of strange mental capabilities without the direction of a master. These individuals were scarce and had limited talent. Anyone who wanted to truly harness his Merea ability properly needed the same formal training that Toran had once received.

"The strength of the mind can overcome any obstacle," Toran said aloud. Today he discovered that a combination of sword and mind could be devastating. If Enrandl had not shifted away, the magician would surely be dead.

As his friends were.

Toran looked at them burning, now beyond his help. A tear rolled down his cheek as he walked away. He would never again adventure with any of them. He wished he had never taken this contract and that he had never met Enrandl.

He put his sword, which had survived the flashfire, back into its sheath. He wore only the jet-black cloak wrapped around his waist. He found a small sack among the treasure and filled it with some coins. The coins held little value compared to the price Enrandl would pay when Toran caught up with him.

Toran retracted his second wish.

If he had never met Enrandl, although his friends would still be alive, he would not have any reason to make him pay for what he had done.

CHAPTER 4

NEW FRIENDS, NEW ENEMIES

Kellik opened the aged book again. He was sitting on a stool, in a tavern with no name, and at a small bar table where the book lay open.

The saloon was large. It had to be in order to house the large stone cooking hearth, which dominated the center of the taproom. The base of this fireplace was made of stones that had been stacked and mortared together up to its slate mantle about three feet high along the length, and it had been squared off at the ends.

The cooking pit had been constructed from various sized stones and mortar (similar to the base) and orbed internally while externally creating a rise at the center of it, which fell off to each side and presented the outside with the appearance of a hill. The image was marred only by the chimney, which stemmed from the top and extended up to the ceiling. Inside, the pit area had two long solid rods used for holding food while cooking it over the fire. A large cauldron hung from a sturdy wooden brace, which one could turn in or out of the pit when needed. There was also a crank and chain for raising and lowering it.

The whole edifice was cold now, but he imagined that during the winter cycles, the fire was never extinguished. The cook and his helpers would not be in to start the evening dinner for several hours, but the smell of the previous evening's lamb still lingered.

He did not have to imagine the crowd this tavern might attract. When he and Saigel had arrived in Kershal, the place had been cluttered with people. Most of them were locals. There were a few outsiders, like themselves, who were passing through to other destinations and lingering a day or two before moving on. It was so congested that Kellik was not able to enter. He stood outside while the smaller of them tried to work his way in and get something to drink.

He waited a long time before a loud roar erupted from inside. Kellik looked in through the doorway and wondered what was going on. The bulk of people gathered around one of the tables near the middle, creating room for him to come in. As the roar died away, one yell stood out above the rest. The accented voice of the speaker who owned it was familiar enough to him.

"Yuh've got no right ta be angry! 'Twus a good match. Yuh owes me thuh two gold."

"I'll not pay until you can be proved!" Kellik heard someone else say. The voice was deep and wavering, but the anger that it expressed had not wavered.

"Proved of whut?" Saigel answered.

"No magic—" A hush fell over the crowd. "Can any … one do this?" With that, Kellik could hear the slurred speech of a drunken man.

"Twus a fair match. Thur was not magic at hand!"

After more silence at the mention of magic, Saigel heard a voice from behind the crowd answer his accusers call.

"Yes, I can." The answer caused murmurs through the previously hushed crowd.

Saigel tried but could not see the owner of the reply. He stood on his chair, which was across from a mountain of a human, and that man did not look happy. He had already plotted a possible escape route because he might have to make a run for the door sooner than later.

"Come on … then, prove the munchikin!" the other bellowed.

Saigel had almost jumped up on the tabletop to parley the subject of magic into an argument about the large man's derogatory comment, but when the gathering parted to offer space for a judge to come forward, his anxiety subsided.

He had heard the term *munchikin* too much and mostly from humans. At first, it had angered him, many times to the point of fighting. However, after hearing its continued use, he decided that he could not take on all the realms. He still disliked it but accepted that he was never going to stop hearing it.

Kellik stepped through the parted crowd, wearing a robe to cover his armor and weapons. He had borrowed if from the tavern's nervous owner—a small balding older man who was not particularly good at keeping the peace when problems occurred. He walked slowly and methodically.

"Who's to be proved?" Kellik said, disguising his voice in a harsher tone than he usually used. He could not believe what he was seeing. His friend, who was barely four feet tall, was taunting a man more than twofold his size for a fight.

"That … one, of course," the large, drunken man replied as if it should be obvious and pointed at Saigel. The accuser was wearing ragged leather armor, and his face was almost as ugly as the armor he wore. "Let the proving be done!" he boomed, although his judge was standing directly in front of him.

Kellik chanted an essence, one which may have been useful two cycles ago in a small cave east of Kershal—the same cave that he and Saigel were returning to. That night in the cave, he had made fire using his flint. Tonight, with divine aid, a flame ignited around his finger. The collective group, which was comprised mostly of local farmers who were naive to the use of magic, gasped. To anyone who had never encountered it, magic's reality was purely a myth that everyone merely believed in.

He knew magic was a rare occurrence in his homeland of The East, in divine or arcane form and, by the reaction of those in the taproom, he made a significant assumption that the people in this region of the realm held the same vague ignorance of mystical forces and that they would probably never see it during their lifetimes.

Anyone in the gathering last night who was close enough to witness his flamelight was going to have a tale to tell for the rest of their lives. Someone here might even become inspired enough to choose, as he had chosen, and explore the vast world beyond their own.

He approached Saigel, who had already fallen into an act of playing along and stood proud on his chair, and said, "If there's magic at hand upon him, the flame will become green." Kellik knew that any other priest and adventurer with enough exposure would understand the essence and that it was merely a quick way to start a fire. He put his hand in front of Saigel, and the flame remained its orange hue.

Now for the tricky part, Kellik thought. He faced the gathering. He had already chosen a soldier from among them for the second part of his ploy. This man could easily be mistaken for an adventurer and might very well have had something with a magical aspect attached to it. Kellik understood the chance that he was taking, and it was another assumption that he was prepared to make.

The idea that no one would recognize this deception yet choosing someone who might be able to do that was on the verge of demented. He gambled on those who were here and that they were already enthralled enough by seeing something incredible. They just might believe that a random soldier, instead of a known local farmer, would have an instance of magic.

Kellik moved his hand toward the soldier. The flame on his finger turned a deep green. The soldier smiled. Whether the smile indicated success or failure was not determined until he spoke.

"The minikin is proved! Two gold is owed," the soldier announced.

"No!" Saigel's opponent yelled. "I'll not pay!" The angry man stood, stretching to his full height before reaching for his weapon.

Kellik's hand went quickly to his sword, but neither he nor the large man he was about to engage had the chance to remove their weapons.

"It was a fair match, Thomas. You should pay," a well-dressed dwarf seated not far from the angered man said. Wearing an extravagant shirt and vest, tailored with the style and design attributed to The Southern Provinces, the dwarf reached for the big man's purse but saw it was not there. "It is so often in large crowds, scoundrels thrive, and purses are turned up missing," the dwarf said as Thom looked down with a startled look. "I am terribly sorry ..."

"Find the thief!" Thom bellowed.

"... But my large friend here has no finance to pay two of any denomination."

"And I'll kill him!" the man continued. If it were possible, Thom seemed angrier than just moments before.

"Surely now, that will not be necessary, Thomas. There is more gold out in the lands to be earned or won." The dwarf calmed his friend down.

"Fuhrget thuh wager," Saigel added. Thom and Saigel shook hands before Saigel went to the bar. Kellik left the tavern, not wanting anyone to suspect him of knowing the minikin.

The well-attired dwarf went to the bar to join Saigel and said, "Fibble is my name." Then he ordered an ale. Saigel looked at the dwarf's long nose and unusually clean-shaven face that was etched with age lines. Then Fibble whispered surprisingly to Saigel in the dwarven language, "I commend you and your friend on your performance, but if Thomas had been less intoxicated, he would have also noticed your exchanged looks. You should practice more if you are going to try anything such as that again, but it was most inventive."

"He invented it," Saigel added. "I didnah know whut was goin' on."

"Well then, I must return to my friend. We have a mission, you understand. And do not worry about Thomas. He will harbor no grievance against you or your elf friend," Fibble said aloud in human speech once more. Then he whispered in dwarven directly to Saigel, "Most inventive." Without a hitch, his language switched again. "Come now, Thomas, we need rest for our travels. Mirzog waits for no one!"

Drunkenly, Thom mimicked, "Mirzog wait for no one. That's because Mirzog's dead!"

Kellik sat down on a bench and sighed. He had been sure that someone would recognize his deception and that he would have to fight his way out of the tavern. It appeared that no one had, and Kellik was relieved.

"Yuh su'prise me," Saigel said later, when he and Kellik had a chance to regroup. "Yuh don't seem like thuh type ta ruse nobody."

"Sometimes you need to make exceptions, especially when a friend's health is at stake."

"True, muh friend, too true," he said and then added, "But yuh still su'prise me."

"You must have your questions prepared and worded properly," Frederick Smythe told him. "The dead do not like to be disturbed—and are certainly not likely to desire an interrogation."

The priest Frederick and Enrandl walked down the middle aisle of the main temple's floor. Frederick was much older than Enrandl, and he showed it. His hair was gray and thin, and his face bore far too many wrinkles for his age. Revolutions of practicing the powers of The Dark Gods' tenebrous designs and essences had taken their toll on him.

"My interrogation, as you articulate it, is primed. Are you an agreeable accomplice to escort me?" Enrandl asked. There was no expression in his tone, but he could not hide an enlightened glimmer in his eyes to mask his deception. It was providence that the priest's attention was elsewhere now.

"Yes." Frederick said. He was shorter than Enrandl, and his hair, though gray and thinning, was neatly cut. His dark-brown robe, which touched the ground, was complete with a hood and several outside pockets.

Enrandl figured the priest into his channel. With a brief spoken word and bow of his head, he raised his arms and shifted back to the dead dragon's cave. Enrandl took out the light disk so that the two men could see.

When the surprised priest saw where they were, he became angry. "What have you done? I am not prepared for this!" Frederick said.

"All apologies," he said and bowed, "but your implied disposition ..." Enrandl feigned the best look of innocence that he could.

"I do not care what you thought my intentions were. I did not know you meant an immediate journey."

Enrandl smiled to himself. An unwilling target of an effect could sometimes resist the display, even if it could be beneficial. The priest had said that he would go, therefore making him a willing companion of the shift. Enrandl had tricked the priest somewhat fairly, so there was no reason to complain.

The stench from the burned bodies hung in the air. The priest looked at them. "Are those your friends?" he asked dejectedly.

"No. The acquaintance of our course has more encroachment upon our leisure." Enrandl pointed. "Our passage will be anodyne. I have frequented in repeated fashion, and whatever may have relocated following my last has limited potential to be entirely established." Enrandl lied to the priest in order to ease any apprehension that Frederick may have and, though he expected nothing, was prepared to defend himself if needed.

When they arrived at the treasure pile, Enrandl noticed the collection was not entirely fused together as he had believed it would be. Someone had raided the pile, as nearly a quarter of the removable treasure was gone.

Enrandl watched as Frederick looked at all the wealth. He knew the priest was wondering how much of a donation the temple would receive for his services. "You have not been here since the last cycle?" the priest asked. "And you have left all of this treasure here?" The priest walked to the pile and nearly stepped on the leopard pelt. It caught his attention before he saw that most of the treasure had been melted together. "With this amount of finance, you could have your—"

"That particular affluence redeems diminutive importance, but your facilities are precisely contrasting, and their requirement is farther on." Enrandl watched the priest pick up the pelt before he continued into the cave. The priest resorted to jogging so that he could catch up with the light. When he could see more clearly, he inspected the pelt as they walked on.

"Beautiful pelt, is it not?" Enrandl asked after several minutes.

"Yes, it is."

"It would compose a brilliant exhibition as a wall mount," Enrandl said.

The priest looked up at Enrandl as they entered the room with the pool, and the sight and smell of the decaying dragon filled their senses. "My object for your attentions." Enrandl pointed to the dead dragon. The form of the beast was unclear because it was at the light's edge. The radiance of its once great scales and size was diminished by decay, but as they approached and Frederick became aware, the priest looked incredulous.

"What would you want to talk with a dead dragon about?" Frederick asked.

"Any response controverts relevance. If you would generously validate the justification of my aspiration," Enrandl said.

The priest looked at the dragon and then at Enrandl. "I did scold you that I was not prepared for this trip. I will need proper prayer." The priest found a comfortable place, set down the white pelt, and began praying while Enrandl walked back to the treasure room, leaving the priest in darkness.

Kellik had not heard the exchange between Fibble and Saigel, which had taken place two days ago, but his friend had informed him of it early the next morning. The dwarf was as good as his word too, because they had crossed paths with the pair the next day. Thom sat in the same place that he had on the night of the match and made no move toward either of them. Saigel was, even then, on the other side of the mountainous hearth engaged in another contest. Kellik's contentment faltered for a moment as he wondered what Fibble had told the human, but the moment passed, and he refocused on the book.

Aside from finance already spent, the book was the only item that Kellik had kept from the dragon's treasure. He was curious to know what the words and symbols meant. A majority of finance from their plunder had purchased a custom-fit suit of leather armor, along with three custom-fashioned swords.

He had recently decided that chain mail hindered him more than it helped. A cold, wet climb, which had taken place several cycles ago, had proved this to him, so he wanted something lighter and more comfortable. The new matched pair of longswords was at the inn across the road, and the bastard sword was sheathed at his hip.

Even in smaller villages like Kershal, judging from the other night's commotion and the problems that it could have caused, no one should be completely defenseless. He kept this sword with him because the others, in his judgment, were not suitably prepared.

The cover of the book was plain and had no decoration. It had been layered over with deep green weathered leather, recognizable by touch and look but not by its odor. The smell of the leather was gone. He had not been aware that this was possible. The paper was even more of an exciting mystery. The cover was old and tattered, but every page was made of a unique paper that looked as if it was brand-new. Throughout the written work, not a single ink smudge was anywhere to be seen.

He could not understand the foreign words. Some of the symbols were vaguely familiar. He flipped through the pages anyway. *It's probably just some ancient language*, he thought.

Whenever Kellik attempted to get Saigel to help examine the book—its writing and intricately drawn symbols—it was his preoccupation since another challenger would approach and not a lack of interest that diverted him to another arm contest. Kellik was learning extraordinarily little about his subject but was finding out something about the community, thanks to his newest friend, Pierce.

The proprietor of this establishment owed GodsLight because of several times when trouble had not destroyed his tavern from previous incidents. When Kellik had asked for—nearly demanded—a robe from the rack behind him for his attempt to prevent the fight between Saigel and Thom, Pierce had graciously loaned one in hopes of protecting his business from harm, yet another time.

Grateful for his help, the owner had decided that any time Kellik was in Kershal, all of his drinks would be free. The offer only extended to him and not to any of his friends. Pierce also offered information, even though he had not been asked. He told Kellik that with his wife and four healthy sons helping, his tavern and jointly owned inn across the road were the main buildings in the village. Several farms and many small homes around the region gave the bar their primary business. Consistent travelers and adventurers, who were going north and south and passing through, provided an excellent complement. There were a few, like Saigel and him, who traveled east trying to cross The Unforgiving but even more rarely returned from there.

A triumphant yell across the tavern interrupted the owner and redirected Kellik's attention. Saigel had won another arm contest. The tavern owner moved off as Saigel approached. Kellik knew that he still held a grudge against the minikin for nearly starting a fight in his tavern.

Either 'e knows how to pick 'em, or he is jus' strong'r than 'e looks, Kellik thought, mimicking Saigel's peculiar accent to himself.

He inspected the loser of Saigel's newest match. When the man finally lifted his head, Saigel hopped up on the stool next to Kellik. None of the normal humiliating cackles came from those around him.

The loser got up from the table and walked away. He was not a big man, but he was taller than Kellik and was well muscled. At this time of the day, few people were in the tavern, but Kellik knew that this man was well respected as he left the nearly silent inn still shaking his head.

"How do you do that?" Kellik asked. "I've not seen you defeated yet."

"Jus' strong'r than I look, I guess. Want a try? Two gold."

"Why only two? You could have a pile of coins by now if you'd bet more."

"Wouldn't be fair. Ones I pick got no chance," Saigel replied.

Kellik tried to count the number of matches Saigel had won over the past five cycles in the several places they had traveled through. When he reached thirty and still had more to score, he declined the challenge.

"Would I have a chance?" Kellik asked.

"No," Saigel answered flatly.

As he watched Saigel's latest opponent leave, another man entered the tavern. His sandy-blond hair was combed straight back and looked wet, as if he had just bathed and had not taken the time to dry his hair. A black cloak that had no other decoration hung from his shoulders. It was in distinct contrast to his gear, except his boots. The boots were similarly black, though not as severely as the cloak. He joined three men at a table near the hearth. Every so often as the four men talked, Kellik noticed the newcomer looking over his shoulder. Not long after the third over-the-shoulder glance, one of them called to Saigel and gestured for him to come over.

"Scuse me. Got a match ta win," Saigel commented.

Kellik looked at the new arrival again. He had a similar build as Saigel's last challenger. He was maybe even taller, but Saigel did not consider his opponent at all. In fact, his friend had not even seen the other until he was beckoned, but Kellik recognized the accepted challenge before Saigel left his bar stool.

"My name is Toran," he began as Saigel walked up. "I understand you have built a small reputation. How does a minikin like yourself walk into a tavern and win ten out of ten matches throughout an evening and into the next morning?"

"I jus' know how to pick 'em, I guess," Saigel said.

"Well, how about a match with me then?"

Saigel looked Toran over. Suddenly, something piqued Saigel's interest about him. It had happened to him on a few rare occasions when something had not felt quite right about the circumstances. It had not occurred to him on the previous evening when Kellik had called out from behind the crowd. He had been a little nervous until he saw Kellik coming forward, but his nerves and this sensation were not the same. He felt it now, and the intensity was substantial. He measured his opponent for a moment longer. If his opponent believed that he had some advantage over him, that belief would typically set Saigel's nerves on edge, but he was not nervous, merely wary.

"Two gold's the bet," Saigel replied.

"Not interesting enough. Thirty," Toran countered.

"Not used to a wager of mor'an two, but thuh furst time yuh don't try sumpthin' new might be thuh last time yuh get thuh chance.

Agreed." Saigel knew that he was right about him. Whatever it was, he was more curious than any other consideration of the human. The table was cleared for the contest, and a chair was vacated for Saigel to stand on.

Upon hearing, "Agreed," Kellik closed his book. Then he joined the spectators around the table to witness the precedent being set there. If Saigel had agreed to wager thirty gold finance, which had not been done in the more than thirty matches he knew of, he did not want to miss this. The small balance of patronage in the taproom, including Thom, gathered around the table, and side bets were made among them.

Saigel did not usually take these matches with much serious intent. He was sure he could not lose unless he wanted to. This human, Toran, was different though. He possessed the same confidence that Saigel carried. Because of his own nerves, the other's confidence, and a thirty-gold wager, he invested all his interest in this match.

They set their hands together, testing each other's grip and adjusting hand positions several times. When they were comfortable with their own holds, they both nodded. Toran closed his eyes and relaxed to the point that Saigel wondered how serious the human was about the match. When Toran opened them again and stared directly back at Saigel, his doubts were erased.

The look expressed total investment.

As Toran stared at the minikin, his vision washed over with a hue of secondary orange. The minikin looked healthy enough for one of his kind but not overly so—at least not enough to complete what he had done in the arm contests the previous nights.

Toran had not left his room at the inn, which was across the road, for days. He had spent a single day for each of his fallen comrades while mourning for them. During this time, he had practiced his forgotten Merea. Most of his previous training returned to him over those days. As he accessed the pigments each sphere provided, there was still something else—something elusive that was just beyond his reach. When the end of the fourth day arrived without his grasping what was evading him, he decided the block was a consequence of his mourning or his increasing anger at Enrandl.

A neutral elven referee, who had been chosen at random, put his hand upon the competitors. When the call to begin sounded, the referee pulled his hand away, and the two contestants just stared at each other.

Toran directed the orange pigment to his arm. The hue to his vision remained the same as the sphere that was bound to him, but his arm glowed more brightly where the pigment now centered.

Recently, he had inadvertently done something comparable to this with a primary yellow sphere to keep from passing out while Enrandl had been searching for him. He could not bind a warm sphere to himself if a cold one was already bound to him. Either he knew this reflexively or because of their incompatibility—the yellow sphere had, on its own, passed through, gone directly to his head, and become centered there. Two warm fields would easily bind together and become centered at the same time without any contradiction. Five days of experimentation while being locked up away in the room across the road and mourning his friends had reminded him of many things.

With the orange sphere surrounding him and a smaller one centered on his arm to enhance his strength, he expected the minikin to struggle vainly against his arm. When this was not the outcome, he started to apply pressure against the small arm.

Saigel kept his arm tense and ready to receive whatever the human was hiding and intentionally holding back. He felt no pressure against his arm but only sensed the man's more intent stare and maybe a little confusion behind it. *No, that's not it,* he thought. He decided it was more like … disappointment. Not wanting to be a source of discontent to the human, he started to apply pressure.

Both pushed against each other simultaneously, but neither arm advanced toward a win.

The strain on Saigel's face was no indicator of his feelings, for in truth, he was excited, and his excitement fueled his curiosity. Toran was strong—perhaps much stronger than he should be. Then again, so was Saigel. Saigel was lucky that the buckle on his belt did not glow according to his exertion; otherwise, everyone near him might know his secret, and in addition, be blinded by the intensity that he was applying against the human. He assumed some magic was affecting his opponent also. He was pushing as hard as he could to move his arm but was not sure how much longer he would be able to.

Toran's disappointment soon became consternation and strain. He tried to force more into the sphere, but its peak seemed to have been reached. Soon his arm would quickly wear out, and his holding this centered sphere to it was not going to be enough. Strength and endurance were separate propositions. He closed his eyes again. *What do I need? Probably the sphere of green,* he thought. A secondary green binding would let him sustain his strength longer. The problem was going to be the transition.

When he had made himself silent at the dragon's cave so that he could hide from Enrandl—but had needed to stay conscious—the violet sphere which had kept him silent had been bound to him, and it had not required a transition to the yellow sphere he had chosen to aid him. He had accidentally centered the yellow sphere on his head.

It had pierced the violet sphere and had gone straight where he needed it without affecting the bound one.

Now he needed to do almost the opposite. He already had the warm orange sphere bound to and surrounding him with the same warm sphere centered on his arm. He knew when he tried to bind the cold green sphere to himself, that the warm and the cold would clash and cancel out the previous sphere in favor of the newly bound one. However, he had to take this chance. If he ceased using the already bound sphere and allowed it to dissipate before binding another, he knew that his strength would be lost immediately.

He created the secondary green orb, and hoped the transition would cause a minimal imbalance between his new binding and the one centered on his arm. The spheres clashed, and in his mind's eye, he watched as the new one shattered the old one, leaving the green bound to him and fortunately causing no breach or disruption to the orange sphere centered on his arm.

Still, neither arm moved.

After three minutes, he was exhausted, and a dull pain started to form in his head, but there was no progress toward a winning position. The referee called for a draw, and they agreed. The draw ended the match, and everyone cried out their mutual disappointment. The crowd fanned out through the room. They were upset that there had been no winner but somewhat satisfied that there had been a good match. Kellik walked over.

"Great match," Toran said, "but I do not recall your name."

"Saigel. Well met, friend," Saigel answered while catching his breath. "Muh friend Kellik. Let me buy yuh a drink since you've been muh toughest competition."

"Your only competition," Kellik added.

Hours passed while Kellik sat with Toran and Saigel, who were talking. Kellik listened to the crowd and flipped through his book occasionally. No more contests were offered to Saigel. Rumors from observers passed to newcomers who had just come into the taproom that evening. They told of the previous match, so the prospect of a rematch drifted around the place.

"Tell me, Kellik, the story behind you and this book. You have been paging through it all day," Toran said.

"It is one of my only souvenirs of our battle with a red dragon," Kellik answered as he pointed at Saigel. "That is also where I met my friend four cycles ago in the unfinished pass across The Unforgiving between here and Dominic's Hold. It was raining, and I found a small cave for shelter. I slipped and fell ..." Kellik trailed off from his statement and looked over to Saigel.

"Please continue," Toran urged as he sat forward in his chair.

"That's all yuh'll get fruhm 'im 'less you want mumblins 'bout some fool pelt 'e lost. Got in 'fore thuh rain, I did, but wus tired an' clumsy. I fell in anyway." Saigel continued the tale from what he could remember and what Kellik had told him. "We're jus' passin' through, makin' thuh way back ta get more treasure."

"If there is any left," Toran replied.

"Whut yuh mean?" Saigel asked.

When Toran began to tell his story of the cave, Kellik came out of his trance to listen. After Toran finished, an astonished Kellik opened the book again and asked, "Do you think it's a book that charts magicians' effects?"

"Yuhr sayin' magic caused us ta fall?"

Toran looked from one to the other after the simultaneously asked questions. "Enrandl did say there was magic displayed there but not what the magic entailed.

"I do not know, Kellik. May I?" Toran asked and held out his hand. When Kellik did not respond immediately, he retracted his hand and waited.

Kellik tapped the table with his thumb several times as he reflected on the story. He had no reason to doubt as he considered letting the human take the book. He shifted in his chair slightly before he pushed the book across the table. If Toran recognized that this transfer of weight was a way to position and allow Kellik more room for a quick response, he did not respond to it.

The coincidence had been far too strong for Toran not to have heard the entire story. Now he picked up the book and thumbed through the pages. He had not forgotten that he did not need to close his eyes to access the spheres. Five days of practice while being locked away from everything else had made him aware of this. Yet his momentary lapse in discipline earlier, to refrain from closing his eyes before the contest against Saigel, had prevented him from doing so.

He expanded a sphere and sifted through the colors, but he could not choose the one he needed. Physical actions had been easy enough to designate pigments to, but he needed to collect information from the book. He could not decide what sphere would let him gain the knowledge—if he even could do so. He let his access fade but continued to look through the impressive pages.

"I really do not know if your fall was caused by the magic Enrandl found." Toran closed the book and then moved on to Kellik's question. "I also do not know any that would get that upset over something like a book of effects." Toran put the book down in the middle of the table. "Magicians are peculiar, and Enrandl is … well, I just think this is something more important than that."

"Find suhm one ta read it?" Saigel suggested.

"Maybe, but if it's enough for this, uh, Enrandl to become so fanatic over, another magician may do the same," Kellik replied.

Toran pondered something for a moment before saying, "I can offer another suggestion to discover its properties, but it would involve some travel on our part … and away from where you are going. Strangely enough, the two of you coming along would only add company to the trip. I was going to Aamber in the next couple of days, but I can leave earlier. I have a … friend who lives just on the outskirts who may be able to tell us something about that." He pointed at the book.

Saigel looked at Kellik.

"Aamber is too far from here," Kellik remarked, and Saigel nodded.

"About eight days by common road but only three days directly," Toran answered, "including the marshes. If we leave in the morning, we could be there by midcycle."

"We'd best get rest then," Saigel said as he accepted, but Kellik looked apprehensive.

Toran waited as the half-elf put his hand on the book, pulled it closer to him, but did not remove it from the table.

"I know. The two of you do not know me very well, but I am sure Higoshi can help you find the book's properties," Toran said.

"We'll meet you here in the morning. Do you have a horse?" Kellik came to his decision.

"There are many farms around here, and many horses for purchase. I would wager thirty gold on it," Toran said with a smile. Kellik and Saigel both laughed as they got up to leave the tavern for the inn across the way.

Toran stayed in his seat. A scenario for his revenge was already forming in his mind. If they had the book that Enrandl wanted, Toran had the magician by the throat. From what Toran had surmised about Kellik, he would not involve himself in an act that led to killing Enrandl. Toran preferred this outcome, but it was Kellik's book now, and some other solution would have to suffice.

"Do you think we can trust him," Kellik asked, as they crossed the dusty road. The sun had just set, and the sky glowed pink on the horizon.

"We'll shurinuff find out, and with GodsLight to shine upon us, yes," Saigel answered.

They went to their separate rooms at the inn. Kellik lit every lantern so that he could be sure that he would have enough light to see. Some projects were better seen with bright light rather than his elven vision. He withdrew his new bastard sword, set it on the bed, and sat next to it. Then he reached over the foot of the bed to get his backpack. From within, he produced a sharpening stone.

His father had given him this before he had left home and had told him that no other stone would sharpen a sword like this one would. He looked at the blade on the bed and marveled at the intricate carvings that the smith had felt necessary to place on it and the others. All three swords had been decorated in precisely the same manner. The etched curves and swirls formed no specific depiction, but they had been elegantly engraved. When he had asked the smith about them, he had been told something about the mark of the soul. Kellik had not altogether understood his dialect and had not been sure whether the comment represented his soul or that of the smith's.

When he had ordered the creation of these swords three cycles ago in Jenerv, the dwarf—Saigel had been adamant that he choose a dwarven smith—had already been in the process of making another weapon. A week later, he had started the first of Kellik's swords, and each had taken about three weeks to complete (including the carvings). None of them had been used since they had been crafted.

Kellik studied the blade of the bastard sword as he had studied his two longswords on the previous nights. In truth, all three should be mostly the same. His former weapons had all been hand-and-a-half swords with longer handles, which allowed for one- or two-handed use. He tended to use the heaviest of the three with both hands. The ones he carried on his back were the lightest kind that he could find because he wanted to have one in each hand. The specific techniques that he needed to employ while using two swords were not as compatible with the long handles as he liked, so one of the specifications that he sought for the new ones was for the longswords' hilts to be shorter without altering the rest of the weapon.

He left the singular blade on the bed and addressed his attention to the twin pair. The smith had well-honed the longswords' blades, and the sword on the bed had been equally as keen when he had taken possession of them. However, when he picked up the sharpening stone, as he had with the sword from the night before, he somehow knew that he could make the matched pair of blades sharper.

Saigel sat on the floor of his room, inspecting the contents of Thom's purse, which now lay on the floor where Saigel had poured it. Saigel usually picked the drunken ones to *borrow* from because they were often the easiest. Several precious-looking gems accompanied the gold and silver finance. Saigel separated the finance and placed it all in their purse. Then he inspected the gemstones. Because they were in the purse along with conventional finance, Saigel did not think that any of the stones had magic, but one could never be too sure. If Kellik were with him now, Saigel would joke with him about using his essence to discover whether any were magical, but for now, Saigel was keeping his secondary talents to himself.

Saigel smiled. It had been courageous of Kellik to risk himself, considering he did not believe him to have a dishonest bone in his body. It was equally impressive that his friend had been ready to draw a weapon and fight to defend him.

The use of such a standard essence in front of a whole tavern of people had been very foolish of him. *Could 'e 'ave had time ta search thuh crowd an' know that none would spot his sham?* Saigel wondered. If so, he had been wrong. Fibble had seen through the charade but had only mentioned the exchange of glances between himself and Kellik. Maybe there had been time to do so. "Nuff. Tis done with," he said aloud to himself. "Time ta sleep."

As he drifted off toward slumber, he recalled watching Kellik use the very same essence to start a fire in the rain a week earlier. They had been in a flat and open field with only one tree for cover. The tree had been blooming and very full of large leaves. The rain had found its way through to soak them nevertheless. The orange flame would not start the fire, but Kellik had used the green one, which allowed fire to ignite regardless of how soaked the gatherings to be burned were.

He smiled one more time. Fibble was right when he had said, "Inventive but very foolish."

Nearly half the day had passed while the priest had slept. *Sunset's proximity should have marked indication*, Enrandl thought. He had picked out some items of interest from the treasure. The book was the only thing that he really wanted from the dragon's hoard, but these other items would have to suffice for now—a beaded necklace, an ivory wand, and a pure white pearl.

He placed the necklace and the pearl into one of his pouches and studied the wand while he walked back to the room with the pool. The priest was still sleeping in the darkness of the cave when Enrandl got there.

"Time to awaken," Enrandl sang as he nudged the priest.

"Okay, okay," Frederick said as he stretched. He must have felt a bit of a chill because Enrandl saw him draping the white pelt over his shoulders for possible warmth. The priest approached the decomposing form of the dragon and took out three sticks, along with three small metal stands. As Enrandl watched, Frederick put the sticks and their stands into positions at the head, middle, and flank of the dead creature. As Frederick pulled a candle out of a pocket, Enrandl decided that, after being scolded for Frederick's lack of preparation, these items must be employed often enough to keep on his person. The priest blew on the wick, and it ignited.

Employing the candle, he lit the three sticks. As the tops of the sticks burned, he pinched out the candle, returned it to the pocket, and then blew out the small flames at the top of each stick. He started to hum to himself. The smoke from the incense that followed brought forth a sweet and pleasant smell, which nearly overcame the scent of the rotting dragon.

Ten minutes later, the priest turned to Enrandl. "Your first question," the priest mumbled almost incoherently.

"Uh, why are you dead?" Enrandl asked. He was a bit surprised and immediately scolded himself for such a stupid question. He expected something grander from the priest's essence. When no spectacular display had been presented, he had stuttered and forgotten his original question. He now reminded himself that divine essences never had the flair and dramatics that his effects produced. Now he had wasted a question.

"She says, '*Because I was killed,*'" the priest replied.

"Who killed her?" he said aloud while wondering how the priest had determined the dragon was female.

"Kellik and Saigel," the priest relayed.

"No. That was not my question," Enrandl said, scolding Frederick.

"I did not know. What is your next question?" Frederick asked, but Enrandl was not paying attention, for suddenly, he could not think straight. *Is somebody beckoning me?* he thought. The priest said something to him, but he shrugged off his words and only focused on the voice inside his head.

Enrandl? A thought was singing in his head. There were a few moments of silence and then, *Enrandl, answer me!* He was jolted as that thought had been suddenly yelled instead of the previous singing. He covered his ears to block it out, but it had already screamed in his head. He recognized it from somewhere but could not place it.

I may not know where you are, but I do have something that you want, it said more calmly.

"Toran?" Enrandl guessed out loud. "Is your identity verified?"

Yes, murderer, it is me. Toran sat in the tavern with his eyes closed and a look of mild concentration. His lips did not move. The aqua sphere that he had used to find Enrandl had been immense, but once he had found him, only two separate and smaller orbs had been needed to maintain the conversation. The taproom had become remarkably busy around him, but Toran was oblivious even to the barmaid who was standing in front of him and asking him if he wanted anything else.

I know where your book is, murderer. If you want it, you will have to come and find me. He formed the words into thought and pushed them from his sphere area to Enrandl's linked sphere. Then as he waited to extract any reply, he tried to place the distance of the connection that he held with Enrandl's mind.

Where is my book? Toran heard.

I am sorry. I must go now, Toran projected. *GodsLight finding me.*

When Enrandl heard Toran's final thought, he yelled, "Where is my book?"

Enrandl's outburst startled Frederick. "Who are you yelling at?" the priest asked. He had tucked the leopard's skin under his arm.

"No one!" Enrandl spat angrily. "Not any longer. Are you ready to go?"

"Yes, but—"

"Then let us go." Enrandl calculated Frederick's presence and shifted them back to the temple. As expected, the priest became angry again, but Enrandl was already prepared to ignore the outburst.

"I can not believe you. First, you drag me off to …" The priest paused, turning away from Enrandl. "Somewhere, when I am not prepared, and then when I do what you ask, you drift off and waste the rest of my time and …" The priest turned back to see the other walking away from him, past the last row of oak pews in the temple. His face grew furiously red, and he let out a muffled scream. Three lesser priests immediately came in to see what was wrong, but the High Priest gestured for them to resume what they had been doing as Enrandl left the temple.

He walked from the main temple to his private chamber. Frederick Smythe sat down behind his desk and began a proper inspection of the beautiful pelt that he had taken from the cave.

Toran relaxed. As the spheres faded, his eyes opened. His focus had been on Enrandl, but he was vaguely aware of the pretty barmaid standing across the table from him. He did not know until he had come back that she had called the owner to come and check on him. A small group of curious locals was milling about also trying to find out what was going on.

"No, I do not care for another ale," he said calmly and looked back down at his maps, which lay sprawled out over the table. Everyone dispersed. The owner and barmaid went back to work.

He drew a large circle. The center—Kershal—represented where he was. The circumference was the last place where he found Enrandl. Contact with Enrandl's mind and judging the gap between it and his was easy, but he could not designate a specific location without access to the correct sphere. He had shuffled through several of them to try out before settling for just distance. He used the spoon and chalk again as a makeshift compass to draw out the large circle.

There was already another circle on the map. It was smaller than the new one. It had been drawn during his brief conversation with Enrandl before the distance between them expanded. It marked the place where Enrandl had been when Toran had first found him.

The bigger circle crossed a large city, Jenerv. Connection with Enrandl's mind had stayed at this distance long enough for Toran to believe that the magician was lingering there for a while.

It is 250 miles northwest, Toran thought. *That is where he usually hires me, and that is where he has probably returned.*

The smaller circle confused Toran. The line crossed no towns. He traced the line one more time and stopped when he reached the mountains east of Kershal. *The cave? What would he be doing back there?* Toran wondered. Toran marked the cave and Jenerv on the map.

CHAPTER 5

TRAVELS

The morning sun spread rays of light and warmth down upon everyone in Kershal. In the stable yard of one of the larger farms in the area, Kellik and Saigel almost looked like a father and a child sitting on the horse that Toran had bought. Kellik had picked the best horse that he could find. It was tall and brown. Because this had been one of the owners most stubborn horses, the price had been reasonable. He had handled the untrained animal with negligible effort. Meanwhile, Toran's black horse had been well trained, so he had paid somewhat more for it. He mounted his horse, and they started the journey to Aamber.

Most of their first morning was spent traveling underneath the teal-green sky, which was occasionally adorned with puffy, silver-tinged clouds. After they passed the many farms that provided Kershal with its income, the terrain gave way to meadows of tall green grass and very few trees. The late afternoon hours gradually brought a newer environment to the travelers. They continued through rocky hills until the setting sun forced them to make camp. They found a flat area with a rock wall to flank them and an easily defensible front.

"I'll get wood fuhr thuh fire," Saigel commented. "And I know Kellik's good fuhr findin' dinner."

"Duck!" Toran yelled before squatting down. The other men followed his lead and dropped to the ground immediately.

Kellik felt a strong gust of wind brush by him. He rolled onto his back, allowed his vision to adjust to the darkening sky, and saw a sizeable winged form fly away. "It's a dragon!" he called out. He stood up while still scanning the sky, drew the two longswords from his back, and waited for a return pass. This situation was one with which he had recently become remarkably familiar.

"Too quiet," Toran answered, "but close to the mark."

Kellik could not find the attacking creature again. He knew that with his superior vision, he would spot whatever it was before the others would, but how had Toran known that they needed to duck?

"Whur's it?" Saigel asked, but Toran shushed him.

"Listen for the wings," Toran said.

Kellik closed his eyes and did precisely that. Along with the residual ring of his new swords being drawn, his ears caught Toran's breathing behind him and slightly to his right. Toran had not stood up from his squatting stance. Saigel was in front of him, prone on the ground. This had been his reaction to Toran's warning, and he was not getting up.

Farther beyond Saigel, the horses seemed to be agitated but not startled enough to run away. The human's advice helped him locate the sound of the creature's wings swooping in from behind him, and he spun in place, swinging his swords up high. Both swords missed the fast-moving form of the wyvern, for it was well above his reach. It flew past him and Saigel's prone figure to snatch the brown horse with the talons of both its legs and then flew away. Kellik's new swords could not find a target to measure themselves against.

Toran broke the silence. "We shall not see any more of him. It seems Kellik *is* good for finding dinner." Kellik did not recognize which of the horses had been stolen, but Saigel snickered. "Let us hope he is as good for us," Toran said.

"That wasn't a dragon?" Kellik asked, replacing his swords.

"I did not get a good look, but I am thinking wyvern," Toran answered.

"Dragons play with thur food and let yuh know 'bout it."

After an hour of hunting, Kellik returned with four scrawny rabbits and commenced cooking them. Orange light reflected off the wall behind them. A stream of smoke drifted in the air along with the smell of rabbits being cooked over the fire that Saigel had started.

When they finished eating, Kellik and Toran decided that the next day, they would take turns riding with Saigel while the other would walk. It would slow their trip some, but there was no other choice.

The three men settled down to rest. Toran rolled out a bedroll on the ground for some comfort against the rocky terrain, and Kellik helped him loosen his armor before they settled down to sleep, leaving Saigel to keep first watch.

Saigel sat away from the fire because it was still too warm from the day's heat to need it, but he did need its light. Several times during his watch and more to stay awake than any other reason, he got up to walk the perimeter of where the fire's light reached. When he woke up Kellik hours later, he reported that nothing unusual had taken place. Saigel wore no armor to loosen or remove and placed nothing underneath him for comfort. His comfort was the cool rock he lay on to combat the still-warm summer night's air.

Kellik had removed his leather armor and had propped himself against a tree, with a borrowed blanket beside him. Some of his gear had been taken along with his horse. He was still lying down on the blanket by the tree when Saigel roused him for his watch. As he looked around, his eyes adjusted to the darkness of the night. He was thankful that the fire had died down because he did not need it to see.

He watched Saigel lie down to sleep. He would have liked to, but he realized that continuing to sharpen his sword might make too much noise for the others to sleep, even though he knew that one of the longswords needed it.

Toran rekindled the fire during his watch. Nothing of interest happened while he was awake. When the morning arrived, he watched the sun rise over the mountains and stretched his arms. Saigel woke up by himself, soon after the sun cleared the horizon, but as usual, Kellik needed to be roused, so the minikin woke him.

Dreams of giant flying creatures filled Kellik's waking mind as he rolled up the blanket and dressed in his armor. Each piece of leather was meticulously crafted and tailored specifically for him. He noticed that Saigel and Toran had drowned the fire and covered it with sand. He laughed to himself. There was not enough vegetation around to catch fire. *Still a good habit*, he thought, as he stretched his arms outward.

Suddenly, the sound of wings filled his ears, he felt a rush of air against his face, and before he could react, something grabbed his arm. He yelled as he ducked. Whatever had attached itself to his arm now disengaged. He heard the sound of its wings as it flew away.

"What is wrong?" Toran asked.

"Something attacked me!" Kellik exclaimed as he looked into the sky. "And then it flew away."

Toran looked up into the sky also and saw a single bird in the air circling above them.

"When Kellik stretched, thuh bird tried tuh land on 'is arm," Saigel commented, pointing to the same bird.

"Land?" the others questioned.

"Yep. Then Kellik panicked," Saigel replied, smiling.

"I didn't panic. How was I supposed to know?" Kellik looked back up at the bird and muttered, "Must be trained." He moved away from the others, stretched out his right arm, and whistled loudly. The bird altered its course and flew downward. Kellik flinched slightly as the bird's wings flapped wind into his face. After the bird had landed, it issued a short screech at him. The falcon's feathers were gray except for the underside of its wings, which were light brown.

"It's a falcon," Kellik said.

"You understood that?" Toran asked.

"No, of course not. The bird's just too small to be a hawk or an eagle."

"Seems tuh have taken a likin' to yuh."

"So it has," Toran added.

Kellik launched the gray and brown bird into the air. It flew up and began to circle the group again. They packed the rest of their gear and continued on their journey to Aamber. Saigel and Toran rode the horse for the first part of the day, and Kellik took his shift later.

During the day, Kellik watched the falcon, wondering why it had decided to follow them. When midday arrived and the group stopped for rest and refreshment, so did the bird. It landed on a high rock overlooking the path they were about to descend. Later in the evening when the three men set up camp, it landed in one of the few trees around them, just as it had on the previous night. The falcon and the half-elf studied each other before Kellik finally settled down to sleep. During his watch that evening, the falcon was not present, but the next morning, he found that it had returned.

The next day brought with it a sky filled with dark clouds and marshes that they had to get through. Kellik was the first one to step onto the damp ground as a light rain began to fall. He sank to the middle of his shin. The dark clouds enhanced the impression of the gloomy marsh, and the trees, which were like overgrown shrubs surrounding them, formed a low canopy above. At first, the horse stubbornly refused to move forward, but after some of Kellik's gentle coaxing, it gave in and entered the marsh.

A few hours later, it was Toran's turn to walk. The falcon had been flying for quite some time, so Kellik reached out his arm and called the bird with a whistle. The gray and brown falcon responded and soon landed on his arm.

"Whut yuh gunna name 'im?" Saigel asked.

"I haven't thought about that," Kellik replied. "Maybe I will ask him."

"Right," Saigel said.

"We shall see next morning." Kellik looked at the falcon. "What do you say?"

The bird only screeched back at him.

The clouds above them grew impossibly darker as evening approached, but it did not start to rain until they had found some dry ground on a high hill, which was out of the marsh's thick muck, and had stopped for the evening. No matter how hard any of them tried, they could not start a fire. Kellik had not foreseen a need for an essence to light the fire in the rain and had not prayed for the power.

The rainfall lasted all night and into the early morning hours. It finally stopped once they had packed all their gear and each of them was ready to continue. None of them had slept very well in the rain, but what sleep they did receive relieved just a bit of the fatigue from the previous day's travel.

Later in the day when it was Toran's turn to walk, Kellik called out to the falcon so that it could rest. The bird started to land but then veered off. Kellik looked around to see why it had done this. He watched the bird attack a monstrous, slimy green creature, which had moved up from behind them. The troll was at least two heads taller than Kellik was. Kellik figured that it was more than that, considering the muck the creature now stood in. It had patches of black fur covering its body, and its sunken black eyes gave the appearance of a nose much longer than it actually was. He was not close enough to smell the creature, but having experienced the foul beasts before, he knew the stench of the filthy things.

"Trolls behind us!" Kellik called out but saw that Toran had already drawn his sword and had engaged a pair of trolls that had cropped up in front of them. He slid off the horse into the mud and drew the longswords from his back.

Saigel took the reins and steered the horse out of the way. After this, he reached into a saddlebag to grab a torch while he watched the first troll grope at Toran with its claws. Both of the ugly creature's claws missed him. Toran, who had already hit one ugly thing two times, struck twice more with blinding speed. With a fifth cut, the troll fell to the ground. Then the second one bit his shoulder.

Kellik, several yards away and to Saigel's left, dodged all of his troll's advances. He was finally finding an opportunity to test the new swords against an enemy. He hit the troll with the first one, but when he swung the second sword, he slipped in the mud and lost his grip on it. The sword flipped end over end through the air in a high arc and stuck in Toran's second opponent, pinning it to a tree.

Saigel tried furiously to light the torch, but he could not even get a spark from his flint. After too many attempts, he surveyed the scene again. In the mud, Kellik tried to get up while the troll held him down. Kellik was not cooperating with the troll's efforts to chew at his ribs. Then Saigel watched the troll, which had already been dispatched by Toran, get back up and begin to advance against him again. He knew that without fire, they had no chance of survival unless they escaped, and for the moment, that seemed impossible.

Toran's second troll, which was still pinned to the tree, was nearly cut in half by the swipe of Toran's sword. It went limp. The body fell when Toran pulled Kellik's lost sword free from the tree. Before Saigel could call out a warning to Toran about the formerly fallen troll, it attacked from behind, knocking him down also.

"We need fire!" Toran yelled, managing to find purchase in the mud and get back on his feet.

"I'm tryin', but it won't light!" Saigel called back, feeling helpless. All he could do was watch. He could see Kellik, who was still hopelessly pinned by the troll, thrust his sword into the troll's midsection while simultaneously trying to throw it off. The troll did not budge and only continued to try to gnaw into the tough leather of his armor. Toran turned to face the troll that had just knocked him down. This time, he was wary of the second troll's possible return.

Saigel had given up on lighting the torch. He knew his weapons, along with the others' efforts, were of no use against the regenerating creatures. Even the magic of his scimitar would not help his cause. Regardless, he drew two knives to throw at Kellik's troll but did not get to throw either one.

Two more trolls jumped up out of the thick muck and startled the horse. It reared. Saigel was thrown off the back of his mount, and he ended up face-first in the mud. Those two trolls ignored the small minikin in favor of feasting on larger prey, as he wiped dirt from his eyes.

Toran's second troll started to get up. Kellik had finally worked his way out from underneath his troll, although it was still biting him, and three more trolls were eagerly approaching either the fray or the downed horse. From his vantage point, Saigel could not decide which one they were moving toward.

He saw a bush that he could hide behind. He was crawling through the mud toward it when a bright flash of red-orange light consumed everything. Toran's trolls fell as parts of their flesh burned. Kellik's troll, the trolls trying to eat the horse, and the trolls that were joining the fight turned and ran.

"Whur'd that come fruhm?" Saigel asked.

"From here!" an unknown voice answered.

Standing a short distance away from them in the direction of the voice, they saw a tall slightly overweight man with short red hair. He was wearing plain drab-brown clothing accessorized by a belt, which had many pouches. His shirt and pants were covered with pockets.

"Just thought I could help," he said.

"Thank The Gods'! We—" Kellik checked his armor. Fortunately for him, the leather, which now bore several teeth marks, had proved itself stronger than the monster's teeth.

Toran interrupted, "You could have killed us all!"

"My, you have a polite way of giving thanks, but luckily I can understand where you may be concerned. You were in no danger from my effect, only from the trolls," the man replied. "I am Alistar, and who might all of you be?"

"Toran. Now explain how we were in no danger."

"You will notice that the display captured all of you yet harmed none. Only the trolls caught in my flashfire were impacted because they were the ones that I intended for the display to cover. I have found myself in too many situations where I needed to channel that effect with myself or companions at risk, so I improved it in such a way that those I choose are no longer at risk."

"I'm glad yuh showed when yuh did," Saigel commented. "Yuh just travelin' through and 'appen ta see us?"

"Not entirely. I make my home here in the marsh."

"Why?" Kellik asked.

"For study and to help travelers such as yourselves who come across trolls," Alistar answered, "because as your little friend here has discovered, there is no way to start a normal fire. As you obviously know, because you were trying to light one, fire aids in their defeat. A reason exists to explain why fire can not be ignited naturally here, and it is my intention to understand why. It is my belief that the troll kind around here perhaps have evolved and may have a natural magical—"

"It is not possible to save every group of travelers that passes through here," Toran said.

"I am sure you would not be surprised to know that few try the crossing here, but you are correct. For the few that do come this way, I help them in any way I can. It is unfortunate, but I have come to believe that the trolls need to sustain themselves also. Your horse does not seem to have recovered. I am sure that it will not go to waste. You only have another four hours by foot in the direction that you travel, and you will be free of the marsh."

Toran walked away from the conversation, and the others introduced themselves. The horse was barely alive from the multiple wounds that had been caused by the trolls. "I think the horse will be fine," he said, already accessing a primary red healing sphere. He knelt down, stroked the horse's mane, closed his eyes, and concentrated. Because his back was turned to the rest of them, they could not see his face, which was contorted ever so slightly, as he adjusted the red-hued mental image of the horse's wounds.

Where the attack had left several large gashes, the horse's flesh reformed and healed together. A couple of minutes later, he leaned against the horse and used it to stand up. After he had done this and had headed back to the group, the fallen horse awkwardly stood up also.

"Its wounds are not that bad," Toran said.

"That is unfortunate for the trolls then, I am afraid," Alistar said as he looked at Toran for a moment. There was something familiar about the human piece of this group. "Pardon my curiosity, but have we met?"

"Not that I am aware of. Why?"

"It is just that I never forget a face, and I seem to remember yours," Alistar commented. "Are you headed to Aamber as your direction indicates?"

"Not really," Toran answered. "We plan on passing through it."

"And will you be coming back in this direction?"

"We do not know. Why?"

"I need some supplies, and I thought that if you were coming back this way, you could save me a trip."

"If yuh give us a list of whut yuh need, we'll shurinuf try."

Alistar reached into one of his pouches and produced a piece of folded parchment. He knelt and handed it to Saigel, saying "You are not like the rest of your kind, are you?"

"Whut da yuh mean?" he answered.

"I have not known many minikins, but you are very different." Alistar opened another pouch and took out a small sealed vial of blue liquid. "I have had something for quite some time. I acquired it from a very brave little one much like yourself, and I have found no possible use for it until now. My acquaintance with him was the only one of your kind that I have ever encountered with a magic user's aptitude, and he was quite a brewmaster. He gave this to me because well, I am not really sure why he did."

"Magic? Whut's it do?"

"Yes, and I am rather curious to have that very question answered. All I know is that I was told it will only work for one of your kind." Saigel looked at Toran and Kellik. Both of them shrugged their shoulders.

"I know you have no reason to trust a stranger like me, but it would be a waste of my time if all I desired was to harm you now."

Saigel took the vial, studied it for a moment, popped the seal, and drank the liquid. "Tastes like mead. Got any more?" They all watched expectantly, but nothing happened. "Well?" Saigel reiterated.

"Sorry that I do not and that there was not a more immediate reaction. Perhaps its effectiveness has expired." Alistar put his hand on Saigel's shoulder, looked at the others, and said, "GodsLight upon your journey."

Kellik inspected the horse's wounds as Toran had. Saigel joined him, and Kellik lifted him up to position himself in the saddle. Toran took the reins as the half-elf mounted. When he started to lead the others and the horse away, the falcon, which had been resting in a nearby tree, called out. It could not have appeared any more natural. It was as if Kellik had held out his arm for the bird a hundred times before. The bird launched from its perch and flew to him. Once it settled on his arm, they continued toward Aamber.

Alistar watched until they were out of sight. He wondered two things. What had the potion done or might still do? And why had he recognized the human?

Three hours later, they left the marsh, and the sun peeked through the clouds at them for a moment before disappearing again. An hour later, they arrived at Aamber's city gate. The guards let them pass through without difficulties or questions. They only wore astonished looks regarding their muddied appearance.

The cobblestones in the road clicked underneath their feet, as though to welcome them on their way through the city. Many townspeople watched and waved. A few who were more curious stopped them to ask why they were in such a state. A bazaar, which had many small kiosks and carts, was opened to their right. Kellik stopped and bought some fruit.

"You have seen some action in the marshes," the skinny vendor knowingly remarked.

"How can you possibly tell?" Kellik said as he smiled and then bit into a juicy piece of fruit.

"There is a bathhouse on Saveth Court."

"And where would that be?"

The fruit vendor scratched his head and gave Kellik directions. Kellik, in turn, suggested the bathhouse to Toran and Saigel, who had been waiting for him near the main road through the city while he had purchased the fruit.

As the others followed him, Toran answered, "We should be able to bathe at master Higoshi's. I want to get there before dark. He lives just a mile beyond this city."

"Whut about Alistar's list?" Saigel asked.

"I am still unsure about him. He obviously was tracking us, and he knew where we were going, yet he waited until we were being overwhelmed by the trolls before acting. We can worry about the list next day." He paused before adding, "If necessary."

"Why doesn't Higoshi live in town," Kellik asked.

"Those who have his talent are not exactly welcomed. In fact, it is feared more than magic by, well, as Higoshi presents it, those who know better."

"And how do you know this man?" Kellik asked and then retracted his question when he realized that Toran had called the man master.

"Whut's he do?" Saigel asked.

"He believes anything can be accomplished with only the strength of one's mind," Toran replied.

The three men reached the northern most gate of the city. The sun was drifting downward toward the evening horizon as they left Aamber. The guards at the other gate reacted the same way that the others had, except one of them asked if they expected to return. Toran informed him that they were not sure what their plans would be, but it would not be that night if they did return.

During their last mile to Higoshi's home, the main road bent to the northeast, but they strayed from the road in favor of a rough trail—overgrown from lack of travel—that continued northward. Not long after this, they approached a small flowery smelling garden ahead of them to their right, and beyond the garden stood a small cottage. The trail led them around the west side of the house, and a ragged, unkempt wooden fence surrounded it. Two trees, whose branches curved and twisted about and over the shack, stood on the east and west sides. Each tree provided part of a covered path, which went from the front yard to the backyard.

As the sky darkened, there was just enough light breaking through the canopy so that those who wanted to use the path could see their way. The gate on the north side of Higoshi's home opened at their approach. Toran shook his head as he continued into the yard of freshly cut green grass. He used several stepping-stones to reach the cottage. There was peaceful silence all around them.

Of course, he knows, Toran thought.

An old man with eyes so squinted that it seemed impossible for him to see, appeared at the door of the cottage. His aged face bore the wrinkles of many revolutions. He was wearing all white clothing, which matched the color of his full head of long, straight hair. Higoshi smiled an almost toothless grin at Toran's approach.

"It is so good to see …" The elderly voice trailed off as the man noticed the sword at Toran's waist. "What is that crude weapon that you carry?" The conversation, which was carried upon the silence, reached Kellik and Saigel, who were sitting upon the horse by the gate.

"Surely you know what a sword looks like, Master Higoshi," Toran answered. "They do come in handy from time to time."

"Not for anyone who has learned to control his own mind."

"It is not that perfect, master," Toran argued.

"I could never train you to understand it, and it seems that you could not even find your own way." Higoshi turned to go back inside his home, paused, and then faced Toran again. "Unless that is why you have returned?"

"No, master, that is not why I have returned. Kellik here has a book that he cannot understand, and he wants to learn all that he can about it."

At the mention of his name, Kellik released the falcon into the air, dismounted his horse, and helped Saigel dismount. He tied the horse to the fence and entered the yard with Saigel right behind him.

"Yes, I know." Higoshi turned again and went back into the shack, saying, "I can not help you with what you want to know."

"What do you mean?" Toran argued and followed Higoshi into the cottage. The inside of the shack was a definite contrast to the outside of it. The wooden walls were clean and neatly adorned with diverse types of art. There was a large sitting room with many chairs to Toran's right. The room had a window, although the trees growing outside blocked any view from it. From the inside point of view, the sitting room could have been larger than the whole shack when it was seen from outside. He remembered trying to measure both the outside and the inside many times, only to find that the sitting room was definitely smaller than the shack.

"The talent that you believe will help you, will not reveal the information you require," Higoshi said. "It only reveals information about its previous owners. You would have known that."

"Then we have wasted our time coming here," Toran mumbled.

"Only if you really believe it so." Higoshi was disheartened. This was not the direction that this meeting was supposed to go. Higoshi had hoped that someday, Toran would return to him on his own. He had imagined that it would be for further training. It had taken his not-so-subtle reminder of Toran's forgotten abilities to prompt him to come back.

He did not make a point of tracking his students, but a minimal effort was required to leave a sphere open so that he would know when one of them was near. During his daily meditations on a sunny afternoon a little less than two weeks ago, he had recognized the faintest hint of a presence. A slight tingle on the outermost verge of his sphere's range caught his attention, but he did not receive anything precise regarding who it might be.

More effort was required for such identification. At this notion, he finished his relaxation, created a sphere, and forced it to pulse outward to locate where the pupil might be. The first pulse resulted in nothing, so he drew in deeper and sent out a more distant sphere. It found his target. Although his first search had not presented him with the unknown student's place, the second discovered the presence not much farther away.

Now that his curiosity was piqued, he decided that he wanted to see who had come, rather than raid the mind of the other. Any of his proper students should be shielding themselves against formal invasion at all times, which meant that any such raid would demand a strengthened effort and be perceived by the pupil in question.

His primary sphere doubled, and with this, he doubled in spirit. The spirit form within the new area could see and hear everything around him, as could his first, but as the spirit sphere moved away, its sensations changed. He was still aware of himself, but the former awareness of the original sphere was diminished. His spirit sphere moved quickly toward The Unforgiving. He passed over Aamber, several farming communities, and then the marshes, before finally arriving at The Unforgiving. His sphere came to a stop in the middle of the mountain, where to his surprise, he saw Toran.

Toran was trying to splint another man's broken leg with some brittle and useless bones. That will not do, boy, *Higoshi thought, although the man in front of him was nowhere near a boy's age.* I have taught you far better than that. *He decided to force a recollection into Toran's mind. This was intrusive, yes, but he was holding out hope that the other man would take his refound ability to heart and seek out his old master to finish what had been started. At this point, Higoshi left him and returned to his body.*

He could see now that Toran had no intention of training further. If only he had not made trouble for himself, Higoshi would have had the time that he needed to make him understand what his fate could hold for him.

The Sagemont affair had been Toran's undoing, and as a secondary result, it had destroyed any chance of another master finishing the training that Toran needed. He had known that something was wrong when Toran returned to the cottage that evening and had used Merea to find out what had happened. While being furious with his student yet knowing he still needed further training, Higoshi was confident that Toran would go where he had directed him.

Toran had never arrived at the other tutor's house. Higoshi knew this, not because the other tutor had informed him, but because Higoshi had assumed another name and appearance and intended to continue the education of his pupil under that guise.

The minikin popped his head around the corner of the open door, and the elf walked up behind him to stand in the doorway. Toran asked Higoshi, "Do you have any suggestions that may help us find the answers we seek?"

"How 'bout Alistar?" Saigel offered. "He'd pro'bly 'elp us." Kellik and Toran looked down at Saigel.

Higoshi walked over to a bookshelf, located a ledger, and went back to Toran. He paged through and found a name. "I have a friend in Aamber that should be able to help. Tonches Guire. He runs a small school for magicians." Higoshi ripped the page from the ledger and handed it to Toran. "Take this to him. He will recognize my writing. Tonches can help you with what you need." He looked out the doorway past Kellik at the darkening sky. "But now, it is late, and his school is sure to be closed. You must stay the night. Toran should be able to show everyone to appropriate quarters."

Toran nodded. "Thank you, Master Higoshi."

Kellik was pleased that their sleeping arrangements were quiet and comfortable and that each of them had his own room. He wondered, as Toran had several revolutions ago, about the size of the cottage, as he fell asleep.

A few hours later, he awoke to the sound of footsteps. When he investigated the hallway, he saw the old man walking away from him and then turning a corner. He offered a good night but received no reply.

Toran slept in a comfortable chair in the library. A book that he had been reading when he had fallen asleep was still open on his lap. Higoshi stood over him, staring thoughtfully. "You have never understood the potential that you have, but soon you will," Higoshi whispered. For nearly an hour, he watched Toran. He did not move but only stared intently at the young man.

After that hour, he returned to his chamber and lay down in his bed. He closed his eyes, a smile spread across his face, and he slept.

CHAPTER 6

SO CLOSE AND YET …

"Ineffectual!" Enrandl's outburst filled the place. He stood in the corner of an elaborate laboratory and stared into a large mirror. Shelves with multi-sized vials and flasks lined the walls. Most of them were filled with a variety of colored liquids. Across the room, there was a single, large table with a complex combination of tubes and bubblers, where he brewed and mixed his different magical potions. There were no windows and only one door, which was closed and locked to prevent anyone from entering the room while he worked.

To anyone who viewed the obviously expensive, six-foot-tall, highly polished, silver with inlaid gold mirror, that person would only see a perfect image of him or herself. The effect now channelled on it revealed a different picture to him. Although the vision he saw now was dark gray and imageless, the display of the effect would usually give him a view of whatever he was trying to scry upon. This attempt to find Toran and the book was not showing him what he wanted to see—and he knew why.

"Supplementary sorcery with obstructive bearing renders this effect irrelevant!" He drew up his staff to strike the mirror but redirected it in midswing. This mirror had been more expensive than his previous one. Still angry, he let the staff fly across the room where it shattered several flasks and vials on the shelves. The magical liquids from the broken containers combined with each other, and a green, billowing smoke issued forth and filled the chamber. He dropped to the floor and covered his head, expecting the worst. An almost sickly-sweet odor of raspberry emanated from the smoke that surrounded him.

Without knowing that another liquid was about to mix with the others, he raised his head slowly. The last fluid mixed, and a loud explosion erupted in the laboratory. Left unconscious by the force of the blast but only lightly injured, he awoke ten minutes later unaware that a series of smaller explosions had pounded away at the interior of the laboratory. A now blue-colored smoke, still wafting of raspberry, was dissipating.

The walls had been blackened, and the only door had been ripped from its hinges (still burning in the hall) by the blasts. The single intact item was the mirror. His three apprentice mages—two human men and one elven woman—arrived at the laboratory in time to witness Enrandl's fury as he finished destroying the mirror with a flame that extended from his hand.

"I require the procurement of a new mirror," he said calmly and after taking a deep breath. The liquid remnants of molten silver and glass formed a glowing puddle at his feet. "One of you, the silversmith on Lakeview Way, has my acquaintance. Require of him its composition to my specification by next or second day. No subsequent will beget acceptance."

The three paused. "Go. Now!" Enrandl ordered. The men ran from the room immediately, but for some reason, the elf faltered, offering him a slight smile and nod before following them.

The magic user could not remember ever having this much trouble with anything that he had wanted. All his life, things he desired had come effortlessly to him. When he had decided to pursue the magical arts, he had seemed to have a natural ability to channel magical energy. His aura seemed to soak it up and pour it out whenever he wished. When his former master had tried to change Enrandl's views instead of teaching him more magics of the realms, killing him had come easy too.

In the revolutions since his master's death, everything else had been easy as well. Still at an apprentice level when his master died by his hand, he continued to teach himself rather than find another master to study under.

He grew stronger and decided to take on apprentices of his own. He found that it was easy to let them learn in the same way that he had. He started by giving them some inspiration and then made them work on their own to grow and leave. His pupils were allowed to pursue magic at their own pace, although he still supervised them. He only taught three at a time. This was as many as he could keep an eye on without something escaping his notice.

He always watched.

He was working on his third group. They were all on their own and doing fine without tutelage, but he was continually aware that one might be waiting to do as he had done and stab his or her master in the back.

Then he found an obscure notation in his former master's library that referenced what his master had spoken of—the mysterious book—which once in his possession would make him invincible by allowing him to draw upon unlimited energy without weakening his aura.

Since then, his life had become complicated. Problem after problem had presented itself to him. It had already taken revolutions to realize the book was real. Then, by magical and physical study, when he determined where to begin his search, every reference to it or about a possible location had been so entirely cryptic, that it took another revolution to solve those puzzles.

His only GodsLight, functional rather than inferior, had been a new effect he had found that allowed him to divine information from The Gods' about the book he sought. He did not expect the divine information to be inaccurate. Finding the correct mountain cave had been a chore, and in addition to Toran sniveling about finance, the book was not present.

The multiple problems disturbed and angered him, but he had come too close to give in now. It was out there in Toran's possession. He was so close and yet so far away.

Where was Toran?

How had he found the book?

How was he evading magical attempts to find him?

Enrandl understood why he might not be able to scry for the book. It was unfamiliar to him. He did not know what it looked like or what history was behind it, other than its existence and primary function.

Toran was a different enigma entirely. Enrandl knew the man, his looks, his mannerisms, and even some intimate details that Toran had no idea that he knew. There was only one reason that Toran could not be found. Something was protecting him from magical observation.

An idea he had not considered now occurred to him. *Could an organized prevarication feasibly source Toran's resolution?* It was possible that Toran was merely using the threat of having the book to taunt him, but Enrandl decided he was not willing to take that chance.

"Curse you!" Enrandl swore. "Where denotes your attendance?" He knew all these problems would be worth their measure when he had the book.

High above them, the sun was bright and warm. Everything was peaceful and quiet. There was not a cloud in the sky. Toran sat on the top step of Higoshi's home, staring blankly out at nothing. Kellik and Saigel finished packing and saddling up the horse and were ready to set off.

Toran had not moved from this position since burying the body out back in the garden behind the cottage. Kellik had offered to help in the task, but Toran refused him.

"There is nothing you could have done. He died in his sleep. Happily, from the way it looked," Kellik said.

He did find a degree of comfort in these words. Higoshi had died with a smile on his face. There were so many memories filtering through Toran's mind, and he was playing those memories mentally like they were happening right now. He stood up and looked back into the empty place. It was dark and lifeless, despite the brightness of the afternoon sun.

When Toran came back to himself, he regarded his weapon, which was leaning against the doorway. *You will not need that,* he thought and started to join Kellik and Saigel. *What am I thinking?* He returned to the door and retrieved it. *Why would I not need my sword?*

He looked in the direction of the mound of soil behind the cottage. He could not see it, but he knew what he could not see. Around either side of the shack, paths went between the trees. Just beyond the garden, which Higoshi had always made Toran keep up, lay the grave of an old man who had taught him so much, and he had let him down. He should have continued to train with Higoshi, but he had allowed himself to be distracted from that path by another.

He wanted to take it all back now. He remembered how much discipline and arduous work he had gone through while training the Merea talent within him. If he could just turn back time and not have joined Conrad on the mission, then leaving Higoshi would not need to have been an option. He knew this was impossible, however, it did not deter him from wanting to do so anyway.

Go now. You have unfinished business to attend to before you can mourn the death of an old man, he thought. He joined Saigel at the horse and helped him to mount. A light breeze was with them on their way. Soon they approached the gates of Aamber again. Kellik's falcon followed above them, and the guards once again, allowed them entrance into the city.

The city's streets also welcomed them again. Toran had been in many different towns, but Aamber was his favorite. He had spent many of his free hours with old friends in almost every part of the city. He knew most of the streets like the back of his hand. He simply followed the directions that he had received from Higoshi and led his companions to where Tonches Guire schooled his pupils in the magical arts.

The school was small and was tucked away between an inn called Keepers Place and a leatherworking shop, at a point where the cobblestone street forked in two different directions. One after another, the three of them walked through the open door. An owl flapping its wings in flight greeted them, and Toran ducked out of the way to allow the bird to exit, but it turned and flew toward the back of the cluttered space instead. It landed on a perch that looked as though it had been set there for the bird.

There was a wall of books to the newcomers' right and shelves of knickknacks to the left. The room was small and had no space for a window. Several candles were burning on a table across the room, giving off the only light other than the light from the open door.

A young man wearing a gray uniform greeted them. He was shorter than average but not by much and had short light-colored hair, which was groomed with the part on the left. "Good day to you!" The young man moved toward them with his hand extended. His energetic attitude surprised Toran, and he backed off for a moment while looking at the young man. While Kellik and Saigel greeted him, Toran looked around and expanded a sphere to fill the shop.

"And this is Toran." Saigel gestured. He was paying attention to the conversation and using the sphere to gain some insight into the shopkeeper, but none seemed forthcoming. Toran shook the other man's hand.

"Are yuh okay?" Saigel seemed concerned.

Toran nodded. "Yes, I am fine."

"Well met. I'm Richard. What can I do for my three new friends?" asked the young man.

"We are looking for Tonches Guire," Toran answered. "Is he here?"

"Normally, I could answer yes," he said while making his way back to the table with the candles. Toran joined him and now noticed two books on the table that he had not seen before. "But he has taken leave to study some prospective students. May I help in any way?" said Richard.

"We have an object that needs studying to determine its magical properties, and a friend of mine told me Tonches could help," Toran explained.

"I'm not sure when Tonches will return. Can I study it for you?" Richard offered. "I studied under Tonches for two revolutions. When

I finished my apprenticeship, I remained to further study and help with the school."

Not a bad sell, Toran thought and then said, "We have a magical book, but we cannot read it. My friend said Tonches would perform this service as a favor to him." Toran could tell by the expression on his face that the favor would not be honored by this man.

"I'm not Tonches, of course, and although he might have done the favor, I'm afraid I must receive some coin for any service I perform."

"Our finances are low, and we have never sought magical advice like this before. Will it cost much to acquire your help?" Toran gestured to Kellik, who in turn, shook his pouch. The sound indicated that there were very few coins within it.

"Tonches makes his services affordable for those in need. This is his school, so I'll follow his lead." The young mage chuckled at his unintentional rhyme. "May I see the book?"

Kellik walked over while opening his backpack and pulled out the green leather-covered book. He handed it to Richard and whispered something in Toran's ear. He received a nod at this and rejoined Saigel, who was still standing at the door.

"Kellik reminds me that we are in a hurry, and you still have not provided us the cost."

"For the study of an item, Tonches would normally collect five hundred gold." Toran's sphere encompassed most of the shop, and he was focused on Richard, but he could still almost feel Kellik and Saigel cringe. "But for you, I would gladly accept two for the same. Tonches would probably not be unpleased with me," Richard said with a small shrug.

Toran knew Richard was not lying, but he could sense some exaggeration. "I thought I was clear that our finances are low." Toran looked to the others, who were both facing away from him and looking at assorted items. Knowing enough of what he needed, Toran released his sphere and moved closer to Richard. He whispered gruffly, "You will concede, my friend, Tonches is not going to have any knowledge about this transaction. I offer fifty. I am sure this finance is more coin than you would garner for the same effect used for your employer."

Toran's Merea had no bearing on the outcome—the sphere was merely for inspiration before he had released it—and though his intimidation was successful, it was not a total success. "It weakens a magic user so much—any magic user. One hundred?" Richard's previous demeanor was now replaced by a sense of urgent need that Toran could not refute.

"That will be fine." Toran walked to the door and tapped Kellik on the shoulder. Kellik went over to Richard and dropped a pouch on the counter. "The fifty I offered. The rest when you have results for us," Toran said from across the room.

"Come back next evening, my friends." His energy returned. "I'll have your results."

"Yuhr quite a dealer," Saigel commented when they were on the street. "Whur'd yuh learn that?"

"Thank you. I used to travel in the company of merchants. Not your ordinary merchants, mind you. More the adventurous type. Each was highly skilled with the sword and had the tongues to bargain whatever they could find that would bring in a decent price. I am usually a good judge of a person's character, which helps during a barter. I just hope he finds out something for us. What do we do until next evening?"

The young mage sat pondering a mysterious book in front of him. The large table in the middle of this otherwise empty chamber was twice the size of the reception area. Specially cleansed for its purpose, the room contained only the table, the chair, him, and the book. It was obviously a magical tome. He had not needed to channel an effect to determine that, but he had to be sure anyway.

He was puzzled by the fact that the display of his effect had not revealed any of the words that marked its unique pages. Although there were many effects that he could not comprehend because of his lack of knowledge in the arts, he believed that this was not a study book charting effects and indicating the proper components needed for channelling them correctly. The book's material, construction, and the failure of his effect to allow him to understand the book's words supplied his belief of this.

He was especially enthralled by the strange paper. The weathered cover had severe damage, but the pages had no sign of deterioration. He tried to smudge the ink in the book but found it was impossible. He also tested some of the pages, at first with drops of water and finally by drenching them, but they would not dampen, soil, or wrinkle. The ink did not run as most ink would do—even in most magical volumes—when treated thusly.

He finally came to realize that he was going to have to channel an effect that he really did not want to use for determining the book's ability. The process was going to take a good portion of the day and into the late hours of the evening and leave him in an exhausted condition. He would need plenty of rest afterward to resolve his weakened aura.

He wished he could have bargained more finance from Toran, but the other had been correct to assume that fifty would have been adequate finance. Tonches was an excellent master who knew his magic, but as an employer, he was not so satisfactory. Tonches did not finance Richard well. What little business he did beyond Tonches's knowledge, in or out of the school, usually garnered much more than Tonches would pay him for the very same services.

Richard left the book on the table and exited the room. He returned with an iron brazier and a small sack, set both on the floor, and opened the sack. Then he poured several rocks of coal from the bag into the small iron vessel. Leaving the brazier on the floor, he went to the table and removed a feather duster from his robe. He dusted the front and rear covers of the book several times. Then he opened the book and began to dust each page individually. After preparing the whole book, a process taking nearly two full hours, Richard returned to the brazier.

With one of the lit candles from the table and some effort, the coals finally ignited within the brazier. Richard waited for the flames to die away and the coals to burn hot. When it was ready, Richard took a stand from under the table and set it up above the bowl of hot coals. Knowing that the display of the effect would not harm even a non-magical book, he retrieved the one to be scrutinized and placed it on the stand.

While the book sat over the coals, Richard left the room. He returned two hours later with a small metal bowl in one hand, a bottle of wine in the other, and a six-inch long silver stirring stick that was tucked above his ear.

He set the bottle and the bowl upon the table. He then took out a small hammer from one of his pockets. Inside the container, there was a small ruby that was worth no more than twenty gold finance. He smashed the ruby into the finest powder he could with the hammer and poured some wine into the bowl. He took the silver stick from above his ear and stirred the wine. After mixing the wine for several minutes, he dropped the stirrer in and let the concoction steep.

He pulled the stand away from the brazier and put out the coals. He had to allow the book to cool before he could take it to the table. This whole purification process was necessary so that any outside influences that might hinder his effect's ability to determine what magic the book held would be removed. He had done this with every item that he had ever studied.

He was sure that other mages had their own ways of purifying things, but this was the way that Tonches had taught him. Until he found a better way, this was how he would do it.

He took the silver stick out of the bowl and drew a symbol on the book with it. After this, he licked whatever wine he could from it and tucked the stick back above his ear. He raised the bowl in both hands and drank the wine.

An hour later, when he had finished his study of the book's magic, his aura was depleted. An evil grin twisted across his face. In the next moment, as he felt the coming exhaustion, that smile disappeared as though it had been a trick of the shadows in the room.

What am I going to tell Toran? he wondered. He needed to possess the book for its magic to work. He would have to say something to him and his friends. Then an idea occurred to him, and he wondered if there would be time. He picked up the book, put it in a small sack, and carried it with him. He locked up the school and walked away.

It was a warm evening, and stars littered the dark sky. He needed no reason to dodge a city patrol by ducking into a busy tavern. He had done nothing wrong yet, but he felt the need anyway. He watched the patrol go by, ignored the commotion inside, and waited a few extra minutes before leaving the tavern. When he did, he nearly bumped into a man who was entering it. The man paid him no attention, and Richard, who did not recognize that it was Toran, continued to his destination.

The effect that had identified the book's magical ability had exhausted both him and his aura, even more than he had thought it would. He moved through the streets as quickly as his body would concede. He finally stopped at a series of shops and knocked on one of the doors. He continued knocking until a light came on from within.

The door opened, and a man, approximately his own age but with darker hair, appeared in the doorway. "It's late. What do you want?" the man asked angrily.

"Michael, I need you to fashion a book for me," Richard said.

"This late? Can't it wait until morning?"

"It's important." Richard showed Michael the book. "It must look like this one. It need not be identical, as I can mask a few mistakes and imperfections, but I need it by next evening. Is it possible?"

"I think I could have it by then, but I have—"

"I'll pay you threefold the normal finance!"

"Threefold? You do not have that kind of coin," Michael said.

"Yes, I do." He grabbed the pouch Kellik had given him and shook the contents in front of Michael. "There's fifty." He knew because he had taken the time to count the coins. "I'll have the rest when you finish it."

"Needs to look like this one?" Michael took the book from Richard. "By next evening? Sure, I will do it."

Richard handed him the pouch and told Michael that he would be back sometime during the next day to check his progress. He returned to the school, collapsed into his bed, and was too exhausted to be surprised that he had made it there. He fell asleep quickly, but not before he smiled at the power that he would soon possess and the riches that it would bring him.

He would leave Tonches, for by then, Richard's ability would far surpass his. He would never have to worry about learning new magics again. He would be a teacher, and he would be the one in control.

CHAPTER 7

CAUGHT IN THE ACT

"Not again!"

As a group, several in the half-drunken crowd let out unhappy sighs, and the rest cheered. Saigel stood victorious on a chair as another opponent left the table having lost an arm contest to him. He had started accepting matches late in the morning and had had several since. Now that night, a large crowd filled the tavern, and most of them were quite interested in the minikin's strength.

Kellik had watched Saigel revel in his victories all day and had bowed his head in disgust each time. Saigel and Toran had both confessed their strengths shortly after their match in Kershal. Deceiving these people for finance was wrong. He did not like what Saigel was doing, but he had seen some logic when Toran had explained it to him.

"The magician at Tonches's school might find something about the book that he feels is more valuable," Toran had explained. "He may then raise his price or not give us any information." Because of their limited amount of coin, they might need some extra finance. It also helped that they both agreed with his idea to donate any excess finance to a local faith.

Kellik held a dual purpose in their ruse this evening. So far, Saigel's strength had met no contention the way Thom had challenged him after the Kershal match, and the spectators just watched and wagered their finance. Kellik would not make a bet until Toran arrived. If anyone did contest a match, he would again pretend to be a magician to prove Saigel's innocence. This time, he would not use his flamelight essence. Instead, he would rely on the crowd's belief that he was a magician.

Toran entered the tavern, ignoring the young man that had just left, and saw the crowd around Saigel. The taproom was small, and if Toran remembered correctly, the owner was a silver-haired elf who made the best wine that most people in Aamber would ever taste. He saw the old elf sitting in a chair on a ledge high up on the wall. Several steps led up to his place. Toran could not remember anyone except the several-hundred-revolution-old elf ever climbing those stairs.

The rest of the place was always kept neat. Several younger elves were always busy making sure spills were immediately cleaned up, and every cup, glass, flagon, or stein was full. There was a hearth in the middle of the tavern's east wall where the cook was placing the remaining half of a cooked boar upon a table. It was probably the last one, considering the time of the evening and the fire being put out. Toran went to the table. "How much for a meal?"

When the cook turned, Toran was surprised to see it was a woman who had sweat, toiled, and cooked all evening. She was elven, just as the rest of the tavern's workers were. Her hair was a light color, of which Toran could not determine because it was underneath the hat she wore. *She may even be pretty,* Toran thought, *under other conditions. But then,* he added, *most elves are.*

The woman cut off some of the ham for him and indicated the rest of the table. Toran saw potatoes and a few different gravies. At least four vegetables accompanied the meal. "Help yourself. No finance required."

"Thank you." Toran left the table after loading his plate and pushed his way through the crowd to the table that Saigel now sat alone at with no challenger.

Toran made several inquiries about the commotion and had learned that the minikin had won several matches but had not lost any. Toran already knew this information for two reasons. First, they had planned this deception. Second, news of the minikin's undefeated record had spread all over Aamber.

Toran approached Saigel as he had in Kershal and played the scene the same way as before, except that he took an occasional bite of his meal. When the match was set, the crowd gathered around and placed their bets. Toran set the empty plate on an adjacent table, and it was soon picked up by one of the elves.

Kellik now entered the betting and found some reasonable odds for the next match. Several groups were offering outrageous odds, but Kellik stayed with what he had already found. With the 110 gold that they would have after paying Richard his first half and the balance due when he was done, he decided that they would make a fair enough amount without some of the long odds, which might not pay out, or even be able to do so when Toran ended up as the winner.

Toran and Saigel played their parts perfectly. Each took turns on the offensive side, but at the finish, Saigel was on the losing end. The amazed and mostly drunken crowd believed what had transpired. Then Saigel did something that Kellik did not expect.

He protested the match.

"Thur's magic at play here!" he snarled, pounding his small hand on the table. Like a wave, an anxious murmur coursed through the crowd at Saigel's declaration. Because of this, Kellik knew his assessment concerning magic's scarcity in the rest of the realms was true. Aamber was larger than Kershal but was still by no means a large city. This town even had a school, small as it was, for learning magic, and yet the reaction was the same.

"I have no magic," Toran said calmly. "Is there a magician about?" He turned to the crowd, which was already amazed at the mere mention of magic, to ask about further magic. When three affirmative calls rang out, including Kellik's, people quickly separated themselves from the proclaiming three. Toran looked at each of them and said, "Come forward and let me be proved."

Two humans stepped forward along with Kellik, who was utterly confused by what Toran and Saigel were doing. The other magicians were similarly clad in green robes, complete with symbols signifying the sky. Apparently, Tonches's school was not the only one around the area.

"Who is to prove me? It was your loss and your choice."

"No. I'll not 'ave magic prove yuh of none," Saigel answered, and Kellik stepped back as did the others.

"What will you have then?" Toran asked.

"I'll match yuh again, but we'yul both change. Takin' off anythin' that might be magic."

"As I have none, it is agreed then."

The accusation was made, but winnings from the match were still collected. Kellik gathered his with no problem. He could tell that some of the others were having difficulties obtaining what was due them from their prospective bets. He could also tell that these were from the ones that had given the worst odds for the first contest. People were bargaining against the new match instead of paying.

He sat back down on his stool by the bar and watched the two of them in their new charade. He could not believe what they were doing and was more amused than surprised as each changed his garb and removed any jewelry he wore. Kellik ordered more ale and turned to the elf who had brought it to him. "These games are for the foolish," he said.

"I agree and wonder who will be victorious now that neither have magic upon them," the elf answered.

"What?" Kellik asked.

"The minikin had several items, and the human had two, but neither have any now."

"How do you know this?"

The elf pointed up to the elderly elf. "He has seen both but knows not what magic works upon them. Now that there is none, we shall see a true victor."

Kellik did not have any more words, so he downed his ale. He did not want to push his luck by asking but wondered why the elves would allow possible cheating in their place.

Throughout the tavern, people were placing wagers on the new match. It was underway when Kellik returned to his stool. He watched as Saigel, this time, pressed Toran's arm to the table. The crowd roared, and Toran sank his head down.

"I've won!" Saigel said triumphantly. "Bring ale fuhr me and thuh human."

The elf behind the bar drew the ale from the tap and was about to take them over when Kellik stopped him and said, "Allow me."

Kellik approached the table and looked at them both. He smiled to himself. If they could improvise, so could he. He held out the mugs of ale to both of them. "There has been satisfactory proof of no magic," he said and then turned to the crowd before handing over the drinks. "But now the two have a grudge between them. Another match with the opposite arm should determine the true winner." Kellik turned back to the contestants and placed their ale on the table. "Drink and then let the stronger prevail."

An eerie silence fell over the crowd as the contestants deliberated. Toran and Saigel looked up at Kellik and then to each other.

"It is correct, little one, that we have no true winner between us," Toran said. "What say you to the grudge?"

"Drink an' have at yuh. That's whut I say!" Everyone roared approval.

When the match finished, several people in the crowd congratulated both Saigel and Toran—Saigel for his earlier wins and Toran for his recent one. The three went separate directions, leaving the tavern at separate times throughout the evening. They met at a previously selected area in Aamber. Because they were sure that no one was following them, they now walked through the darkened streets together.

"Well, that should have been profitable," Toran said, starting the conversation, "and very inventive, Kellik."

"I found a place to donate any excess," Kellik added while smiling. "Thank you, but you could have warned me that you were going to be inventive yourselves."

Saigel had agreed with Toran about the excess finance, but they could not convince Kellik to keep the winnings. They wanted to split any excess evenly, letting Kellik donate his share, but in the end, it seemed that Kellik was going to hold fast to his idea of donating.

While traveling in a group of three, the last thing that any of them would have expected, even late in the evening, was to be accosted by thieves, but as they turned a corner, Toran realized an immediate twinge of danger. He looked up too late to warn Saigel of the man already dropping from above him. Instead, he pushed him aside.

"Hey!" Saigel complained. As he fell down, pursued by his attacker, Toran saw another man, much larger than the other, come out of the shadows in front of them to charge at Kellik.

The elf had been quick to draw his two longswords, but Toran was still shaken by how he had known they were in danger. He had not heard or smelled anything to alert him, but he had somehow known. His moment of wonder thwarted him, and he was not prepared to defend himself.

Saigel kicked his attacker and tumbled farther away while another dark figure came from the opposite corner of the lane behind Toran and knocked him unconscious. Kellik had felled his opponent only moments before that same assailant had moved swiftly across the road and brought down his friend also. Saigel now stood alone, and it was two against one.

"Surrender and you will not be harmed!" one of them demanded.

"To whut end?" Saigel replied defiantly.

"My employer would have an audience with you."

"To whut *end*?" Saigel growled the final word.

"We'll take you by force if you don't cooperate."

"I surrender." Saigel dropped his sword.

Collecting all the loose weapons did not take their captors long. With the two men weighed down—one carrying Toran and the other with Kellik—Saigel could have made a clean run. He decided against it and stayed with the others. They turned a corner and went into an alley. Saigel began to feel sleepy. Finally, he could not stay awake and collapsed.

Kellik's falcon, circling high above and following them, now landed on a building, which overlooked the place his elven partner had been taken. Moments later, it slept also.

Michael had not gone back to sleep after Richard had left the book with him. He had spent the next couple of hours studying its construction and had found its materials to be quite ordinary, except for the fabulous paper that was bound within it. The spine had no decoration. The most exciting thing that he could find out about the book, besides the paper, was that there was no binding whatsoever.

"You are magically held together, I suppose," Michael guessed aloud. "How am I to duplicate this if I do not know how it is held together?" He picked up the book again and opened it. "Perhaps if I break it down to study its construction firsthand … but no, I do not have that much time. Bah! Besides, if you are magically held together, I would not be able to refasten you, let alone my ability to unfasten you in the first place. I must find a way to secure my copy without it looking like it is bound.

"Then the cover. How am I to age the cover? Perhaps I have taken on more than I can handle. No. I will find a solution. Richard said he would cover any imperfections or mistakes." He looked around his shop at the equipment and tools of his bookbinder's trade and then shook his head.

He regarded the heavy wooden mallet. "I will not use you because I need individual sheets, and without the many folded sheets of paper sewn together, there will be no swell for you to knock down. And my press. Well, I might as well replace the fruit cage in you and make myself some cider while I decide the most probable course of action to take in finishing my current task."

He went to the window and saw that the sky was getting lighter. Dawn would come soon, and then he would be able to get some materials for the cover. By knocking on the front and back covers during his initial examination, Michael had discovered bother were simply two thin wooden boards. "Probably breach wood," he determined. Breach trees were common throughout all the lands, except in The East where they still grew but not as abundantly as in the other kingdoms. The wood was strong enough for a good cover, but Michael frowned at the thought. He preferred to use a stronger wood for his covers, such as a good march, not nearly as common but much stronger and less apt to warp from numerous soakings like this one had had.

Of course, he could find both easily, and the leather would not be a hard match. This was more his hope than his confidence. While at the leather shop, he would stop next door to let Richard know how he was coming along with the duplicate. With this in mind, he sat and counted the number of pages. Then he used a wooden gauge to size the paper. He went over to the shelf and counted out the same amount of paper sheets.

The "trimmer," as Michael called it, consisted of a sharpened blade of curved metal attached to a lever. The lever was then fastened to the table edge. An adjustable wooden marker, which had also been fixed to the table, was held in place by a setting screw. The table had gauge marks for varied sizes of paper and had already been set, coincidentally, at the correct paper height measurement. He cut each piece of paper separately. The scraps fell unheeded to the floor to join the others from projects that had been done previously. Then he reset the marker to make his second cut for each page.

"Now with all of you the correct size, I need a way to stitch you without indicating a stitch." He thought for a long moment. "It may not last as long as a stitched book, but I could glue you together at the binding. More than likely though, the first or second time you are opened, several pages will fall out."

Michael gauged the original cover size before he left his shop to get the boards and leather for the new one. The morning was warm, but clouds filled the sky. The rain was not threatening yet, but by the afternoon, it might become a possibility. The boards were easy to find and sized to fit. The leather was much more difficult.

The leatherworker next to Tonches's school had no leather that was even close to the correct one. So he would have to go somewhere else. Before he continued his search, he did stop in to talk with Richard as he had planned. It took Richard several minutes to answer the door, and he still looked as exhausted as he had the night before.

"I am having a problem with the binding of the book because there appears to be none. The pages are attached somehow but are not stitched, as is commonly done," Michael said and then explained his idea of gluing the pages together and the drawback of doing so.

"Maybe I can come up with something to help them to stay together, but for now, do what you can," Richard answered. "I need to get some more rest. I'll speak with you later."

"Very well, my friend." Michael tried several other leather workers before he found compatible leather for the cover. Nearly half the day was gone by the time he returned to his shop.

"A bucket of water will be necessary for drenching," he said, as he started the cover. He laid out the leather over the table and placed the boards on it. "Now you must be marked," he said to the leather, "so that my folds will not be too long around the boards. After I get you marked and cut, I will fold each of your edges in on each board. Then I will stitch the final fold in you with a single thread," he continued while pointing to the board on his left, "to you.

"Then when all of you are together as a book, that thread will hold the leather in place. This is not how I would generally work the two of you together, but since nothing else I am doing will bind you all as a whole, I figure this will have to do. I do usually take more pride in my work."

Enrandl stood before his new mirror inside his still-ruined laboratory. Even with the short notice, the silversmith had fashioned a beautiful replica of his last one, except for the gold inlay. Enrandl channelled into the mirror and centered his concentration on Toran. The dark-gray, formless picture in the mirror told him that Toran was still protected from being scried upon.

Now he turned his thoughts toward the magical book. He assumed that the tome would be similarly protected, but the mirror's picture shifted. Where there had been darkness before, colors now appeared.

The colors swirled into a definite form of a book. He gazed, stricken by surprise, as the thought of a possibility settled in.

Are my senses sincere? he thought. *Has the potential of my goal been actuated?* He had never seen the book or even heard a description of it. Yet there in the mirror was a book. He knew that the book he wanted, its abilities, and his concentration on it were delivering this picture. *The uniqueness of qualification must be paramount in such gesture.*

The book sat on a table. He made the magical vision scroll around the room, where he found a young man with red hair dressed in simple everyday clothing. He appeared to be constructing a different book.

Enrandl quickly channelled another effect into the mirror. "Who are you?" Enrandl demanded. The man in the mirror shook for a moment and stepped backward from the table where he had been working. "Respond to my query! Who are you?" Enrandl demanded.

"I am Michael of Florin. Who is there?" he said as he backed away from the table and looked anxiously around him.

Enrandl ignored his question. "What method have you conspired to align your custody of my book?"

"A friend brought it to me," Michael said. Being sure that there was no one in his shop, he moved back toward the table. "Were it not his to lend?"

Enrandl looked Michael over once again. He assessed instantly that the man pictured before him had never in his life dreamed of working magic. He ignored this and continued, "You will proffer custody of my possession to no one prior to my arrival. Does my insinuation satisfy your comprehension?"

"Who are you?" Michael asked.

"I am Enrandl Quemont. No individual but me! Do we have an accordance?"

"Yes. Yes, I understand," he answered, nodding.

Michael stood paralyzed for a moment after the mysteriously threatening voice had stopped. When he regained his senses, he picked up the original and wondered what Richard had gotten himself into. The bookmaker glanced around his store again to be sure that he was alone before returning to work on the copy. He had gone over the allotted time for this construction. Richard had been by several times during the day to check his progress, so Michael was already working as fast as he could. His friend was going to get this book and its duplicate no matter who this Enrandl was.

It was another five minutes before his copy was finished. Although he could have done better if there had been more time even considering the makeshift binding he had used, the forgery would still fool most people. He took both books, put out all his lanterns, locked up his business, and went to the magician's school.

Enrandl appeared from his channelled shift and found that he was standing alone in the darkness of Michael's left-behind shop. Furious to find it in its current condition and with Michael nowhere to be seen, he started to demolish the interior of the store both magically and physically. Nothing escaped his wrath, including the front door, which was blown outward from its hinges into the road beyond it. He was careful not to let anything catch on fire and burn everything down. This had to be witnessed by the bookmaker. When he was finished destroying the bookbinding shop—though he could not put a name to the city he was in—the angry magic user stepped out onto the streets of Aamber.

CHAPTER 8

LIKE COMING HOME

The smell of apples and oranges greeted Kellik when he awoke. He had been asleep sitting in a chair with his head on the table. As he raised his head slowly and looked around the room, he saw what appeared to be a large dining room. On the table before him lay a large feast. There was a turkey, which had been cooked golden brown, for the main course. The apples and oranges, which he could smell, were sliced and peeled in front of him.

Toran was across the table from Kellik but was still unconscious. He had been placed in a chair in much the same way that Kellik had been. Saigel was nowhere to be seen, and it concerned Kellik.

He wondered where his friend might be. When he checked for his weapons, he found that they were gone. He was about to get up from his chair to explore the dining room when the door at the far end opened.

Three men entered. The first man was older and dressed in a regal-looking, green cloak, decorated with a silver lining. His straight posture suggested nobility. He was much older than Kellik, even considering Kellik's extended life span.

Toran started to stir as the cloaked man said, "I see one of you has awakened." He sat down in the chair at the head of the table. The other two men, dressed in black leather armor, stood flanking his chair on the left and the right.

The man on the older man's left would stand out in any crowd. He was nearly seven feet tall and very muscular. In fact, he was so muscular, Kellik thought that he would not be able to walk into an old armory and find a ready-made suit to fit him. More than likely, he had to have a custom-made one. His current armor was a bit too small for him, as if he were growing out of it. His dark-brown hair was pulled back in a long ponytail. A sword was strapped to his back. Kellik knew of only one man who was larger than this one—Thom—and as far as Kellik knew, he was three days west of Aamber.

The man on the right side of the chair was not nearly as impressive a sight as his partner was. He was much smaller in height and build, and he had short red hair. Two swords completed his armament. From his view, Kellik could not tell what type of sword either man carried.

"Where am I?" Toran asked, without looking up.

"I am corrected. Two of you are awake here, but where is the little one?" the man replied.

Kellik saw Toran stiffen slightly.

"I'm 'ere," the minikin's voice originated from behind the two guards. They spun in place and drew their swords.

"Put your weapons away!" the older man ordered forcefully without yelling. "They are all unarmed."

Not all of us, Kellik thought, as he took note of their weaponry. He saw Saigel's brief smile as he walked to the table, he sat down in a chair next to him, and the guards sheathed their swords.

"Please eat. You must be famished. Sleeping for nearly a full day can make one very hungry."

"And a bit sore. Where are we?" Toran was now aware that the others were with him but still did not raise his head.

"Will he keep asking?"

"Normally," Saigel answered. "'Til 'e's answered."

"Very well, then. You are my guests in the home of William Sagemont."

Toran rubbed the back of his head, "We probably would have accepted an invitation. Did you say we slept an entire day?"

"I fear I could not take that chance. You three have cost me a large amount of finance with your little ruse. You played well, from what I was told, but it was unfortunate that you met in the wrong part of town and under the watchful eyes of two of my servants. Oh, and yes, you have slept a full day. I must apologize for not waking you earlier, but I had some business to attend to."

"What do you want from us?" Toran continued to question him.

"I would like you to work the same performance again."

"Won't be believed again," Saigel commented.

"Of course, not here in Aamber, but it may succeed perhaps in Jenerv, where it has not already been seen." Kellik watched as William looked at them all in turn. Toran was not sitting up, but he was facing Kellik and Saigel and rubbing the back of his neck. "If my guards have caused undue damage, I can have you healed."

"I am just stiff from being slouched over in a chair all day. We have some business to take care of here before we travel to Jenerv. How late is it?"

"Well after sunset. I will leave Seane and Paul here to accompany you," he gestured to his left and then right, "for the business here and on your journey to Jenerv. Thank you for your time, gentlemen, and please do eat something." William stood and headed for the door.

"Wait—" Kellik started, but Toran cut him off with a wave.

"Thank you. We will be on our way to Jenerv as soon as we finish our business."

William left the room. They ate in relative silence under the close watch of the two guards. Once Kellik tried to start a conversation, but Toran just shook his head and went back to eating. When they had finished the meal, their escorts brought them through the main hall of what Kellik thought was a castle. They retrieved their weapons at the foyer, but with a warning. The smaller of the two said, "Do not try anything foolish."

Outside, they found that the night air was refreshing. Kellik looked back at the home they had just left while Toran informed the new companions of their tardiness. He noted to himself that since leaving home, things had not been as they had appeared to be. He had experienced things he would not trade, even if he had the chance to.

It had all started at the cave where he and Saigel had fought the dragon. Then there were Saigel's arm contests, Higoshi's cottage, and this obviously expensive home, which looked like a run-down warehouse from the outside. *Is this how everything is, away from home?* he wondered and then heard the flapping of wings. He turned with his arm out. The falcon landed there on it and moved to his shoulder. The group moved quickly to the school.

"Fine looking bird," Seane said.

"Thank you. Why did you agree to help him?" Kellik asked Toran. "It's just not you if you do not haggle."

"I know that type of man. Bartering is not in his nature, and if we did not agree to help, we would not be alive now."

Paul was nodding in agreement with Toran's answer as they came to the school. It was dark, but Toran knocked for several minutes, just in case someone was sleeping and did not hear him.

"Have to return next morning," Kellik said, putting his hand on Toran's shoulder.

Seane and Paul escorted the three of them to an inn where they were told that William would be paying for their rooms. Kellik wondered how these two were going to watch all three of them in separate rooms and stay awake all night. The three went their separate ways.

As Toran went to the window of his room, he scratched his chest. *William Sagemont.* He could not believe the old man was still alive, but what was he doing here in Aamber? *Only careful planning is going to get me through this one,* he thought, *and William not recognizing me.* He had known the voice as soon as the man had started speaking. He intentionally feigned soreness so that he would not have to lift his head too far.

The Sagemont family had been friends with his own during his early studies with Higoshi. Toran had been to Jenerv several times with his father and had met William. William had always given him the impression that he liked him and had something fun for him to do while he and his father conducted business. When he was younger and before he started his training with Higoshi, it was horse riding and carnivals. As he grew older, the activities became more attuned to his age. He never knew what business his father and William were doing together but was usually too busy to wonder.

One summer when his father had died during a hunting trip with William, William had personally come to Higoshi's cottage, although it had been nearly a week's travel, to tell Toran what had happened. They were hunting (no business this time), and his father was walking his horse through a small forest with the rest of them when something startled it. William told him that his father had fought to calm it down, but the horse had trampled him for his effort.

William informed him that from that day forward, if he needed anything, he only had to ask, and it would be given to him. Toran had accepted his offer but had rarely asked anything of William. Many would have taken advantage of such an offer, but he had not.

Because he was powerful in an underground society, William had many enemies. One of those enemies had commissioned a friend of Toran's to steal some valuable jewelry. Without knowing whom they were stealing from, he had accepted when his friend Conrad had asked for his help.

In all the times that he had met William in Jenerv, he had never been fortunate enough to visit his home. There was always business to attend to, or his father was in a hurry. Conrad had not expected anyone to be home. So, when they discovered that someone was there, Toran's recently learned Merea ability to render both of them invisible was needed to keep them concealed.

They successfully found the treasure but encountered William before they could leave his home. Toran's concentration faltered when he saw William, the bubble popped, and the two became visible. The short confrontation that followed ended in his friend's death and what Toran thought was a mortal wound unintentionally inflicted upon William.

He escaped with the jewelry and went to Higoshi. His master could hardly contain his anger when he had returned. He directed Toran to another master and sent him away but not before explaining why. It was not because he no longer wanted to tutor his favorite pupil but to save him from any wrath that may have fallen on him or the school from William Sagemont.

That left him with no family. His mother had died during his birth, so he never even had a chance to know or mourn her. His father had then been taken by the unfortunate accident, and he could no longer go to William and continue in his favor. Finally, he was banished from his training with Higoshi, who was the last person that he considered as his family.

He had only one option left to him—to continue his training with the new master Higoshi was sending him to. He had every intention to do so but never made it to that destination. He joined a company of merchants that were headed the direction he wanted to go. From them, he learned the weapon play of the sword. The merchants became his friends. They were not his family, but at this point, he would take what he could get. He could never figure out how Higoshi had learned what had happened. With his new training, the question was soon forgotten, but he figured that Higoshi had just read his mind.

Read his mind, Toran thought. He left the window, went to the door, and listened. One of the two guards was still in the hall. Toran stood and created a sphere of pigments. The multi-colored hues, which danced about the sphere as it expanded and tried to discover the person outside the door, were less vivid as his latest ones. He found that the sentry outside was Paul. He could sense others within the sphere: Kellik and Saigel, who were in the rooms on each side of his, and almost everyone downstairs in the taproom, but he focused on Paul. Once he and Paul were inside the sphere, he saturated it with primary blue.

Surface thoughts were easy to comprehend, but Paul seemed extraordinarily easy. Toran was impressed with his attention to the duty of monitoring the three of them, and this dedication may have left his thoughts more vulnerable. Paul, unaware that his mind was being searched, was easy to explore. Toran focused and centered a smaller sphere on Paul's brain and moved through it quickly. After just a few minutes, Toran found all the answers that he wanted. Paul was oblivious that his mind had been raided.

Seane and Paul were on their own during the day, but at night, additional sentries would be placed there to cover any possible escapes.

Seane was down on the lower level resting for his shift. Concerning how William had discovered their con, Seane and Paul had been at the tavern during the ruse. They were placing bets for William. Unfortunately for Kellik, Saigel, and himself, they had been in the right place to see the three of them meet. They quickly found an associate and commenced their ambush on them in an alley not far from William's home.

Then one of his own thoughts invaded his concentration, and all the spheres collapsed instantly. What he remembered forced him to go to the bed and sit down. Rediscovering the Merea talent, which had been buried deep within him a long time, had taken little practice (mainly a concentrated effort). He knew that with practice, surface thoughts of most beings were easy to read. He had not only learned the surface thoughts of Paul's mind but had probed much deeper to find the secondary information. This thought brought another to him: Predicting the ambush was another talent he had never been trained to use. He had tried to learn the ability to sense danger approaching, but even with Higoshi's tutoring, he had found that he could not master it.

The thought probe that he had just completed was something he had never even attempted to learn, and yet he had used it as if he had been familiar with it all his life.

You will understand, Toran thought as he lay down. Higoshi had said that to him so many times and even on the day before he had died. *The strength of the mind can overcome any obstacle.*

He fell asleep and immediately began dreaming of his old master. It was a recurring dream that he had been having since the night of Higoshi's death. Every night he dreamed of training sessions with his old mentor, but it was not always the same training. The dreams were similar enough so that he could remember most parts of them in detail. Each began the same way and then branched off differently.

"Toran," Higoshi called. "Toran, listen to me. The colors will fade. Embrace them now to learn control, but you do not need them."

"Master Higoshi?" Toran found himself on a bed of grass during a breezy spring day. The surroundings were vaguely familiar to him. The leaves from several trees rustled gently in the light breeze. "Where am I?"

"That is not important. You must prepare yourself. Call forth a sphere and concentrate!"

"I do not understand, master." The colors and forms of the trees shifted, and for a moment, he could see the wind that moved past the leaves. When Toran looked up at his master, Higoshi looked somewhat younger than he remembered, and he was no longer lying on a bed of grass. Higoshi was still gray-haired and bearded. His eyes were squinted, and his skin was a little darker than its normal paleness but less wrinkled.

"The colors will fade. The formation is the key. How will you ever learn if you can not concentrate?"

Toran was now sitting on a small platform inside Higoshi's home. Still not understanding what was going on, he watched Higoshi as he walked a path circling the platform.

"Toran! I can still see you," Higoshi scolded.

Toran became angry and concentrated. The sphere surrounded him, and he tried to draw the turquoise to him, but he was having difficulty. It was as if he had no idea what he was doing, and that made no sense. *Maybe my anger is blocking me from access to the sphere,* he thought. He relaxed and remembered what Higoshi had taught him. He centered his mind on what he wanted. The sphere engulfed him (bound to him), and he could see its blue-green hue in everything around him.

He could almost hear Higoshi say the words, "When your mind is set on the task, will it to happen."

The whole scene played on through his mind. His eyes were closed. The invisible blue-green barrier surrounded his body, and in his own mind, he no longer envisioned himself within the sphere.

"Very good. I knew you could do it," Higoshi said, indicating that he was, in fact, invisible. "Practice will teach you the limitations of this talent."

His view shifted again. Toran knew that between the shifts, he was dreaming. But as the new exhibition unfolded, he became lost in the commotion of it. The scene was the memory of another training session when he had learned and finally mastered the use of another Merea talent.

There was only one problem, and he did not realize it while he was sleeping. He was not dreaming of memories. During his dreamscapes, everything he learned played through his mind as if they were memories of Higoshi's teaching, but while he was awake, he knew they were not. The talents to sense danger and explore deeper into someone's mind for information were not his memories. Both had come to him during his dreams on the previous nights, as did the talent of creating and controlling different instances of the weather that he dreamed while unconscious at William's home. With his training session completed, he continued to sleep, dreaming normal and pleasant dreams.

Richard's hands moved as fast as his eyes could read in the lamplight. He turned to the next page, skimmed over it, did not find what he was looking for, and turned to the next one. He understood that it would be much easier just to leave Aamber with his prize, but without access to effects for him to channel, the book's powers were all but useless. For that reason alone, he had not left in the first place.

Several books lay around the small room. Some were on his bed, some were on the table he was sitting at, but most were strewn across the floor. The target of his search was in one of his study ledgers, but with his lack of organization, he was not sure which one. He had been amazed when he had seen Tonches use the effect recently.

It was fortunate for him that he had not seen Tonches channel it a revolution ago. All of the effects that he had stolen from his master over the past revolution would have taken less than three cycles for him to copy. With the numerous books contained within the hidden library, another revolution would be required to finish all of them without the aid he was searching for. He had intended to take as much time as he needed while working at the school so that he would be able to finish stealing all of them, but now his goal had been altered.

If he had copied the effects with help, his task would have been completed much sooner, and Aamber would have been behind him well before Toran and his friends came to town with the book. Then he never would have even known about it.

"There it is," he whispered, "there it is." He carefully studied the next three pages before he closed the book in front of him.

Richard had found the underground library in the school by accident. It was beneath the primary classroom. He had been cleaning the room when he had tripped on a loose nail in the floor. Ten minutes later, after finding a hammer, he returned to pound the nail down. When he did, he heard a hollow echo from below. At first, the sound had confused him, but after feeling around, his confusion disappeared. He found the countersunk handle in the floor and opened the door to the lower level.

Tonches had used an illusionary display to hide and cleverly disguise the trap door to be just as the rest of the wooden floor was. Below the door was a ladder leading him underneath the school. The library below had numerous volumes describing effects, which Richard had not even dreamed existed.

Richard wondered why Tonches had never set traps in such a place. At least he could have hidden some rune or sigil among the books—one that when an enterprising young mage such as him had found would explode when transcribed.

Tonches is mostly a trusting soul, so why would he? Richard added to himself.

Richard had told Toran that he had stayed on at the school to help Tonches, which had not been a lie, but he did have other reasons—all the effects that Tonches would never know he had copied into his own books. Whenever his employer had to leave town, Richard would have the opportunity to copy more of the formulas into his own growing library.

The last time he had had a chance to do any copying from Tonches library, he had made sure that this effect was the next one he found and among the others copied. There had been no chance since then to explore its formula. Now he had the opportunity, and he hoped for GodsLight that he would be able to understand its complexity. As he studied, he found that it was a simple enough effect for his usage, and no one would be able to stop him.

He closed the book and looked out the window. The moon was in the middle of the sky. It was late, and he still had a lot of work to do. The school was across town. Richard kept this room at the inn paid for so that he would have a place to store his books without Tonches gaining knowledge of what he was doing.

Richard left the inn and followed the main road that always had torch posts burning throughout the night. He turned the corner of the school's street but practically dove back around it. He crouched down and peeked around the corner at the front of the school, where Toran, Kellik, Saigel, and two others, whom he did not recognize, stood. Toran was knocking on the door.

He had to sneak around to the back and go in using the school's rear door. From there, with Toran still knocking, he went into the classroom with the hidden library. He found the handle in the dark and went down the ladder. The knocking at the front door stopped.

He was positive that no one would see any light down in the library. He lit three candles., The two books were in the middle of a small table. The magical one was to his right, and the copy that Michael had wonderfully crafted was to his left. He still had the problem of the pages possibly not staying together because he had not found a solution for that, but whatever Michael had done was working for now. With a few minor illusionary touches, the book would be perfect in appearance.

He opened both books to their first pages and then removed a quill and an ink bottle from one of his pockets. He placed the quill on the copy, opened the ink bottle, and placed it on the table between the books. Then he positioned his right hand over the actual book as if he had a quill in it. He put his left hand out flat in the air above the duplicate as he channelled. He moved his imaginary quill, tracing what he saw on the page, and he spoke a phrase that would enable the effect to display.

A moment later, the feather he had placed upon the duplicate book rose in the air. It dipped into the ink bottle and began writing. He drew back his left hand to give the floating stylus room, and no longer mimicked writing with an invisible quill. Now he merely looked at the symbols in the original. As his eyes moved across the symbols and letters, the small plume quickly copied what he saw into the other book.

When he turned a page of the first book, a page of the duplicate would follow. Richard's effect ceased its display, and he found that only a few pages had been transcribed. He was going to need several channellings to complete the whole book. He channelled as many as he needed to finish the work, and by the time he finished, morning had come, his aura was considerably but not completely drained, and there was no chance for him to sleep before his customers would come knocking once again.

This time, he was prepared for them.

The evening air was warm, as on the previous evening when Enrandl had arrived in Aamber. He had spent the entire day waiting for the bookbinder to return. He stood outside and across the road from his shop. When Michael finally returned, the magic user watched and allowed the destruction to sink in before crossing the street. The bookbinder's surprise when Enrandl entered the store was apparent, and the fear in his eyes made Enrandl smile.

"Where is my book?" He advanced upon Michael, who backed away until he hit a wall and could retreat no further. Enrandl grabbed the man's shirt and lifted him off the floor so that the smaller man was on eye level with the magician. Before crossing the road and while the owner was still looking over the damage, a quick effect to enhance his strength had allowed Enrandl to do this, when ordinarily he could not have.

When dealing with a thief one dark night, he had decided that he needed more of a physical presence from time to time. He was still experimenting with the idea. While this gave him some satisfaction, he was still unimpressed with his display and decided that it needed more experimentation.

Michael had not seen Enrandl's eyes until that time, but he would not have described them to anyone as *kind*.

"Where is my book? I will not reiterate," he growled angrily.

"I gave it back to my friend," Michael stuttered.

"I apprised an ordinance to such exploit!"

"He came for it. I …" Michael paused. "I had to give it to him."

"You will facilitate a consultation to associate us then."

"I can't do that," the trapped man said.

"Your life is forfeit to the merit of your justification." Enrandl glared at Michael.

"He has gone out of the city and will not be back until next midday."

"A prevarication I can not quantify."

"You do not have to," Michael replied.

"Very well. The recovery of your associate's attendance will have a perceptible destination." Enrandl released him. His tone was calmer now, and Michael, with disbelief, watched the look in his eyes change. "Reclaiming my property is of paramount significance worth munificent reimbursement."

Michael paused as he took in Enrandl's words. "How generous?"

"Very." Enrandl could almost smell the man's greed.

"I'll take you there next morning," Michael decided.

"Excellent." Enrandl smiled.

CHAPTER 9

THE CHASE

It was early the next morning when the three met Richard at the school. The streets were already busy by the time the three men were allowed into the building.

"We apologize for missing our appointment," Toran said.

"A GodsLight that I bid you thank you for. My research was not complete, and the extra time was what I needed."

"You look tired," Kellik said. "You must have been up late and worked long hours to help us."

"I believe I told you the effect can drain a lot from a magic user."

Toran nodded, and Richard handed the book to him, hoping no one had seen his hand was shaking. He put both of his hands in his pockets to prevent any further opportunity and felt a piece of parchment in the left one. He knew that the book was close but not as good as he had hoped it would be. The fact that they had shown up this morning with two more friends made him more nervous. Toran handed the book to Kellik, who tucked it under his arm. The falcon was resting on his shoulder.

"I found nothing unusual about it. It's a simple study book," Richard said.

"A simple study book?" Kellik asked. Richard noticed a strange expression on his face as if a foul odor had drifted past him before Kellik continued. "Why would he want this book so much?"

"I have no idea because they are all weak effects. I even listed them for you," Richard handed Toran the parchment, and immediately put his hand back in its respective pocket. "Effects a beginner would be learning from."

"Maybe it's not thuh book he's lookin' fuhr," Saigel added.

"It had better not be," Toran added. "If good men died for something simple like this …" His expression finished the sentence for him.

"I'm sorry it does not seem to be what you expected."

"Yes, so are we," Kellik said and headed toward the door. Saigel and Toran followed him. They met Seane and Paul outside and walked several paces away from the school.

"Whut now?" Saigel asked.

"I do not understand," Toran said.

"That's it! I can't believe it!" Kellik remarked and then brought the book up to his nose.

"Neither can I. Why would he kill my friends?" Toran said.

"Maybe he din't want ta pay any of yuh." Saigel looked up.

Toran started to reply, but Kellik cut him off. "No, Toran. I mean this isn't the same book. I can smell the leather—"

"Whut?" Saigel said.

"What do you mean?" Toran finished.

"I've looked through this book," Kellik said and then stopped himself and flipped through the pages. "No, I mean *my* book, hundreds of times. I know this isn't it." He licked his thumb and rubbed one of the pages. The writing underneath his wet thumb smeared slightly. "It's a clever copy but not clever enough because I've never been able to smell the leather on the cover before."

They all turned back toward the door of the school in time to see it close and to hear the lock.

"There has to be a back way out. Kellik, find and cover it," Toran said, pointing toward the end of the block of buildings. Kellik put the false book in his pack and then went off, taking the order without a word. Paul followed along with him.

Toran moved and stood at the door. Without closing his eyes, he summoned a sphere with a picture of the storefront in his mind. A moment later, a shimmering ball of colorless light appeared in front of the door because Toran had willed it. Saigel and Seane looked on in wonder. Within just a few seconds, the ball stretched into a vertical line of the same colorless light. The others stood and watched as the line separated into two lines and widened until an oval shape as tall as the door behind it formed. Through the oval, the inside of the school was visible.

"Go," Toran ordered.

Saigel stepped through first, and when Toran saw the little man was disorientated, he said through the portal, "That will pass, Saigel. Just breathe." Then he sent Seane in, and when he was through, he staggered side to side for a moment as if someone were trying to push him over. Toran had experienced this before, and he was more prepared for the disorientation, but it still affected him slightly. When he followed them, he took a deep breath and shook his head to clear his senses.

"Whut 'appened?" Saigel asked almost drunkenly.

"It is not as bad when you are not bypassing solid objects. Sorry. I will explain later. We have to catch Richard."

Seane had also now come back to his senses. They advanced into the school as the shimmering oval of light disappeared and the front door to the school appeared once again in the correct place.

They found their way through the classrooms, one of which included the trap door to Tonches's library. They finally reached the back door. It was locked of course. Toran stood back and started to concentrate again when Seane tapped him on the shoulder, breaking his concentration.

Outside, Kellik turned the corner and looked for Richard. A small crowd making its way along the busy lane blocked any vision of the escaping magician. The falcon shifting position to stay on his shoulder gave him an idea. It obviously had some previous training, but he did not know the extent of it. He raised his arm to point into the air. "I hope you understand this, little friend. Search."

The falcon flew from his arm at the command. It was less than a minute before it sounded off. Kellik looked up, spotted the falcon, and then looked down. Richard turned away from a closed door and ran down the road. Kellik pointed in his direction, and he and Paul ran after him, ending up at the door.

"Allow me," Seane said. He took a few steps back and rammed the door with his shoulder. The muscular man broke the door. Its hinges exploded, and the rest of it went crashing to the ground. When he hit it, the crash startled several people. One woman screamed, turned away, and ran off. Seane stepped into the street and motioned for the others to follow him.

Those who had stopped for the commotion and those who had ignored it carried on with their day. There was no sign of Richard. Seane must have seen something as the rest of them left the school because he pointed and started running.

Toran and Saigel followed. Although he was quick for a minikin, his short legs meant that he could not keep up with the rest of them. He soon fell behind in the pursuit, and Seane, too far ahead, did not notice his disappearance.

While he regained his breath, he thought about where he could find the others. Because he was not paying attention, Saigel turned and bumped into a tall human with tangled, black hair, wearing a glittering, blue robe.

"Relinquish to my resolve, you insignificant pest!" the man spat angrily at him. Saigel had much more important things to contend with, but it was too hard for him to ignore the insult. He was about to respond when someone else spoke.

"Richard's school and your book are across town. He should be there soon," the other voice said.

Saigel stopped his retort (insult and all). *Richard and thuh book?* he wondered. They were going the wrong way if they were heading for the school. Saigel considered this for a moment, decided he could not refute the coincidence, and followed them.

Not far ahead of his pursuers, Richard turned into an alley. He was in an unfamiliar area of town. Not knowing where to go was slowing him considerably, and he needed more of an advantage. He decided to double back to find some more familiar territory to work with.

Toran and Seane quickly caught up with Paul and Kellik. William's employees grouped together a few paces behind the others. Toran overtook Kellik but stopped chasing Richard when he turned a corner and caught sight of the magician. Kellik came around the same corner, looked back at Toran, and then continued to run. He was followed momentarily by Seane. Paul stopped and stayed with Toran this time. Toran smiled as he conjured a sphere that was only visible to him. In the sphere, he opened another shimmering doorway, which was visible, and then he stepped through the oval portal.

When Toran materialized directly in his path, Richard skidded to a complete stop. He closed his sphere with the shimmering portal at both ends and watched. The magician glanced back at the rapidly decreasing distance between himself and Kellik and decided to turn into an alleyway. Kellik was noticeably confused at Toran's sudden appearance, but he maintained the chase around the corner.

Toran had closed the opening before Paul reached it, and before he started after Richard again, he looked back to see Paul's reaction to suddenly being considerably far behind the rest of them. The man was nowhere in sight.

Now returning to a better-known area of the city near the bazaar, Richard chanced a looked over his shoulder for his pursuers. The young magic user did not notice the black-armored man dive at him from the other side. Paul missed but clipped Richard enough to knock him off balance and into a fruit cart. Fruit soared out of the cart in every direction, and the furious owner started to run after him. Toran, who was already running, brushed past the angry vendor, which caused him to turn slightly. Kellik came around the other side of him and spun the man around in the opposite direction. The pudgy cart owner fell into his already-broken-open, giant, prize-winning watermelon face-first. He looked up from the squashed fruit along with several others who had fallen during the commotion as Seane hurdled over him.

Michael and Enrandl heard the commotion but ignored it. "Where are we going?" Enrandl asked.

"Up there and around the corner on Sinderstone Way." Michael, who had just seen Richard fleeing, pointed. He had no intention of leading Enrandl to his friend and pointed in a direction contrary to where he was. Michael knew the city very well and could direct the magician around for hours while Richard made his escape.

He had told Richard about the peculiar conversation that he had had with Enrandl Quemont, and Richard had decided his best course of action was not to be in the city any longer. He did not know where Richard had planned to go, but he was going to meet his friend just outside of the south gate and go with him. A bookbinder was always needed somewhere, so he harbored no worries about his business, considering that it was in shambles now anyway.

"Wait," Enrandl said. "A curiosity vexes me presently."

Against Michael's urging, Enrandl went in the direction of the commotion, and he knew the magician would be led away no longer.

Through the crowd, Saigel had also seen what Michael had. The minikin ran directly toward Richard. When his turn to tackle him presented itself, he did not miss it. Richard fell into another cart. There was a loud snap that sounded like wood had broken, but the toppled cart remained intact, so there was no mistake that something on Richard had broken. Toran went directly to the magician, and Kellik stopped to help Saigel. The falcon landed on the overturned cart.

Toran knelt over Richard and searched him for the book. "He does not have it. The book must be back at the school," he told Kellik. "Where is the book?" Toran asked Richard, wanting confirmation, but Richard said nothing.

"What does the book do?" Lifting the man up, Toran noticed that the magician's neck did not look right, and Richard's eyes closed. "What does the book do?" Toran yelled at the dying magician. He set Richard's body down while he formed a sphere, but Richard was gone before he could attempt to heal him. He looked up at Kellik and shook his head, but Kellik was paying no attention to him.

"Toran," Enrandl said as a slight breeze began to blow.

He felt the chill in the magician's tone. If he had not known before, he knew now that Enrandl was not happy. Toran looked at Kellik as he stood there above him, and the thought of the fake book in his pack made him smile. He buried that smile before he stood up and turned around to face Enrandl.

"Where is my book?" It surprised Toran that the magician had asked this question in a calm tone.

"Give me the book, Kellik," Toran said.

"But …"

"Please just give it to me."

Kellik reached into his pack and produced it.

"Is this the book you are looking for, murderer?" Toran said as he took the book from Kellik with a half grin on his face. "Thank you. Is this the reason my friends died?" When he turned back to the magician, there was no hint of that smile.

"No," Enrandl answered flatly. "My treachery was envisioned by your avarice."

Toran's rage burned. "You lying troll!" He wanted to cleave Enrandl's head from his body but checked his impulse. For his dead friends and those whom he currently considered friends, there would be a better time to confront Enrandl. Toran conjured a sphere.

"Have your cursed book, and may you choke on it a thousand times!"

Michael watched his creation fly through the air as Toran threw it at Enrandl, but the magician dodged it. He knew it was his because he was an artist, and he could recognize his work anywhere. When it landed in the dirt behind the magician, he checked it over his shoulder. Michael watched his creation hit the ground and beamed with pride as the glue held the pages in place. He was marveling at his achievement as a shimmering oval opened where the others were standing.

Enrandl retrieved the book as Toran turned away from him to face Kellik. When he opened the portal, Saigel would know what to do—but Kellik would not. They started walking away with Paul and Seane several paces behind them as the magician inspected the book, as Toran knew he would, to verify its magical presence. He did not expect Enrandl to find any and wanted to get them all away from there as soon as he could.

"Stay close," Toran whispered, putting his hand on Kellik's shoulder.

"Why?"

The shimmering door opened in front of them, and he ushered his friends through. The falcon, which had flown toward Kellik, darted through behind them just before the shimmering door disappeared.

When the oval closed, a flashfire exploded where the shimmering had been. Paul and Seane, caught in the display, both collapsed to the ground.

"Pray to The Gods' that we do not meet again," Enrandl threatened.

"The magician called him Toran?" William asked for the third time.

"Yes, and then Toran threw the book and turned to leave," Seane continued looking directly at William. The big man bore several burns on his body, and he had not changed his scorched but serviceable leather armor. "Toran, Kellik, and Saigel stepped through the opening. We were trying to follow when it disappeared. The fire exploded after that. Paul did not survive."

"I want all of them found! Including the magician," William told Seane.

"He must have shifted after he killed Paul. That is all I could gather after I woke up."

"Fine, but I still want them found." William leaned back in his chair and ran his fingers through his white hair. *How could I have not recognized him?* he thought. "There is an old man who lives just outside of town to the north. Go there first. He would not stay in town, and if he is staying anywhere, that is where he will be. When you find him, bring him to me."

"His friends?" Seane asked.

"Kill them," William ordered flatly and then paused before saying, "Better yet ..."

At the cottage, Kellik was cooking the deer he had killed after they arrived. The smell of the meat crept into all the rooms. Saigel was watching Toran meditate in the corner. The minikin had Kellik's closed book in his lap. It had only taken a quick search to find it at Tonches's school. In his hurry, the devious man had left the hidden door to Tonches's library open and the book behind, obviously thinking he would be back to get it later.

Kellik was singing an elven tune that he had learned when he was young but was not doing very well. Kellik stopped singing and brought the others their dinner.

"I wonder when Enrandl is going to figure out that he does not have my book," he said.

"And when 'e does, whut's 'e goin' ta think?" Saigel added.

"He already knows," Toran answered as he opened his eyes.

Enrandl stood before a smoldering mass that had been the false book. In his anger, he had burned this book with half of his laboratory table. Why was he having so much trouble acquiring this treasure? How could he fall victim to this trickery of Toran and … Kellik? He knew that name from somewhere, but where had he heard it?

Then he remembered.

The dragon had told Frederick that Kellik and Saigel had killed it. Could Saigel have been the minikin? The other two men who had fallen to his flashfire must not have been associated with them;

otherwise, they would have been allowed to escape also. That made them of no consequence to him.

How Toran had found the book had been a mystery to Enrandl until now. Kellik and Saigel must have absconded with it from the hoard of treasure. Enrandl continued his pattern of thought and deduced that Toran must have met Kellik and Saigel and then learned where they had found the book.

You are a sagacious adversary, Toran, but your evasions will expire, and you will pray for GodsMercy they had not expired.

His mind formed an idea, and this idea blossomed into a larger scenario. Toran was going to pay dearly for his deception and so too were his friends.

CHAPTER 10

TO WHERE AND BACK AGAIN

When the knock at the door woke Toran, he sat up in bed in a panic, and he was disoriented. He tried to recall where he was. As he recalled the previous night's events, an answer came to him. *Higoshi's*, he thought. *We stayed the night at Higoshi's.*

Toran looked around the room with fondness and familiarity. It had been his room during his time here as a pupil. The morning sun spread rays of light throughout the room. The headboard of his bed had an elegantly carved dragon sprawled across it. The window above it allowed the sunlight to enter the bedchamber. Accordingly, the room had been done correctly as was the rest of Higoshi's former home. Everything was in its own place. The bed was in the center of the room, directly across from the door. It had a small table next to it, which was adorned with an unlit lantern. Toran remembered that he had not put the lamp out before falling asleep. For some reason, it had gone out of its own volition far before it had been depleted of its oil. A closet stood centered on the wall to his left.

He lay back down for a moment and remembered rearranging the room several times during his stay here. *That was never a popular subject with you.* Toran thought of his mentor. His memory recalled how many times that he had tried to prove that thought. The proof matched the number of times that Toran had moved the furniture. Every time he had, the furniture in the room had been reset to its original position when he had returned to it.

"Let's go," Saigel interrupted his musing.

"I am on my way out," His scratchy voice managed.

The impression of last night's dream was much more detailed than any previous ones that he had had, and it was reasonable to assume why. This was Higoshi's former home. Toran's dream, despite its clarity, had been more confusing than any of his previous ones. Once it had branched away from its customary beginning, he had been learning to draw energy into his body so that he could then refocus it in another direction. However, he was having trouble mastering this ability. His continual attempts and failures made the night's vision seem longer. The absorbing sphere was not the problem, but each attempt at redirection caused a collapse of his sphere, leaving the energy to fizzle into nothingness. Eventually, by the end of the session—and the dream—he could command the talent.

It was not necessary for him to do so now that his old master was gone and buried, but he found himself making up the bed and straightening the room anyway. His respect for Higoshi apparently reached beyond death. He went to the other bedrooms and found that Kellik and Saigel had not bothered with theirs. It did not upset him enough to make their rooms up as well. Then, out of curiosity, Toran decided to walk through the rest of the cottage and to make sure things were in their place before going to the front room. This included Higoshi's room.

He had struggled against a strange urge to use this room on the previous night but had settled with his own room. When he entered the chamber, his head filled with thoughts. He could not remember ever even being in this room yet seeing it and being in there did not feel alien to him. He almost felt at home. He wandered around the combination office and sleeping chamber, dusting several things and replacing items that he knew had been knocked over by squirrels from the tree on the east side of the house.

He made a second check of his friends' rooms and even of his own, after finding nothing else in the cottage out of place besides the unmade beds. When Toran entered the sitting room, he saw that they had company.

"Whut took yuh so long?" Saigel asked.

"Just keeping things in order."

"Seane decided to pay us a visit," Kellik's voice emanated from the kitchen. "He didn't even knock."

"I am sure he meant to," Toran said, as he realized that William must have recognized him. There was no other way that Seane would have known to come to this place since there were no tracks to follow. His hand went to his sword, not to draw it, but to be ready to do so. When he did not find its hilt, he remembered that the sword was still in his room.

"Sorry to show up uninvited, but we still have some business in Jenerv to take care of, and William gets upset if his business goes unattended."

He noticed that Seane was wearing a new suit made of leather. He looked at Saigel, who was leaning against a chair and was not far from the kitchen. Kellik's falcon stood perched on the chair next to the minikin. He was not sure what to think. If William knew that he was there, could Toran trust this servant?

"Please, no more quick escapes by magical doorways."

"It is not magical." Toran turned away from him and concentrated. A transparent sphere formed and engulfed Toran. He pushed it outward. He found Seane's mind, but it was difficult to search through. His surface thoughts were sturdy and comfortable enough to learn, but wherever Toran risked going deeper, his progress was blocked.

Seane's surface thoughts were accurate enough. He was still going to accompany them to Jenerv for their performance, so Toran did not dwell too much on the reason that he could not explore the other man's mind deeper. He knew that some thoughts were naturally blocked because of undiscovered Merea talents, and he believed this to be the reason.

Instead, he was thinking about how Seane might have found them. If William had directed him here, maybe William did not care what Toran had done in the past. Toran instantly judged against this probability. Seane may have found a magician to help him find them, which was more probable.

"Yeah, we shud'uv came that way ta here fruhm Kershal." Saigel walked over to Toran and broke his concentration.

Toran looked down at the minikin. "I am not sure how far I can go. It has been a long time since I used the talent."

"Well, it sure helped, but now we still have to find out about the book," Kellik added.

"I don't think William will allow any other deviations," Seane said.

"Without knowledge, where is the harm? Besides, he is located along the way to Jenerv." Toran already had an idea in mind as he lied to Seane.

"Who's on thuh way?" Saigel asked.

"Alistar."

"How are we going to find him, and how do you know he can help?" Kellik said as he walked out of the kitchen.

"Whether he can help or not, we shall see."

"Do you think it safe to go to another magician?" Kellik asked. "I thought you did not trust him."

"We need to know, and Alistar is on the way to Jenerv."

"Yuh gunna trust him now?"

"We are going to have to trust someone. At least we know him," Toran said, "somewhat. As for finding him, we will go to the edge of the swamp and have your falcon search for him." The falcon, still perched on the chair next to Saigel, looked from Toran to Kellik and then back to Toran.

Saigel spoke up, "Now thur's an idea. But is it trained fuhr that?"

"It did help to find Richard in the city," Kellik answered, "I think. But it's time we found out for sure." Kellik approached the falcon and began chanting. The falcon watched him intently. He had not used this essence since the last time when he had needed to talk to a dying leopard. Several revolutions had passed, but he had never found another chance to use it until now, but he always kept the power available. He finished the chant, and they began to speak.

The falcon greeted him with a feeling of warm acceptance. Because he had minimal practical experience using the power, he struggled with how to ask the falcon to help them. He started with the same sense of need as the leopard had imparted to him before. The falcon replied with the same warm acceptance again. Then Kellik tried to picture Alistar in his mind, to recall their encounter with him regarding the trolls, and then to convey the need to find him. The falcon's reply made his head spin, but he realized the confusion was not his; the bird simply did not understand.

The falcon did comprehend the need to find Alistar but did not know who he was. Kellik concentrated harder on Alistar and the magicians face, and after a few more attempts, there was finally an understanding.

He had wanted to ask the falcon its name but had not been able to figure out how to do so. He had spent his extra time since finding the bird, trying to find a way. Up until now, no ideas had come to him. The falcon, as if seeming to know his dilemma, tried to help.

Kellik shuddered as he felt a slight and grave fear, followed by a cold and wet sensation. The combination induced the impression of gray rain clouds, night air, and wet feelings similar to being drenched by the rainfall during his climb to the cave at the pass. Then the falcon imparted a surprise upon him so suddenly and strongly that the others saw that he was shaken by the emotion. The shock, quickly followed by a semblance of breathtaking awe, felt like something beautiful and deadly. Then the falcon communicated all the same emotions in rapid succession.

"A storm," Kellik said.

"Thur's not a cloud in the sky. Thur won't be—"

Kellik cut Saigel off with a wave of his hand. "Is that your name? Storm?" Kellik immediately knew that he was wrong when the bird took him through all the emotions again. "Another name for a storm. Somebody help me."

"Blizzard," Saigel offered.

"No snow. Just rain and lightning."

"How about a tempest." The power of his essence faded, but the falcon must have caught Seane's word before it did.

When the bird stretched out its wings and flapped them before adjusting its stance to settle again, Kellik knew that Tempest was its name. "Tempest it is then." He took some extra time and used another essence to verify the falcon's name. He attempted to teach Tempest some commands. Once he was able to communicate his speech and emotions directly to the bird, he found that Tempest must have been well trained at an earlier time, and she grasped the new training with little effort.

In most cases, she knew what Kellik wanted because the skills had already been taught by her previous owner. Not long ago, this master had passed on. When Kellik asked why the bird had settled with him, Tempest told him that an urge had drawn her to him. After the first day with him, she had liked him and had decided to stay.

It was almost midday before they left. It took two trips, but Toran succeeded in opening the shimmering doorway to the edge of the swamp, and they all stepped through.

"Is it not inordinately tepid for this particular feline's peculiarity?" Enrandl asked Frederick. The leopard paced in its cage, growling and occasionally clawing at the bars.

"It is protected from the heat. I have not yet had a chance to restore the rear leg, as you can see." The priest was suddenly proud. "Not knowing how long it was passed, I was really quite surprised when the resurrection was successful. Magnificent creature, would you not say so?"

"Certainly. Without interrogation. Your expectation of credence is the conjecture of this to be … have been, the pelt you acquired during our excursion?"

"Certainly. Without interrogation," the priest answered, and Enrandl's eyes sparkled at the response. He went to the cage and studied the cat. Success was within his reach. He had come to Frederick that day, to inquire about that very thing: raising the dead. Now it was directly in front of him.

"The pelt obligated sufficient aspect of effectuating your ritual?"

"It is easier when there is a whole form, but even the smallest piece can sometimes successfully bring the dead back to the living."

"Excellent. Although you verbalized a particular restriction of time constraint?"

"I am sure The Gods' would grant me enough power for many more revolutions, but the most I ever did was bringing back a young woman who had been past sixty revolutions."

Once again, Enrandl's eyes sparkled. "Such prolonged extension," Enrandl said, almost to himself but not entirely. "And my obligatory compensation to your ideology for such an augment?"

"I am not sure. What do you have in mind?"

"I will eventuate a hastened advent." With that being said, Enrandl left the priest's chamber. Frederick sat back in his chair and wondered what the magician was planning to do. He knew that the donation would be quite large and that Enrandl would find the finance to pay for it. Frederick had known Enrandl since he was an apprentice magician.

He was probably the closest thing Enrandl had to a friend. The man was power hungry and ambitious. He would pay any amount of coin if he wanted something badly enough.

After gathering a bag full of small pieces of wood, Enrandl channelled a shift to the cave. He stood before the rotting form of the dragon for the first time since he had concocted his plan. He had been having doubts because his designs had changed several times since the previous day. He speculated on the possible consequences of raising a dragon from the dead, but why would he when he could transform the rotting form into something less dangerous and less conspicuous—and Frederick's words had triggered the turn.

A young woman past sixty revolutions, Enrandl recalled.

The dragon had not even been past six cycles, according to Enrandl's computations, and that was well within Frederick's period. The only real problem was the quantity, if any, of the dragon's true spirit, which would be transferred to the new form. If the dragon could not remember what had befallen it before it became a human, the whole plan would be useless. The consequence of his failure was such a slight gamble that he was willing to accept them for the probability of success. She would be just another human instead of a dragon that he would have to contend with.

Enrandl took the bag of wood and set it down on the ground. He pointed at the bag and pronounced, "Ee-tine-ghi." A flame burst to life on the end of his finger, shot out toward the bag, and caught fire immediately. After watching the fire burn and the smoke that curled upward from the flames for a few moments, he removed a vial of thick silver liquid from a pouch. He spoke the required magical phrase just before shattering the bottle on the fire. With both his arms working together, he began to force the display into a circle.

The smoke from the fire followed his hands and circled with them. Enrandl guided this smoke to swirl around the dragon. While the smoke surrounded the dragon's dead form, it shrunk and twisted. Eventually, an abnormal amount of smoke—more than the bag of wood should produce—filled the air and engulfed the dragon's changing form. When the smoke dissipated, the change was complete. Enrandl looked upon the now human form, which was still mostly decomposed, and he smiled because he had taken another step toward his goal. He rolled the remains into a large blanket and shifted with the body back to the priest's temple.

When he walked back into the High Priest's chamber, Frederick was nursing a claw gash on his left arm. Enrandl almost laughed but controlled himself and laid down the dead body.

"How long has it been dead?" Frederick asked before he unrolled the blanket.

"Research consigns its demise in the parameters of six cycles."

"Well, you will have to wait until next day. I must see if The Gods' will grant me the power to perform the resurrection."

"Distinguish your council. My return is posited, and I have a resolve to attend," Enrandl replied.

The three sat under a tree to shade them from the direct sunlight of the day. Saigel was on his back, looking up at the clouds. Seane, who had fallen asleep against the tree, was just waking up. The falcon had been gone all afternoon. As the sun reached the horizon, it had still not returned. Kellik became worried.

Occasionally through the dense and mottled trees, Kellik spotted a troll or two, but the creatures did not advance upon them. Without any fire at hand in the swamp, as much as he wanted to, he would not go after the trolls. Kellik had heard many stories about trolls, and from them, he had garnered a natural hatred for the disgusting creatures. Several days earlier when they had encountered them, he had recognized them but had not been impressed by the trolls of The Westlands.

In The East, trolls were far more immense than these cousins of theirs, and the mere sight of one could paralyze a toughened warrior. Kellik had been affected in a comparable way by the red dragon he and Saigel had encountered. The exception had been his reaction to the beast. The awe of that creature had caused him to not realize that they were in danger, but an encounter with even one of The East's troll kind would have left him stricken with an uncontrollable fear. These trolls commanded no such presence but still suffered from the same weakness against fire. Without fire to destroy them, setting off into the swamp to kill them was suicide.

Kellik found it odd that he had grown attached to Tempest so soon after encountering the bird. He hoped that nothing had happened to her. He figured that they would not receive any results until the next or maybe even the second day. If he learned that even one troll had ended Tempest's life, with or without fire, he would find a way to go through the swamp and eradicate each one of them, unless they vanquished him first.

When Alistar appeared out of thin air with Tempest perched on his arm, Kellik stood there bewildered.

"I thought Tempest would have to lead you to us," Kellik said.

"Not at all. I recognized your feathered friend when he landed. Then I merely used a scrying effect upon you and shifted here directly." Toran returned from gathering wood and greeted Alistar.

"How is my little friend?" Alistar asked Saigel. "Has the potion done anything for you yet?"

"Nothin' I'd say," Saigel answered.

"Should affect you in some way you know." Alistar saw Seane. "Well, now, what have we today? No trolls to contend with and a new player to the game. I am Alistar." Seane introduced himself and then continued to build a fire with the wood that Toran had brought.

"Did you, by chance, return with the supplies I requested?" Alistar asked.

"I am sorry, but we had to leave town rather quickly," Toran answered. "But Kellik has something we hope you can look at for us. We know it has magical properties, but we are having a tough time determining what those properties are." Kellik took the book out and handed it to Toran. "The last magician tried to steal it from us, and another has been searching for it." He offered the book to Alistar.

"Oh my!" Alistar exclaimed when he looked at the book. He took it from Toran's hand and repeated himself with less enthusiasm. He said, "I would wager there to be more than one magic user searching for this book, if they knew it existed."

"Do you know the book? What does it do?" Toran asked.

"Do I know it? By The Gods', I fashioned it."

"You wrote it? Well, what does it do?" Kellik asked.

"*Wrote* is perhaps not the strongest word to describe my function in its creation. The magic user who possesses this book can channel infinite amounts of magical energy through his aura without being weakened."

"Whut da yuh mean in-fin-ite magical energy? I don't unnerstand," Saigel said.

"A beginner can channel only a small amount of energy through his aura each day to display effects, and these effects are weak and fairly simple to understand, but the source of the magical energy is limitless. More complicated and stronger effects require more energy to be channelled than he can channel when starting out. As this magic user grows and learns more about the magical energy encompassing him, he finds that he can channel greater amounts and some of the stronger effects.

"There are many mages who study for revolutions," Alistar continued, "and they are still only able to channel tiny amounts of energy because their auras just will not allow more. Others can study for the same amount of time and have more access to the energy around them."

"That book gives a magician the ability to channel as much energy as he wants?" Toran sat down in the grass and absorbed what Alistar had said. He wondered what would happen if Enrandl ever got his hands on the book. "It makes sense that Enrandl wants it."

He now stood and went to Kellik, seeing a way to enlist his help in destroying Enrandl. "But there has to be something else. He cannot be that shallow. Whatever that something is, I have no doubt that he plans to continue, with or without it. We have to stop him."

"Stop him fruhm whut?" Saigel asked.

"Stop him from what?" Alistar asked.

"I do not know," Toran said. He turned to Alistar, "There is a magician named Enrandl that is trying to find this book. He killed several friends of mine in the process of searching for it. More recently, we encountered him in Aamber, where he tried to kill *us*. I do not know what he could be planning, but I am sure it cannot be good for anyone but himself."

"As long as we have the book, he will continue to search for us," Kellik commented. "I don't like being a target. If Toran has judged him correctly and if he'll do as predicted, just keeping the book from him won't suffice. I agree with Toran." This agreement made Toran smile.

"You have other business to take care of in Jenerv," Seane said.

"Enrandl stays in Jenerv often. Maybe we can take care of both." Toran looked at his friends.

Alistar could see that they agreed. "What about the book?" he asked. "If you take it with you, Enrandl may get it away from you. But if you leave it here with me, he will not be able to get it."

"We may need to bait him with it, so we should probably take it with us. I do not think he is going to be fooled by another false representation."

"Can yuhr door take us ta Jenerv?" Saigel asked Toran.

"I am still not sure how far I can go, but short jumps can get us there soon enough."

"If you would permit me, I do still need supplies, and Jenerv will suffice as well as Aamber. I can take us all," Alistar said.

The others agreed, and Alistar gathered them all around him. He stated a quick phrase before raising his arm above his head and making a circular motion that mimicked gathering them all in. He snapped his fingers, and the group shifted.

They all now stood in the middle of a large chamber, facing a startled brown-robed man who was sitting behind a desk. There was a door just behind him and to the left. An obviously out-of-place cage was on the wall to their right, occupied by a sleeping pure-white leopard. Behind them, a large wooden set of double doors seemed to be the main door to the chamber.

Alistar watched as the High Priest recovered from his initial surprise, surveyed the group, and focused on him. "Alistar, it is good to see you, old friend! You are looking healthy. I had never expected to see you again."

"Frederick Smythe. In a way, it is good to see you also," Alistar replied without the enthusiasm of the priest.

"Who are your friends?"

With the commotion, the snow leopard had been roused from sleep, and it stretched. It began to pace the cage. Kellik, who had been watching the leopard during its rest, noticed something about the beast and immediately went to the pen.

"They are just fortunate people who needed some help to reach Jenerv," Alistar answered. "This was the only place I knew well enough for a definite shift. We will be out of your way soon enough."

"Where did you find this cat?" Kellik inquired. When Frederick's attention was drawn away from Alistar, he stared in awe as Kellik petted the leopard—like it was something he had not yet been allowed to do.

"I captured it several cycles past while I was in the Northern Reaches."

"That can't be true. This cat has been dead for several revolutions."

"You are obviously mista—"

"I'm not mistaken!" The anger in Kellik's voice surprised everyone in the room. "I watched this cat die!" His irritation subsided, and his words became sullener. "It was an accident, and I pleaded with The Gods' to spare him. I thought they had not heard me. I saved the pelt for revolutions and then lost it. Where did you get it?" As he finished speaking, his anger grew again.

"If you must know, I found it in a cave, along with a pile of treasure."

"He does not belong in a cage. Do you plan to set him free?" Kellik asked the priest.

"I was thinking of keeping it as a pet, actually."

"You're not serious!" He wanted to argue but remembered why they had come and realized he was overstepping his bounds. He moved away from the cage.

"I admire your concern, but it is not something you need to concern yourself with. It is not possible to release every animal that is in captivity."

Kellik remembered Alistar's words when a comparable situation had presented itself: *It is unfortunate, but I help the ones that I can.*

"I apologize." Kellik backed down. He was still angry, and his tone expressed his anger.

"Your sincerity is appreciated," Frederick quipped.

"We have to be going," Toran said, breaking the momentary silence.

"And I apologize for disturbing you." Alistar went to the desk as the others went to the door. "Many things have changed, but it is good to see you again."

"Please visit anytime."

Alistar turned and followed the group out the door. Then he led them through and out of the temple. The sun had gone down, and the city's streets were growing dark. The bustling crowds had already dissipated, leaving mere stragglers who were hurrying to get off the streets.

"I hope to see you back my way again sometime," Alistar said when they were outside. "You should have no trouble finding somewhere to stay. May The Gods' shine brightly upon you."

"And you," Toran said.

Enrandl stood on a dark street in the town that he still had no name for. He watched Michael cleaning his store and allowed him to complete the task. He did not like being lied to, and this man was going to regret having lied to him. He started across the street as someone turned the corner and went into the store. The two men talked for a while, and then both of them left.

Enrandl thought it was curious. He followed the pair as they walked through the complicated streets and alleys. After turning another corner, Enrandl suddenly felt tired. He yawned and then noticed that Michael had fallen down. He stopped to consider this for a moment as the other man lifted Michael onto his shoulder.

Hours later, he awoke to the sun's first light of morning slowly creeping its way through the streets. He wondered what had happened.

As he stretched from his slumber, he noticed that he was not wearing his blue robe. As a matter of fact, he was not wearing much clothing at all, and all his pouches were gone. A few of his ingredients had fallen out of his pockets, and they were now lying next to a dead rat.

He let loose a turbulent yell that carried until he was out of breath. He picked up a small crystal, which had fallen from a now-missing pouch, and pulled some fur out of the rat. The rat, which was not really dead, suddenly jumped to life, startled Enrandl, and scurried away. He held the rough crystal in the palm of one hand, pointed down the alley, and snapped the other hand's fingers with the fur between them. At the snap, the fur sparked, and the crystal shattered.

The crackle of electric, blue energy filled his ears as blue light streamed and displayed the force down the alley. The energy left black, scarred, and shattered stone in its wake. An unfortunate passerby, who had come to find out the source of the yell, had ended the path of the bolt. His body convulsed several times, before and after it fell to the ground. Enrandl channelled a shift back to Jenerv.

CHAPTER 11

CHANCE MEETINGS?

William awoke in the morning refreshed from his night's slumber. It impressed him that the bed was surprisingly comfortable. The room in the local establishment was below his usual standards, but as he was intent on not drawing attention to himself, it was enough. He had retired from his position of provisioner of the territories' black market, but he still had many enemies, which had been created while he had held that title. He was more likely to be recognized in Jenerv than in Aamber.

As he had grown older, he had decreased his active involvement with the black market. At this point in his life, he was mostly out of any business that transpired. Once, he had been in charge and had kept everyone under his control. Now he allowed others to deal with the problems of the underground while he controlled only the small town of Aamber's meager dealings.

He had decided early in his reign to step down at some point rather than be removed by some ambitious bastard who felt an aging old man was becoming useless. His unprecedented decision had been entirely unexpected by everyone who was below him. He did not fear those employed by him as much as he could predict their actions. He took pleasure in the timing of his retirement when he found out there had been a coup forming against him. He thought it quite strange though. With all the contacts and personnel he believed loyal to him, combined with the considerable amount of information they could garner, it was only after he stepped down that he had learned about the planned attempt.

He held no grudge against his successor for the conspiracy, and he had even advised him in several ways during his succession. At one time in his life, he had been cold and ruthless, and he probably would have executed the man personally for plotting against him. He decided that his best action, in this case, was to leave the other man alone.

In the end, he moved to Aamber and took over its small operation. Not in command as it were, he maintained a wellspring of informants and contacts. From them, he gathered everything he needed to know about the magician known as Enrandl Quemont.

When his late-night conversation with the bookmaker had concluded, William had displaced himself to Jenerv. When he was a much younger man, he had accidentally discovered this rare and untrained Merea talent, which was quite similar in most respects to the effect of shifting.

As young men are, especially when it comes to impressing a young woman, he had been tempted to do daring acts, which had accosted his own mortality. On one such occasion with a pretty maiden in mind, a daring horse chase toward a high, rocky promontory pushed the limit too far. The winner was the person who last arrested his horse's progress toward the cliff.

It was to have been a duel to impress the woman. Instead of swords—everyone knew William was terribly unskilled at this—the chase was agreed upon. Meanwhile, a previous agreement had also been made. The arrangement had been struck between him and a companion to counterfeit the race and make him look like the winner.

All was going well. His partner had reined back his horse appropriately enough for appearances of ending the race, but William was too daring for his own good that afternoon. He wanted a much grander conclusion. When he finally stopped his horse with barely enough room to spare, he heard a leathery snap underneath him, and he was thrown forward away from the halted horse along with the damaged saddle. The only thing that he could remember of the fall toward his watery grave was that he wanted to be home, safe in his bed with that chamber's familiar surroundings about him.

In that instant of terror, with that picture so distinct in his mind, Merea took over for him. He had the fraction of a moment to see an immediate violet-colored sphere engulf him and project him to the place he so longed to be. Then there he was, lying right where he had imagined. When the fear and shock of the experience subsided and he realized that the events could not have been a dream, he laughed long and hard until his throat burned, with no voice to continue.

This was not his only talent, and very few knew of it. His ability was transparent in comparison to any who had actually trained with Merea. He welcomed this untrained power to take him from one place to another. It proved extremely useful at times.

He liked doing his business in person. During earlier revolutions when he could not do so, he had settled for and assigned others to transact his business. His desire to enact his transactions in person instead of sending envoys in his place was overruled by caution.

He had come here to meet the magician Enrandl. The man was not new to the territory, but he had remained relatively anonymous for his magical skill. A small school for learning magicians, which also served as a home, was all Enrandl held—at least here in The

Westlands. He may have more holdings somewhere else, but that was not important. It was important to William that Enrandl did not get in the way of his current plans concerning Toran Hensh. The man needed this information for his own sake.

There was a small wooden chest at the base of the bed, which had been covered with simple decorative swirls and floral carvings. He opened it. From inside, he brought forth a ragged and ripped disguise. The man on the street that he had purchased the clothing from would probably never have to wear such rags again, depending on how he spent the finance William had supplied to him.

William replaced his usual clothes with the relics from the derelict man. He scrubbed his fingers vigorously through his hair. Then he pulled up the edge of the bed and rubbed his hand across the floor. After doing this, he smeared his face with the residue. When he opened the door that led out into a narrow hall, his gait included a limp and his left arm swaying in a successful attempt to make it appear useless.

"Halt! Who are you?" A young man outside stopped him. William concluded that it was one of the new ones. His small operation still had a high turnaround rate where his personnel were concerned.

"It is me, you dolt!" His words, a few hand signals, and his body language explained the situation to the other. The guard apologized and watched William continue down the narrow walk.

The open lower level of the tavern was an elaborate scene. There had apparently been a great brawl, but William experienced no disturbance in the slightest.

When he turned the corner and started down the stairs, he caught sight of another one of his men hunched over a table but apparently quite aware. Again, actions were used to gain the information he wanted to know, not about the fight—he had no interest there—but about the coordination of that morning's endeavor.

With an affirmative answer that all his sentries were in place, he left the inn through the back door and limped into a large alley. The main street was to his left, and it was bustling with activity. He knew that Enrandl liked to travel the back ways, and he used this one frequently.

He turned to the right and followed a path that he knew Enrandl would share that morning. He recognized his sentinels, even though they were well disguised and nearly invisible to the average passerby. William found a corner and crouched there to wait. He pulled some trash around him to enhance his disguise. It was not long before the blue robe emerged from around a corner, and Enrandl was upon him.

William leaned forward, barely far enough into the path of the magician to reach him, and said, "Got some finance for a poor, hungry, old man?"

But Enrandl barely looked at William as he kicked him back into the corner. "Uncouth detritus, I would not dissipate any leisure to exterminate you!"

William had grasped the blue robe as he fell back against the wall, and when it ripped, Enrandl spun in place, furious at the assault. Getting his attention was the intended reaction. He had known that the ripping of the robe would accomplish this, and he had used a bone arrowhead held in his hand to start the tear. Enrandl reached down, caught William by a tattered collar, and tried to stand him up, but the shirt ripped, and William, who was now bare chested, remained sitting on the ground.

"The intentions of my leisure emerge variable," Enrandl threatened. William offered no struggle as the torn shirt dropped. His quarry knelt down to his level, reached for his neck, and then tightened his hands there.

"I do not think so," William countered with a chuckle.

"Your vindication for such an aversion?" Enrandl asked, with William's throat tightly in his grasp.

William looked behind the magician, which prompted Enrandl to make quick glances over both shoulders. He discovered his surroundings now included black-leather-armored men—six of them to be exact. Two of them had bows aimed at Enrandl, and the other four had longswords. They had approached from behind him without so much as a click from a heel hitting the cobblestones beneath their feet.

"I trust my bowmen not to miss," William said, "so I will not make an adequate shield."

"You have contention to conspire with me?" He let go of William's throat but did not stand as he attended to his torn robe as an alternative.

"It has come to my attention that we share a certain common interest. I was hoping we could talk about it."

William sensed the arrogance as Enrandl looked him over again, shirtless with the rest of his tattered outfit. "What entente deems our prevailing regard?"

"We both seem to have a problem with Toran Hensh."

"He is merely a pittance." Enrandl inspected his torn robe with more interest in it than his comment.

"I am not willing to believe you. I have one documented occasion where you tried to kill him and his friends. Instead, you succeeded in killing one of my men and destroying several business carts in a bazaar. For that death alone, I should have you executed."

"A futile venture. Toran entreats inconvenience. Regardless, should his effacing barter my concomitant, I will afford it."

"Of that I am sure, but you will not until I have finished with him," William stressed.

"Who are you?" Enrandl asked simply.

"All you need to know is that you should leave Toran alone until I am through with him." With a wave of William's hand, one of the men approached Enrandl and handed him a pouch. "I apologize for ripping your robe. This should compensate you."

Enrandl watched as he stood, picked up the ragged shirt, wrapped it around himself, and limped away down the alley. The effort to make his arm appear useless was wasted on the magic user. The other turned a corner as Enrandl watched his men disperse. Then he stood and inspected the pouch. He found the exact finance needed to contract his seamstress to fashion one of his custom-made robes but not enough for someone to gather its components. Enrandl again wondered who this man was and what Toran had done to get his attention.

Her eyes opened slowly. She was lying on her stomach with what should have been her left foreleg curled up under her head. Her first sight, when her eyes finally adjusted and focused, was of an enormous black-haired human with kind gray eyes. He was wearing a glittering dark-blue robe. She thought that she might be dreaming. How did this human get so big? She might have been shocked by this but did not have the time. There was more here to contend with.

She took another moment to orient herself to the surroundings and found a problem. Her olfactory and aural senses were severely limited. Everything was wrong. She turned her head to look around and found that she was moving differently than what she was accustomed to. Her long neck should have lifted and come about without the need to turn her head, but only her head turned, and she could not raise it more than a few inches.

The room, which she remembered as a cave, was sparsely furnished. She was lying on top of a soft rectangular mound where her treasure should have been. Beside her was a type of construct that she had never seen before. It was a small wooden plateau supported by four smaller wooden pillars. For some reason, she understood that this was a table. The walls held no decoration except a curtained window. Each item she viewed during her inspection of the room was familiar, but to her recollection, she had no reason to know them because she had never seen them before. She wondered why she recognized these things. A dresser, a desk, and the table, complete with an oil lamp, was the only other furniture besides the bed.

Wait! Where is my treasure? It had not registered as missing at first because she had believed that she was dreaming. She thought that her reality had finally become clear until she pushed herself up and looked down. When she saw the mattress beneath her and the two, five-fingered human hands, she panicked. She instantly forgot her treasure with yet another startling revelation. She looked over the rest of her and then roared. The roar came out as a high-pitched scream.

Instinct overcame rationale, and her left claw (hand) slashed out toward the only target she saw. The attack did not come close because she became unbalanced while attacking him and fell flat on the bed with her face buried in a pillow. She pushed herself up on her arms again and pulled her body up underneath her.

Her first words did not concern treasure or anything she had just gathered about her surroundings. The accusation she directed was meant for the only target she could see. "What have you done to me?" She rolled slightly and sat up. It was an odd position, but it seemed like it was all that she could do with this form. Her new legs dangled off the side of the bed. "And where am I?" She tried to stand like the human on her unfamiliar legs but immediately fell to the ground.

"A prominent revelation. Your resurrection satisfies my desideratum," Enrandl answered.

Kayrahawkatzeena paused at the wording of his answer, used the bed to help herself up, and tried to stand again. She noticed that the human was giving her no help. From her new perspective, this human was not as large as she had initially believed because she was much smaller than she should have been. With her sense of balance thrown off by the human form, she decided to sit back down on the bed and climbed onto the mattress in the most familiar way she could manage. "What are you saying? I was dead?"

"Your residual impressions are deteriorated then? Are any recollections prevalent?"

She thought hard. "Lightning. I remember being struck by lightning, day past." Her right hand moved to the area under her left arm where she suspected the wound to be but felt nothing.

"Day past?" Enrandl said and then laughed. "Six cycles have elapsed since your demise."

"Demise? I hesitate to believe you human," she said, although this was not exactly true at that moment.

Enrandl went to the window. "Six cycles ago, winter previously expired. Experience midsummer." He pulled back the curtain, and light burst into the room. "The snow on the mountains has receded."

She carefully braced herself against the bed until she had some semblance of balance. She then followed him to the window very slowly and awkwardly but kept her balance. Walking or at least the knowledge of it was familiar, although very new for her to complete. She braced herself with the wall.

The sun outside was bright. She observed that the snow was indeed gone from the mountains as the human had said. "I suppose I owe you some compensation for the life you have given me, but why am I in this form, and how do I get back to my own?"

"The restoration of your true existence aside, should I entreat any quantity of finance, compensation would be problematic," Enrandl said.

"What does that mean?"

The magic user looked into her eyes as he chose his words carefully. "Those two that assaulted and terminated you had the impertinence to revel in their accomplishment and lavishly spend all the treasure with which they absconded. Their conjecture of your magnitude and adroitness were so extraordinary that I had to experience such for my—"

She recalled a memory and interrupted him, "The elf and the minikin?"

"Yes, and as you were truly magnificent with the consideration of your deteriorated aspect discovered, I discern they are powerful warriors to have vanquished you."

"Not powerful. GodsLight was the only power that day," she retorted. "Why have you brought me back then?"

"A judicial providence for yourself and a munificence for me as compensation."

"Kellik and Saigel," she said. Enrandl was glad to see her eyes grow with anger at the thought of their names. "You have my attention human."

"Enrandl, thank you. Kellik and Saigel have encountered a new companion. His name is Toran. He possesses an article that I find requisite. Your succor brooking me to my design for your attaining an adjudication of your leisure toward Kellik and Saigel."

"Why am I in this human form?"

"Honestly, less extravagance for a relocation and a paucity of conspicuousness. Imagine the anarchy a red dragon, with all her splendor, would generate in the port upon your revival." He could see her imagine just that. "Your restoration will be resolved when we are accomplished."

"You will get what you want, and I will have my justice. Where do we start, human?"

"Enrandl," he said, and she repeated it. "First, we educate your traipse to a formal gait."

In the corner of a tavern called the Wild Boar, which Seane had chosen and had explained had a reputation for the most potent mead in the province, Saigel stood on a chair feigning the strain of the match in front of a large crowd. For William's benefit, the three were to play their ruse the same as before, and it was going well. There was only one minor alteration. This was because they could not convince Kellik to bet. Everything was progressing smoothly until Saigel saw William walk into the taproom.

Somehow, even in the tattered disguise that William wore and with the "strain" of the match, Saigel noticed him. He began to feel that something was wrong. The uneasiness nearly cost him his match and the whole con, but he resumed his concentration and won. Kellik was across the room at the bar. *Can't get a message ta him,* Saigel thought. *Just have ta wait till Toran gets here.*

He sat at the table rubbing his arm when he realized why he felt uneasy. Toran had told his friends what had transpired between him and William, explaining that he had believed this to be the reason they had been captured. When they had been released to run their game elsewhere, the belief had changed.

Saigel was convinced that because William was here now, Toran had been recognized. He assumed that nothing good was going to prevail. When Toran walked into the tavern, Saigel's heart sank, and he cursed himself for not having fought Paul and Seane when he had had the chance back in the alley of Aamber. If he had been able to defeat them, they would not be here now. He cursed himself again as he realized, as before, that he really would have had no chance against them.

Another opponent sat at the table in front of him. Saigel looked him over and also watched Toran, who was headed his way (walking past William in the process). Saigel waited until he could make good eye contact with Toran before speaking to the new challenger, loud enough for the whole tavern to hear.

"I've wasted 'nuff time with two-piece bets. All wagers will be thirty." He stared directly at Toran and saw Toran's confused stare in return. "I've not been an' won't be defeated," the minikin continued. "Yuh'll have to meet muh wager or not challenge me." When he finished his speech, the man at the table reconsidered, stood, and walked away.

It was late, and Enrandl needed a break. Most of his afternoon had been spent with the dragon-woman, along with some of the women he knew, which included one of his students. They were doing their best to coach their charge into being more human, and more importantly, more alluring for Toran's enticement. He supposed that her transformation from the dragon's form had supplied her with a natural beauty. That would benefit his conclusion. A few times, he caught and reminded himself that she was not a woman.

The student that he had instructed to help them, the elf Shevail, seemed distracted and performed her efforts with a strange reluctance. He had been schooling her in the magical arts for quite some time. She was an excellent pupil. Although she was intelligent and quite capable of doing the tasks he assigned to her, her training was taking longer than expected, based on the intellect she exhibited. Her attitude and actions this day had surprised him.

He could not fathom why her usual bearing had changed. Where she would typically be amiable with others, today, she was curt and even rude to the women around her. She was always respectful to him, but he noticed several of her annoyances directed at him. He finally thought that the reason she acted that way was that she was not moving forward in her studies. He could understand that response. He would probably have the same reaction if he had been forced away from his learning when he had been a student.

He arrived at the nearest establishment and walked in. He was not accustomed to venturing out into Jenerv for evening events, but for just a while, he wanted to be away from Shevail, the other women, and the …? He undoubtedly needed a more suitable designation for her.

Toran retreated to the bar, a few people away from Kellik, who obviously shared Toran's confusion. He closed his eyes, instantly extended a sphere out, searched mentally through the crowd, and then reopened his eyes. He was finding these acts of Merea simpler to perform. He did not link with any minds but his friends' minds, even though he knew that he could tangent all of them. His broad search found Saigel.

What are you doing? Toran silently asked.

Saigel's thought replied, *William's here disguised as a beggar to yuhr left. Yuh walked right past him.*

Because of Saigel's description, Toran found William quickly, and a surface glimpse of his thoughts, without delving too far, revealed information about what was to happen. Another challenger sat at the table and placed down a small pouch.

"'Nuther fool," Saigel said. "Have at yuh then." The neutral referee came over and started the match.

We've got to go, Saigel added silently. *Truble's brewin'.*

Toran gestured to Kellik, who had heard the telepathic conversation, indicating the door. The two of them were headed that way when Enrandl walked in.

"Criminal!" Enrandl immediately accused, pointing at Toran. "He is postulating this gathering for his plunder."

It took the crowd a moment to comprehend what he had said. Soon everyone in the tavern who had heard the accusation, whether it had been understood or not, searched for his or her purse. Several called out that their finance was missing. Saigel's opponent had reacted also, pulling his hand away and checking for anything missing. Many tables and chairs were toppled following this revelation, and several people in the crowd tried to get to Toran.

Toran and Kellik had finally reached the door, but Enrandl was blocking their escape.

Dagger in hand, William positioned himself behind Enrandl, grabbed his robe near the neck and pulled. "You have a lot to lose by this action, foolish magician!" William thrust the dagger toward Enrandl's rib cage, he appeared to have missed somehow, and he was taken aback by his failed effort, but the exploit had afforded Kellik and Toran a way past the magician and out the door. A group of the Wild Boar's angry patrons hurried after them.

"My equity will reign," Enrandl insisted as he grabbed William's wrist and spun around to break out of his hold. Enrandl twisted William's arm during the maneuver, and William winced in pain and dropped his dagger so that Enrandl could not sink it into his back. One of the passersby bumped into him, and Enrandl lost his grip.

Armed now with a dagger of his own, both free of each other's holds, Enrandl lashed out at William, but the old man moved with the stealth of a man half his age and blocked Enrandl's attacking arm at the wrist.

Several more of the crowd rushed out to chase the accused thief and his accomplice, as Kellik seemed to have joined Toran, pushed past Enrandl, and knocked him to the ground. William moved quickly to him and stepped on the hand wielding the dagger.

"GodsLight shines brightly on you this day," William said, "but their DarkLight will find you. I assure it." When he finished, he made his way out the door with the pursuing crowd.

When Saigel had heard Enrandl pronounce Toran a criminal, while his opponent was distracted, he grabbed the bag with what would have been his winnings and tried to find a back way out of the tavern, but he had not been successful. A good portion of the crowd had remained in place because they had been satisfied that their belongings had been intact.

Saigel hid behind an overturned table, watching Enrandl get up and inspect himself and the taproom before going outside. He allowed a minute or more before he came out of his hiding place and headed for the entrance, declining any arm contests along the way.

Outside, Enrandl had apparently waited for him. When Saigel came out of the tavern, he grabbed him and lifted him off the ground. "Your existence is my forfeit," he said, "for my demand contentions my desire. Courier this communication to Toran." Saigel remained quiet. "The tome no longer constrains significance. He will be ended. Convey an urgency to slumber beneath this wary suspicion. His mortality has no extension."

Enrandl set Saigel down, and the smaller man looked up at him. "I'll deliver yuhr message, but I'm sure it's returned tenfold."

"We have accordance on this measure," Enrandl replied and walked away. Saigel spat in his direction before leaving.

Toran had almost cursed at Kellik for splitting away. He had been about to give them an escape route via a shimmering portal to a safer area, but then his friend had turned off without warning. Luckily, Kellik had not been followed by any of them. Instead, the crowd had chosen to chase the one who had been genuinely accused. Toran led his followers for a couple more minutes and turned several corners to be sure that they could not turn back and chase Kellik. Then he finally used his escape.

Toran now stood outside the walled city of Jenerv under a tree for shade. Kellik had instructed his falcon to stay here and wait for them. Although the falcon was not present, Toran figured it was hunting for food. He sat back against the tree and concentrated on a sphere to find Kellik. When his search found him, Kellik informed him that he was currently searching for Saigel.

Toran sent a message: *You need to get out of the city. Come to the tree line. I will find Saigel and tell him the same.* He expanded the sphere and searched for the minikin. When he finally located Saigel, Enrandl's message was relayed. Toran told him that they would discuss it once they were back together.

CHAPTER 12

KINDLING

Toran sat on a wooden step outside a different tavern from the previous night, waiting for his friends. The salt-tinged air from the sea drifted into Jenerv on a warm breeze.

The Sea Witch was two districts away from the Wild Boar, where they had narrowly escaped from William and Enrandl. He had chosen the port's quarter near the docks because he guessed, from the social and economic value of the area, that no one from the Wild Boar would be around to see him. In any case, two days had passed, and in a large city like Jenerv, two days was a long time. If encountered, the few townsfolk, even if reminded of the incident during casual conversation, would not recognize them.

The day had been calm and overcast. He wrapped his cloak around his neck for extra warmth. Earlier in the morning, a light rain had wet the ground enough to form small puddles. Four children, three human and one elven, were playing in one of the larger puddles.

A young man ran across the street and hurdled over the puddle and the four children. The kids looked up in awe as he flew over them and then watched for a moment as the dark-haired man disappeared into an alley before they resumed their play.

Out of nowhere and from a busy street nearby, a woman appeared. What immediately caught Toran's attention was her crimson hair. She had a braid from her neckline down to the middle of her back. She wore casual clothing in multiple colors. Reds, oranges, and yellows were delicately positioned to enhance her outfit. It was pleasing to the eyes but not half as pleasing as her face, when she turned to see him staring wide-eyed at her.

When she smiled and turned in his direction, Toran looked behind him, expecting to see someone there, but he was alone. Halfway to him, she stumbled because of a hole in the street but did not fall. He was about to go to her when another man stopped to help her. She composed herself and proceeded to Toran.

As she came closer, he saw that she was beautiful, although her features were thin, and it looked as though she had not eaten for a cycle. Her cheekbones were so high that if it were not for her crimson hair, he would have judged her an elf. It was still possible, but he could not recall any elf with such hair as hers. He stood and greeted her with a smile, noticing that she looked nervous. "Greetings."

"And to you." She hoped this was the polite reply. Kayrahawkatzeena had never felt so uncomfortable in her long life. She had only been in human form for a couple of days. Although Enrandl had many young women around to help her, she was still uneasy with the boundaries and capabilities of her new form. Her depth perception was incredibly different, and the limits of her peripheral vision were unnerving. She was steadily improving but walking still gave her problems.

Enrandl had said that she should get out and explore the city so that she could become more accustomed to being human. Uncomfortable as it was, she decided to accompany Shevail, one of Enrandl's students who was a beautiful elven woman with pitch-black hair, on some errands. The elf was shorter than Kayra was.

Enrandl had suggested this much shorter name for her human form. She liked the sound of her new one, even though Enrandl had only recommended it. *To decrease objectionable query regarding her lineage and disposition of her origination*, he had declared it.

Shevail had been teaching her common courtesy. During the past two days of her teachings, Kayra noticed small hints and assumed that

Shevail was fond of Enrandl and was somewhat jealous of her—yet still went out of her way to help her. It was primarily this example that had brought her to understand common courtesy. About an hour ago, Shevail had wanted to go back to the school, but Kayra decided to stay and walk around for a while.

She wandered throughout the city and marveled at the complexity of human life around her. She customarily slept (sometimes for several cycles at a time) during the time that humans woke up and conducted their business. Here and there during her walk, people stared at her, and it was beginning to make her feel uncomfortable. When she spotted this human doing the same thing, curiosity got the better of her, and she needed to know why everyone was affixing so much regard to her.

"My name is Kayra," she said.

"Toran," he replied. There was a moment of silence as the two stared at each other.

She did not know what to say. She had just ventured out to do what Enrandl had suggested, and she had only approached this human to find a reason for his apparent attention. Now she stood face-to-face with the one Enrandl was searching for. She began a sentence in her own familiar language but stopped herself after three words and started again with human speech.

"Do you think it is going to rain more?" she asked.

Toran looked up, judged the increasing cloud layer, and shrugged. "I do not know, but just in case, why not join me inside?"

He stopped at the tavern entrance. There was no door, yet he stood next to the opening and motioned his arm to it while bowing slightly. His motive was unclear to her; however, a smile brightened her face as she walked by the handsome human.

The tavern was not busy. In fact, only one other person occupied the place aside from the keeper who was moving about and changing various things to new positions. It was evident to Kayra that he kept his place neat.

The two of them sat in a secluded corner near a fireplace that had a warm fire. The place had no bar area. Several tables were arrayed neatly around the room. There was very little decoration to be seen, and a doorway that led to a room in the back.

The other person was a bearded minstrel who sat in another corner. He was singing a melodic tune and playing a decorated lute.

From the back room, a chubby woman with straight blonde hair came into the parlor and approached their table. She glanced at them before offering a thin smile, which clearly stated that she did not care to be there. "What will you have?" she said flatly, gathering just enough charm and effort to wink at Toran.

Toran ordered cider for himself, but Kayra declined when he offered to buy one for her.

"I am more tired than thirsty," she explained.

Toran eyed her with concern and asked, "Why are you not resting?"

"I have been trying for days to get help." She and Enrandl had gone over what she should say to build Toran's interest toward a manufactured peril. "I can not go back out there on my own. No one will help me."

"Help with what?"

"Second day past, my brothers and I were attacked east of the city. They were slain. All our possessions were stolen, and I barely escaped with my life. Some of those things were priceless family heirlooms. Along with justice for my brothers, I would like to have those things back."

Toran straightened up in his chair. "My friends and I may be able to help you." His smile widened.

Surprised at first, she eventually smiled in turn. First, it was just a simple grin. She was pleased at his eagerness to help her. Then her smile widened as it had before coming into the building. There was something almost familiar about this human. He made her feel like she was someone else. She could not think of anything to say. Her cheeks became warm, and she looked away and felt their warmth with her hands. In the corner of the tavern, the bard began another tune. This tune was slower, but it still had a good rhythm and a happy tone, and she determined that there was nothing wrong with her face.

She looked back at Toran and thought he was going to say something to her when she realized he had changed his mind, and he was considering the music also.

"Would you like to dance?" he asked.

"Do what?" She was lost again. *Dance? What is dance?* she thought. *Enrandl's women friends never said or showed me anything to do with dance.* But how can she refuse? If she did, he may not agree to help her. She wanted Shevail to be there and to help, but she was not. Something in the bard's song pulled at her, and for a moment, she almost believed her own story. She thought she needed his help and did not know what she would do without it. She barely heard him repeat himself.

"Do you know how?"

"No, I have never …" She lapsed into silence.

"Let me show you then." He stood and reached for her hand.

The music may have drawn her, but she accepted his hand, stood, and followed him to an area where there was room to move. The music filled her ears, and she looked into Toran's eyes. They were soft and yet confident. They showed that he was concentrating. He was saying something, but she could not hear his words.

She could hear only the music.

Although she did not hear his words, she followed everything he did. She danced gracefully as if she were flying through the air. Every turn and cut about seemed to mimic a relaxing flight pattern that she might have flown.

The musician played on; his words woven beautifully with the melody. Toran was all she saw. The music was all she could hear. When the music and the dance stopped, Toran and Kayra stood close to each other. Their lips were just inches apart and moving together.

Suddenly, there was applause. Kayra and Toran looked to the source of the clapping. There stood Kellik and Saigel. The latter was atop a table. Anger flared in her eyes. Tearing herself away from Toran, she inhaled deeply. The exhale was not the fire that she instinctively intended. Everyone in the taproom looked at her as if she had gone mad.

Then her legs no longer wanted to support her, and she collapsed to the floor where she had so gracefully danced only moments before. Toran went to her, and Kellik and Saigel slowly approached.

"Whut was that?" Saigel asked.

"I am not sure, Saigel," Toran replied.

"I am not injured," she said finally. She had taken a moment to calm her anger. Her collapse had given her time to accomplish just that. There they were, standing just a few feet away from her: Kellik and Saigel, the only two who had ever entered her lair and left (against her will).

"You dance beautifully," Kellik remarked.

"She has only the knowledge I have given her," Toran said, apparently proud of himself.

"Thank you," she answered as Toran helped her into a chair. "These are your friends?"

"Yes. This is Kellik, and this is Saigel." Toran turned to the other two and said, "Meet Kayra."

"Pleased," Kellik said.

"Well met," Saigel added. He was now back up on a table.

Their names had already been burned into her memory. She remembered the battle. She controlled her anger as the images passed through her mind. Her perfect memory seemed to be one of the few abilities that remained intact in her human form, but it mainly applied to events she knew as a dragon. This caused her to pause, and she wondered how the minikin had survived. She had seen him charred, burned, and collapsed on the ground.

Then she regarded Kellik. Something had protected him from her fire. She looked him over. He looked different than when she had fought him. The leather armor he was wearing now stood in contrast to the shining chain mail he had worn before. She recalled the ring he had found in her cave while she had listened to their approach. She looked at his hand. She had only been able to glance at it during the battle and remembered its look. He was still wearing it.

*"Jus' a silver band," Saigel had remarked quietly, "*pro'bly *dropped by suhm fool soul passin' by. Yuh spied it. Yuh keeps it."*

She closed her eyes and rubbed them slightly to hide her concentration. Another ability that she had retained was her effect powers. Unlike human wizards who used extravagant gestures and complicated phrases and sometimes combined these with complex material components to bring about their effects, all she needed was a moment of silent thought, and her channelling of the source energy was complete. She could not be sure if the ring had been the source of his protection against her fire, but she knew the ring at least emanated a magical presence, and it was a good possibility.

She looked all three of them over and found that Kellik had one other item of magic glowing inside his pack. Toran had two pieces of magic: one under his shirt in his chest area and his black cloak. Saigel glowed magically from several places: the belt around his waist, his short sword, and a couple of small things within a pouch. The most interesting item was a scimitar-shaped aura on the minikin's back, as if he had strapped it there in position, but there was no visible scimitar.

Saigel noticed her stare and looked around. When he did, she stretched her arms and mocked a yawn. Her arm passed through the area of the scimitar but contacted nothing. She noted this and turned to Toran. "The dance was—very nice, but your friends are here, so maybe we should continue our talk," she said.

They returned to their table in the corner, and the bard began another tune. This one had a more cheerful tone. Toran explained to Saigel and Kellik about her problem, and they agreed to help.

"When do we leave?" Kellik asked.

"I need time to gather some extra information, but I should be ready to go by second day, in the morning. We should be able to leave then."

"I'll get provishons," Saigel added.

"Very well, then. We shall meet here on that morning," Toran added.

"I must go now. I will see you then." She looked into Toran's eyes, not really knowing why, but once again, she had the feeling that she was someone else. She refocused herself and then turned to go. The three said their goodbyes, and Kayra left the tavern with a wicked smile spreading across her face.

Standing in the rain outside the tavern as his eavesdropping ears had heard most of the conversation, the dark-haired young man—who had earlier hurdled over the four children and a puddle—smiled and walked away. The rain started to fall harder.

Enrandl sat behind a large wooden desk. The smile his face was wearing suggested pleasant thoughts. It was not an expensive desk, but it served his purpose. Various works of art, from paintings to mere sketches, adorned the walls. Each one resembled him. The elf was quite the artist, and he wondered where she had the time to have become so proficient at such with all of her magical training.

There was only one other chair in the room, which was on the opposite side of the desk. On the desk was a simple candle, a few empty flasks, which were each labeled with different notations, and a stein, which had his image carved on it and was filled with a steaming liquid. The stein and the exemplary liquid it contained were also both created by—what was her name?

The door to his chamber suddenly crashed down, which erased his smile and replaced it with an angry scowl. The two men, who rushed in after the door had fallen, now stood on opposite ends of the room. Enrandl stood and started to say something when William strolled into the room. The magic user sat back down.

"Well, we have an abundance of circumstance," Enrandl quipped.

"Yes. This meeting is unfortunate for you, as I am not as easy on people who cross me." William looked around at the artwork, silently judging the others' narcissism.

Enrandl stood again. "You have an audacity to infiltrate my domain and intimidate me!" Enrandl leaned forward with his hands on the desk. "Your lack of etiquette defines a contempt for respect," he finished angrily.

William stood calmly as the magician finished his scolding. Then he said, "If you would like to converse about respect, I would ask you why you felt the need to disrupt my business second day past?"

"I had no rumination of reference to that occupation!" Enrandl continued to scold.

"Ignorance is not an acceptable excuse," William said, still staying calm. "You entered that tavern with intent to harm or otherwise interfere with Toran's business after I warned you not to."

"My liability, solicitude, or dilemma bears no resemblance to our intertwined enigma regarding Toran," Enrandl eased back off his hands and now stood unaided by the desk.

"It will be imperative unless you cease your interference."

"My alternative?" Enrandl goaded, gesturing to the guards.

"Oh, no, the alternative is much worse," William smiled and turned toward the door.

After the two guards turned to leave, Enrandl channelled. Three red-orange arrows of magical energy sped to the one guard and two to the other. Both men fell to the floor.

William immediately turned and saw the downed men. "You have already killed one of my employ. If either of them should perish, death will be your *only* alternative." William's words were calm and cold.

Two more men entered to carry the bodies out. William had known what Enrandl would do and had planned for it. This time, William backed out the door while watching Enrandl closely.

"Poor marksmanship," William reprimanded, correctly assuming that he had been the target of the effect. "At point-blank range with magic, that should never miss." William shook his head, turned, and went down the hall. "Poor marksmanship," he repeated.

Enrandl beat his fists down on the desk, upsetting everything on top of it. The steaming liquid from the stein burned his hand, and he winced. He wondered who this man was, where he had come from, and most importantly, why he had come now when Enrandl was so close to getting the book.

Death will be my only alternative, Enrandl thought, mimicking the words. *Ha!* There would come a time when his plans would be complete. Then he would deal with William Sagemont.

William walked away from Enrandl's home. Before going in, he had contemplated and confirmed that—even though Toran had stolen property from him and had left him for dead—his more recent encounters with that magician had become a priority. He had decided to foil the man's plans at every turn, if he could, including helping Toran if necessary. For a moment, William watched a beautiful crimson-haired woman walk past him, but his thoughts drew his attention away before the woman entered Enrandl's home.

"You conspired what?" Enrandl scolded her. There was not even time to rearrange his desk before Kayra walked in with her news.

"I made the plans with Toran to leave in two days."

"I have not gauged a suitable environment for the machination!"

"And I gave you two days to find one," Kayra answered. She turned to walk away from him, but he hurried around his desk, grabbed her, and spun her around.

"Unhand me!" she said. The spark of rage he witnessed in her eyes calmed his own anger as he released his grip on her arm. She could become disinterested at any time, and he did not want to risk her doing so when he was this close to his goal.

"I apologize. I get trepidatious when circumstances are deprived of consistency." Enrandl tried to sound sincere but failed. "We have a diligence of application that requires attentiveness. I will effectuate a qualified venue."

"I am sure you will," she replied and turned to leave.

When she was gone, Enrandl sat down at his desk. He found himself lost in the confusion between pleasure that his plan was progressing and anger that Kayra had progressed the project too quickly. He needed to find something nonetheless, very soon. He needed a place that was large, confined, and isolated. His body stayed motionless while he tried to produce an idea. Then he found what he was searching for. *Yes! That is perfect,* he thought. *She will think so too.*

He was so lost in his thoughts that he did not notice the liquid, which still had steam rolling off it, had dropped from the desk onto his blue robe, where it would leave a stain that he would not be able to remove.

The next morning, William sat at a table in his private dining room with a plentiful breakfast before him. The dining room was vacant of decoration except for a mantle on the east wall. The mantle was also empty. Two other people occupied the room, standing by, looking to William, and waiting for direction.

"Find a way in there and get me some answers." He was speaking directly to a young man dressed in light-blue robes. It was his blatant attempt to look like a beginning wizard at Enrandl's school. "I want to know what, where, and when he is planning such an enterprise." "Seane, have we found them yet?" William asked, after the other young man had left.

"If we had, you would know, sir. Our meager number here is limiting our search."

"Yes, I am sure it is, but they must still be in town because I have no reports from the gates about them passing. Your men are instructed to report and follow?"

"Yes."

"Very well. Keep me updated."

Seane left William's room and then reemerged a few minutes later. "We may have found them."

"Where are they?"

Another man walked into the room. He was taller than William was, and he carried himself like nobility. Although his clothing appeared worn, it had been plush and expensive at one time. The lute on his back was obviously not as worn as the clothing. His middle-aged features were hidden behind a dense beard of black hair. He strode to the middle of the room and stood before William.

"Who have we here?"

"I am Paul," the bard answered, "and I have information that you may like to have."

"Enlighten me," William replied curiously.

"The three you seek were at the Drunken Dog Tavern in the east quarter. The human met with a beautiful crimson-haired woman. The minikin and the other came after the dance and spoiled a wonderfully created romantic moment, if I do say so myself." Paul paused and then said, "They were moments away from a kiss when the other two interrupted, and my, my, the girl was upset."

"Excuse me," William said, but Paul appeared not to hear him.

"If I could just have that one back … But they are leaving the city in the morning, probably to the east."

William stood up and walked to the window. "How do you know this, and how did you know I was looking for them?"

"I have, shall we say, sources. I am told you may have the ability to help them."

"Yes, I can, but I need more specific information."

"Too much of that is uncertain, so I can't help you with that, but I can tell you that they are walking into a trap."

"Where and when?"

"More uncertainty. I am afraid I also can't answer that," the bard replied.

"Then we are going to have to follow them." William looked at Seane and then back to Paul. "I thank you for your assistance and have one more question for you. I have recently lost an employee and would like to offer you a position to fill his."

Paul took his instrument from his shoulder and played a few chords. As the music from the lute poured forth into the room, it seemed to glow with varying shades and colors of the rainbow. "You have not even heard me play."

"I do not need to hear you play. You seem to have a way to find information, if it is true."

"It is accurate, as much as I could give."

"I must tell you, that you would have some impressive boots to fill. The man you would be replacing was quite good, and his name was also Paul. Now it may be a coincidence, but you show up with valuable information and bearing the same name. The coincidence is too close. I feel the need to offer you a position in my organization."

Paul thought about William's reasoning. "Maybe we should discuss some terms."

"Sit with me and eat." William gestured to Paul and Seane.

After an hour of discussion regarding what Paul's new responsibilities would be, he made his decision. "I thank you for your offer and for the confidence that I would be able to perform the job, but I must decline."

"But we have not even come to terms of finance yet. I am prepared to be quite generous."

"Finance is not a factor in my life."

"Which means that you are already wealthy?" William guessed. He did not have the look of wealth; his clothes had been exceptional at one time, but they were well out of fashion. "Or perhaps can access finance when needed?"

"I can sustain on what I garner from my performances."

"Then would it be possible for you to disclose your sources so that I may have informational access to allow me to help them?"

"I can't," Paul answered.

"You are definitely not a man to be trifled with, my friend. I have one more idea though. I realize that you will not become a permanent employ, but how about a temporary arrangement?"

"What do you have in mind?"

"You said earlier that you would like to have a moment back—that moment when the man and woman were going to kiss."

"That was more just a—"

"I know, but what if you were to help me help them? Then you might have a second chance to maneuver them together."

William knew that Paul had not thought about the possibility until it had been pointed out to him. He was sure that appealing to the romantic side of this man just might close the deal.

Paul shook his head with confident denial. "There are many who would benefit from my music, and I must return to them." Paul stood and turned to leave.

"Thank you for your help." William offered, and the bard stopped at the doorway.

"I do suppose that if you hired me for specifically the purpose of bringing these two together, it would be worthy of my effort and time."

Paul was unquestionably the romantic William understood him to be. He was confident that the bard, on his own, was intending to do what William was now hiring him to do. So he said, "Done."

CHAPTER 13

ALWAYS A FIRST TIME

The three friends stood waiting for Kayra outside the Drunken Dog Tavern. It had been two days since they had agreed to meet with her, and it had rained hard both days. There were still a few clouds left from the previous night's rain, and the ground was nearly all mud. The morning sun had burned off most of the clouds early, but the few that remained dropped whatever precipitation they held.

When she finally arrived, she was wearing the same clothing from their last meeting. The three horses that trailed her, one smaller than the other two, explained her tardiness.

"You never said anything about horses. We would have gotten them ourselves," Toran said.

"I could only get three, but they will make the journey quicker and cleaner." She gestured to her boots covered with a thick layer of brown mud.

"Saigel and I are used to sharing a horse, but I see you have a smaller one for him." Kellik looked at Toran. "That must mean the two of you will be sharing?"

"I suppose so," Toran replied with a smile.

"It is all they had," Kayra added.

"I do not mind if you do not." He helped her into the saddle and then mounted the horse behind her. Even with a smaller horse, Saigel was still too short to climb up on his own. Kellik helped him before he mounted also.

Three guards at the gate, half-groggy from an unauthorized nap, gaped at Kayra as she passed. One of them, who believed that he was still dreaming, grabbed her, only to have his hand swatted away. He now had four new long gashes that quickly began to bleed. Laughing at their injured companion, the other two guards opened the gate.

They traveled along the road for hours, following Kayra's directions. When the remaining clouds had evaporated, they passed through a thick grove of trees and approached a river. The sun was slowly drying what it could, but under a canopy of trees that the sun could not breach, minimal drying had taken place.

"Halt!" a voice called out. They stopped the horses and looked around. "There is a tariff to pass through my forest," the voice continued.

"Whut?" Saigel asked.

"What is the tariff?" Kellik asked.

At the same time, Toran was asking Kayra if this was where the attack on her had happened. She thought quickly about the surrounding trees so that she could cover her lack of an answer. Enrandl had mentioned nothing to her about a new ambush, and the group was still a day and a half from Enrandl's spot.

"No. We are nowhere close to it."

Meanwhile, Kellik had bargained with the voice and had found that only a small finance payment placed on the ground would get all three horses through the grove.

"It's crazy to pay," Saigel argued.

"Come now, Saigel," Toran said trying to calm him, "it is only fifteen silver. Let us pay and go on."

"That fifteen would buy good meals," he said, reluctant to agree. They paid by leaving the coins on the ground. Kellik continued to watch behind them for someone to appear and collect the coins, but they were soon too far down a small decline to see.

They stopped later for a few minutes to stretch and eat a small lunch. Afterward, Saigel stood on a large rock, and for the first time in his life, he mounted a horse on his own. Kellik followed. Toran was holding the reins of the horse for Kayra when two men dropped from above and knocked Kayra from the horse. The older man, whose clothing was already soiled by dry dirt, slipped in the mud beneath his feet. There was a loud snap, and the unfortunate man yelled out in pain. The bandit with dark hair protected by leather armor moved to aid the other.

Neither Kellik nor Saigel remained on their horses for long. Each dismounted and drew his weapon. Toran, who had still been holding the reins when the spooked horse charged away, was dragged for more than ten yards—and slathered with deep brown mud—before he could let go.

Meanwhile, Kayra was still lying on the ground and instinctively wanting to swat with her tail and knock the man down. She overruled this instinct and kicked out at the back of his leg as hard as she could. She achieved a partial result with her foot.

He was not knocked all the way down but grimaced, twitched slightly in pain, and knelt on one knee. He would have been thrown a distance away if she had been able to hit him with her tail.

He stood, approached her while prematurely raising his sword, and left the other bandit in the mud. When he was above her and his sword was ready to strike, which left no way to defend herself, she could see her death in his eyes. It was the first time in her long life that she had known fear.

She had been beaten that day cycles ago, when she had fought Kellik and Saigel at the cave, but during that battle, her confidence that she would prevail had been resolute. She knew now that The Gods' had shined brightly upon them that day.

But today was her day for GodsLight.

The sword was barely halfway down to her when Toran arrived and parried the fatal blow far wide of its intended target. She gasped in relief. There was a look of silent thanks between them before Toran pursued his foe.

He swung his sword, pressed his opponent back, and put himself between the bandit and Kayra. The bandit tried to avert his intentions, but he was forced to move away again.

"Go," Toran ordered Kayra, but she remained on the ground still paralyzed with shock. She had never felt so frail and close to death before. Now she had been saved by a mortal, who had risked his life for hers. As Toran worked his opponent farther away from her, the other man kept trying to circle around back to Kayra, but Toran continually blocked him.

The bandit engaged him with a complicated yet predictable series of attacks. His misfortune was that this series showed Toran how inexperienced he was. The routine was something a beginner does. Through experience and some good luck, Toran had not encountered a highly skilled swordsman before he had discovered that the maneuver was useless against a more battle-hardened foe.

Toran sidestepped, parried twice, and then sidestepped again to avoid the sequence. Trying not to be too overconfident, Toran tested his opponent. He moved forward and used the same attack combination. To his astonishment, the man perfectly executed the same sequence that Toran had just used. Toran thought his own defense was unique, and yet this young fighter was performing it the same way he had.

This one learns quickly, he thought and decided to let the youth have the offensive for a while. He found his opponent to be well practiced but soon tired of toying with him. Within a few clashes of sword against sword, Toran unarmed the younger fighter and knocked him out.

"You will be a fine swordsman someday," Toran predicted. There was no sign of the other man who had dropped from the tree. He could not have gone far with a broken ankle though. When he looked for Kayra and his friends, he found that two of them were unconscious and that she was nowhere in sight. He could see that two of Kellik's swords lay far from him. Saigel looked as if he had not even drawn his weapon.

Where is the other bandit? Toran wondered.

"Look out behind you!" Kayra called out.

Toran dove to his left, tucked, and rolled in the mud. When he returned to his feet, he found the older man, who had stark-white hair, opposite him with both ankles apparently intact. He was covered with fresh mud, which had joined his previously dried, dirty appearance before the fall from the tree. Indeed, this man had fallen and had possibly broken his foot.

"If he no longer lives, you will soon not," the man threatened, but his words seemed forced out as if he wanted to say something else.

"Fair enough, for if they are dead, you soon will be." Toran indicated Kellik and Saigel. "What do you want? We paid the tariff."

"You owe more than a mere tariff. You owe me your soul!" The words no longer seemed as if they were being forced out, and Toran was taken aback and confused by the statement.

The two men circled each other while Toran regained his poise. He was still unfamiliar, but Toran had to assume this man was either one of William's hirelings or one of the groups from the Wild Boar.

The attack came quickly and familiarly. The younger man had used the same routine. Toran followed through with his aggressive defense and soon discovered a problem. After his final sidestep, which would generally put him clearly away from his opponent, he found the aggressor in front of him and still attacking.

Toran's sword was fortunately positioned for a parry against one of the continuing strikes. When he tried to adjust his stance so that he could protect his now unprotected flank, the sword was torn from his hand by a leaf-filled tree branch. The blade flexed and flipped out of his hand and away several feet from the tree.

"Now, Laitian will have your soul!" the man promised.

The same branch that had stolen Toran's sword proved to be his savior when his opponent miscalculated and cut his sword into the tree, rather than cutting into Toran. Now the sword was stuck, deeply lodged in the branch. "No!" His yell echoed throughout the forest.

Toran moved away from the old man, who was struggling in vain to pull his sword loose. When the old man failed to pursue him, Toran assessed the situation. Kellik was up and tending to Saigel. All the horses were gone. Toran looked back to his former opponent and found the older man still striving to remove his sword from the tree and ignoring the rest of them. Toran saw Kayra emerging from the forest. She had finally come to her senses, had moved away from the fight, and had stayed hidden for the duration. Kellik and Saigel approached as Toran retrieved his sword. "What happened to you two?"

"Still not sure," Saigel replied. "Everythin' happened so fast."

"One minute he was on the ground nursing his ankle," Kellik said. "Then he was up and was quickly disarming me." Kellik looked at the man, who was still at the tree trying to retrieve his sword. "Then, I am not sure what happened. Looks like season change is coming early."

"It also looks like the rest of the way is on foot," Toran added. Saigel and Kellik began moving.

"What about them?" Kayra asked, walking closely next to him.

Toran removed a pouch from his belt and dropped it on the ground amidst the growing pile of dead leaves that continued to fall from the tree. Although he was not accustomed to giving finance away to people who tried to rob him—not to mention ones that wanted to kill him for some reason—he still felt sorry for the younger man. "I want this to compensate you and the boy for your loss. Apologies for not finishing this, but you seem too occupied, and we need to move on."

Toran and Kayra walked fast to catch up to the others. Toran still could not understand the man's obsession with the sword, but he figured it to be necessary.

They were entirely out of sight when the sword was finally dislodged from a rotting, leafless, and dead tree surrounded by a green flourishing forest.

The sun was moving into its late-afternoon position as several clouds passed in front of it, periodically allowing the weather to cool by the time they decided to stop again and rest. They had found one of the horses on their way and decided to use it to carry what little gear they had left. Saigel sat upon a rock next to Kayra while Kellik and Toran hunted for dinner. Kayra was staring off into the distance, recalling how

Toran had saved her life, and trying to figure out what it was about him that made her feel so strange whenever she looked into his eyes.

"I know how yuh feel," Saigel said.

"What?"

"Lost muh family too."

"Oh really." She sounded disinterested.

"Whole society, really," Saigel added.

Kayra looked up with a little more interest and asked, "How?"

Saigel's minikin society had lived down in The Southern Provinces with no cares or worries, until one day deep in the woods, one from his society had made a startling discovery. A minikin named Jobal was finishing a routine outer-rim sentry assignment when he heard the loud crash of a falling tree. He investigated the area and found where and why it had fallen.

Inside the heart of the tree—and several others that he had inspected—instead of wood he found a strange white substance. To Jobal's surprise, it appeared to be paper. He cut open the tree and saw that the entire inside of it had been transformed. When he inspected the stump, he found where the paper had come from.

In the stump, he found hundreds of worms eating out the insides of the tree and excreting the paper substance. Jobal was amazed. An inspection of the paper later discovered that it was sturdy and unable to be soiled. Saigel explained that this was ten revolutions before he had been born.

The minikins harvested the paper and used it as a trade item. Word traveled, and they soon became immensely popular with magicians and scholars, who came from all around to their village to buy their paper. Over the revolutions, these minikins tolerated others around them and eventually became the first group unguarded against the rest of the realm, where most other of their kind would shy away from the popularity.

Twenty-some revolutions passed before one particular human came to them. He was a greedy and selfish one, but everything was normal at first. He would arrive every couple of cycles and take all they had. In time, his nature overcame him, and their arrangement changed several times without notice.

He started to come more often, and he was beginning to take charge of the minikins and their worms. He chased off potential buyers with physical and magical threats. Then the man and his friends had come one last time and murdered his whole society. Saigel was the only survivor. He had been found by the dwarven clan Stonecrusher as they were passing through on their way home from a business venture. They took him along and raised him until he decided that it was time for him to search for the magician, who had been responsible for him becoming an orphan.

Toran and Kellik returned with some rabbits and a small deer. "You never told me about that Saigel," Kellik said as he and Toran sat down. "But you know—"

"Yeah, well, maybe yuh ne'er asked. I'll ne'er fuhrget what happened, and I'll find 'im someday."

"How are you going to find him if you don't even know what he looks like?" Kellik asked while reaching for his pack.

"I'll know him when I find him," Saigel added gravely.

Kellik took the book out of his pack. "Saigel, look at this."

"I seen it. Justa book."

"But you've never opened it," Kellik countered. He opened the book and handed it to Saigel. "This paper matches what you've just described, my friend." Saigel was amazed at what he saw. Kellik continued, "The ink won't smear at all. I have tried. The paper is immaculate compared to the cover. It could be made from your society's paper."

A tear dropped from Saigel's cheek onto one of the pages. Saigel wiped it away and realized that Kellik might be correct. "I'm not denyin' thuh paper. Could be magic ink." Saigel closed it and handed it back to Kellik.

"You keep it," Kellik offered.

"No, yuh." He hopped off his rock and walked away.

"I am sorry you had to go through that," Kayra called to him before he could go too far, but he did not answer. She looked at Toran and then at the ground. "We should get going. There is a lake not far from here. We can make it before dark."

"I think you are forgetting that we no longer have horses," Toran commented. "We should make a camp soon, and I have been meaning to ask, was it goblins that attacked you and your brothers?"

Kayra knew that she should answer him quickly but was not sure how. She tried to recall exactly what she had told him before, but her memory had been starting to fail her since she had become human. She considered again that her perfect recollections only applied to her dragon memories and not all the recent events of the past few days. Information that had been consistently taught to her was easy enough to remember, but lesser matters or things she might have said were not easily recalled. "I … I am not exactly sure I remember. I must have been knocked unconscious before I recognized who was attacking us."

"We have been in goblin territory for the last half of the day—since we left those bandits. Some big battles against them were fought around here. I was just guessing. You never said who attacked you."

"I apologize, but I really do not know. I suppose it could have been goblins." She shrugged her shoulders.

"I have heard tell that even Mirzog the Mighty was finally killed somewhere in this territory," Toran added.

"Wow!" Kellik replied. "I have heard of him. The fiercest goblin king ever. Won hundreds of battles and all but single-handedly—"

"Bah! Yuh've pro'bly heard 'e fought like 'e was demon possessed too?" The minikin had come back to the group. His eyes were a bit red but were no longer tearing.

"That is how I heard it," Toran answered as Kellik merely nodded his head emphatically. "Do you know different?"

"Tales expand thuh farther they git frum thuh source." Saigel sat back down on a rock. "I'm not sayin' he wasn't. Since I seem ta be thuh storyteller today, I'll spin ya 'nuther one."

Saigel began to explain:

The Stonecrusher clan that found him had its own experience with Mirzog. Its encounter with his eminence was the reason that the former goblin ruler decided to forego battle with dwarves in an attempt to conquer the mountains of The Westlands.

It was several revolutions after Saigel's adoption by the clan. He had barely been involved with fighting the goblin king but held one of the most potent treasures from the battle.

No single Stonecrusher family claimed him as its own, but instead, all of them took responsibility for raising him. The first of them had the daunting task of finding a way to allow the minikin to see in the underground mountain darkness like they did. It took a group effort to create and enchant a special pair of spectacles for him.

One family after another took him in and educated him with the trade for which that family was responsible for keeping the whole clan together. He quickly became a favorite with each passing family. He was eager to accept the knowledge that they taught him. In the end, none of them understood what he was learning on his own.

The acts started small, and sometimes; he did not even register what he had acquired until later. From dwarven family to dwarven family, he learned to procure what he desired. It was not something the dwarves had taught him but something that was natural to him, of which they were unaware.

A piece missing here, an object vanishing there, and that was that. One way or another, items disappeared. When this happened, because of his growing natural talent, he escaped accusation for anything that went missing or anything that mysteriously reappeared without explanation. With each family, he found things that he desired but understood that he could not keep. He respected each family because they had saved him from an uncertain future. He could not conceive of any way not to be blamed for the final prize because when he left, it would never again be seen by the Stonecrusher dwarves.

The night before Mirzog's attack, Saigel was restless. An agitated feeling persisted with him throughout his morning chores with Brutus and right up to the attack. The weapon smith lived alone, except for Saigel. When the goblin raid began, they were heating up the forge to continue working on their current smithing lesson.

At the first alarm, Brutus, uncertain of the extent of the danger, instructed Saigel to stay with the forge and to protect himself if necessary. There were plenty of smaller weapons around for him to do so. Brutus ran off to see what was going on.

It was not long before he could hear the distant clash of weapons and battle cries of both dwarf and goblin, even though he could not understand them. The battle lasted most of the day, and Saigel did not want to stay cooped up inside the forge, but he did not stray far. He climbed to the top of the forge house and watched what he could see of the battle from there, including the end of it.

He had never seen a goblin before. He decided that if they were not ugly, they were not very impressive creatures to look at. Most were barely taller than he was. The dirty, haphazard armor they wore looked as if it had been randomly pieced together from various discarded articles. They had pointed noses and teeth too long for the little mouths on their faces. Their sharp teeth continually cut into what served the goblins as lips, leaving behind gashes with fresh blood.

He did find himself impressed at the way the goblins worked together against their foes (his clan in this case). The pack tactics that they employed was a work of art that he would never forget. The admiration of these creatures was heavily tempered with his revulsion that they were killing members of his family (something he had experienced before).

When he saw the goblin king come from around a rocky corner, he knew he was experiencing something special. Mirzog could have been a small human.

He barely resembled his kin, except for his nose, teeth, and accompanying blood trickling his lips.

He was now being forced backward by a group of four dwarves, which was led by Brutus. They returned Mirzog's blows and blocked his strikes. Mirzog fought alone with a sword in each hand, as if he was a pack of at least five of his comrades.

A sudden concussive force erupted from all around them, shaking the whole area and showering all of them with stones from the rocky cave's ceiling. The rocks flew as far as Saigel's rooftop. Everyone on the cave floor who was caught in the blast was forced in multiple directions and driven to the ground, including the king. Mirzog's swords skittered along the cave floor several feet away from him.

He was back on his feet with incredible speed but was still separated from his weapons. He was near the place where the blast had thrown Brutus. The dwarf was getting up slowly as the goblin considered his options. Looking all around him, including a dismissive glance at Saigel, who was watching from the top of the forge house, he seemed to decide. He reached toward his back and closed his eyes. A blinding flash of light burst outward, distracting everyone momentarily, and Mirzog was back in action.

He had taken the spectacles off after the burst of light blinded him. When Saigel's vision cleared, and he could see the caves washed in the scimitar's light—three of the four dwarves in Mirzog's area would never see light again—the goblin was advancing on Brutus. Saigel wanted to help, but he could only grab a couple of stones by his feet and hurl them in the direction of the king.

Before Mirzog could skewer Brutus, he twirled in place and used the weapon of light to block the path of the first stone. The second stone, however, was not as easily prevented and struck the goblin directly in the eye. Mirzog tried to shake away the sudden pain, but the distraction was just enough for Brutus to disarm him, sending the weapon across the cave. With no one to wield its magic, the light of the weapon extinguished.

It may have been the first and only time, but with a loud scream and an evil, one-eyed glare at the forge house's roof, Mirzog the Mighty was forced to retreat. In this unique instance, he did so without retrieving the magic weapon.

"The sword was given ta Brutus 'cause I was 'is ward at thuh time. A gesture ta thuh both of us," Saigel said. "Always put back whut I took, till thuh scimitar, but I left thuh seein' specs in its place."

Kellik was about to comment when a large brown form lumbered out of the trees toward them. Everyone except the half-elf froze where he or she stood, as the bear approached.

"Just be calm." Kellik's voice was low and calm. "It is probably just hungry."

"Fuhr us," Saigel commented.

Kellik reached into his sack and produced a rabbit from there. He held the rabbit out in front of him, offering it to the bear. The bear stood up on its hind legs and roared at him, yet Kellik still moved slowly forward. Finally, Kellik placed the rabbit on the ground ten feet away from the bear. He remained standing just a couple of feet from the rabbit.

The bear dropped back down on all four legs and moved forward. Everyone watched as the bear stopped to sniff at the rabbit and then regard Kellik. The beast was several hundred pounds larger than Kellik—and close enough that the smell of the bear's dirty fur was evident—but he stood still and showed no fear. A low growl issued from the bear a moment before it accepted the rabbit and started to eat it. Kellik now backed away from the bear and joined his friends.

"Let us go before he finishes," Toran said.

Darkness overtook them before they knew it, and they stopped for the night. They chose a spot just off the road. There was no clearing for all of them to gather together, but they made a fire to cook the deer and settled among the dense group of trees for the night. Tempest found a spot in one of the surrounding trees. They cooked and ate the deer and placed what was leftover in a pack. They were all tired and agreed that the watch schedule from the previous night had been a good one. The night passed uneventfully during each of their watch shifts.

The next morning after everyone was awake, something startled Tempest, and she flew away for a few minutes, but none of the group could find any sign of what might have done so. When Tempest returned, Kellik was about to chant the essence that would allow him to speak with the bird, when the brown bear from the previous day found them again. Kellik knew it was the same bear because it smelled the same, and he recognized a patch of white fur on its left paw, which he had seen the day before. The bear just sat down in front of Kellik and watched him. Kellik was speechless, and he moved toward his friends. The bear got up and followed him.

To Kayra, it seemed familiar that Toran automatically handed Kellik the pack that had the rabbits from the previous day's hunt. He did this like he had done it many times before. She watched Kellik remove a rabbit from it and approach the bear. The bear sat down. The elf looked apprehensive, yet he still approached the bear, placed the rabbit in front of it, and took a few steps back. The bear smelled the rabbit and then lifted it in one paw (the left one with the white patch of fur) and threw it back to Kellik. The dead rabbit landed at Kellik's feet.

"Maybe it don't like rabbit," Saigel said. "Try the deer?"

"I do not think it is hungry," Toran said.

"Then what does it want?" Kayra asked with a small hint of fear in her voice. As a dragon, she would not have even thought twice about the brown bear. As a human, she was slowly becoming aware that there were many different things around her that she could not merely breathe fire upon and not worry about anymore. She abruptly realized that she wanted to be a dragon again. She wanted her power back so that she could do just what she wanted to do—breathe fire on the bear and not have to worry about it.

Toran touched her shoulder, and all her fear disappeared. It was replaced with a strange confidence that he could and would protect her from any peril that she faced. She knew again that she was someone other than Kayrahawkatzeena, a mighty middle-aged dragon who was stuck in human form. She was moving behind him and shielding herself from the bear when everything beneath her began to shudder and shake. She yelled as the ground fell out from underneath her.

Enrandl stood at his mirror and channelled yet another scrying effect into it. He had tried several times to scry on Kayra. He hoped that she would be his way to get past whatever magic was preventing his spying on Toran and the book, but each time, his effect was blocked by more magic. Of course, this was an assumption on his part. He decided that he needed to create a more powerful way of scrying, one that prevented effects or magical items from blocking his magic, but he did not have time to do it now. He ceased his influence over the display and walked away from his mirror.

The laboratory had been refurbished since the explosion of mixed liquids and looked as if it were in better condition than it had been before. Shevail came through the door and offered Enrandl his portrait-carved stein with its steaming refreshment.

"Thank you. I invariably appreciate this delightful concoction of yours. Have you a denomination?"

"No, I have not, master," Shevail answered. "I do not even have a name for the plant that the main ingredient is derived from."

"It is truly a delectable potation."

"Thank you, master." Shevail bowed and backed out of the laboratory. She closed the door and then leaned against it, breathing a heavy sigh. She smiled and ran down the hall to her sleeping chamber. Inside, there was only a bed, a chair, and an easel with a painting canvas upon it.

She went to the easel and sat down on the chair. Light shone into the room via a window on the southern wall. She looked at the sketch of Enrandl that she had drawn and picked up her charcoal. An hour later, another figure had joined Enrandl on the canvas. It was an elven female with long hair. Shevail smiled wider and hugged the drawing for a long time. She released the canvas and went to bed. "I love you, master," she said and then added, "Enrandl."

CHAPTER 14

MIRZOG THE MIGHTY

Saigel sat among the trees as tears rolled down his face. They were cleaning streams that ran over his muddy cheeks. Tempest was perched on a branch of a fallen tree, next to a sunken depression where there had once been solid ground. When the groundshake began, the bird had immediately launched into the air. The minikin had only had time to watch the earth open and swallow all his friends. He had not known what to do to help them. When the ground had stopped its movement, he had tried to dig for them, but after an hour, he had deemed it hopeless.

The brown bear that Kellik had tried to feed had also been swallowed up during the groundshake. Saigel had not known Kellik for long, several cycles were about the extent of their time together, yet from the moment they had met, he had considered him a friend.

Toran was a slightly different story. Saigel liked the man well enough but found himself shaking his head at some of the human's actions and decisions. Their meeting had been just a little more than a week ago.

Because he had known the woman even less time than the others, she held even less influence on him. She had also been one of Toran's decisions that Saigel could not grasp.

Now they all were probably dead, and he was alone again. Everything was pointless to him as he stared at the cave-in. If family and friends were swept away as their village was destroyed or swallowed up as the earth shook and collapsed, what was the point of anything? He was seriously considering returning to the dwarves and living out the rest of his life with them. The separation had been of his choosing, and he could accept that loneliness. It was also a separation that he could countermand. Continuing his search for the one who had murdered his clan would not bring any of his society, family, or his buried friends back. He could do nothing for them.

Then he recalled what he had just learned about the book that Enrandl wanted so badly. It had probably been made from the same paper his society had died for. He had disregarded the item when Kellik had tried to give it to him. Now it held some importance, and he needed to find it, and with some GodsLight, his friends.

Maybe I gave up too soon, Saigel thought, hopped back down into the gash, which had been created by the groundshake, and began to dig again. A breeze blew through the trees as his worn and dirty hands continued pulling stones and mud from the depression. For a moment, he thought he could hear music. He figured that it was his imagination enhancing the sound of the leaves blowing in the wind. Just in case he was mistaken, and the sound had come from somewhere below him, he doubled his efforts.

"The minikin is starting to dig again," Paul informed Seane. A slow smooth tune rolled out of the lute as one of his hands held its strings in chords and his other plucked and strummed across them.

"How can you be sure the others are fine?" Seane asked.

"I learn a great many things about many things when I am playing. You can believe me, for I speak truly when I tell you that they are safe for now."

"That is an impressive instrument you have there. I wish William would find us soon. I do not know if we should help or not."

"Aaron and Collin are about to return and confirm that the minikin has started to dig. The groundshake was natural. The magician had nothing to do with it. You are safe not to interfere."

She opened her eyes to a startling sight—darkness—and felt an odd sensation course through her. At first, she thought the cold wetness covering her legs was the source of her chill, then realized this was not something physical she was sensing. The darkness surrounded her and she could see nothing. It was yet another new experience for her in this human form that caused her unease. With dragon eyes, she would not have had a problem seeing anything in these surroundings, but once again, she reminded herself that the comforts of her proper form were not available to her. She took a few deep breaths to calm herself.

"Toran?" she called out while she felt down by her legs. She found that moist soil covered them. Her legs, which she had uncovered from the mix of mud and dirt, were moving freely by the time Toran answered.

"I am here. I think, that is," Toran answered. "Kellik, can you hear me?" he tried. "Saigel are you there?" His questions were answered only by the silence. "I am going to light a torch. Just stay where you are."

"A wise proposition, that," she answered. The torch was lit, and they both could see each other. She was lying atop a mound of earth. He had rolled onto what appeared to be stonework. She watched him steal just a moment to inspect the walls and floors around him. Broken stone and wet soil were all he found during his brief inspection. Kayra found a way down to him and found that he also appeared to be uninjured.

"My guess is that Kellik and Saigel are either on the other side of that mound or buried underneath it, but in both cases, we have no idea how far."

"What do we do?" she asked. She knew this was not part of Enrandl's plan, unless he had changed it without her knowledge. She wondered what Toran had that Enrandl wanted so badly but decided that it was his business. If she felt the need to possess whatever it was that enthralled him, she would take it from him.

"I think we should try to find a way out of here."

"I am not going to stay here by myself, so lead on." She put her hand on his shoulder.

"Here," he said, handing her the torch. "I will be more valuable with a weapon than a torch." She took the light without argument. Toran drew his sword, and they continued down the passage.

The bear roared, and its large paws broke apart three more of the diminutive skeletons, but even as they fell to the ground, three more bodies of animated bones moved in to take their places. Kellik was behind the bear, and he did not have much room to move around it. The mound behind him blocked the other direction, so he stood with his weapons and nothing to do but wait for the bear to finish destroying them or be killed itself.

The three-foot-tall skeletons were tiny in comparison to the sizeable, snarling form that they were assaulting. Unfortunately, the bear was being hit and cut by the advancing, little skeletons. When all its great strength had failed, the animal finally collapsed. There were several skeletons on the other side of the bear. Kellik was getting ready for their charge when a voice echoed against the walls around him.

He could not understand the powerful words, but with the essence of the exclamation, every skeleton exploded into powder right before Kellik's eyes. Dust was still settling all around the dead bear and himself when he heard footfalls approaching. He kept his swords ready for whatever might come and crouched behind the bear. He knew that only a priest of The Light Gods' could utter such a command and have such a powerful result, but he wanted to be certain.

"See, I told you that crypt robbing could be fun," a harsh and familiar voice said.

"I am sure you think this is fun, but … Oh my!"

"How in the name of The Gods' did that get down here?" the same familiar voice said.

"I am sure I do not know. The gates were locked."

Kellik did not recognize the second voice, but he was sure that the first one was Thom's—the giant of a man who Saigel had an arm contest against and beaten in the village of Kershal.

"Oh, look beyond. I told you that shake would cause a cave-in. Now how are we supposed to bypass that?" Fibble said. He was still dressed in his fine clothing and was armed with a large hammer.

"Must be where the bear came from," guessed Thom. "Well, we'll find another crypt to plunder. This one is spent."

"Do not give in so soon my friend. This was your idea, after all, and there may be many other ways through these structures. There must be hidden passages to secret chambers that someone wants no one to find. You talked me into this and are not getting out that easy," Fibble said and started to climb over the bear. "Besides, with all those animated bones, there must be something quite interesting hidden somewhere. I am sure of it."

Kellik moaned and started to stand up.

"What is this?" Fibble said, looking down upon him from the top of the bear.

"Where am I?" Kellik asked, feigning a shake of his head.

"Have no fear. I am here to help."

"What have you got Fibble?" Thom asked from the other side.

"Kellik is my name." He tried to sound weak.

"Are you injured? Did you fall in the shake?"

"I think I am okay, but my friends are …" Kellik did not know what to say because he had no idea what had become of any of them.

"Do I know you, Kellik?" Thom asked as he climbed over the bear also.

Kellik recognized his armor and face. "I believe we met in Kershal."

"You speak true. Fibble told me all about it. I like your style."

"Thank you. I was above ground, and I did fall in with the shake. I am not sure where my friends are."

"We shall endeavor to find them," Fibble replied.

Toran and Kayra found the end of the passage and a small sarcophagus. Toran shook his head and said, "At least we know we are going to die in a crypt."

Kayra knew that in her natural form she could have dug her way out of this place, and even from this perspective, she wanted to try. She did not want to die this way, and she knew somewhere deep inside him, Toran did not want to either. "We have to try to dig our way out of here," she offered.

"We will not give up. It just seems hopeless," Toran replied.

They walked back to the cave-in and started to dig. After an hour, they stopped to rest and looked at their progress. They had made a large hole with their effort, but they were exhausted. They fell back on the pile and looked at each other. They were covered from hair to feet with soil. Kayra reached out to wipe a smudge from Toran's face but only ended up smudging it further. She looked into his eyes and felt his gentle hand on her soiled cheek. His face moved closer, and he pressed his lips to hers.

She had seen several humans do this during her time in Jenerv, and while wondering why they did it, she thought the sight had been revolting. Now as she experienced it, she thought it was exhilarating. When he stopped, she found herself wanting more. She kissed him back with so much force, he fell backward (he had been unbalanced to begin with).

She was still kissing him when a flood of mud poured over them, and Saigel appeared through the soil, and daylight filled the crypt.

"Ain't this a sight fuhr sore eyes," Saigel said. "I'm interruptin'?"

"Yes and no," Toran answered. "I am glad to see that you were not buried beneath this mess. Is Kellik with you?"

"I wus hoping 'e was with yuh."

A muffled yet determined yell through the wet mound called to them, saying, "Saigel?" They heard first, and then, "Toran? Kayra? Can you hear me?"

"I believe that could be him now," Kayra answered, "but not from up there. From this way." She pointed in the direction where she and Toran had come from and not at the cave-in site.

Saigel slid down to their level, untied the rope at his waist, and picked up a broken piece of stone about the size of his fist. Kayra watched as he started to knock the stone against the stonework walls, which were just beyond the cave-in. He quickly found what he was looking for. She also heard the hollow sound from behind the round rock in the wall.

"Thur's a passage beyond 'ere." He put his ear to the wall. "I hear sumpthin' movin' too." The grinding of stone accompanied his comment, and the circular stone recessed into the wall and then revolved downward. An open passage appeared just as Saigel had predicted.

"Did I do this?" A voice came from the opening. Then a dwarven head emerged. "Quite accidental, you know. It would seem I have a knack for locating hidden places suches as this." There was a pause before he said, "Oh! The partner."

"What have you found now?" Thom's voice called from behind Fibble.

"Our little friend to complete the pair and apparently his addition."

Kayra felt that she was in the way and stepped across the path. She tried to see beyond the dwarf. Toran took her place behind Saigel. *Does he look puzzled*, she thought as she regarded the human's expression. Suddenly, there was Kellik, pushing his way past the dwarf and meeting Saigel with a brief hug.

"I thought we'd lost each other," he said. Saigel was about to reply when they all heard a faint booming noise echo through the passages around them.

"Fibble, what was that?" Thom's unseen voice asked.

"If it was none of us, and if it was not—" The dwarf was interrupted by another eerie rumbling of the same sound. This time, it was slightly stronger than the first. It resounded for a third and then fourth time, with continued repetition comprising a slow cadence.

"Perhaps our goblin skeles were guarding more than Mirzog's dormant treasure. Let us take a look!" Fibble disappeared to the other side of the previously hidden portal.

"Skeles?" Kayra asked.

"Skeletons. Unnaturally animated bones of long-dead creatures. These being goblin? I am guessing?" Toran answered her as Kellik nodded.

She derided herself. Of course, she knew what skeletons were. She just had not heard the word *skeles* referring to them before and had not taken the time to ponder the word before she had asked. She felt something odd as Toran explained. It was a pang inside her, which she could not put a definition to. It was not anger exactly, and the sensation only lingered long enough so that she missed what Kellik was saying.

"A large number of them too. They overcame the bear before Fibble blasted them all to dust."

"Blasted? GodsLight?" Toran asked.

Fibble appeared again with only his head poking through the opening. "Yes, yes. I venerate The Light Gods'. Are we going to investigate the drums? Thomas has discovered a downward spiral staircase, which must have revealed itself also when I opened this portal. I am believing the source of the drums to be coming from below us somewhere."

Saigel led the group down. An orange glow from his torch flickered on the stone around him. The low booming sound of a drum became slightly louder with every other step and continued to beat out the cadence as they went farther into the tomb.

Then from somewhere in the shadows below, a chant commenced between the booms of the drums:

"Umhbahg toraahd girach seeresh, Mirzog!"

The rhythmic pulse of the drums and the dancing firelight of his torch united. There was only enough room for one of them at a time to go down the circular stairs. Fibble was directly behind the minikin, followed closely by Thom, Kayra, Toran, and Kellik, who was watching their backs. Fibble seemed to be correct, as the drums and chants continued to grow steadily louder as they approached the bottom of the staircase.

A long, dark corridor stretched out before them. A faint luminescent light revealed an open arched portal at the far end that blinked at them all. It resembled an eye that was watching and patiently awaiting their approach.

"Umhbahg toraahd girach seeresh, Mirzog!"

Saigel motioned for everyone to stop and moved ahead of the group. As he walked, his sharp hearing caught Fibble whispering to the rest, "That sounds like a resurrection chant." After carefully and quietly examining the path, it took him a few stealthy minutes to reach the end of it. He put his torch down several feet away before approaching the arch.

There was a broken-down, two-door iron gate. It had once filled the whole archway but would do so no longer. The first door, which was decorated with violently deranged goblin shapes and gargoyle impersonations, was still in place but hanging horizontally on its twisted lower hinge. The upper hinge had been destroyed beyond recognition. The other half of the gate was completely torn away from the wall and halfway down the steps inside. The drumbeat continued and the goblin chant greeted his look around the corner.

Here was the tomb of Mirzog the Mighty.

After a brief glance, he decided that the sound of the steady drumbeat and chanting would mask their own sounds. He was sure that the others could approach without alarming anyone who was involved in the exhibition before him. He motioned the others forward before he took the time to study the area more completely.

Stone had been roughly hewn into an inverted ziggurat of thirty goblin-sized steps that led to the scene that was still farther below. It encompassed the chamber and strangely resembled a small square auditorium. In the dim light, every surface was flickering sporadically like stars in the sky. Across the tomb, there was a second gate, which he assumed was similar to the one near him, but there were no passages in the walls to his left or right.

With just enough light for him to see movement in the four corners, Saigel saw the drummers, each beating on a large drum. The progress of their strokes caught his attention, and the four instruments boomed in such complete unison, only one beat was heard at a time.

Standing below on the main floor in the mostly dark chamber were twelve living goblins that surrounded a raised shrine, which was in the form of a sarcophagus. Each wore tattered but priestly vestments that were intentioned for a ceremonial ritual. The goblins were spaced evenly around the altar, and they were chanting the same litany as the drummers played on: "Umhbahg toraahd girach seeresh, Mirzog!"

At one of the short ends of the altar, a fire fought against the darkness and allowed Saigel to see what he could. The last place that he looked, before the others joined him at the arch, was the top of the altar. Lying there was the skeletal remains of a goblin.

"Thas gunna be 'im," Saigel whispered just before the small fire at the foot of the altar exploded into the air. It blazed upward—now resembling a pillar—scorched the ceiling, and immersed the entire chamber with bright orange light. This further compounded the starlike flicker that was going on all around the tomb.

Everyone except for Kellik was well situated to observe the rebirth of Mirzog, but he was the only one with the misfortune and horror to see the demon rise.

He was standing too far in the rear of the group to witness what was going on or to have seen the fire near the altar, but no one had picked up the torch that Saigel had left on the floor (now behind them all), and when the torch's fire flared along with the one in the ceremony, it created a pillar of its own and caught Kellik with its full force. He bellowed an unintelligible sound as he immediately pushed through all of them to the front to get away from the flames with all the haste he could marshal.

"What the …" Toran was the first inadvertent victim of Kellik's panic. The human was walloped and was pushed three feet forward. This required him to execute a spectacular (yet unsuccessful) attempt to spin around Kayra. Unfortunately, he remained standing, and he was not able to stop his momentum toward Saigel.

When Kayra, who was positioned slightly to Toran's left, was hit by him, she was turned in the opposite direction of his attempted dodge and fell backward into the rear of Thom's legs. The large man fell to his knees behind the dwarf and then flat on his chest, forcing Fibble to stumble down the first few steps into the room.

At the last moment, Toran stepped and leaped over Saigel. In the air, he turned sideways and caught sight of a drummer who had given up his part of the cadence to charge Fibble. The airborne maneuver finished when he landed flat on his back. He thanked The Gods' that he had landed on the broken gate—breaking it into more pieces—rather than on the hard edges of the stonework steps.

With the brunt of his momentum stopped when he crashed into Toran, Kellik stumbled on and bumped Saigel into the room and down a few steps along with Fibble. Kellik looked around at everyone. The dwarf stood with his back to one goblin drummer charging at him while Toran, from his back with no breath to call out a warning, tried to warn him by pointing at the goblin. Saigel had not been able to get up immediately from his brief roll, and the drummer from the far corner charged at him. Meanwhile, Thom and Kayra were in a pile in the hallway to his left. His eyes were drawn to the main floor, mesmerized by the enfolding sight, and he could not look away. The last two drummers kept pounding out their cadence.

Boom.

A branch of flame separated from the fiery pillar and arched itself to engulf the first of the twelve goblin priests, but he continued to chant, "Umhbahg toraahd girach …" His vestments were scorched and smoldering but not igniting.

Boom.

Then the fire shot out from the priest and crossed the altar to another priest. Like the first priest, he accepted the burning flame stoically and continued the chant, "Seeresh, Mirzog!"

From priest to priest, the fire wove its way back and forth as the remaining drummers pounded out the cadence. None of the goblins broke his concentration or stopped chanting. Finally, a twelve-pointed star of fire, with each goblin being one of those points, was formed above the goblin skeleton. The priests threw their arms into the air, and their chanting ceased, but the drummers played on. The only noise other than the drums was the sound of Fibble, Toran, and Saigel struggling against the other drummers.

As if the fire was finally overcoming the goblins, they all started to waver and drop to their knees. When the sarcophagus's lid drifted upward, each goblin rose again in the same order that the flame had chosen them. As all of the goblins held their open palms toward the altar, the fire on them passed from them and underneath the elevated lid.

Boom.

"Umhbahg toraahd girach ..."

Boom.

"Seeresh, Mirzog!"

The cover crashed back down and fragmented into four parts. The skeletal body bounced once, broke apart, and fell in pieces all around its coffin, along with the broken lid. Fighting ceased, and although the fire still raged on, a profound silence encompassed the tomb. The star of flames designed by the goblin priest transformed from an orange chroma to a bright white hue. With an imploding pulse of energy, which was enough for everyone around to feel it, the white lines of flame were sucked into the coffin and extinguished, leaving only the radiant tower from which all of the fire had spawned. The ossuary instantly began pouring out a virescent mist.

The wispy haze filled the main floor while a jet of darker, thicker smoke rose to the ceiling and formed a massive, ghostly goblin-shaped form. The ghost shape mostly solidified into a towering and attenuated figure, which emanated even more foul emerald smog that floated and followed its motions. It stretched out its thin arms with an eerily loud sound of bones cracking. The skin of the beast had become deep gray and was stretched so tightly to its skull and body that there might as well have been no skin at all. Its emaciated frame resembled sickly and decaying tree branches.

The demon Mirzog, which now stood at its full height of twice its pre-resurrected size, nearly reached the ceiling of the tomb and towered over the twelve paralyzed goblin priests. What should have been intelligent eyes in its dark sockets, whether he was eight feet tall or not, was instead pure anger in the form of black fire. As if it was using those flames as replacements for its eyes, Mirzog surveyed the surroundings. The singed acolytes who stood in the resurrection circle around him all recognized that this was wrong, and they began to scatter.

One unfortunate creature was not fast enough. It was grabbed in one of Mirzog's abnormally large hands as the demon's mouth opened unnaturally wide, revealing several rows of teeth that were not typically part of a goblin's mouth. With one bite, Mirzog decapitated the goblin. The demon goblin spat the head at another fleeing priest. It struck with enough force to knock the priest to the ground. Mirzog dropped the headless body, and with one step, he crushed the fallen priest under its bare foot.

Priests and drummers alike seemed to know that there was only one plausible exit available to them—the one Saigel's group had come through. All of them scurried up the small stairs in that direction.

The demon opened its arms wide and directed a stream of the murky smoke that encompassed it at a group of fleeing goblins. The eddied swirl caught three of them, lifted them from the ground, and wrested the doomed priests toward the demon. Razor-sharp claws grew on its fingertips, seemingly on a whim as the priests were drawn to it. His cruel claws tore all three apart in only a few seconds. Not one drop of goblin blood hit the floor because the smoke absorbed it and the demon Mirzog soaked it all in.

Muscles in its body pulsed, expanding and contracting as they grew. It bellowed out a pleased growl as if it wanted more. Then as Kellik watched, something happened to the demon goblin. It paused in confusion, as if it was lost, and looked around the room again.

The rest of the goblins filed out the broken gate, ignoring everything in their path, including the enhanced torch's fire, which still burned as tall as the corridor. Kellik could see that the beast was definitely searching for something other than the priests. He was not as mesmerized by the actual creature as he had been by the summoning of the monster and was no longer under that control either. He watched as Mirzog's eyes and concentration fell on Saigel and saw a kindred recognition of each other.

"Thief!" A scathing and atrocious voice carried the word out for several seconds as it rumbled all around them. Mirzog took one ground-shaking step, reached the minikin, and grabbed at him, but Saigel ran down the steps between the demon's legs to escape. Mirzog maintained its effort to reach the little man. It bent at the waist, and its long arm followed the minikin's path. It made the same brittle-bones sound that it had before as the demon's bent body also followed Saigel between its own legs. Then the beast jerked and twisted at its waist. Green smoke swirled around it as Mirzog folded underneath itself, snapping and cracking the entire time, until incredibly, it was facing the opposite direction without even turning.

"Fibble. This is part of your expertise, I assume," Toran told the dwarf as he pointed downward. Fibble was brushing himself off and was seemingly about to give chase to the fleeing goblins. He did not see what was going on behind him. He surveyed and considered the creature that was facing off against the minikin.

"Oh, my! That is quite a sturdy fellow. Where did he come from?"

Toran said, "I do not—"

"It came out of the coffin!" Kellik told them. Kayra was back on her feet and joined him where he stood.

Fibble shook his head, and replied, "Evidently, Mirzog's resurrection did not proceed as our little friends would have liked."

Thom stormed past them and their conversation, taking many stairs at a time to engage the creature below. When he reached Mirzog, his large sword cut down the middle of its back, burning a large searing gash there. Temporarily distracted from its target, the demon snarled, unnaturally turned its head halfway, emitted odious smoke and supernatural clamor, and glared at Thom with its eyeless, fire-filled cavities. Then it bent one arm of its arms impossibly backward toward the human.

Everyone watched the large man as he was heaved from the floor. His sword clanged down behind the feet of the demon, and the demon threw him across the chamber. When he collided with a wall several feet above the highest step, it buckled and caved in under the force. Debris collapsed all around. Instead of falling, Thom, knocked unconscious when he hit the wall, remained embedded in the broken structure.

Only Kellik and Kayra, however, witnessed the filthy green smoke surrounding Mirzog as it swarmed to the gash at its back—thronged the wound—and congealed there, leaving no evidence of injury to be seen.

Kayra cringed at the image and shook Kellik's shoulder. "That thing just healed itself." She gagged and choked as she recounted what the others already knew, asking, "Did any of you see that?"

Fibble moved to help his friend, but Toran tried to redirect him. "I will see what I can do about Thom. You are more suited to deal with that thing."

"Not true in this case," the dwarf corrected as he continued toward Thom. "I have my essences prepared for encounters with undead identities, and that there is nothing of the sort," Fibble called back to him.

That is not very reassuring, Toran thought. He followed the dwarf as he contemplated Fibble's comment. When he caught up to him, he asked, "What are we dealing with then?"

Mirzog had refocused on Saigel. The minikin had stopped with the small coffin between them, but it was not going to be an obstacle for long.

"Something more otherworldly. Demonic, I imagine. I must ponder the dilemma." They reached the unconscious man, and after a brief examination, Fibble said, "I do hope Thomas will be fine."

Toran mused, "It is concentrating on Saigel for some reason. Thom was just a momentary distraction."

Saigel called out, "I know whut ya want, and yuhr not havin' it!"

Mirzog roared disapproval at this, reached across the coffin for him, and instead ended up with a piece of the broken lid in its palm.

Toran reacted in the instant that Mirzog roared. It was similar to the response he had experienced to the ambush by William's men. Instead of the less complicated evasion that he had used then, he quickly conjured a sphere around the piece of the broken lid. Then he levitated it into the space in front of Saigel, where Mirzog grabbed it instead of his friend. The demon was distracted just enough for Saigel to escape. Toran released control of the sphere but could not see where Saigel had gone.

Mirzog apparently had the same notion. Toran watched as the beast dropped the rock and peered over the coffin in search of its enemy. Meanwhile, Fibble muttered something about iron and containment essences.

"What was that about iron?" Toran asked the dwarf.

"Iron should be able to hurt demons, and it is a major component for containing and banishing them."

"Iron can kill this thing. Now that is useful." Toran returned his attention to Mirzog as Fibble tried to protest. Toran had not heard the dwarf's complaint, as in the same moment, a sphere-propelled piece of the iron gate was hurled at the demon. The iron bar burned through the middle of Mirzog's back and impaled it there, with one end protruding from its chest.

The beast roared and turned its head to face the members of the group while it grabbed the iron weapon. The fetid hand burned and smoked as it touched the iron. Mirzog flinched slightly as he pulled the bar the rest of the way through his chest and then dropped it. The bar clanged loudly on the floor. Drifting green smoke rushed to its hand and the hole in its chest, exhibiting the same nauseating healing it had before. That was when Toran realized that the wound Thom had inflicted no longer existed.

"I did try to tell you—"

"That Thom's sword is made of iron?" Toran reasoned, "And that thing healed anyway. I should have kept listening. Well, maybe I just need to hurt it more."

Mirzog had already contorted its body around to face the rest of them, and it was taking a step forward. Kellik and Kayra retreated to the hallway. Toran sent spheres to the remaining eleven bars, which were scattered around him, and flung them all toward Mirzog before dashing away from the dwarf and his stuck companion to join the others. The missiles pierced the demon from the middle of its chest to its upper abdomen, and it paused. The iron bars burned at each penetrated area, but Mirzog ignored them and endured the pain while its putrid green smoke combated the continual burning and smoking from each piece of intrusive metal. It was obviously content with its capacity to heal itself. The beast deformed itself more and started to become smaller as it made its way to the broken gate.

Kayra gagged "Why does it have to make that noise?"

"You said something about containment?" Toran called to Fibble.

"Yuhr not goin' anywhur!" Saigel yelled. He had not left the coffin. "We're keepin' yuh right 'ere whur we already got yuh!"

At the minikin's voice, Mirzog stopped and redirected its convulsive movement back to the center of the chamber. Its eyes of fire were the first things to make the turnaround. It glared at Saigel while the rancid smoke and the rest of its body noisily twisted around the iron bars and back into its larger goblin shape.

"'Cause demon or not, yuh still got a gob brain 'tween yuhr ears. And they like thur shineys!" Saigel looked at the demon. "Don't ya?"

Why is it so cautious? Toran wondered.

A plume of green smoke reached out to Saigel, but he put something in front of him that caused it to move back and dissipate. He was holding the twelfth iron bar from the broken gate.

"Gunna make yuh play fair, Mirzog." Saigel continued to taunt him. "Toran, I'd be barrin' that gate 'bout now. Fibble says iron constrains demons. This 'ole sparklin' place is doin' just that, with that 'ception."

Toran immediately conjured a sphere that encompassed the eleven bars inside the demon and extracted them from its body while Mirzog lunged for Saigel. The painful extraction paused the beast, which roared in pain, allowing enough time for the minikin to defend himself. When the demon's claws scratched at him, they were knocked away by the last piece of the gate in the minikin's hands.

Toran suspended the iron bars in the air instead of forcing them into the entrance's stones. If he had sealed the demon in, that would have left them in there with it. He created another globe and expanded it across the room to find Fibble. *If it cannot heal, will iron kill it?* he asked the confused dwarf.

From across the room, he heard, "Yes, I believe so." The same mental answer came from within the sphere.

The demon was still on the main floor and preoccupied enough with Saigel's continued taunting that Toran felt it was safe enough to forego holding the bars in place. He let them fall noisily to the ground and expanded the sphere he had contacted Fibble with. The sphere soon engulfed the entire room. While Saigel started to protest about the exit not being blocked, Toran expanded this sphere even farther outward. It continued to grow larger until, within it, he saw the tree line outside far above him.

The idea had come from another one of his dreams: his training session with Higoshi while he was unconscious at William's home. He did not need very much wind. Even a small breeze would suffice for his purpose. He caught what he needed and contracted the sphere back down with its center on Mirzog, but most of the tomb was still inside it. He did not realize how quickly he had done it, for Saigel was still telling him that he needed to block the exit.

Within the globe, he caused the wind to swirl. The demon did not even notice until the velocity of the wind increased. It pulled the putrid green smoke away from the demon. When the wind was swirling fast enough, he formed a vortex to draw it away even farther. Mirzog tried swiping at the gale around it, but to no avail. In these fits of turning and swatting, it saw what else was happening. Toran had lifted all of the fallen iron bars and had hurled them back at the unprotected demon, giving it barely enough time to dodge all of them except one. The demon caught that one iron bar, and the rest of them ended up stuck in the wall farthest from Toran.

Its hand was severely scorched by the contact with the toxic metal, but it launched it back at the trouble-making human. Toran conjured a sphere to intercept and halt the missile in midair, well before it reached him but not before a separate searing sensation tore through the back of the demon's skull.

Saigel had climbed up to the rim of the sarcophagus. After several balanced running steps, he had jumped from the edge of it with a slight boost from the swirling vortex of wind from the sphere he entered, which he could not even see. There was a brief flash of bright light, just before he skewered Mirzog with an upward motion, from the base of its skull to its brain. Then he set his little feet on the middle of the demon's back and pulled upward, bringing his weapon out of its skull, right between its fiery black eyes. "Guess whut elseses made of iron?"

With the putrid healing smoke held at bay by the wind of Toran's vortex, Saigel's usually hidden magic scimitar (the weapon that Mirzog had lost when it was alive and in true goblin form) launched an unstoppable flame that coursed through the demon from its head down through its whole body, until there was nothing left behind but ash. Saigel landed on the floor, and the light of the scimitar faded slightly before he returned it to his back, and it disappeared from sight. Everyone sighed in relief, Toran released his sphere, and silence settled around the group.

Saigel climbed the stairs to join Fibble and his friend. When Thom had hit the wall, many of his possessions had been jarred loose from him, and the dwarf was gathering them together. Saigel was almost to the top of the ziggurat when he had bent down and picked up something. He said, "Looks like it tried ta git away. He gunna be okay?"

Saigel handed Fibble a small pouch. It sounded like it contained a fair amount of finance. Fibble accepted the pouch with a smile and nodded back at him. Suddenly, before the dwarf could answer the question, Thom awoke with a gasp. He panicked and tried to free himself from the wall. Fibble calmed the alarmed man's overreaction and helped him down. Thom looked around for Mirzog, but Fibble and Saigel had to explain to him, twice, that the demon had gone and would not be returning.

When they were all at the top of the spiral stairs that had led to the tomb, Kellik said, "That's twice you have bested Mirzog: as a goblin and as a demon. I'll bet it wants nothing more to do with you."

Saigel shrugged and replied, "Couldn't 'ave duhn it muhself. Let's git outta here."

"Thomas and I will be staying. Once we adjourn to allow his head to cease its pounding, we still have exploration to do."

"GodsLight to you both," Toran offered.

"And to all of you!"

CHAPTER 15 

INTO THE FIRE

Crickets chirped in the night air around them while the moon cast a silent, pale reflection on the lake. Orange firelight illuminated the surrounding trees. Four men were relaxing around a fire and cooking two meaty rabbits as their shadows danced among the branches of the same trees. These men had done what they had been ordered to do. They had followed their quarries nearly a day after climbing out from the rift created by the groundshake.

A problem now presented itself, and Seane was relaying that problem to their employer. *They just vanished in front of our eyes.* William listened to the report from Seane. *We followed them to the lake. They bathed, got dressed, and when they started on their way, they just disappeared.*

William's eyes were closed, and his pale-blue sphere was extended outward to Seane for this mental conversation. This was a secondary Merea skill that he had discovered was quite useful—and from what he had learned over the revolutions, it was the most common untrained talent—when speaking with people who were far away. The extended conversations could always be used to estimate how far away his target was, but a direction never seemed to accompany this conclusion unless the one at the sphere's reach was also talented.

There was no magic? William projected to Seane's mind.

Nothing. They were walking beyond the lake, and then they were gone, Sean responded.

Search the area again. I will contact you next day so that I may displace myself to you. William, sitting comfortably in his home, discontinued his conversation with Seane. The other had no Merea, and William did know where they were approximately, but the attempt to travel to them was going to be precarious. Displacing one's self without a personal knowledge of where one was appearing was not ordinarily done. For magicians who did not have precise locations documented and memorized, shifting was impossible.

The difference with Merea was that when someone used spheres, controlled them, and had a firm familiarity with the target, it was possible to use a person for displacement. He knew and trusted that Seane could get an accurate description around him so that he could visualize and attempt this. However, it was still reckless and only done in emergencies.

He cleared his blue sphere and refocused it out as far as he was able. First, he focused on Toran but expected not to find him. When he had first realized that the man who had almost killed him many revolutions ago had been thrust into his retired life, knowing Toran definitely was a trained talent, he had tried to find him but had had no success, as with this time. It was feasible that the other had recognized William and that he now protected his mind from being perceived or communicated with. Then again, as best as he could recall, Toran had not known about his talents—and he would have no reason to know. Still, there had to be a reason why he could not be found.

Then he changed his focus to Kellik and found him quickly. He was a couple hundred miles away. He did not want to converse with Kellik but only wanted to know the distance. He did not know the elf very well. He had met him, and he could plausibly visualize him well enough to gather his surroundings and appear in front of him, but it was far more reliable to do so with Seane. For the time being, he was operating to keep his involvement a secret.

Without a direction to follow, the number of miles was useless information to him. He stood and paced back and forth in his library as he thought about where they could be. The library's extensive collection had hundreds of books and a wide range of subjects. William fancied himself a collector. He engaged in many interests, with one unfortunate exception in this case: geology.

Not one of his many books had any maps, especially not maps of the area. He decided that he would start to procure them. Aamber's library would not be open for hours. As an idea struck him, he suddenly checked his pacing and left his home.

The rain clouds had not yet reached Aamber. They probably would not arrive until the following day. He walked casually through the streets until he arrived at and entered an inn called the Sleeping Lyon. He knew that even at this late hour, his best men were following him so that they could protect him.

While most of the buildings in Aamber were crowded together and had multiple levels, the Sleeping Lyon was by itself, was on a corner, and only had one level. It was a large building with a double-door entry. At one time, it had been an expensive home with many rooms, but a few revolutions back, the owner had converted it to an inn after a fever had taken his family. William had financed the renovations when the owner had lost all of his holdings, several revolutions after that.

He saw that several patrons had not made it to their respective rooms. Some had passed out near the doorway, and several were lying near the dwindling fire.

Once inside, he nodded to the owner, who was straightening the taproom, and proceeded farther into the inn. He stopped at one of the rooms and entered.

After closing the door, William brought out a small green crystal that was three inches long and held it in both hands. This gem was a gift given to him by an old friend long ago. He whispered something, and the stone began to glow. A pale-green light filled the room. He broke the crystal, and then the glow disappeared. He placed the pieces into his pocket, sat down on the bed in the dark, and waited.

"It has been a long time," he whispered to himself. "I am not even sure you are still alive, but I need your magical assistance, old friend." He did not have to wait long.

A masculine voice, which was strange yet familiar, addressed him from behind. "I have come because you are an old friend, but I fear our views are different now, and I may not be able to help."

"It is enough that you came at all." William turned around and smiled at the man who was standing in the shadows of the darkened room.

"How may I help you?" the man said.

"I need to locate someone," William answered as he stood.

"You need to locate someone," the voice said. "I need to know for what purpose."

"It is a small group. Their lives may be in danger. I need to help them."

"Help? You want to help?" the man in the darkness mocked him. "What do you have to gain from the help you are affording?"

"I have mellowed with age, Alistar, and not everything I do needs to gain me something in return."

Alistar moved slightly out of the shadows, but William could still only vaguely see his face. "Do you gain from helping them?"

"Yes. The satisfaction of forgiving someone who caused me a great deal of pain many revolutions ago. He is in a dangerous predicament with an adversary he may not be prepared for. I would do what I could to lessen the danger."

"Then why all of this darkness?" The room erupted with light. Alistar stood before him in a fancy red robe, which William could have sworn was glowing. "It seems I have been meeting all of my old friends lately. First Frederick and now you."

"Ordinarily I would inquire about old friends and how they are doing, but there are four people in danger of walking into a trap."

"Please describe them. I will need as much information as you can give me."

"An interesting group actually. A pair of humans: one male, the other female. An elf and a minikin. The human is called—"

"Wait. Does the elf have a falcon?" Alistar said.

"Yes, his name is ..."

"Kellik," they echoed each other.

"I have met, and more pointedly, I have saved these fellows from a group of trolls while they were in the marshes, except for the woman. I have not met her."

"Can you locate them?"

"Of course." Alistar produced a small silver mirror and a tiny bag from one of his pockets. He set the mirror upon a dresser and from the second item, collected a pinch of fine powder made from glass. Then Alistar waved one hand as the other sprinkled powder over the mirror, and it reflected an image other than his own, but the picture was gray and showed him nothing.

"Now that is odd," he remarked.

"Odd? What do you mean?"

"I tried the leader of the group, Toran. I do not believe he likes me much. Do you know him?"

"We are acquainted."

"I get nothing with him as the source of my display. Let me try my favorite little friend and see what I can find." The picture brightened to life, and he watched. Saigel and the red-haired woman that he had been told about but did not recognize appeared to be in a small village in the middle of the day. "It is day. They are in a small, deserted village."

"How can that be?" William mused. "Daylight passed hours ago, and they are only about two hundred fifty miles away, by my calculation."

Considering this, Alistar forced the scene to pan back and forth. Then, suddenly, the mirror went dark. "Wait, what is this?" It was not a natural darkness, as if he was losing the display. He could feel the display still under his control. He should see either gray from something blocking his effect or himself reflected in the mirror, which would indicate that the magic had run its course. He swept the vision back to the village scene.

"Interesting," he said. He adjusted the picture into the darkness again, this time upward, and continued until he saw a dark sky and a mountainside ledge with a large cave opening. "Here we are. They are in the mountains. The village scene must be an elaborate illusion."

"But where are they?"

The mirror's image turned toward the sky as Alistar commanded it to, and he studied the stars. Then he went to the window, and the light in the room diminished. "By the stars, they should be somewhere in the mountains south by east from here."

"This is part of a trap! I assure you of this, and I need to get my men there to help them," William said as the light of the room brightened again. "May I ask one more favor?"

"You need to be shifted to the mountains," Alistar said knowingly.

"No. Although I will need directions that are as close to the location as you can give me. The other favor I ask is that you get me to my men who are east of Jenerv. I can get to the mountains from there. I am sure you have other business to attend to."

"I have a newly invested interest in what I am finding to be a most popular association of people, so if you will have me, I will accompany you along the way."

William described Seane well enough so that Alistar had a clear picture of him in his mirror. From there, Alistar studied and memorized the surrounding area so that he could channel a shift there.

Paul was playing his lute when the two arrived suddenly but did not seem surprised by their appearance. He stopped playing and started waking the others.

"We have little time. The trap has been set in motion," Paul told William.

"How do you know?" William asked, but Paul gave no reply as he continued his task.

When everyone was ready to go, Alistar gathered them all around him. A whispered phrase and a circular arm gesture completed the requirements, and the channelled shift to the village was enacted. The magic user felt the energy course through him, but there was no display from the effect.

They had not moved.

"Bah! I should have known!" Alistar exclaimed.

"What is wrong?"

"There is only one possibility," Alistar said. "I felt the energy channel, but we obviously did not shift because I did channel successfully."

"We are in a hurry here, Alistar," William pointed out.

"Sorry. The village scene is an illusion that does not exist. Memorizing that area served no purpose. I will not be able to shift there."

"Now what?" Seane asked.

"We must fly," Alistar answered.

"That will take too long," William said, aggravated. "We can not help them."

"Not as long as you might think. Give me a moment." Alistar searched his pockets. He pulled out one feather for each of them and a piece of string, which he used to tie them together. When he was finished, he asked everyone to move close to him. He put his hands out with the thumbs crossed together in front of him with the tied feathers between them and started flapping his fingers like wings. When the channelled display commenced, they faded away to almost transparent outlines of their previous forms. Like living ghosts, they began to float gently into the air.

Seane panicked. "What is happening?"

"I have no time for explanations, as William has said. In this form, I can move at a very substantial speed on my own, but with the combined thoughts from all of us, we can move faster than that. We can increase our rate tenfold. All you need to do is think about the direction that I begin us in, and whenever I change direction, concentrate on following me."

They started slowly, with Alistar giving instruction and assuring them that they were not going to fall. They rose above the tree line. Once they began moving fluidly and imagining Alistar's direction, they moved so fast that, had they not been mostly transparent, they would not have been seen by anyone viewing them in the moonlit sky.

The sun was high in the sky, but a cover of trees granted them shade. The trees gave way to an open clearing, and Kellik, with Tempest on his shoulder, Toran, Saigel, and Kayra saw a small village ahead.

They all had felt the temperature drop some time ago and had attributed it to the canopy above them. However, none of them realized that the lake, which should still be visible behind them, had been gone for the same length of time.

There were several huts with a single path going through the middle of them. Toran was in the lead with Kayra just behind him. Kellik and Saigel checked out several of the dwellings and were about twenty feet behind the other two.

"This village is abandoned. I wonder where everybody went." Kellik remarked.

"I don't 'member this bein' here," Saigel said.

"Has anyone else noticed that the sun has not moved since we left the lake?" Toran continued to look up at the sky as he walked down the empty path. Then he walked into something hard, even though there was nothing there. The others approached him as he stepped back and inspected what appeared to be a clear path through the village. When he reached out in front of him, his hand felt cold rock.

"Weapons!" he ordered. "This is a trap." The others obeyed, and Toran moved back to Kayra and put his hand on her shoulder. "Stay with me."

"I will," she replied.

Toran felt her shoulder grow and its texture change. He turned around to face her as her skin started to take on the same deep red hue as her hair. Scales began to form over her body, and her hair shrunk away as she grew larger and larger. Her clothing ripped and fell from her body. Soon she was a full-sized and completely red dragon.

While Toran got ready to protect himself from the dragon, he felt six sharp pains at his back. He collapsed to the ground, unconscious.

Saigel watched the magical arrows hit Toran and looked to the source as a burst of loud and deep laughter filled the village scene.

He could not tell where the attack had originated. Then the scene disappeared and revealed a familiar cave. The pile of treasure along the far wall had diminished. Now that the illusion was gone, he could see the path through the deserted village they were following had been perfectly formed to disguise their way through the caves. There had been no interruption until Toran had walked into the side of the cave while believing to be in the middle of a village clearing.

The dragon turned away from Toran's unmoving body. "Do not move!" she commanded them.

Kellik and Saigel stood motionless. "Weren't thur two exits to this place?" Saigel asked.

"Yes, but I see that there are none now," Kellik said as he indicated the way they had come.

"Every exodus has been obstructed!" Enrandl's voice boomed through the cave, "No outlet exists for liberation!"

"Where is my treasure?" Kayrahawkatzeena asked.

"What little we took, we spent," Kellik answered. "There was still a great hoard of treasure here when we left."

Enrandl became visible and strode toward them. "What little we took, we spent," Enrandl mimicked. "Your conviction to that veracity supplies commendation. A deviation from insight is evidentiary to a possession of mine. Conceivably, a persuasion of my associate for your lives' forbearance should its recovery be actuated," he said, holding out his hand.

"I got it in muh pack," Saigel revealed as he reached back. "Come 'ere, an' I'll give it—"

"No! Do not move." The dragon brought her tail around from behind her and snapped it above Saigel's head.

"Temper your disposition, my crimson-scaled companion. Whatever is the dilemma?"

"There will be no tricks, little one. Kellik has the book."

"Kellik, is it? Such a complimentary bestowing of acquaintance." Enrandl's hand moved toward the elf as he removed his pack and produced the book from inside of it. Saigel watched the magician's eyes glow as the book he had sought was removed. The same eyes became surprised as the book flew across the room.

Kellik dived and rolled away to give himself space and time to draw both of his longswords. The dragon came at him quickly, allowing him barely enough time, but Saigel remembered Kellik's story. He knew his friend had experienced her agility and would have given himself plenty of time before the dragon would be upon him. Sure enough, he parried her claw attacks and ran underneath her before she could crane her neck down to bite him.

Enrandl ran off to retrieve the book. Saigel drew his scimitar and pursued. He caught up to the magician as he bent over to pick up the book and cut his weapon across Enrandl's left calf. This strike did not cut his leg, but Saigel was happy that its force was enough to at least topple him. Enrandl fell to the ground and rolled onto his back with the book in his left hand. Saigel was trying to reclaim it when he noticed something at the magician's neck. He was wearing two different necklaces: one beaded and the other a gold chain with a simple talisman on it. Saigel concentrated on the one that caught his eye—the one with a simple charm hanging from it.

It must have fallen out when Enrandl fell because Saigel recognized it as soon as he saw it. It had not been there when the fight had started. Anger coursed through Saigel, and his scimitar was quickly at the fallen man's throat (the book was forgotten).

"Whur'd yuh get that symbol?" Saigel demanded.

Enrandl looked surprised by the question, but the minikin did not care. "What?"

Saigel grabbed the necklace and tore it from Enrandl's neck. "Thuh charm on this necklace. 'Twas muh society's symbol. Whur'd yuh get it?"

"A trinket of my mentor. Its embellishment entertained me. His departure from existence yielded a transition of possession."

Saigel, being preoccupied with his interrogation, did not notice Enrandl removing something from one of his robe's pockets. He wanted to exert revolutions worth of pent up anger on this villain, so instead of merely cutting across his neck with his weapon, he raised it to decapitate him.

Before he could achieve this goal, Enrandl swung the book at him. Saigel lost his balance, and Enrandl hurriedly pushed him off and away. He saw the human roll even farther away from him, stand, and throw a white pearl at his feet. Where it shattered, a thick cloud of billowing, white smoke issued forth. Saigel charged into the smoke after he recovered his balance. His sword cut through the smoke aimlessly. When he appeared on the other side of the cloud, he had contacted nothing.

The smoke dissipated, and Enrandl was gone.

Across the cave, Kellik and his dragon opponent, who was now several times larger in her dragon form than he was, repeatedly exchanged blows. The creature could not seem to connect her attacks against his defense, and he continued to make no offensive movements. Kellik was staying within his defensive mode for his own reasons, and she was actually making it easy for him. All of her attacks were from claws and bites. Her tail remained behind her. Her talons and bites came predictably one after another, and they were easy enough to dodge or shunt aside with his swords. More importantly, she did not breathe her dragonfire. Whatever reason she had for not doing so, he was still waiting for the flames.

They both heard Saigel call from across the room that Enrandl had escaped, and they slowed their combat down. Saigel relayed the fact that the book had gone with him. The information had been directed at Kellik, but there was little chance of the beast not hearing him also, and the dragon ceased her attacks.

"He has taken my treasure?" Her question was roared. She acted like she was ignoring the elf until he rested and lowered his sword. He paid for this mistake as her powerful claw knocked him nearly halfway across the cave. Then she turned on Saigel. "I will have justice on the two of you, and then I will deal with that traitorous man."

She inhaled deeply and prepared to breathe her fiery death at the minikin when the sound of sweet music reached her ears. Saigel looked around as if he heard the tune but did not know where it was coming from. The song struck her deep inside as it had when she had first heard it. Suddenly, she found herself back in the tavern dancing with Toran. She recalled every move and every note and chord that had been played. The music continued while she relived the whole dance in just a few moments. She slowly exhaled without fire and followed the musically induced memory.

The enormous red form moved to where Toran lay unconscious and stared at him. She wondered why this human brought out her strange behavior, and what the source of the music was.

Kellik, who had been making his way back across the cave, and Saigel listened and watched in amazement as the dragon curled up around their friend while the music played on. Kellik no longer cared where the music was coming from because it was keeping the dragon calm. He decided to use it to his advantage and approached her cautiously.

"Excuse me, but why do you want justice against us?" Kellik asked politely.

"Foolish elf, you do not even realize who I am or where you are, do you?"

"I do know where we are, and we thought we killed you."

"Then you know why I desire justice."

"No, I don't. We were defending ourselves with no other choices but to fight or to die. There is no justice for you to gain."

"You prove nothing to me, elf!" The dragon growled at him and then again calmed down.

"You can't gain justice against us for something we had no control over."

"You stole my treasure."

"Had we known you still lived; we wouldn't have taken any of the treasure." Kellik paused but then was quick to add, "We would have been too fearful that you would wake up and come after us before we could gather any of it."

"You have no way to prove your honesty," she said, but Kellik could tell that his logic was getting through.

This occurrence overshadowed his general acceptance by primary animal life, but he was sure that reasoning more than empathy was working to his advantage here. They would have been fearful of her, and they all knew it. She had to know that their previous confrontation had been forced on them by the trap she had designed—and that she would have done the same thing in their place. He understood that the dragon was still looking for an excuse to exact her revenge on them, and he needed to redirect that search.

Saigel spoke up. "How 'bout Enrandl? He stole yuhr book, and 'e knew you're alive."

"He's been trying to get that book from us for some time now," Kellik added, "If justice is what you desire the target of your justice should be aimed at him." When Kellik finished, the dragon stayed silent.

"We want to stop Enrandl, but we do not know what he is planning to do." Kellik paused to let the dragon intervene. When she did not, he continued. "Do you know what he may be planning?"

"He has not revealed any plans other than trying to get something from Toran. He is far too single minded to plan anything beyond getting that."

Her belief contradicted what Toran believed of the magician, and Kellik quickly commented, "But he didn't get anything from Toran,"

"And 'e did take thuh book," Saigel added.

"Then it is possible," Kellik said carefully, speaking to Saigel, "Enrandl used Kayra to get the book from us."

Kayrahawkatzeena knew Kellik's words to be accurate, but she saw through his ploy. "I have been conned into helping a human before, very recently. I will not be deceived again." The music that still played softened the fierceness of her words unintentionally.

"We would not dream of any deception." Kellik looked over at Toran. "First of all, we must see what is wrong with him."

"He was hit by Enrandl's magic. I can hear his breathing, and it is steady. He will survive."

"Then where do we go?" Saigel asked.

Kayrahawkatzeena looked down at Saigel and remembered how the minikin had hurt her in their earlier battle. She now knew the secret of his magical scimitar and wondered if that scimitar could hurt Enrandl as much as it had hurt her. She decided that picturing her claws tearing the magician apart was preferable. What amazed her was that she had not given away Saigel's secret to the magician when she had had the chance. The minikin had reached for the scimitar, saying he was going to get the book, but she had only told him not to move.

"You can accompany me to Jenerv where he has a permanent place to stay."

"You know where it is?" Kellik looked at Saigel and then to the dragon for her answer.

"I do," she replied.

"But how do we get you into the city like this?" Kellik wondered aloud.

"His dwelling will burn, and I will tear him apart! My form does not matter."

"But if you attack in this form, you'll be fighting more than just him. You'll have most of the city to contend with. Don't you see the problem with that?"

"Are you suggesting that I become human again? Even if I had the ability, I have found that your small forms are far too mortal for my comfort. I will never submit myself to that again."

"I may be able to help with that." Across the cave, Alistar walked through what appeared to be a stone wall and approached the group. He was followed shortly by Seane, William, Paul, and two more of William's guards. The bard halted his song as they walked forward.

"Alistar? How did you find us here?" Kellik looked utterly confused.

"You seem to have attracted quite a following of concerned people." He stopped and waited for William to catch up with him.

"Not again. We tried to get your money for you, but Enrandl cut us short. What more can we do?"

Alistar looked wickedly at William.

"No, you wrong me. I have not come for those reasons. I am now here to help." Toran stirred as William finished.

When Toran opened his eyes and saw nothing but the enormous red dragon curled around him, he yelled and clambered over her tail and away from her, trying to make enough room to draw his weapon. Saigel rushed to his side and stopped him. "No. It's okay. She's with us." His eyes looked up hopefully.

"More pointedly, you are with me," Kayrahawkatzeena corrected him.

"What is going on?" Toran asked.

"Enrandl has the book. He was associated with Kayra," Kellik said as he gestured to the dragon. "He lied and used her to get it. She knows where he is, and now she is going to help us find him."

"What now? Where do we go from here?" Toran asked. He looked at what was once a beautiful woman, in his opinion, although his hand never left his sword. He could still barely believe that Kayra had transitioned to this enormous creature right before him.

"Maybe Alistar and William can figure that out," Kellik offered.

Toran's surroundings were still not clear to him, for his attention was fixated upon the dragon. The fact that the people whom Kellik had mentioned were standing behind him had not yet registered. "William? Sagemont? We cannot trust him! He wants to kill me!"

"I am wronged again," William defended himself.

Hearing the man's voice, Toran spun to face him with his sword drawn, while Alistar gave William an angry glare. The elder's guards were quick to respond and blocked Toran from their employer, who shouted, "No! Sheath your weapons. I have forgiven you, Toran. Please believe me. I wish only to help if I can."

Toran wanted to argue. While William's men backed down at his command, Toran noted Alistar's residual stare. There was something there he did not understand, and because of this, his confusion about Kayra being a dragon instead of a woman—and the haze that was leftover from his unconsciousness—he could not find an appropriate argument.

He could easily have used Merea to find the older man's intentions, but he decided to take William at his word. "If Enrandl has the book and what Alistar has told us is true, we have to get it back. We have no idea what he may be planning."

Alistar said, "We still have some time. There will need to be time for reading the book and setting up a preservation for it."

"A preservation?" Kellik asked.

"Yes. The book must be read thoroughly and then placed where it will not be disturbed. Only then can its magic be used."

"What if the book is disturbed?" William asked.

"As long as the book remains within its preservation area, there is no problem, but if it is removed from there, all channelling aptitude is lost."

"Lost?" everyone but Alistar repeated.

"The aptitude to channel would be gone, yes."

"Then that person couldn't use the magic of the book again," Kellik assumed.

"There would be no purpose. The book's magic allows unlimited channelling of the source, so without that ability, like I said, it would have no purpose."

"You said you fashioned the book. Why did you never use it?" Toran asked.

"I did."

"But yuh lost it, and yuh still do magic," Saigel said.

"Ah, my little friend, you see, that is the mystery. In fact, my magic is unique. I found that the lack of access was not entirely permanent. The energy merely progresses differently now. After several revolutions of determined experimentation, I was able to channel again, but with the new process, I needed to rework every effect."

"Improving some of them in the process," Toran added, remembering the recent experience in the swamp, of being caught inside an explosion of Alistar's flashfire that should have affected everyone in range of the display, but instead, had only burned trolls in that area.

"I still had all my knowledge, but channelling would no longer function for me. I could still feel the energy. I was resolute to create another style and, in a few instances, correct the effects and improve some of the drawbacks within them."

"How long did that take you?" William asked.

Alistar replied, "Too much time and too many changes. I am not the same man you once knew."

"And all of your magic is custom made, based on how it was channelled before," William reasoned.

"Correct. That is why I say my magic is unique."

Toran asked, "So how did you lose the book?"

"I can only guess that it was stolen. When I awoke one morning, I found my ability gone, and instantaneously, I knew why."

"And if you created it, why did you include such a terrible consequence?" Toran continued his questioning.

"Another mystery. It was certainly not intended on my part. An error during the creation may have created that curse. It may even have been The Gods' Right Hand."

"Then we just need to find out where he keeps it?" Toran asked.

"He will not know about the curse. I created the artifact, and I had no idea that it was cursed. He could keep it someplace simple, as it just needs a dedicated area."

"You do not know Enrandl. It will be somewhere that is grand," Toran replied.

"I could scry upon it, but he will know you are coming after it and will have found a protection for it."

"But 'e thinks we're dead. Killed by her." Saigel pointed up at the dragon.

Alistar reached into his robe and produced his mirror and bag for scrying, and as he predicted, magic already protected its location.

"We will find him in Jenerv. A good place to start," William offered.

"What about Kayra?" Kellik asked.

"Yes, that is where this whole conversation started. Well, she would be rather hard to get through a city gate. She could go over it conceivably, but oh, the commotion and panic she would cause. All I can do at the moment is to diminish her and make her look like a fire lizard."

"How long would I be diminished?" The dragon looked directly at Alistar.

"About a day or so or until I cancel the effect."

"That will be fine," she said.

Alistar heard reluctance evident in her tone and said, "I must return home. You should all get some rest. I will be back in the morning." He turned to the dragon. "But first, for you, I could make you human again … or we can proceed with the diminishing."

With a subtle sideways glance at Toran, she again flatly declined the desire to be human. Assuming this would be the case after hearing the previous conversation, Alistar already had two small black statuettes in his hand. One was somewhat larger than the other one was. He made a fist, shook his hand next to his ear, and heard them clicking together. Then he moved the smaller icon to his other hand and made fists with both hands.

There was a shattering sound. When he opened the side holding the larger of the two pieces, only black dust remained. He blew the powder out of his hand at the dragon. As the airborne dust shimmered and expanded to embrace her, she began shrinking, which continued until she was only two feet tall, with an extra foot of tail behind her.

"I must go now and will return soon." Alistar channelled his shift, and with a brief flash of light, he vanished.

"I just never understood why." William said, "Why you would want to steal from me when I would have given you anything?"

He and William had separated from the group, but Toran discerned the watching presence of his friends, who were still not convinced of the older man's intentions. "Until I saw you, I did not know it was your home being robbed," Toran said, "and Conrad had just wanted my help on the contract."

"Someone hired him to steal the amulet."

He understood from William's tone that it was not a question as much as a fact, but he answered it for clarity. "Yes."

"I only recall one person who knew that I owned that," William said. "I spent many cycles recovering from the wounds you gave me, and not just the physical ones. I loved you as if you were my own son, and at least now, I know it was not a deliberate attack against me. Not by you anyway. What did happen to it?"

"I never knew who hired Conrad so I could not take it to him, and it was too much burden for me to bear."

"I am sure." William put his hand on Toran's shoulder. "I have forgiven you, Toran. Of that, you can be certain, and you have also given me somewhere else to turn my anger."

CHAPTER 16

ASCENSION

The search was finally over.

Enrandl sat cross-legged in the middle of the old ceremonial chamber of Frederick's temple. It was the same room in which he had discovered the book had actually existed, and this time, it was his.

The chamber decorations were mostly the same way that he had left them a few cycles ago, but he recently made two alterations to the chamber's appearance. Numerous books were now scattered amid the candles that circled the floor. They were study books that held the secrets and incantations of how to channel each of the effects that he knew. All of them would be infinitely accessible when he was finished with his project.

He did not require the presence of any of them for him to command the power he was about to obtain. Knowledge of an effect's formula was all he would need, but he liked the idea of them all being there.

The candles burned warm and bright. The prize possession, which had been so troublesome to possess, was on his lap. Its aged cover was open, revealing its immaculate pages, which Enrandl now began to read.

The second alteration was a small shrine in front of him. It was a place for the book to rest on when he had concluded the reading. The shrine now began to glow with violet light. Soon afterward, the candle's light phased into the same violet hue, giving the room a dark and eerie tone. This adjustment of lighting did not bother his progress.

It was a day's worth of reading later, and he had not taken a break to eat or to rest. The book had begun to glow as Enrandl turned to the last page. When he completed reading it, the book lifted from his lap into the air, closed itself, and drifted to the glowing platform. It settled there, the purple light from both disappeared, and the candles returned to their usual tint. His preservation was complete. Enrandl stood, brushed his long black hair out of his eyes, and smiled as he looked around the chamber at the several books that were there.

He left the room, closed its heavy door, and traced the line between the two doors with his left index finger. He then placed his hands upon the door handles and manipulated them to lock. Each door was outlined magically, and when done, Enrandl walked away. He left the temple and returned to his school.

None of his current students was around because he had given everyone the day off. He went to his bedchamber and lay down, seeking the rest he knew that he needed. It was no use because a particular idea occurred to him, and it would not be deterred.

An hour later, Aamber's lamp-lit cobblestone streets clicked under his hard boots. The summer's night air was warm but comfortable, and Enrandl strode through the small town as if he was flying. He could feel the enormous quantity of magical energy that flowed around and coursed through him, as if he was the pawn of the channelling. However, he knew that it was all there for him to command.

The few people he met along the way to his destination greeted him with a smile that was equal to his own, but he ignored them. The source of his smile was from his knowledge that he was indeed truly invincible. Before he had left his home, he had embedded several magics upon himself, to make him further so.

None of these puny townspeople could come close to matching the power that he now held, and it was actually a challenge for him not to destroy everything in sight. His control surprised himself, but he had many things to do back in Jenerv and one little loose end here in Aamber to tighten up. His destination was a small bookmaker's shop. Nothing would be destroyed until he got there.

He found the shop, and it was currently closed. He stood across the road, allowing a wagon to pass in front of him before he moved his hand to begin the channelling motion of his effect. The flashfire exploded inside, and the walls of the small shop blew outward. Books and papers flew in all directions, and fire erupted from within.

"Open but vocation is invalid!" Enrandl yelled. Then he laughed uncontrollably as he watched the flames quickly spread to the next shop. It also caught on fire. The magic user reached into one of his pockets and produced two sticks. He promptly started rubbing them together and blowing gently across the top of them for his channel. As he did this, the smoke and flames from the burning buildings multiplied. The display resulted in a fire so out of control that even with all the new power he commanded, Enrandl himself might have had a stressful time putting it out. At this, Enrandl laughed even harder, uncontrollably adding a harsher, shriller tone.

Michael came running around the corner. Until he saw the burning buildings, he did not know that it was his shop and surrounding ones that were burning. Through all of the pandemonium, he heard the laughter. It persisted over the frenzy of people running for water to douse the flames and women screaming. Nothing drowned it out. He looked around for the source, and when he saw Enrandl, he knew why he had come. He also knew that the magician would not stop at the destruction of his shop. Unfortunately, Enrandl had also seen him. Michael turned to run.

"Your expeditious retreat precipitates my resolution," Enrandl said quietly to himself and pointed his finger at Michael. His aura poured out the magic so easily through him that he wondered if he had actually channelled. He thought that the mere thought of wanting had been enough to cause the effect to display. Further experimentation of this concept in the future was in order.

As Michael continued to run, his limbs slowed down. Then he had problems even getting them to move. Soon he could not move at all, and try as he might, the muscles in his body would not budge. Though movement appeared impossible, feeling and thought were not. He had a feeling of dread regarding something that he assumed was coming. It was walking through the chaos of people scrambling this way and that. He knew that horrible man was approaching him.

Powerless to prevent it, he felt a hand placed on his shoulder, and instantly, the chaos of the crowd was gone. He was in a quiet alley that looked familiar, although Michael could not remember the reason why. Then Enrandl was standing in front of him, staring with his kind gray eyes, and smiling at him. He tried to smile back, but not a single muscle would move.

"Deliberation regarding your predestination might conclude you fortunate. A fiery demise among your elected vocation implored opportunity." Enrandl turned away from him. "That conclusion would be inaccurate. Elucidate me a solution. We experienced an equivalent proximity some evenings ago. Sauntered this precise lane, concurrently, though not collectively." Enrandl spun around to face him again. "Your discretion of my observant gait was ignorant. What intention was concluded hereabouts?"

Although he could not move his lips to speak, he would not have been able to answer anyway because he did not know. He had fallen asleep there—exactly as Enrandl had. If he had been able to speak, he could have told him about his conversation with William Sagemont when he had awakened. Was that what the magician wanted to know?

"Your resolution to my query determines your providence." Enrandl produced an ornate dagger from under his robe. "A thrice of indication seems appropriate. One."

The paralyzed man struggled to speak as Enrandl moved behind him. "Two."

He thought a mumble of muffled word had escaped his throat, but he was mistaken. Enrandl held the blade of the dagger to his soundless throat.

"Three."

Enrandl used the dagger to cut the man from ear to ear, and then he walked away. Michael stood paralyzed as his blood spilled down his shirt. "I venture the absence of utility subjects interest." The lifeless body collapsed when the effect's display was released.

Using his normal hand motions to channel, Enrandl shifted back to Jenerv. There were exploits to be accomplished in his home city. While he had strolled through the streets of Aamber that evening, he had decided that his school was too small and that something of a grander fashion and scale was in better accordance with him now. Of course, he would still need the underground link to Frederick's temple, which was miles away.

Then he wondered why and considered the underground link to the temple for a moment. Since he could merely shift to the book's chamber whenever he needed to, he wondered why he needed a tunnel. He decided that he did not like the idea of shifting there for one main reason. If he could do so, then others would be able to do so too. That room was going to need stronger protections to prevent such things from happening. In any case, secrets and hidden passages fascinated him, and he decided to leave it, regardless.

He walked into the street while not caring about what was going on around him. He was nearly run over by a horse-drawn wagon. The driver barely managed to dodge him. He turned back to his home and started a channelling. For this, he picked up some dust and brought out a vial that did not appear until he reached for it. He put a couple of drops of the liquid in his left hand and mixed it with the dust. Then he put the vial back into the invisible pocket. He stirred the combination with his pinkie finger and then held out his hand.

The building in front of him grew and changed. A crowd gathered around as he stood there for the rest of the afternoon, channelling endlessly until his new home was complete.

He was not aware that some of the more powerful magic users in Jenerv were watching him perform this overwhelming feat of talent. He was equally unaware, although he already believed it, that all had decided that they would not want to be opposite him in battle.

Once done, he discovered that a small group of the city's militia had approached him. He said, "Ah, I was challenging your alacrity of representation. A more rapid manifestation is required to characterize your professions continuance."

Toran had the dream again. The recurring ones did not happen every night, but each of the dreams began the same way. Toran was learning how to use his invisibility talent. Unlike others, when the invisibility session was finished, he received only one new training session. This evening branched into several types of training in several other courses and abilities rather than just one. Then as he slept on his side, he was bathed in white light, and the ghostly form of Higoshi came into focus above him.

"I needed more time to teach you, but your foolish antics, revolutions ago, forced you away from me. It is most unfortunate you had to learn this way."

"What do you mean?" His eyes were closed, and he shifted onto his back before the apparition continued.

"You will understand. The strength of the mind can overcome any obstacle."

"Even death?"

"Remember. You *will* understand." Higoshi's ghost faded away.

Toran woke up and heard one last word: *Remember.*

"Higoshi," he whispered.

"Awake and face the day!" Alistar yelled. The group jumped up from their slumber.

Toran, already slightly awake, was the first one to his feet. Saigel was next. His short sword was on the ground but near him. Seane and Paul just sat up, and Kellik and the two other guards remained asleep. William was nowhere to be found.

"Whur could 'e 'ave gone?" Saigel asked, after everyone had settled their nerves.

"He may have gone back to Aamber," Seane said, yawning. "He has a way to travel. Somehow, he can shift like magicians do but without channelling," Seane answered.

Toran knew without magic that the only way this was possible was for William to have used a Merea ability, and was probably best that he had blocked his mind against Merea detection. He did not remember doing so, but knew that protection was in place. Obviously, Seane had no idea what Merea was and for some reason, he reflected on his latest dream for a moment. When he had first started having them, he had figured that they were only dreams. But now, he found that he was curious to experiment. He wanted to attempt to use what he had learned during his dreams to see if any of those talents were actually available to him.

Without trying, he had already read the less conscious thoughts of someone else and reacted to an attack moments before it had even been sprung. Then he realized he had already experimented. Gathering the wind to defeat Mirzog was a conscious act and not an accidental one.

Further experimentation would have to wait. Now he did not have the time. William's other men, Aaron and Collin, were awake and getting ready. Kellik called Tempest, who after a few moments, darted in, followed soon afterward by the diminished dragon.

The two were now approximately the same size. Kayra's new form was slightly larger. They played predator against prey throughout the cave. After trading predator positions several times, Tempest finally headed for Kellik, landing on his outstretched arm. Kayra flew toward Toran, but he waved her away. She unexpectedly landed on Kellik's shoulder opposite the arm where Tempest was perched. Unlike the bird, she lay down on his shoulder and circled her tail around his arm to remain stable.

As soon as everyone had made the final adjustments, Alistar gathered everyone within the display. Then he moved his arm in a circular motion and channelled a shift to Jenerv.

The group was now inside the temple again. The chamber had not changed in appearance since the last time they had been here, except this time, Frederick was not present. The sleeping leopard stirred and raised its head.

Kellik immediately went to the cage, chanted an essence, and said, "Hello, old friend, if you are indeed who I believe you to be?" The cat purred in positive recognition of him, and Kellik felt a warm empathic feeling that he judged to be friendly.

He figured out how to open the cage, and when the cat was free, it jumped up on him, knocking him down in the process. The leopard stood atop Kellik, pinning his shoulders down with its forelegs and his legs with its hind ones. The rest of the group drew their weapons and were ready to attack the white leopard. The cat hissed at all of them just before it licked Kellik's cheek and bumped its head against the half-elf. Amazed, they put away their swords, and the leopard let Kellik get up, but it still acted warily toward everyone else.

"You're welcome," Kellik said. Then Kellik impressed upon the leopard's mind a likeness of the priest. The cat let out a low growl, obviously disapproving of Frederick, but there was also some gratitude.

The leopard circled once, and Kellik could not believe that he had missed it. The leg had been repaired, but the cat still regarded the priest with displeasure.

Kellik did not understand it. He had caused the death of the leopard, and Frederick had been responsible for its new life and reformed leg, yet the leopard preferred him over the priest. His essence was still in effect, so Kellik introduced each of the men in the chamber while expressing the same warm feeling that the leopard understood as friendship.

Kellik turned to Toran. "You continue your search for Enrandl. I have a ..." he paused, then said, "A thank you to deliver."

"How will you find us?"

"I will have Tempest, Kayra, and the leopard with me. I'm sure that I will be able to find you."

"No," Kayra's tiny female voice said. "I will stay with the others." She flew from Kellik to Toran, but he waved her away again. Her altered course brought her around the chamber once and then to Alistar, who accepted her, and she assumed her position on the magician's shoulder and arm.

"Very well, but Paul should go with you. In case you encounter resistance."

There were two exits to the chamber: the main double doors and a door behind Frederick's desk. The leopard led Kellik and Paul to the door behind the desk. Toran's group went out the double doors.

"It is good of you to come, Frederick," William said. He was sitting behind the large desk in his office. The desk was bare, and not even a scratch adorned its top. "Alistar said he had seen you recently, but I did not have the chance to inquire about how you were."

"I am fine, William. I must say that I was surprised to hear from Alistar and now you. It has been so long."

"Yes, too long." William looked at Frederick and pitied his appearance. He did not know that revolutions of practicing the powers of The Dark Gods' were the cause of the priests' deteriorated looks. William only marked that the priest had not aged well. "How long has it been?"

"Too many revolutions to count, I would say."

William eyed Frederick with suspicion. He wanted to be direct, but he was not sure that he should be. It had not taken William's informants long to find out that the man who had taken his place as the leader of the black market was well acquainted with Frederick and at one time was one of his lesser priests. Frederick was the only person, other than himself, who knew that he had possessed the amulet necklace that had been stolen by Toran.

William chose the direct path. "I can not believe you would resort to stealing from me."

"What do you speak of?"

"The necklace we found. Why would you steal it from me? You know that I would have lent its use to you."

Frederick looked flustered, but at this point, William could not tell if it was from being caught or because an old friend had made an unsubstantiated accusation.

"By The Gods', did you think I would not find out?"

"I do not know what to say," Frederick answered.

"Why not tell the truth?"

"The truth is that I have wanted that necklace ever since we found it. But you refused to part with it."

"It was my choice," William replied angrily.

"I know that, but ..." His reply trailed off.

"So you hired someone to steal it from me."

"Yes," Frederick replied with no remorse.

"And where does it go from there?" William had surmised that Frederick had planned for his successor to have control for a while—and then he would slowly take power for himself. That change seemed to be still in process, but it had not happened yet. Perhaps his reasoning was incorrect. "You conspired against me just because you wanted a piece of jewelry?"

"You are well informed, William, for someone who is out of date and a little too late. You stepped down and out, remember?"

"Yes, I remember. I will wager that you were quite upset that I did this before you had the chance to have me murdered."

"I must admit, old friend, I was dismayed that you had made yourself unreachable before my plans came full circle, but that is all in the past now, and I need not worry about it."

"Oh, you will need to worry. I promise that you *will* need to worry."

"I must be going, William. I do hope we can speak again on more neutral ground."

"I doubt that will be possible," William replied. As he did, three of his guards stepped into the room with their swords drawn. From somewhere underneath his robe, Frederick produced a quarterstaff. William's men were strong and experienced, but William had ordered them not to kill the priest, so with some effort, Frederick was able to parry and block his way out of the chamber and to escape down the hall. William called for the men to cease and let the priest flee.

He walked back to his desk and sat down. There had been a point in his life when he would have fought the previous encounter on his own and not have had someone do it for him. He wondered why he had not fought now. He knew his skill would surely outmatch Frederick's, but he had not wanted to fight. Perhaps he was not as sure of himself as he thought he was.

Maybe he was weak.

A long-extinguished fire ignited within him. If he had been weak, he would be so no longer.

CHAPTER 17

INAPT PUPIL

When Toran's group left the temple, they expected to be on a sunlit and busy city street, but they did not appear to be outside, and there was far less activity than they had predicted. The morning sun, which should have been glowing in the sky, was still visible, but a mostly gray canopy clouded its warm light. All doors and windows of the nearby buildings were closed and shuttered.

"Whut's goin' on here?" Saigel asked.

"Where are all the people? The shops should be open," Toran added.

"There seems to be some type of a dome over the city," Alistar answered. Each of his index fingers traced circles around his eyes as he channelled. His eyes sparkled for a moment. He looked up at the canopy. "There are magical emanations from that ceiling," Alistar said.

"Look there!" Collin called, pointing to a massive stronghold with four towers located in the center of the city.

"I do not recall that being there before," Toran commented. "Our search begins there." The rest agreed with Toran, and they headed for the structure. They made their way through the unusually quiet streets, heading for the new stronghold. From time to time along their route, a shutter or a curtain opened and someone looked out at them.

They were halfway to the structure when a voice called out to them, "Halt!" Toran could not tell where the voice had come from.

"Whur'd that come from?" Saigel asked what Toran had been thinking.

A moment later, they found out when three of the city's militiamen walked out in front of them. "The law says no unauthorized travel before the dome is removed," one of them started. "I need to see your permits?"

"We are … new to the city and did not know," Toran replied.

"You'll need to come with us and tell your story to the captain."

"Who made this new law?" Seane asked.

"Enrandl Quemont has taken control of Jenerv. Where have the five of you been?"

"I did say we were new," Toran said.

"He's the most powerful magic user that has ever existed."

"We must be allowed to speak with him," Toran commanded, shaking his head at the guard's comment.

"You'll need to speak with the captain first," the guard said, obviously not taking well to Toran's tone, "on the charges of unlawful travel."

Toran drew his sword, followed by the rest of his group except Alistar. The leader and his men also took out their weapons. The leader warned them, "I'll advise you not to do this. It's another offense you'll have to answer charges for, but I'll forget it happened."

The warning was met with Toran's sword, but the issuer of it successfully blocked the attack. Seane had no room to maneuver, so he backed away and waited for an opening.

Aaron and Collin, who were working as a team, paired off against one of the militiamen, and Saigel ducked and dodged to avoid another opponent's first attacks against him. With his scimitar already drawn, Saigel decided to use his short sword also. His small size gave him an advantage over taller opponents. The minikin charged forward, but instead of attacking, he dove ahead, tucked himself into a ball, and tumbled between the legs of the other. While the surprised guard adjusted to engage him again, he had time to draw his second sword.

Aaron seemed to have already decided that Collin did not need his help, so when three more of the militia came from behind them, he disengaged from his current conflict and joined Seane to head off the incoming attackers. Toran and the leader were steadily trading attacks back and forth in their fight.

Alistar had moved behind the whole scene. He could see even more militia coming from what seemed to have been nowhere. Kayra was still wrapped around his shoulder.

"There seems to be no end to the reinforcements," Alistar remarked. "Time to help out." He waited until everyone was in range—there were now more than nine of the city's militiamen fighting them—then he channelled. His flashfire engulfed everyone except for himself and Kayra. After the flash was gone, only three men of the opposing side were standing.

When the rest of the militiamen saw that all of their companions were down and that none of their opponents were even injured, they all ran in separate directions.

"Thank you, Alistar," Toran said, barely looking his direction, and he guessed why.

"A simple thank you with no arguments this time?"

"None." Alistar saw the corner of Toran's smile, and his sideways glance caught Alistar's eye. Toran bowed his head, and they moved on.

Torches lit the way every twenty feet in front of them, except for a few empty sconces. The construction of the corridor looked like it had been built too long ago to be standing. It was braced frequently, and while everything looked sturdy enough, they moved through the halls cautiously.

Kellik, Tempest on his shoulder, wondered where the leopard was leading them. Paul walked between them and started to play his lute. Kellik followed while watching behind them.

"Stop playing. You are making too much noise," Kellik ordered.

"For your information, the tune I play happens to be making us invisible, and the sound is being displaced to appear ten yards behind us, including our talking."

"Well then, I'm sorry. Keep playing," Kellik said.

Paul could see the doubt in Kellik's eyes. The bard was not worried though. He knew what the magical instrument could do and that it was working because it told him so.

"Against the wall. Someone is coming." Kellik watched in amazement as three men started to run past them as if they were not there. Unfortunately, the leopard did not know any better and attacked the first of the three before he could pass. Kellik drew his swords as

Tempest flew from his shoulder. Paul stopped playing and gripped the lute as if it were a club.

The first guard, who had been caught by surprise, fell to the ground. The leopard immediately tore out his throat. The second guard swung his sword at Paul. The bard parried with his lute.

Tempest flew toward the third, disrupting his movement so that Kellik could move around Paul and engage him with swords. Both found their mark, and the guard fell.

Kellik turned around in time to see Paul, now wielding a quarterstaff, strike at his foe. He missed with the staff, but he continued to spin and kicked out, catching the man in the ribs. As his adversary doubled over, Paul hit him in the back of the neck with a downward stroke of his weapon. His opponent fell to the ground and did not move.

Kellik was just about to comment on Paul's weapon when another priest came around the corner.

It was the High Priest.

Frederick caught a glimpse of the scene before him and retreated immediately. The leopard started after him. Kellik and Paul were also going to give pursuit when another guard (one the leopard had just darted past in favor of chasing Frederick) came around the corner and struck the first victim he saw. The powerful blow to his chest knocked

Paul back into a wall. His head hit the wall first, and he fell to the floor, unconscious.

Kellik brought both swords around to attack the guarding priest, but his first swing was parried expertly enough to cross up his second. He was compelled to back away and compose himself.

The guard came in aggressively with his club. Within moments, Kellik's defense was too wide to protect himself. The priest jabbed him hard in the chest, pushing him back farther, and prepared to attack again.

When the cat struck, the staggered guard toppled to the ground, flat on his face. The white leopard, which was now stained with blood, clawed and bit at his back while he yelled in pain. When the guard was finally silent and no longer moving, the cat started after Frederick again.

Kellik looked for Paul, but the bard was nowhere to be found. He shrugged his shoulders and found Tempest on top of an empty sconce. He motioned in the direction that the leopard had taken, and the falcon flew off. After one more unsuccessful search for Paul, Kellik followed Tempest.

"I don't feel invisible," Saigel remarked in a harsh whisper.

"Shush. I will explain later. Just keep moving," Toran replied. He was concentrating on creating one sphere that would be large enough for all of them as the group moved to the main doors of Jenerv's new citadel.

Saigel did not feel invisible because in reality, he was not. Toran's invisibility talent was not quite perfect. It *did* effectively block the light around them, which *did* make them invisible to anyone who was looking in their direction. It would be ideally seamless if his sphere was small enough to render only him from sight.

The problem was that while the required larger sphere, which was around the group, obstructed light to their advantage, its size also blocked more of what anyone could see behind them, creating a disadvantage. If they did not keep moving, there would be a significant gap in someone's view of where they were.

Toran had considered conjuring separate spheres for each of them and altering his vision in all to make them individually not seen. That amount of concentration on each sphere to counter each of their individual movements would be something that even Higoshi might be hard-pressed to successfully achieve.

Back at the cave, when Toran had used the same talent to hide from Enrandl, there had been an abundance of shadows and darkness to suppress any distortion—and he had counted on Enrandl's continued movement to change the direction of light around him. A much smaller sphere, like the multiple ones he had just considered, had been required to keep the magician from seeing him.

The guards who were here were mostly stationary, but if the group could stay close together and keep moving, there should be no complications considering the scale of the current sphere.

Two guards had just opened the main entrance for two regally dressed people. Toran and his group followed, walking closely behind them. One by one, they passed the threshold and beyond the guards.

Once inside, the royal pair was led to the left by a dark-haired, young woman, possibly an elf. When they were out of sight, Toran ended his talent.

The inside of the new structure was vast and empty. A wide spiraling staircase stood at the center of the foyer, leading upward with halls to its left and right. The large and mostly unadorned walls were white and smooth, and an unknown light source illuminated the interior of the place.

"We are visible again, so try not to be seen. Okay, Saigel, Alistar, and Collin, go up as high as you can and work your way down. The rest of us will start down here and work our way up."

Saigel led the way as Alistar followed with Kayra on his shoulder. The group headed toward the stairs. Saigel's short legs plodded upward, but Alistar was slower, and he cautiously looked around him. Collin followed, watching behind them to see what direction the others took. They paused briefly at every landing along their way to the top.

Each landing spanned outward from the stairway in both directions, exhibiting the same appearance as everything else, so they continued to the top. Three levels from where they had started, the stairs ended. Saigel looked left and right. He asked Kayra if she would scout to the left, and the miniature dragon untangled herself from Alistar and flew from her perch without a word. Alistar immediately moved on down the opposite passage.

"I'm gunna leash yuh, so yuh don't get inta truble," Saigel commented when he caught up to him.

The group came to an open archway and peered around the corner as Kayra landed on Saigel's shoulder. Inside a massive chamber, Enrandl, wearing his customary blue and glittering robe, sat. He appeared to be in a type of trance, but when the group entered the room, he spoke to them without opening his eyes, "Accordingly, your predestination was not so tombed by the blade which should have devised your mortality, Alistar."

"Yes, I am fortunate to have friends who arrived in time to prolong my life. You really should finish the tasks that you begin."

"A tactical fallacy I propose to render effectual presently," Enrandl answered. He stood and faced them.

Saigel looked at Alistar and then Enrandl and said, "Yuh two know each other?"

"Yes," Alistar answered. "He was my student."

When Enrandl replied to this comment, Alistar noticed something in Saigel's stricken expression, and it distracted the elder magic user—Enrandl's words fell on deaf ears.

Saigel stammered, "His master had muh society's symbol, and 'e killed 'em—all but me."

"I did what? Oh my! I could not have known ..." Before Alistar could explain any further and without even a sound, he felt six separate magical darts pierce his side, causing him to wince in pain. "No respect for your old master?" he said as he turned.

"Long ago, my agency of respect had but a minuscule degree, and at present, you are drastically absent of measure to my acumen. Conceivable existence of an equality to myself challenges all credence!"

"We shall see." Alistar's hand reached into a pouch and produced something that he placed in the other. His voice was barely a whisper. The phrase Saigel heard seemed familiar, but he did not hear it in its entirety. He watched as Alistar blew a colorful powder from his hand to finish the channelling of his effect.

At this, the minikin was nearly blinded by the display. He looked away, and Collin covered his eyes, as every color imaginable, along with its clashing counterpart, issued forth from Alistar's hand. These bright clashing colors danced and swirled into a considerable orb and then flew toward Enrandl. The globe of colors struck the magician and engulfed him.

Whatever display Alistar had sent this effect to accomplish failed because when it was all over, Enrandl emerged unaffected and unmoved by it. "I surmise a conjecture that you have a more reinforced regimen to contend amidst me, *master.*" Enrandl stressed the last word sarcastically.

The sarcasm obviously pricked at Alistar, and as a result, it angered him. He immediately began another channelling, and while Enrandl stood waiting, Saigel found that he could maintain its inference and predict what display the effect was about to present. Almost as the minikin had predicted, a fifteen-foot ray of glowing yellow light shot from Alistar's hands toward Enrandl. It was not as intense as the previous effect had been, but Saigel closed his eyes to shield them from this bright new color. He wondered why Alistar was not using fire or electrical insurgence against the other magician. When this display was concluded, Enrandl remained utterly unscathed.

"A feasible instance for an adjudicate resistance now?" Enrandl mused and began to channel.

While Saigel watched Alistar hurry to retrieve something silver from a pocket in his robe, he decided to act. Saigel drew a dagger and hurled it at Enrandl. The blade struck his left leg, and although it bounced away harmlessly, it was enough to distract and interrupt his concentrated effort. In this way, it stopped his effect from forming a display.

"Little scrub! What courts your challenge here?" Enrandl pointed his finger at Saigel, and with a silent channel at him, six more magical darts, similar to the ones that had struck Alistar moments ago, flew from his fingertip.

Alistar intercepted their path with his mirror held out before him. Instead of the missiles hitting Saigel, they began to swirl around the magic user instead. Saigel decided to retreat from the magic battle back to where Collin was standing.

"An admirable provision! My query presents: How sufficiently does your capacity intern?" Enrandl duplicated Alistar's second effect. The yellow ray of color shot forth and joined the missiles in their swirling pattern. Enrandl nodded his head, seemingly impressed with his former master and the displays circling around him. He took fur and a crystal from his robe, and with a snap of his fingers, he channelled again.

Across the room, the contingent audience watched as a bolt of sizzling electrical energy joined the previous displays in their dancing exhibition around Alistar. Impressed but a bit flustered, Enrandl began to channel again, when Alistar pointed his finger at him. The orbiting arrows, which had initially been intended for Saigel, pulsed forward at Enrandl and hit him squarely in the chest, although they appeared to do nothing to him.

Alistar then directed the electric blue energy to fly at and charge the other magician. Once again, the bolt struck its target and delivered no harm. Alistar released the final effect that had been dancing around him. Ordinarily, the other person would have been shuddering in pain and fear from the yellow beam of intense light, but no affect was registered.

Saigel could see that Alistar was lost. His effects had done nothing to Enrandl. When he had reflected back the other man's own magic, it had been delivered uselessly.

Alistar was still busy pondering, but Enrandl did not waste any time. The explosion of fire erupted directly upon Alistar, and he was visibly charred. His clothes were singed, and he had several burns covering his body. Saigel, with Kayra stretched across his shoulders and tail around his arm, looked up to Collin. "Alistar is losing. I'm going to find the others." He looked to Kayra. "Yuh stays also. Maybe yuh can 'elp ... somehow."

Kayra unwrapped herself from him and launched into the air. Saigel ran off, and she landed on a ledge above to watch the magic battle.

Alistar pointed in his opponent's direction, and a large area of the floor around him began to glow. Enrandl looked down and raised his arms above his head. When the area disappeared, he plunged toward the level below. Alistar, pleased to see that his magic had utility, still needed to act quickly since he had not completed this task yet.

Over his revolutions of relearning his effects, he had found many different ways to add to and adjust them. In this case, he had disintegrated the floor, and it had worked perfectly and had dropped Enrandl down, but his version of the original had an added option. He could restore the disintegrated area. He had added this option to his effect as a safety precaution in case a companion was accidentally disintegrated, which was irreversible.

He had wanted to use the floor to trap his enemy. The absent area had begun to glow, and as Enrandl had fallen, it had reappeared again like it had never been gone. Alistar sighed with relief but then noticed that Enrandl had not been trapped there as he had planned.

"Behind you!" Kayra's little voice warned, but it was too late. Alistar felt a cold chill advance through his body and collapsed. As the necrotic energy pulsed through him, he could feel the absence of his aura that Enrandl's effect had created within him. He knew that he did not have much ability left to channel.

Enrandl stood leering above him. "Your vanquishing by my stead was inevitable. The junction of book and my advocation establishes that none shall conquer me," Enrandl gloated.

Just then, Kayra swooped by him and scratched his cheek. She thought that her small claws had connected with his face but decided that she must have been mistaken, for no wound had been inflicted. She landed next to Alistar.

"A captivating associate. Such an admirable discontent that your pairing will be presently eradicated," Enrandl said.

CHAPTER 18

DECEPTION

"They had to have come this way," Toran said, and neither Aaron nor Seane disagreed. There had been no doors or other passageways since they had divided in separate groups. The sparse decorations throughout the halls had not changed since they had arrived. They had encountered no one—not even the couple they had followed in here on the previous time or the concierge who had led them away.

As they considered all the evidence, they thought that either no one had taken up residence here or that they had recently moved in.

It had not taken them long to make their way through the hallways of this floor.

The stairs to the next level were already beckoning to Toran as he watched Seane, who led, turn another corner and come to a stop. Toran walked up to him and looked around the corner to see two twisted iron torch sconces. They were equally unnecessary on opposite walls of the blocked hallway because of the unexplained illumination. Each had wooden torches. One of them burned silently, and the other one was black and smoking, as if its last effort had finally concluded.

"It ends here." Seane turned to the rest. "End wall and two torches."

"Wait." Aaron's deep voice followed. He rounded the corner and stopped beneath the sconce that held the smoking torch, which was opposite the one that was still burning strong. While Toran had already thought about their lack of purpose, Aaron seemed to have other thoughts. When he reached up and pulled the sconce downward, a grinding noise echoed around them. A few seconds later, the end wall slid away to reveal a flight of stairs leading down into darkness.

"How did you see that?" Seane asked.

"Seemed obvious." Aaron shrugged his shoulders.

"Excellent find," Toran said. Of all William's henchmen, this one seemed to have the most promise, but Seane was usually the closest to him. "Whoever designed this place did not think to disguise things very well. Hand me that torch."

Toran took the lead now and started down with torch in hand. He soon decided that the fire on it was not real. There was no heat or scent associated with burning, and it barely served him with light to see.

At first, the stairs and the structure beyond the false wall were similar to what they had left behind. This abruptly changed about halfway down. Everything was significantly older and not at all polished. Even the air grew staler as they descended, contradicting what they were leaving behind. He discerned this with each step that he took.

As they all heard a vicious growling coming from below them, Toran's thoughts about the torch and scenery left him, and he drew his weapon before proceeding down with more caution. Near the bottom landing, they found a familiar white leopard viciously assaulting an unmoving body.

"That's the cat that Kellik set free," Seane revealed when he could finally see it. At his words, the previously unaware leopard looked up from its distraction. The bloody maw issued another low growl directed at them, and the leopard began to advance.

"Do you think it recognizes us?" Aaron asked. "You know Kellik introduced us."

"I am a little more worried about where Kellik is," Toran set his sword down and slowly approached the leopard as the others hid their weapons because they assumed they might be taken as threats. They kept them as ready as possible.

"Hello there," Toran said calmly and in a higher voice than usual. He had watched his friend calm a wild, hungry bear in the forest. He tried to emulate the same posture and soothing tones that Kellik had adopted when dealing with the bear. He hoped that earlier introductions had tamed the cat enough to accept his calm words. He stopped and knelt before it, sparing a momentary glance at the severely injured body of Frederick, the priest.

He closed his eyes and concentrated on easing his nerves. He was about to produce a sphere to help him do so when he opened his eyes again. The leopard was directly in front of him. He could smell Frederick's fresh blood wafting on its breath. The cat was now moving cautiously, and it had stopped growling. It tilted its head slightly as if it had reached a conclusion. When Toran raised his hand slowly toward it, the white leopard nudged it with its forehead.

"Be wary, but we should be okay." His words were interrupted by an irritated growl as the great cat looked up. Toran tumbled backward away from it and then clambered to his feet. When he saw the leopard had not moved, he looked around, released his held breath when he saw Saigel standing on the stairs above them, and knew the cat must have just reacted to the sudden appearance of the minikin.

"We found him!" Saigel said. "Alistar's fightin' 'im, but it don't look so good."

"What do you mean?"

"Fahlla me!" Saigel turned and ran back up the ancient stairs. The others followed him. Upon hearing what Saigel had said, all of them had forgotten entirely about the leopard.

It followed them anyway.

They could have overtaken Saigel while running and climbing three flights of stairs, but his lead finally brought them to the chamber where Alistar and Enrandl were battling. It was less of a fight at this point, as Alistar, undoubtedly weak from his wounds, was lying on his back and pointing at Kayra. Enrandl stood next to them.

The display was soon apparent as the small dragon began to grow. The rest arrived to join Collin watch the transformation from flying lizard to massive dragon. They witnessed Enrandl's look of surprise at this new revelation. When her accustomed frame filled nearly half the chamber, they watched him slowly back away from this dragon, which had her complete attention directed solely on him.

Saigel immediately ran to Alistar's weak form as the others tried to decide whether they should help or stay out of the way. The wizard was unsteady and barely conscious when the minikin reached him. His eyes were slightly open.

"Saigel," he said and then coughed. "I ..."

"Don't talk. Save yuhr strength."

"Listen." He coughed again. "I was … different when I did what I did. If I could change things …" He coughed again. "Emergency." Alistar passed out.

Emergency? Saigel thought. *That makes no sense.* He stayed by the unconscious wizard and noticed something in his hand. A foot-long, crooked wooden stick was halfway out of his pocket. It looked like Alistar had been trying to get it out of his robe. Saigel grabbed it and wondered what purpose this wand served. "Emergency." He repeated as he stood up and gave the rest of the scene his full attention. He did not notice the faint red glow that surrounded the motionless body.

Enrandl backed away several steps as he processed what had just occurred. It was not a fear of the creature present before him that gave Enrandl pause or its attentiveness regarding him. Something in the dragon's eyes caused him to know for sure that it was Kayra, but her attendance here did intrigue him.

He had not given the fire lizard any thought. It was a pet or a familiar, and its presence had not even registered before it landed next to Alistar. The first time that he had seen her dragon form had been at her cave. The flowing mesh of scales had lacked the luster that they now radiated, as her body had then been withered and gaunt from cycles worth of decay.

The last time he had seen her had been at the same cave, when she had been about to exact her justice on the elf and minikin. She had been fighting with the elf, and Enrandl had paid little attention to her. Once he had gathered his prize, he had shifted home, with the assumption that she would take care of them and Toran. Now she was here, fully reformed from the much more decrepit carcass that he had initially transformed into a woman, and her aggression was aimed at Enrandl.

Out of his pockets, he gathered ingredients to start a channelling, not knowing that Kayra had begun concentrating on an effect of her own. Fire erupted around them both, but when the display of Kayra's magic was complete, the dragon and the human stood unscathed by the flames.

Kayra had neglected an attempt to evade the flashfire as she had targeted Enrandl and allowed both of them to be engulfed by the display. She knew why the burst of fire from this display had not hurt her. Her scales yielded her protection from all sources that duplicated fire. Most dragons were provided the same protection from their own unique weapons, but humans were not usually immune to such.

Her second tactic would be a less defensible one.

Kellik appeared to have some form of protection against it, and Saigel had recovered from the jet of flames she had launched at him cycles ago, but neither of them would be caught in the dragonfire she was about to produce.

Unaffected by her magic, Enrandl finished his own channelling, but there was no immediate display. He started to move, and though it was only several steps, he did so at a far quicker pace than he had expected. He knew the effect well enough. He knew what the display entailed, but he had never used it before now. Being so unaccustomed to the new rapid transit, he promptly tripped over his own feet.

Kayra had reacted precisely and quickly and had tracked his new haste. Before he could stand again, Enrandl heard her inhale deeply and knew her deadly dragonfire was intended for him as he struggled to get up in reaction to his fall.

What her previous attempt with magic had not accomplished, her dragonfire did. Enrandl had rolled across the floor but was again standing. His blue robe was singed but still serviceable. His long black hair was mostly melted away, leaving sparse patches of his standard locks. Burns covered most of his body, including spots on his head where there was no longer hair, but his mind raced in spite of the pain.

If what he believed was correct, he had some time before she could send fire at him again. He glanced in the spectators' direction, deliberated on them and their weapons, and presented himself with a concept while the dragon moved closer to him. More reserved but still at a quickened pace, he moved farther away from Kayra and set himself for another effect. Instantly, he took a small piece of rope from his pocket. He straightened it between his hands and tossed it in the group's direction. Before it landed on the floor, he mimicked gripping it and pulled it to him.

At Enrandl's choice, Aaron suddenly found that his sword was hard to handle. It kept pulling away from him, and then it was rent from his hand. It flew across the room and skidded to a stop at Enrandl's feet. One part of his plan had been accomplished. Now he hoped that he had time to finish part two. The magic user hurried to complete the channelling of another effect before Kayra could attack him again.

He took a pinch of something from a pouch and then placed the combination of hair of oxen and fox on his tongue. Then he made fists of both hands and flexed the muscles of each arm, shaking each arm down one at a time, as he channelled.

Enrandl began to grow.

His height increased by four inches, and his build and mass increased dramatically. Muscles developed everywhere; including in places he never even knew he had muscles. The dragon engaged him just as his transmutation was complete. He rolled under and away from her craning neck, reached for Aaron's sword, and continued this dodging tactic until he was able to stand on his feet again. The dragon's claws reached out toward him, but he slapped them away with the sword he now wielded.

Seane had given Aaron another sword, and the two advanced on the magician from his right flank while Toran and Collin angled in from the left, but Enrandl moved faster than anything that they had seen before. In a brief time, he had fatally wounded Collin with a thrust to his stomach. While the man fell to the ground, Enrandl parried each attack from the others in the particular order that they had come. Then still at an improbable pace for a man of his new size, he ran across the room to get behind Kayra.

The dragon whipped her tail around and caught the man's legs, toppling him. Then she craned her neck around as she sought a chance to send more fire his way. Enrandl was on his feet and moving before she could even inhale, so she tried to turn herself to face him, but he managed to get underneath her and to strike at her belly.

His three quick strikes were ineffective against her scales. She kicked him out from underneath her, but this seemed to enrage his resolve, and before she could turn to face him, he was underneath her again. This time his sword struck true, and she roared in pain. She tried to force him to retreat, but he kept pushing forward with quick relentless strikes that cut away at her midsection. The chamber was massive, but so was she in her full form, and her size decreased her mobility no matter how hard she tried. She could do nothing to displace the human from underneath her for more than a few moments, and with each new wound, she was getting weaker.

This one human was hitting her faster and harder than Kellik and Saigel had in tandem, cycles before while fighting in her lair. She recalled her disbelief that she could be so wounded. When Kayra finally succumbed to her injuries, another recollection came to her. She could not help but imagine the pool in her mountain lair. How she wished for access to that water.

She had had the opportunity during the extended battle with Kellik to ease her pain and heal herself before chasing him outside. The water itself did not provide the restorative property, but the pool that contained it caused it to have the ability, so, even if the water were available to her here, a refreshing drink would give her no respite. She made one last effort to lunge forward and trap him underneath her as she collapsed to the floor, but Enrandl managed to dive away from her to safety.

Hoping to reach Collin in time to help, Toran ran to him, but he was too late. He knew that if he had remained where he was and had not taken the time to cross the room but had simply conjured a sphere upon him, the healing still would not have been soon enough. When the heavy thump of the dragon falling to the ground caught his attention, he turned to see what was going on.

"No," he whispered softly. "No!" His yell echoed through the chamber. He grabbed Collin's sword with his free hand and charged with his own sword in the other. Toran engaged Enrandl, but the magic user was already prepared for him and thrust his sword out at him to halt the charge. Toran parried the thrust, spun, and brought his other sword around to the magician's neck. Enrandl's lack of experience with swordplay registered, as he was not prepared for such a maneuver. He stood defenseless as Toran's perfectly placed strike cut across his throat.

The stroke bounced off Enrandl's skin, not even leaving a scratch.

Kellik found it hard to believe that he had lost the trail of the cat, and worse than that, he had no idea where he was. He had been wandering down these passages for far too long. Once the leopard had gotten the notion to get Frederick, the chase had started. The priest proved himself a feisty prey who knew his temple and the catacombs beneath quite well enough to evade and hamper even the cat's keen senses. The leopard seemed to have doubled back numerous times during its chase. One of those times during his attempt to follow, Kellik must have taken a wrong turn, and that was when he lost them.

He finally came across a bloody scene where he could see white fur and a large amount of blood staining the floor. He hoped it was not the cat's blood that was presented before him. On his immediate left, a flight of stairs led upward. He studied the scene with more prudence, found paw prints, and breathed a sigh of relief. If any of this blood had been the cat's blood, at least it had still been alive when it had gone up the stairs. Human prints had joined it there, and their excursion up the stairs had been recent.

Was someone with the leopard, or had the owners of the prints visited here before or after the cat's presence? Kellik wondered about this as he followed the leopard's tracks. When he reached the top landing, he found that his way was blocked. He knew that there had to be a way through there, otherwise, it did not make sense. He touched the blocking wall and adjoining side walls, where he quickly found a loose stone. As he pushed the rock inward, it activated the sliding wall, and he went through.

He was amazed at the contrast between the tunnels he had been in and the immaculate presentation where he was now. The only blemishes in the perfection were a few bloody prints leading to more stairs going up, and even those had begun to fade as it had dried on the leopard's paws. He followed the stairs up to the second level, and when he reached the landing, a dagger hit him in the back. The hilt was within his reach, and as he pulled the blade free, he winced in pain.

He saw that it had come from an elven woman on the landing below him. She put something in her mouth and then dropped her arms one at a time with dramatic flair.

The bird had flown from the intruder's shoulder as Shevail had been midway through her channel. The half-elf knelt down to withdraw a dagger from his boot as his falcon dove directly at Shevail and almost crossed up her gestures enough to disrupt her effect.

She did not know who this one was, but she knew that Enrandl was only expecting two visitors. She had already greeted them; he must be an intruder, and she was going to protect the man she loved.

The falcon flew up and out of the way. Shevail disregarded it, and she had to duck quickly to avoid the half-elf, who was now halfway down the stairs and diving toward her. As she ducked, he flew over her.

He tucked and rolled, bounced off a wall, and lost the dagger she had thrown at him in the process. It slid across the landing several feet away from him. The intruder tucked his own dagger into his belt, drew a type of sword she did not recognize from the sheath at his hip, and advanced upon her. She knew how inexperienced she was with weapons, but she was sure that the effect she had channelled before engaging with the elf would support her competence. It was an effect that she had secretly watched her master practice, and it worked well for him.

Early on when her magical career was new, she had discovered that she had had a penchant for a specific type of magic, which her master had not realized. She was quite competent in the art of scrying. During her studies with him, Enrandl directed her the way that he taught all of his students. She had ample time to study alone and to practice his teachings, but she took the time to work on her specialty also.

Most of her attempts were to scry upon him, and in doing so over the last cycle, she watched him progress and develop a new effect. This effect had the display of making him stronger and more agile, and she was an exemplary student who had watched and learned from him exceptionally well. Her build was more athletic than his was, so her physical transformation was not as evident on her body as it was on her master's, but the strength and agility were definitely magnified.

They exchanged several effective blows and countered each other's attacks. Shevail was slower than Kellik was but still managed to keep up with the pace of his sword and strike offensively as well. She knew GodsLight shone on her because the intruder was obviously having a difficult day. He was slowly pushing her back when he slipped. His right foot shot out in front of him, and he fell on his back. His sword skidded across the floor several feet away from him as her dagger had done to him earlier, but this one slid to the stairs and tumbled down to the landing below.

She moved in to strike, but the elf kicked out his leg and tripped her. They both hurried to stand up. Now her opponent drew the longswords from his back and took control of the fight. He was attacking at will, seemingly quite comfortable with the way the two swords worked together to balance each other. She managed to deflect all of his attacks, but she had no room for any offense.

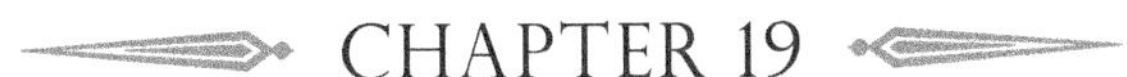

CHAPTER 19

ONE CURSE AND ANOTHER

Toran was stunned by the revelation that he had not defeated Enrandl with one swift cut. The evil laugh that followed sent a chill through him. Nothing in the heat of battle was ever guaranteed, but he knew that his stroke should have ended this one.

Enrandl was swiftly advancing on him now. His swordplay was still awkward and incompetent, but he was dancing and weaving so quickly that even armed with two swords for defense, Toran was still hard-pressed to protect himself.

Steadily retreating now, a few of his parries missed. In the hands of a skilled swordsman, what he thought had been deadly cuts had left only minor scratches by the inexperienced magician. Enrandl pressed on, and now Toran was slowing.

Escape! The thought appeared out of nowhere, but Toran mentally asked, *How?* Not waiting for another answer, he caught enough of a break from dodging and blocking to summon and expand a sphere around the two of them. He produced an image of where they were in comparison to each other. Then he altered the perception in his mind to a preferred formation. When he rendered the change and his new placement relating to the other was adapted, he was surprised by a Merea talent he had never learned—not even in his dreamscape training—but had just executed perfectly.

Enrandl watched Toran vanish before his eyes. Thinking him to be invisible, Enrandl angrily slashed out in front of him anyway, finding nothing but air. Then he was astounded when Toran's swords were both deflected off his back. He turned around, swinging his sword out and around him, in time to see Toran disappear again before the weapon could strike him. Enrandl immediately turned around another time, expecting Toran to be there, but he was not.

Standing behind Enrandl, Toran recovered from the momentary shock at his successful displacement as he watched Enrandl swing out at the air in front of him. Toran struck the magicians back with both his swords—to no benefit.

Before any countering action by Enrandl could come and knowing he would respond by swinging around at him, Toran recalculated his sphere to now encompass only himself and allowed the other to see him for just a moment. Toran then remodeled the sphere to observe himself absent from the scene (the light around him blocked by the sphere) and caused the change to happen. He stepped back to dodge the arc of the sword and assumed that the magician would predict another displacement.

When the magician, as predicted, turned around for the second time, Toran quickly dropped one of his swords, placed his free arm across Enrandl's chest, and pulled him back over his outstretched leg.

Enrandl fell across the leg while Toran stood above him and witnessed the conversion of the man back into his usual self. He released his sphere, became visible again, and swung his remaining sword down, hoping that the previous body was the reason that his attacks had been blocked.

One more time the sword bounced harmlessly away.

Saigel was keeping his distance across the room and still standing beside Alistar as Tempest flew in and landed next to him. "Whur'd yuh come fruhm?" Tempest began to walk away, and then the falcon flapped its wings and flew out the entrance to the chamber. Saigel followed.

Kellik's attacks became slower as he tired. He needed to end this soon. He was trying to push Shevail backward toward the stairs but instead, found himself being pushed back. The woman's one sword was now moving faster than his pair. He was wondering where her burst of speed had come from when he realized that he had been duped. She was holding back to wear him out, and it had worked, as he was now being pressed backward, and he knew he could not keep going. At this continued pace, he would soon be out of energy.

"Kellik!" a familiar voice called to him.

The elven woman was surprised, and her attack routine momentarily faltered. Kellik took advantage by dropping his sword and punching her across the chin. She collapsed to the floor. With his hands on his knees, Kellik took a few deep breaths and then turned to see Saigel coming down the stairs. The minikin had been at the top of the second landing. Kellik retrieved his swords and met him halfway.

"Havin' problems?"

"Nothing I couldn't have handled … without your help, of course."

"Bah! Who's yuhr friend?"

"I've no idea; she just came out of nowhere. What's going on? Where is everybody?"

"We need to get back upstairs," Saigel replied. "Toran and Enrandl are fightin' toe to toe."

"Toran's not a magician. Where is Alistar?"

"Dead," Saigel said sadly. "His magic didn't work."

"Where is everyone else?"

"Stayin' back but watchin'. If 'e is powerful like Alistar says, I don't know why Toran's tryin' ta fight him."

Do not give in now!

This time Toran understood that it was not his own thought. Higoshi had spoken to him, and he was hearing the suggestion clearly in his former mentor's voice now.

But how can I fight him? Toran answered. *I have no magic.*

The strength of the mind, Higoshi's voice stated in his head.

"Can overcome any obstacle," Toran finished aloud.

Toran's private conversation allowed Enrandl to get up and step away from him. He prepared another effect.

Interrupt him, Toran reminded himself. He centered his mind, and a sphere was there, which was dedicated to containing both him and Enrandl inside its field. He formed three small bubbles inside the area between them and sent them directly at Enrandl, one after another. He knew these would probably not hurt, but in the middle of the others' motions, Enrandl's head jerked to the left as if he had been struck.

Then it jerked right and left one more time as the unseen, yet near-solid spheres hit him in succession.

This angered Enrandl, and he immediately searched for his attacker. When he found no one, he turned back and regarded Toran. He thought that he might have moved up and punched him. When he saw that Toran had not budged, Enrandl looked around him again and then refocused on him.

Enrandl initiated another effect, but when he began his incantation, he was hit three more times. He looked back at Toran who still had not moved, but he was staring at him. Enrandl had heard of Merea but had never experienced it. He did not know if the man across from him knew Merea. He did remember that Toran had done nothing in the way of magic when he had disappeared. There was no one else near him. He was not using any magic. If Toran was going to find a way to interrupt every effect that Enrandl attempted, he would no longer channel any.

He withdrew a foot-long ivory wand from one of his pockets and pointed it at Toran. He usually saved items of this power as a last resort. With the endless flow of energy that the book gave him, he presumed that he would never need such recourse. Toran was convincing him of the error of that assumption.

Saigel was about to inquire about Paul and where Kellik had lost the leopard when they heard an explosion. They ran the next two flights to the top landing. When they approached the chamber, they found a different opening to it. A gaping hole was where a wall had once been. Debris from the wall covered the floor in the hall.

When they approached, the cat recognized Kellik and met them at the pile of debris. Saigel shook his head and smiled as Kellik reached down to pet the leopard.

On top of the pile of rocks, Toran lay unmoving. His body twitched before he opened his eyes. His first sight was Kellik and Saigel standing above him. A second bolt of electrical energy hit the wall above their heads, sending chunks of stone crumbling down.

With Kellik's help, Toran was trying to get up as Enrandl approached. Toran did not see his sword anywhere and assumed that it was buried under the pile of rubble. He looked around him at the debris and then back at the magician. As he expanded a new globe around him, what he saw with his eyes soon separated from his new vision within the sphere. He selected several rocks that had settled on the floor around him.

Pieces of stone, which had just served as a wall to the chamber, were suddenly thrust into motion and were pelting Enrandl. He dodged the larger pieces, but most of the smaller fragments hit him and stung his flesh. He did his best to hide this from his enemies. The effect had completed its display, and his protection from all physical attacks that were directed against him was now gone. If he got close enough, he would be vulnerable to Toran's sword.

Enrandl moved back across the room while Kellik finished helping Toran to his feet. The three of them, along with the leopard, regrouped and started across the room to catch up with him.

A rumbling noise echoed around them, and the cat stopped altogether. It shuddered for a moment before the floor underneath everyone began to quake. It was not only the floor but the chamber and the whole citadel that was violently shaking. Everyone, including the leopard, stumbled around, but Toran stood almost motionless.

In the instant that the floor had started to move, Toran had introduced a sphere bound to him. A view of him floating above the shaking floor was quickly modeled into reality. He was levitating and drifting toward the magician.

The others scrambled for cover as parts of the ceiling began to fall. Cracks in the floor formed all around them, creating gaps down to the level below. Everyone except Enrandl, Toran, and the leopard escaped to the hall through the hole that Enrandl had created with his first blast from the wand.

Toran was still comfortably floating toward Enrandl, who was stumbling around from the groundshake. The panicked leopard had lost all sense of direction and had tried to leap across a large crack.

When the cat hit the crumbling floor on the other side, the rock underneath it cracked and began to fall. The leopard tried to jump back and landed on the edge it had initially leapt from.

The cat joined the field of Toran's sphere. He felt it land and envisioned its rear paws slipping out from under it, but there was no time for him to force a change in what he saw. The ground stopped shaking, and he set down on the now still floor. The leopard's front claws scratched at the stone but could not gain purchase. Slipping farther backward, it would soon fall.

Toran ran to the cat as he dedicated his current sphere to activating an increase of strength as he had done during his first match with Saigel. He reached the edge just as the leopard lost what little grip it had. Toran caught one leg in each hand and pulled.

Only then did he realize his mistake.

He had caught the forelegs from the underside. The claws of the terror-stricken leopard dug into his forearms. Toran yelled in pain but continued to pull. He tried to alter the strength sphere in favor of one to block the pain, but the claws dug deeper into his arms, and blood flowed from the wounds. He could not even conjure another sphere through the pain that he wanted to ignore.

Heal yourself, Higoshi offered. His voice came quickly but irregularly, as if they were both experiencing the same pain.

I cannot. The claws, he said with his mind.

Trust me, Higoshi said. *There is no time to argue.*

Still concentrating on the bound sphere for his strength, he found enough presence of mind to master the pain, and his healing spheres centered on his arms where the claws still dug into his skin. His anatomy lessons had never included foreign objects within the body to be repaired, but he formed the vision and willed the change to happen. New skin and muscle formed and grafted around the nails—as if they were supposed to be there—and he was amazed that it worked.

The pain was gone, and he pulled the leopard up without difficulty. Before he could think of a way to extract the claws from his arms, Enrandl stood above him. "Presently, the scope of your existence retains conclusion."

Toran felt exhausted, both mentally and physically. He had never used so much Merea at one time. He had too little energy to react as Enrandl placed his hands upon him, but nothing happened.

Paul woke up feeling dizzy and opened his eyes slowly. He was lying on the floor half in the torchlight of a hallway and half in a chamber lit by many candles. He remembered being knocked back (his chest still ached) and hitting his head (also aching), but he did not know how he had arrived there.

A vent hole in the wall across from him did not have a screen. The screen's many missing pieces were broken and scattered among other discarded relics on the floor. His only guess was that a weak spot on the floor from the level above—possibly another vent connected to the one across the way—must have given way when he fell on it, which brought him down through the now broken vent screen. From there, he must have hit the heavy doors, which guarded the room, hard enough for the hinges to be ripped from the deteriorated walls. That allowed the inward collapse of the doors they had once held in place. The doors remained locked in one piece, as if removed from where they stood and placed on the floor in their current condition. Numerous candelabras had toppled over as casualties of the fallen doors. The flames from the corresponding fallen candles in these holders had been extinguished.

He reached for his sword, and after he did, it began to change. The hilt metamorphosed, creating the head of his lute. The blade of the weapon changed from a sharp-edged weapon to a rounded bridge with strings stretching from its head to its body. He played a short, soft, and comforting tune while the instrument pulsed with all the colors of the rainbow. The rainbow's glow extended to surround the bard.

"Yes, it is better now," he said to the lute, "but where am I?" He waited for a moment and then said, "Really?" His summation of what had happened had been correct, but there was an additional aspect to where he had ended up. Paul turned his head and investigated the room from the hallway. Most of the candles' flames, other than the fallen ones, had been blown out when the doors fell, but he was still able to see with the remaining light. The book that Alistar had spoken of was in the middle of the room.

That book was giving an evil man unlimited power.

"Just take it?" he asked. His head still throbbed, and his fingers were playing the same comforting tune. He rose from the floor and walked to the altar where he stopped playing and slung the lute onto his back. He closed the book and picked it up. A purple radiance appeared around the book and the altar, where it had been sitting, but he felt no harming influence from the glow.

When the illumination disappeared, and Paul left the room, the candles all went out at once, and the chamber was only dimly lit by the hall's torches. Paul stood in the corridor and placed the book in his backpack. Then with the instrument in his hands and while playing an upbeat tune, he said, "We should get out of here, but which way, and where should we go?"

Enrandl backed away from Toran and the leopard. At first, he could not understand what was wrong. He looked to his hands, wondering why the display had not come forth. Then the realization edged its way into his mind. It was something that he had not been warned about. The book had been removed from its preservation, and he could no longer channel effects through his aura.

What method of consequence accounts for displacing a book? He let out an anguished yell and backed even farther away from Toran. He could not draw the magic energy from around him, but he could still release it from an object. He drew out the ivory wand again and aimed it in Toran's direction. An electric bolt of crackling energy shot above Toran's head. "Just a taste of your death." Enrandl lowered his aim.

I am too weak, Toran thought.

This time, Higoshi finished for him, *You have enough left for this.*

Toran steadied his nerves and concentrated, trusting in his mentor that he had enough Merea left to defy his enemy one more time. The protective globe arose well before the electric bolt left Enrandl's wand. He watched both the image of the electrical strike in his mind. He actually saw it enter the sphere and strike him directly on his left side, and yet he felt no pain. The energy was absorbed by him instead, and his body began to radiate with blue-white electric light. Remaining calm, he altered his concentration. The sphere expanded, reaching out to include Enrandl. When Enrandl was within its influence, Toran guided his vision of the crackling electricity that surrounded him to a view of the wands electrical burst volleyed back toward the magician.

Then he executed the change.

The envisioned picture pulsed into reality. With no time to dodge it, Enrandl stood amazed as he watched the bolt return in his direction and strike the wand in his hand.

Earlier, Toran had not noticed the rocks that he had shot at Enrandl hurting the magician, so he believed the protection on him was still sound. He thought that if the same shielding was the reason why magical displays were not touching him, he should aim for something that could be influenced. The chosen target began to tremble and shake. It exploded into thousands of pieces with a charged outward blast that narrowly avoided catching Toran and the leopard in the wake of its destruction. Enrandl fell to the floor and did not move.

Wrong again, Toran responded to Enrandl's last comment. He smiled through the pain in his aching head and looked around and at the leopard.

"Are you all right?" Kellik called from across the way.

"Yes, but I am going to need some help finding a way to get these claws out of me."

"Open your doorway, and we can come to you."

"I will, but you will have to hurry. I do not know how long I can keep it open." Toran struggled but produced a sphere to surround them all. Glowing balls appeared simultaneously at opposite sides, by him and by the others. It extended under his control. Finally, and much slower than when previously viewed, the sphere opened into the oval doorway. Everyone came through, and then Toran released his sphere with a gasp. They helped him with the task. When the leopard's claws were extracted, he healed himself just enough to stop further bleeding.

No one had approached Enrandl. "Kellik? Sword?" A sword was offered, taken, and Toran approached the motionless body.

"He dead?" Saigel asked.

"If he is not, he soon will be," Toran answered. The body was a torn-up mess strewn with the impacts from pieces of the exploded wand. He was standing over the fallen man with his sword, when amazingly, the magician's eyes opened slightly. When the understanding of what was about to happen seemed to coalesce, his eyes went wide with fear.

Toran savored the expression and delayed the strike to let it settle into his victims mind a fraction longer, but that pause cost him his triumph. With the brief time allowed to him, Enrandl found and touched the beaded necklace around his neck.

"Kerashtin," Enrandl said. Before Toran's weapon came down to skewer him, Enrandl was bathed in an orange light—and he vanished. The sword struck only the stone floor, barely missing the only thing remaining in his place.

Toran picked up the beaded necklace the magician had been wearing, and he studied it as Saigel approached.

"Whur'd he go?"

Toran grimaced as he tried to search for Enrandl's mind, but no sphere would rise for him to send forth. His last access to stop bleeding from where the cat's claws had been removed had exhausted his Merea. His head ached terribly now, but he found enough strength to scold himself through the pain.

"I cannot believe I let him escape. Now I will have to continue my search."

"I do not think so." Alistar's sudden appearance among them startled everyone, and the leopard's hackles arose instantly. "I am sure … it will not be necessary. He has lost his way."

"Yuhr alive?" Saigel was visibly affected by this realization more than any of them.

"Yes. My thanks to you. May I have my wand back?" Saigel retrieved it from his belt and handed it to him. "Perhaps that potion you drank did do something for you."

"Emergency?"

"Yes, GodsLight that you understood the reference," Alistar answered. "If you will recall, I told you that the minikin I knew was a magic user. That little drink was either his concoction for giving another the use of magic or perhaps the reason he was able to control such at all."

"I didn't understand. I repeated you. Gunna last long?"

"Then I am more brightly shone upon than I have imagined. You will have to keep trying and find out, little one."

"How can you be sure he's lost it?" Kellik asked.

"I saw the look in his eyes," Alistar began. "An effect had been channelled before he touched Toran, and the display did not come forth, not because he had done something wrong or that his aura was too weak. He simply and unexpectedly had no more craft. I have experienced that sensation. Someone disturbed the book in its preservation, and he is a magic user no longer. He is no more a threat than anyone you would meet on a common road."

"But you learned your magic again and can use it. How do we know he won't?"

"It is not as easy as that, Kellik. To the best of my knowledge, we are the only two to have ever commanded the book, and it took me several revolutions of research just to discover I was able to do such a thing. Then, before I could, I had to rework every effect that I wanted to relearn. It is my belief that wherever he is now, he will not be heard from for quite some time."

"I wish I could be certain. I would like to know that he is no longer a threat," Toran said sullenly.

EPILOGUE

EVERYTHING IN ITS PLACE?

Snow-covered mountains dominated the scenery. Winter would not arrive for two more cycles, but the mountain range at Philter's Crossing always had at least a thin blanket of snow. The sun was occasionally caught peeking down to spy on the landscape, employing fractures in the cloud layer for its attempts and where it would temporarily reflect its brilliant light on the white scenery as it surveyed what was below.

During one of these incursions, a glowing ball of colorless light disturbed the cold rushes of air that, along with the snow, remained a consistent aspect of the pass. This ball stretched into a long glowing line starting on top of the ground, expanding upward, and creating a shimmering oval. Two men and a large white cat stepped out of the portal.

Kellik was the first to appear. He was wearing a heavy winter coat and leggings to contend with the temperature he was expecting. Several journeys through here afforded him enough understanding of the region to know what to expect. He had advised Toran that if he was joining him and the cat, being outfitted with similar precaution would be beneficial. The leopard, which he had dubbed Snowfall, was next to appear through the mentally created doorway, followed closely by an unprepared Toran.

Warned as he was, the third person in the trio shivered at the frigid winter climate. The freezing air chilled him through instantly. Kellik just smiled at his friend as the other promptly crossed his arms across his chest for what little warmth he could muster. Then he looked down at Snowfall.

The words would not be understood by the great cat, but Kellik thought that they were necessary. "I'm truly sorry for everything, past and present. I hope you'll still be able to survive."

"I hate to rush you, but ..." Toran said.

Kellik only felt partially sorry for his shivering friend and said, "I know. Farewell."

Snowfall growled lightly back at him, as if the beast did understand.

Through his discomfort, Toran's concentration had remained on the portal. Before making this excursion, he chose not to travel the way of his recent and short displacing talent that he had discovered (with Higoshi's spiritual guidance), so they all had to settle for several trips through his well-practiced ability for semi-distant jaunts.

Toran knelt down to the cat's level and scratched behind Snowfall's ear, but when he tried to stand again, a massive paw caught his shoulder, drawing him back down. The cat's impossibly warm tongue licked his cold face, and the wet spot quickly began to freeze. "You are welcome," Toran replied, wiping his cheek as it slowly went numb like the fingers he had tried to dry it with. Thinking about the scars on both his arms from Snowfall's claws, he added, "You have left quite an impression on me also."

Snowfall turned away from them as the sky started dusting new snow all around and the sun, caught in its current act of intrusion, again hid behind the clouds. Those clouds created a complimentary deception as the leopard tracked farther away from them. It passed an unusually out of place mound of snow, and the cat was soon too blended with both the new falling snow and white ground for either of its recent companions to see its presence. When Snowfall was gone,

Toran and Kellik both stepped back through the disturbance, and it disappeared.

When they had made their last trip, finally arriving back in the sitting room of Higoshi's former cottage, to their surprise, they had found Alistar waiting to greet them. "I was hoping I would find you here," he said to Toran. "There is someone who would like to speak with you."

On her cue, Kayra, who was again transmuted into human form, came around the corner from the kitchen. "She has given up quite a bit for you since she was revived. You should listen to what she has to say," Alistar whispered to Toran. Then he nodded to Kellik, indicating that they should leave the two alone.

Kayra was wringing her hands together and looking anywhere in the sitting room but at Toran. After a moment, he seemed beyond impatience. "I have nothing to say, so if you do, then speak."

"I … I wanted to apologize for my deception. It was *his* plan to make me this way. Then I met you, and …" Her voice faltered. She took a moment and swallowed to clear her throat. She had planned her words carefully beforehand, but now she could not remember what she was going to say—or in what order she wanted to say it. *What could I possibly be thinking?* she wondered. *I am still much too new to this.* She froze in her speech, but Toran did not waste the silence.

"You," he accused, "you set us all up! I really cannot see how Kellik and Saigel can forgive so easily."

She shuddered and shied away at his outburst, staring at the floor. She spared a brief glance up and found that his expression had changed. His anger was still present, but where it had been recently directed at her, it was now tempered. He was looking beyond her, not allowing it to show completely.

Quickly looking back down before he may have seen her, she continued, "I forgot myself, Toran. I was so carried away in my need for justice against … *him*, that I lost everything … everything that this human form has brought to me. I forgot about our dance and how it made me feel."

"What could being human have possibly brought you?"

"You. I have only begun to undertake these emotions, and they are still quite good at confusing me. I have no words to describe them, but until your friends interrupted us that day, I had forgotten who or what I was. I believed. I mean to say I was lost or absent, maybe even removed from myself. I was as absorbed in our dance as I was to my need for the justice that I wanted—the justice that was due to me against your friends."

Her eyes started to water, and she continued. "But they were forgotten entirely. There was nothing but you. We were the only two who existed. You, me, and the dance."

"You lied before," Toran said, his anger no longer showing. "Why not now?"

She wiped her eyes. "If I were lying, would I have had Alistar return me to this human form again?" There was a perceptible irritation in her voice.

"All effects are not—"

Kayra cut him off with anger in her tone, "Permanent? This one is—or will be—permanent! When enough time goes by, even Alistar will not be able to reverse it—as *he* did."

"Then you are going to stay human? Why?"

"As long as I live." She reached out a hand for his, and a soft music began to play. "For the dance. One I hope we can continue to replay." She looked into his eyes, "May I take this one?"

He stared at her for a moment.

"Have," he replied and smiled at her confused look. Another tear streamed down her face. He wiped it away and accepted her hand. "Not take. You were asking, 'May I have this dance?'"

"Oh …"

"Then … may I have this dance?" Kayra asked again.

Paul was standing in the room with them. They could not see him because the magic of the lute and the song that he was playing did not allow them to. But Kayra knew he was there. He waited patiently to delicately begin weaving another song into his previous one. He could hear both of them combined perfectly, but the others heard only the exact same music they had heard at the tavern of their first dance. The exception was the lack of his voice singing, but the result was the same. He watched them dance around the room as gracefully as they had that first time.

When the song ended this time, there was no interruption.

"Thank you," William said curiously, setting a simple wooden box on his desk and watching the woman leave. "What could this be?"

His curiosity did not overrule his caution as he examined it thoroughly. He found the lid sealed with wax. He was almost prepared to seek a magician to help him assess the seal and verify there was nothing unnatural about it. Caution still did matter to him, and this item could have some magical trap placed upon it.

An experimental scratch at the wax with his dagger verified nothing. Instead of waiting, he impulsively cut away the rest of the seal. He was gratified that nothing extraordinary happened. He then carefully removed the lid, and what he saw caused him to gasp. A tear welled up in his eye and ran down his cheek. He brought forth a leather strap exhibiting a highly polished copper charm. The charm depicted the four primary compass directions seen on a map. There was a difference between this charm and a map's legend. The variance would have been obvious to anyone who compared it against real compass directions—even someone who did not have a single geography book in his library.

The navigation points of the charm were in their opposite positions.

William stood and smiled with absolute disregard for the tear drying on his cheek. He had gone so many revolutions without this piece of jewelry, and now he could put it to effective use. It was a better method than to personally benefit from the magic of the object. He walked over to his bookcase.

On the fifth shelf, as close to the center as he could place it, there was a book. He removed it from the shelf. Paul had brought this same book back from Jenerv before he had resigned from William's service, the power and curse of which were too real and too much for any magician to possess. It was a potential that even the kindest-hearted one of them would kill to possess. His friend had conceived, produced, and at one time, commanded it. Now at his own explanation, he was cursed from its use ever again.

A powerful and evil young man had barely learned what kind of power he had possessed before its pages had similarly cursed him. His magic could return in time (if he was still alive), but it would take many revolutions of studying and experimentation to do so. William wrapped the necklace around the book, hiding the symbol behind it, and placed it back on the shelf.

Alistar watched while the picture in the mirror turned gray. The item that he saw William place upon the book was performing its magical function to mask it from him effectively and presumably, from anyone's attempt to now scry upon it. The gray in the view began swirling into colors as Alistar altered the display to a second subject.

The new scene was mostly dark, except for the moonlight's reflection on a small lake near a cottage. Included in the scene was Saigel sitting on a short pier, staring into his hand. He adjusted the center focus of the mirror, directing the view while almost knowing what he would see the little man studying. The symbol of Saigel's lost minikin society glinted in the dim light reflecting off the lake. He looked at the minikin's face as the little man placed the token into a pocket of his shirt.

A long time ago, he had done Saigel a grave injustice. Although he could not conceive of doing something so terrible now, he was powerless to change what had already happened.

"I am honestly sorry, my small friend. I hope that I will be able to make it up to you someday." The image shifted again until Alistar was looking back at himself when the effect display ended. "Someday," he repeated.

Darkness surrounded Enrandl. At first, he wasted his time pounding his fists on the walls, yelling for someone to let him out. He had no idea where he was but only that he was not where he was supposed to be. The necklace he had found in the dragon's treasure pile should have shifted him to an island that he visited often. The island was where he centered his thoughts, and the item's magic supposedly worked in a similar function to shifting. He tried to convince himself that there had been a simple defect in it, but his persuasion failed. The jewelry had a cleverly masked curse. The curse was so strong that his own effect—with a display that should have illuminated any magical property the necklace may possess—had been unable to detect it. When he invoked the necklace's magic to send him away from Toran, he had been sent here instead of his intended destination.

He felt his way around the room before sitting again. He judged the diameter of his prison to be about ten feet. The walls were smooth and cool to the touch. He had not felt a single crack or flaw during his inspection, and he could not reach the ceiling.

He would have channelled himself some light to see by, but he knew that was no longer an option for him. Without that ability, there was no escape from wherever he was. His effects were gone. They had been stolen from him. He felt exposed but not from anything that would confront him. Everything he had was gone, with the probable exception of his defense against hostile magic. That ability had not come from the book, but there was no way for him to know for sure if it was still present.

One thing amazed him most of all, and he could not comprehend the eventuality. He should be angry and even furious at his situation—a wave of anger that he could only level at himself—yet here he was, sitting calmly in the dark, resigning himself to his prison with no thought of being so enraged.

Perhaps one day, he would be free.

Perhaps then, he would be angry.